CHASE THE SHADOWS

SUPERNATURAL LEGACY 2

EVERLY FROST

Frost, Everly
Chase the Shadows

Cover design by Claire Holt with Luminescence Covers
www.luminescencecovers.com

For information on reproducing sections of this book or sales of this book,
go to
www.EverlyFrost.com
everlyfrost@gmail.com

DISCOVER THE EVER REALMS

Seven series. One world.

Suggested Reading Order:

Bright Wicked
Storm Princess
Assassin's Magic
Soul Bitten Shifter
Supernatural Legacy
Dark Magic Shifters
Kingdom of Betrayal

Fan your flames.

CHAPTER ONE

a deep silence fills my mind.

Despite all the pain, and the fear, and the broken hopes, I'm quiet in the face of death.

Solomon Grudge's revelations should be a heavy hammer crushing my perceptions of who and what I am, but his words are like whispers that I try to catch, to hold on to and make sense of, as he prepares to end me.

I took the angels' most valuable prize. One of the first Avenging Angels born in centuries. A baby whose heart was filled with the purest rage and a need for justice. She was destined to be their greatest warrior. Then I stole her and doomed her.

Me.

He took me. He doomed me.

And then, for some inexplicable reason, he gave me back.

Now I will die at his hand.

I'm suspended in the air in the center of the alley at the side of the angels' Cathedral. A solid band of dragon's gold, an inch wide, is wrapped around my throat. It's twisted into a knot at the back of my neck, its loose end rising into the air behind me. It's attached to nothing, yet it won't break or fail.

The dragon who controls it is crouched on my left, closer to the open end of the alley. He hasn't come as near to me as the other dragon shifters who surround me. It's difficult to make out his features even in the bright moonlight because my vision is blurred with sweat and tears, but the smoothness of his skin tells me he's the youngest.

If one of my wings weren't damaged, I could fly upward and defy this gilded noose. But my black feathers are strewn like inky snow across the cobblestones and my left wing flutters hopelessly at my side. Only my pointed toes and the uneven beats of my right wing are keeping me from strangling, but it won't be long now.

Mere heartbeats.

My air is already gone. My fingers are bruised from trying to keep the band from crushing my neck. One of the other dragons is directing a web of dragon's gold onto my back, which will force my wings to retract. Once again, it's difficult to make out his features, but he's the oldest, judging from the speckles of silver in his hair that catch the moonlight and seem to dance in the air around his head.

So, too, do the pristine white wings of the legion of angels who are watching from the rooftop above the alley. The moonlight glows around them as if to accentuate their purity. They're wearing golden armor, dressed for battle, their heads held high, their features a blur of piety and virtue at the edge of my vision.

Their leader, the Serene Commander, is finally stirring at the closed end of the alley where Solomon knocked her unconscious. I estimate that she will recover in time to see me die—or in time to try to kill me herself.

My death has been sanctioned by the Celestial Ascendent, the angel in command of all angels here on Earth, and if Solomon and his men don't finish me, the Serene Commander will have to try.

Solomon stands opposite me while the remaining three

dragon shifters have fanned out to guard his back. They're all shirtless, wearing scuffed, brown pants and boots.

Solomon's heart thuds heavily within my senses as he steps closer and reaches for my neck with his enormous fist, his calloused palm brushing the underside of my chin.

He is one of the strongest dragons I've ever fought. An imposing figure at well over six feet tall with broad shoulders and enormous biceps. His dark-blond hair is pulled back into a messy ponytail, his eyebrows are drawn down, and his lips are set into an uncompromising line.

His hazel eyes glow in the moonlight as he meets my gaze and doesn't look away.

I lured him here tonight, planning to end him and the Serene Commander. I wanted to take them both out in one clean sweep and stop the war between the angels and dragons.

For my sins, I will pay with my life.

I can't speak. I have no air. But as I focus on Solomon, my lips move in the shape of my final question. *Why?*

Why did he steal me? Why did he give me back?

His jaw clenches and, for the briefest moment, his gaze becomes far away. His fist softens around my neck and his voice is a murmur. "There was a time when I also asked why. But I soon learned that there are no good answers. You must prepare yourself now, Cruel One."

He calls me *cruel* because that is the meaning of my true name: *Asper*.

Cruel is how I've lived my life. Trusting no one. Hating all. At every turn, the angels and dragons proved me right.

Until I met Callan Steele.

I close my eyes.

For a moment, I disappear into the memory of Callan's fiery presence, the heat in his gaze, the warmth of his touch. The vehemence in his voice when he told me that I have the power to choose my path.

He was right.

I will always have a choice.

And right now...

A furious scream builds within my chest, an impossible heat driven upward by an inferno of retribution that sweeps away the whispers of uncertainty and the deep, paralyzing silence.

My eyes fly open.

I choose fury and blood.

Gripping the sides of the noose and using it as an anchor point, I swing my legs up and around Solomon's waist as fast as I can. As soon as my thighs close around him, keeping me elevated and protecting my neck from snapping, I let go of the noose with my right hand.

His eyes widen at my sudden move, but he doesn't lift his arm fast enough to avoid my fist. I smack his jaw in two rapid jabs at close range that snap his head back. The recoil would have propelled me backward if not for the strength of my legs locked around his waist and my left hand still gripping the band at my throat.

Solomon's fury is instant and just as violent as I hoped. After all, Callan once warned me: Hit a dragon and the dragon will hit back without mercy or hesitation. I'm fucking counting on it.

Solomon's hand closes like a vise around my neck while his other fist smacks into my side, trying to make me unfurl my legs and push me off him. I'm ready for the blow to my stomach, my muscles already fully tensed, and the hasty tightening of his hand is hindered by the band of gold.

With his fury directed at my body, he isn't paying attention to my wings. One may be broken, but I can still use it to my advantage.

As he lands another blow on my side and his balance shifts, I give a savage beat of my wings. The breeze whistles through the large gaps in my left wing while my right wing catches the air.

His own momentum is against him, so that the movement of my wing sweeps us both to the side.

That's when I unhook my legs and thump my right forearm down on his outstretched arm, using all of my strength, aiming to break his wrist.

I don't crack the bone, but he does recoil, letting go of my neck as he stumbles to the side, trying to regain his balance.

He crouches, lowering his center of gravity, recovering fast and I know I've only got seconds—not least of which because the dragon controlling the noose is yanking it back in the air and taking me with it like I'm a fucking doll.

I've kept my left hand around the band the whole time, my fingers jammed between the gold and my throat, but now I return my right hand to it in a flash. I tuck my wings so the wind resistance doesn't knock me around in the air and use the noose once more as an anchor that stops my neck from breaking despite its intended purpose.

The only way I'll survive is if I can get this band off my neck and stop the dragons from chaining me again. I have no idea how I'll escape the other chains they control, but right now, I'm focusing on one thing at a time.

The noose first.

As I'm jolted back through the air, I claw my fingers and wrench at the thick, golden band. My palms are suddenly burning hot and I'm not sure if it's because of the friction against the band or because of my rage. Or possibly because the ruby heart charm on the bracelet I'm wearing is suddenly glowing like a beacon and emitting a searing heat where it rests against my skin.

The bracelet once belonged to Callan, but for some reason, it switched its alliance to me. It's mine. Just like the bracelet that's currently wrapped around my wing where it protected the bone from being cut during my fight with the Serene Commander.

Now, both bracelets remind me that if I controlled dragon's gold once, I can do it again.

A savage scream sounds within my mind, a command, as I direct my will at the gold around my neck.

Get off me!

All I hope is that the gold will stretch and allow me to breathe, but I'm aware that it's warping beneath my touch.

My fingers sink into it like putty.

I don't care what shape it's taking as long as it allows me to breathe.

Let me breathe!

At the scream within my mind, the band loosens and pulls apart between my hands like dough.

I don't have time to be shocked.

In the distance, the dragon who was controlling the band gives a shout of alarm. He was already crouched, his muscles straining, but as soon as the golden band breaks, he jolts to the side and grips his head as if he experienced the break like a massive thump to his skull.

At the same moment, the tension on the band—the upward pull—stops and the band drops to the ground with me.

I land at a crouch, my left hand still gripping the would-be noose as it drops more slowly than I do. My right palm slaps the stones when I reach out to balance my landing. My bruised fingers ache, but they're the least of my worries.

Before I can make another move, the loose end of the band drops onto my bare shoulder. It feels like it's on fire. So hot that I scream as it burns through the strap of my bra on that side and settles against my shoulder. It feels like it's cutting across my spine.

The pain radiates out from the band across my back from my shoulder blades to my waist, an agonizing, searing heat, but despite the burn, it suddenly feels very important that I don't let go of this gold.

Opposite me, Solomon has paused mid-stride, his focus flashing to the dragon who was controlling the noose. His voice betrays more concern than I was expecting. "Micah!"

The younger dragon raises his hand as if to say he's okay, although his forehead is creased, his lips are pressed together with pain, and he remains crouched where he is. He has light brown hair, tanned skin, and cedar-brown eyes. When he was standing, he appeared as tall as Solomon at over six feet and as broad in his chest and shoulders.

Solomon swings to me, a snarl on his lips.

His muscles bunch as he launches himself at me.

I should be focused entirely on him—on the oncoming threat of his fists and his strength—but my mind is consumed with the fiery golden band resting across my left palm while I remain kneeling on the cobblestones.

Its living nature is as strong as sunlight. As if its heart is bared to me, I feel its anger like hundreds of sharp needles pricking my palm. Callan told me that gold must be nurtured for hundreds of years before it will take on the living properties of dragon's gold. It must be cared for. Nurtured. He was angry at the way some of his clan treated their gold, the way they would force their gold into the shapes of jewelry against its will.

This band is fucking angry. It doesn't belong to Solomon or any of his men. It isn't loyal to them. I'm not sure how I can be so sure of that, but its rage is like a flame shooting up my arm and into my heart.

A rage like mine.

Be mine, I whisper to it inside my mind.

In the next instant, Solomon is upon me. My leg muscles bunch, my instincts shaping my response as I launch myself upward, using the strength of my good wing to direct my body to the left.

His right hand darts out to catch me, but at the same time, I swing the band at him, intending to use it as a whip, aiming it right at his face.

The breath stops in my chest when the gold morphs at the same instant, the band abruptly elongating and sharpening.

Solomon's reptilian pupils constrict with the first sign of real fear he's shown since I met him. "Fuck!"

He twists to protect himself, his wings thumping out and shooting across his body at the last possible moment. The blade hits the brown membrane and rakes down it, making a shrieking sound. His wings must be as tough as stone because, despite the screaming noise it makes, the weapon barely leaves a scratch.

The sudden appearance of his wings knocks me off course, but I spin midair to compensate and throw my good wing out to stop me skidding too far when I land. The tip of my wing bone grinds along the ground as I come to a halt at a crouch, gripping my new weapon.

It finishes forming before my eyes, a beautiful weapon with a larger blade at the top end that I just used to strike Solomon, and a smaller blade at the other end. Both blades have wickedly sharp tips.

I have limited knowledge of medieval weaponry, but I know my polearms, and this one is a glaive. It's comprised of a pole shorter than a spear's and it has two deadly ends, the larger one sharp enough to cleave a dragon's head from their shoulders, the smaller one deadly enough to use like a dagger.

The glaive feels as light as air within my hold, and it catches the moonlight as I snarl up at Solomon.

He twists back to me, his wings lowering only far enough for me to see his furrowed brow and furious eyes.

His focus flashes from my glaive to the older dragon, who is in control of the clip attempting to settle onto my back.

"Leon!" Solomon shouts. "Clip her wings. *Do it now.*"

So far, Solomon hasn't ordered any of the other dragons to

fight me, but I'm acutely aware of the three remaining bands of dragon's gold that hover in the air at the edge of my vision. Any one of them could be used as another noose, but it seems Solomon is more interested in hobbling me before he tries to kill me again. I'm stronger with my wings than without them—even with one broken—and he must know it.

The older dragon, whose name seems to be Leon, leaped out of the way during my fight with Solomon, but his arms remained outstretched in the direction of the clip. Now, his biceps are pumped and visibly straining. Sweat drips down his brow. His hair is dark brown and swept back with a wave in it. His skin is light brown while his eyes are the darkest brown with russet flecks in them.

When he speaks, his voice is gravelly, like a worn-out engine —the kind that perseveres no matter how hard it works. "The clip is fighting me. It won't close."

A cold smile grows on my face.

Damn right it's fighting him. With every beat of my heart, I'm willing that beautiful spiderweb of gold to stay the fuck away from me.

I reach back with my free hand, manage to catch hold of the upper thread of the spiderweb clip, and rip it off my back. I fully intend to sling it to the ground, but it clings to my fingers as if it's as sticky as a real web.

I pause as I discern its soul like a living and feeling creature. It isn't as hot with rage as the band that transformed itself into a spear for me, but it's subtly vengeful. It doesn't like what they were trying to make it do.

My vocal cords were so crushed by the band around my throat that my speech is a hoarse whisper, but I manage to speak clearly enough that Solomon won't misunderstand me. "This gold doesn't belong to you anymore. It's mine now."

The second I stop trying to shake the web off my hand, it slides up over my palm like a living creature, slipping neatly past the ruby-heart charm bracelet and curling around my forearm. Multiple strands join to form thicker threads that create an armored lattice covering my arm from my wrist to my elbow.

Solomon is on his back foot, his cheeks ashen. In his shifted form, his wings are extended and curved around his broad shoulders while his enormous biceps glisten with iridescent scales. The color of his wings is the deepest earthy brown, the membranes glistening as if they're covered in dew.

He is ferocious and the greatest danger to me right now, more so than the Serene Commander and all her angels, but he somehow manages to look thrown as his focus runs across the spear and the band on my arm and back up to my face.

"Fuck, no," he whispers.

I have no idea how I'm doing what I'm doing, but I give him a cold smile. *Hell, yes.*

I only have seconds before the dragons come at me again. I'm acutely aware that they're regrouping on my right. Leon and Micah have both closed in with the other three behind them, blocking my escape on that side.

On my left, the angels are also mobilizing. Half of them remain on the roof, while the others are rapidly dropping to the cobblestones beside the Serene Commander, their wings a flurry of white feathers. I don't see any weapons on them, but that doesn't mean they aren't carrying concealed daggers.

Aria drops to the alley with them. She has bright blue eyes and auburn-blond hair. She smells like an overabundance of flowers, a cloying scent that reaches me across the distance and irritates my senses. She lands right beside the Serene Commander, who has risen to her feet.

During my fight with the Commander, I scraped my fingernails through the mahogany wings she had painted across her eyes and temples, but those wounds have healed, and now her skin is flawless. Her eyes are cornflower blue and her hair is like spun gold. The band of flat gold that rests across her forehead glimmers in the light, and her white dress flows around her as she steps toward me, the mahogany leather breastplate she's wearing accentuating her slender curves while her high mahogany boots *click-clack* on the cobblestones.

The heat of her hatred is like a whip across my body as she calls to the other angels, "Lana Harlowe dies this night. The angel who brings me her head will earn everlasting glory."

Aria and the other angels give a unified cry, their voices low and ethereal, before they each crouch and retrieve a silver dagger from their boot.

Their cry is followed by the snarls of the dragons. I'm not sure how much longer the tenuous truce between Solomon and the Serene Commander will last. Possibly only as long as it takes to kill me.

Well, fuck that.

It doesn't matter how much my body hurts, how stiff my neck is, how tired I am, or how likely it is that I'll never make it out of here alive. I know what I am, and I will die as I am.

A wild thing.

Rising to my feet, I take a beat to spin the weapon in my left hand, roll my shoulders, and draw a cleansing breath to empty my mind of the cold fear that threatens to conquer me.

Then I brace for the onslaught.

CHAPTER TWO

*T*he dragons move faster than the angels.

The three gold bands streak toward me and I'm not sure which dragons are controlling them now. Possibly only Leon, since he's standing beside Solomon, his hands moving in the air while Micah and the other three charge toward me.

I dart to the side, using my glaive to deflect the first band, catch it like a ribbon, and drive it toward the ground. The other two bands fly on, one shooting toward my face, the other toward the glaive—the first no doubt to wrap around my throat, the second to disarm me.

The band coming at my face is of the greatest concern.

My reflexes fire, my right arm rises, and the lattice that covers that forearm glints in the light. The oncoming band of gold hits the lattice as I swing my arm, intending to deflect it, too. Even if the damn band wraps around my arm, it's better than around my neck.

The attacking band hits the lattice and bounces right off it. It's as if it hit a wall. It rebounds into the pavement, where it lies completely still at my feet. I don't have time to comprehend what happened, not trusting that the band won't rise again, before I'm forced to defend myself from the second band flying at my weapon.

My right arm darts into its path.

The attacking gold hits the lattice and bounces onto the ground, where it also lies still.

I glance at the lattice, which emits an innocent glow of pure light, yet once again, I sense its subtly vengeful nature. The layers of its heart are mired in conflict. There's loyalty and rage, but also a sense of belonging that surprises me.

In the distance, I'm aware that Leon lowers his hands before he exchanges a quick glance with Solomon, and it seems he won't try to lift the bands from the ground.

The other dragons are on the front foot, but Solomon holds his hand up to them in a *stop* gesture and gives them a firm shake of his head.

The whole thing happens in the space of heartbeats, and I'm not sure why Solomon has suddenly decided to hold back, but then the angels are upon me in a flurry of wings and daggers.

Aria reaches me first, her silver blade flying at my face. I knock the glaive's pole into her arm, driving her hand wide so I can land a fist to her chest, a punch that pushes her backward. In the next second, I duck beneath the swing of another angel's dagger, spin, and swipe her feet out from under her with the blunt side of my glaive before I whirl back to deflect three more blows.

There are so many coming at me at once that it's impossible to land killing blows—and there's a part of me that hesitates to kill them, since they're only following orders—but even so, they're at a particular disadvantage fighting me.

None of the angels can look me in the eye.

My corruption hurts their souls. At least, that's what the Serene Commander always told me. It's their downfall in this fight because they're focusing on a point past my face, which is upsetting their aim.

Aria twists back to me, regains her balance, and darts back into the fray, but this time, she seems determined to look right at me, her bright, blue eyes darker than mine. She uses her wings to gain air and speed down toward me, her dagger held in both hands and aimed at my chest.

I tilt my head back, glaring right up into her eyes, and she recoils as if I struck her, her wings beating frantically as she tries to get away.

"Witch!" she screams as she collapses to her knees on the ground, clutching her head as if I'd driven blades into her mind. "Filthy, vile witch!"

I sense the dragons startle behind me. I suppose they're wondering if I somehow magically struck her across the distance, since I didn't physically lay a hand on her. Or they might be wondering why she'd call me a witch. Although I suspect she means *bitch* but doesn't want to say it in front of the Serene Commander.

Her screams don't deter the other angels, who continue to slash at me, their attacks coordinated in the way of warriors who have trained together all their lives. If they weren't my opponents, I might admire their synchronization.

I continue to duck and deflect their assaults, using my glaive defensively and my free hand to hit back, knocking several of them unconscious in the process. The rest aren't deterred when their brethren collapse around them, and in the distance, the second group of angels drops from the rooftop, preparing to follow up the first.

The rush of air at my back tells me someone else is racing up behind me, and I spin just in time, surprised when I'm tackled by one of the dragon shifters.

It's Micah. I catch sight of his light-brown hair and cedar-brown eyes as he lifts me off my feet, but it's the shape of his pupils and the scent of his nature that surprises me enough to make me freeze a little.

I'm immediately struck by the scent of the forest, very similar to Solomon's scent, but there's a darker thread within it. In the brief moment that I inhale, I'm hit with the speed of racing paws on the mossy ground, a nose held low to the ground, and the overwhelming need to catch his prey.

He's a dragon shifter but he's also, somehow, a... *wolf*.

Undeniably a wolf.

I'm also struck with the knowledge that he has never killed anyone. There is no copper tang on my tongue as he prepares to ram me into the stone wall at the side of the alley. If he had succeeded with the noose earlier, my life would have been the first he would have taken.

It seems he's determined to rectify that.

I don't hesitate for more than a second.

Driving my latticed forearm down on the top of his shoulder, I connect with his collarbone in a blow that should break it. A ripple of charcoal-gray scales shoots across his chest, hardening his skin and protecting him from my attack. That doesn't stop me ramming my arm down on his shoulder twice more as his wings thump out at his sides in sync with the transformation of his skin.

Usually, when dragon shifters shift, it's all or nothing: always scales and wings at the same time. Most can't choose one or the other. Callan is the only dragon who can breathe fire, and Solomon is the first dragon I've met who can transform different parts of his body at any given time.

Micah appears to be like other dragons, his scales and wings manifesting at once. His dragon skin is dark gray, but the inside of his wings are the color of ash, silvery and luminescent, mesmerizing in the moonlight.

While the angels scatter on either side of us, I'm aware of Solomon's alarmed shout. "No! Micah!"

The younger dragon drives me back against the opposite wall of the alley and I hit the rock with a *thud* that would have rattled my bones except that, right before I connect, I extend my wings. They slap against the wall on either side of me, protecting me from the worst of the impact and allowing me to brace against the stone at my back.

Using the strength of my wing bones against the wall and ramming the end of the glaive against the stone with my left hand, I shove myself forward before Micah can pin me.

Because he tackled me around my waist, he lifted me up so high that his head is at my waist and it's easy to drive my right fist across his temple so hard that the scales on his face *crack*.

He roars with rage, reflexively opening his arms and recoiling backward.

I don't stop. Don't make a sound. Conserve my energy. The moment his arms open, I flip the spear into my right hand—my strongest hand—and prepare to drive its tip down through his torso on my way to the ground.

It will be an efficient kill. Fast and brutal. But certain.

"No!" Solomon's roar meets my ears, and his voice sounds different than before. Desperate and afraid in a way I wasn't expecting. "Not my son!"

His son?

I don't know why that should stop me. Micah tried to kill me. So did Solomon. I shouldn't show either of them mercy just because they're related by blood—or because Solomon's voice betrays his fear for his child.

And yet...

In that heartbeat, all I can hear is the Serene Commander telling me that when she sent me to kill dragons, she sent a monster to kill monsters. She told me I'm incapable of love, that the absence of true feeling is at the heart of my corruption.

But... I am no longer what she made me.

I am who I choose to be.

I came here to kill Solomon, not his child.

At the last possible moment, I angle the glaive to the right so that it grazes down Micah's bicep instead of impaling him. The blade cuts through his scales like a knife through butter, but it's a shallow scratch, nothing more.

A decision I may well come to regret.

My weapon's tip collides with the ground and slices into the stone, where it remains in an upright position.

I land at a crouch beside it, my chest heaving, my focus flashing to Micah, who has flinched and frozen next to me. I fully appreciate the span of his wings now that they curve around me, forming a bright wall of silver that closes in around me.

His eyes have widened, his lips are parted. His arm is bleeding, but he hardly seems to notice. "You didn't kill me."

The hairs on my arms shoot up as my senses suddenly flood with the kind of electricity that precedes a lightning strike. The scent of a storm.

Solomon appears above Micah's wing, his own wings spread and beating the air. He retracts them as he drops right onto my position.

I barely have time to dart to the side as his big fist flies toward my face. His hand hits the rock behind me, smashing the stone surface. Shards fly across me, one of them slicing the skin on my forehead above my right eye, another nicking my neck, but the sting tells me they're shallow cuts.

While I dart to the left, Micah moves to the right, retracting his wings and leaping out of his father's path.

I'm forced to leave my glaive behind, but one of the discarded golden bands lies right ahead. I drop and roll, snatching it up as I leap to my feet and spin back to Solomon while he rages after me.

This band feels cold. Empty. As if its living nature has perished and now it's nothing more than a malleable ribbon of metal. Using it like a whip, I slash it across Solomon's chest and face as he plows toward me.

He doesn't even bother to protect himself, storming onward while I backpedal. "You destroyed my people!" he roars. "Now you try to kill my son!"

My arms move of their own accord, my reflexes in full swing as the band cuts across his scales, but my desperation levels are growing.

I've been fighting for too long and the exhaustion in my muscles is making me slower, the pain in every limb making me want to scream.

Escape is becoming less likely with every passing second.

If only I could fly...

But I can't.

I've never run from a fight. It's not in my nature to stop. Even with Callan, I had to *bend*; I veered off my original course, but I didn't give up or give in.

My chest is heaving and sweat drips down my face, or maybe it's blood. I'm not sure which anymore, but I fucking hate it either way.

The angels have gathered behind me. The dragons are blocking the alley in front of me. Micah has returned to Leon's side, both of them waiting with shuttered expressions while Solomon pursues me around this moonlit space like he's—

It suddenly dawns on me why he stood back when the angels attacked.

He's waiting for the moment when I'm too tired to fight anymore. He let the angels wear me down and now he's baiting me like the caged and wounded animal that I am.

I would scream with frustration and despair if I had any energy left. If my vocal cords would let me.

Standing at the center of the angels, the Serene Commander watches me with her head held high and a faint smile on her lips. She's barely had to lift a finger since Solomon arrived. She knows I won't last much longer.

With growing desperation, I plot a path around Solomon,

across the alley, and to the spot on the wall where the Serene Commander's spear remains embedded. I can leap up to it, use it as leverage to reach the nearest protruding brick on the uneven wall. Make it up to the roof one brick at a time.

I mentally scoff at myself. The angels or the dragons will fly after me and pick me off that wall in two seconds flat. I'll be lucky if they don't stab me in the back—literally.

My next option is to fight my way through the group of dragons blocking the entrance, except that's what I've been trying to do...

My teeth grit hard and a snarl emits from my lips as I duck Solomon's next fist.

If I'm going to die, I'm taking him with me.

I will fight him with every last shred of strength within my body because he took from me the life I should have had. He condemned me to grow up in a cell beneath the Cathedral's walls, listening to the far-off music of other angels' lives and wondering what the fuck I'd done to deserve my fate.

I dart around him, aiming for the glaive I left in the ground, my legs pumping and muscles screaming as I reach for it. My hand closes around it just as I sense the air shift behind me and hear the thump of his wings.

I inhale the scent of the oldest tree in the forest and feel the brush of Solomon's earthy wings across my face as he collides with me, tearing me away from the weapon.

He throws me against the wall, where I try to use my wings to my advantage again, but it seems that move will only work once. My attempt to evade him only takes me into the path of his other fist, which smacks into my abdomen, pushing the air right out of my chest.

I hit back at his side, but it carries only half the strength I had at the start of this fight. I try again, but he grabs my hand and shoves me back into the wall, knocking his knee into my stomach—a second blow that pins me there.

I gasp for breath. My wings scrape against the stone, making a tearing sound.

My arms shake and the muscles in my legs are screaming.

Solomon's furious features dominate my vision as he stares down at me. "It's over, Cruel One."

I shake my head, wishing I could shout, but my only response is an exhausted, pained whisper. "It can't be."

Despite standing in the bright moonlight, he doesn't cast a dragon shadow. He's the first dragon shifter I've met who can conceal his true nature this way. So can his five men. It's possible that he doesn't have a dragon shadow, but I find myself wondering, if I could see it, would his dragon's nature reveal itself to be as merciless as he is?

"We are but playthings in fate's game," he replies, more softly than I was expecting.

I want to deny it. To scream at him that my life is not a game dictated by fate, but the series of events that brought me to this point can only be the cruel work of destiny. I nod. "True."

I finally retract my wings. The bracelet that was wrapped around my left wing bone lifts off it and flies back to my wrist, slipping neatly into place. It can't help me now, but I'm glad it's back where it belongs.

I exhale. Inhale. Taste the night air on my tongue and tip my head back to see the stars. Beautiful stars.

Dammit, I fought so hard.

Returning my gaze to Solomon, I allow my weight to settle within his hands while his palms close around the side of my head and my neck. I lean in to the danger, the same way I would crane toward Callan's fire, inviting peril, as is my nature.

"Then end it," I say, refusing to lower my gaze or close my eyes. "If you believe my death will stop the conflict with the angels, then do it. I want this war to end."

A deep silence fills my mind again and I wonder... *Is this peace? Or is this rage?*

For me, I'm not sure that there's a difference.

Solomon studies me for longer than I expect, a furrow forming in his brow that deepens with every passing moment.

With each breath I draw, his scent envelops me. When I first inhaled it, I knew it was familiar. *Deeply* familiar, as if it were part of my foundations. Now I know why: It would have been one of the first I ever inhaled. A dragon's scent that, somehow, makes me feel like I've found my origins.

The power of his presence transports my mind to the darkest part of a forest, where the branches of the oldest trees spread across the sky, the sunlight is dappled, and the moss is soft beneath my toes.

The sensation is so strong that I can *feel* the cool forest air brushing my back and arms. Raindrops are dripping from the canopy above me onto my head, through my hair, and down my forehead and cheeks.

The feeling is suddenly too real, and I'm horrified to realize that it's not raindrops, but tears dripping to my chin.

Fuck it. I let them fall.

"I didn't believe her," Solomon says, a sudden, soft statement. "But now I think she was telling the truth."

My forehead creases. "Didn't believe who?"

He pauses. "Your mother."

My lips part with a quick inhale. *My mother?* Nobody has spoken to me about my mother before. Or about my father. When I asked the Serene Commander about my parents, she was tight-lipped and refused to tell me anything.

Before I can speak again, there's a commotion among the dragons where they remain on my right.

At the same time, darkness drops across me.

I can't make out what's causing it until Solomon takes a hasty step back, lifting his hands clear of me.

Following his line of sight, I tip my head to meet the gaze of a blood-red dragon that's descending down the wall beside me.

CHAPTER THREE

*T*he beast is as insubstantial as the moonlight. A dragon shadow.

Its barbed tail flicks across the wall while its head lowers to mine, its teeth bared in a soundless snarl.

I recognize this shadow, and my heart stops for a beat before a lithe, female form drops to the ground beside me—apparently having jumped from the roof above.

"Well, damn. This seems a little unfair." Beatrix rises from her landing, the straps of a pair of high heels clasped casually in her left hand.

She is a Dread dragon, a member of the ruling Cohort. Strong and clever enough to be a beta if she wasn't so conniving. She has high cheekbones and dark hair cut at an angle along her jaw. She's wearing black jeans and a black T-shirt and her eye makeup is heavy, as if she were going to a club, accentuating her large, dark eyes.

At her sudden appearance, a ripple of shock runs through the angels while the dragons' agitation manifests in growls and fierce glares.

Beatrix seems oblivious to their anger. "It looks like we

weren't invited to the party of the year." She glances around with an exaggerated pout. "Angels *and* dragons. All having fun without us."

"Us?" Solomon backs up, glancing warily around him, before spinning to a figure crouched on top of the alley wall opposite the Cathedral.

Felix Lamonte is just as cruelly beautiful as Beatrix, his cousin. His hair is as dark, but longer and swept back into a bun. He's tall and agile, and his dragon shadow dominates the space on that side of the alley, its serpentine form seeming to cling to the wall below him.

Appearing not to care about the imminent danger from both the angels and the Grudge dragons, Felix grins at me across the distance before nonchalantly pursing his lips and kissing the air in my direction.

"Fucking Lamonte cousins," Micah says, looking from one to the other before Leon reaches out to place a warning hand on his arm.

"Ooh, I see our reputations precede us." Beatrix licks her lips at the younger Grudge dragon while she looks him up and down. If she's surprised that he doesn't cast a dragon shadow, then she doesn't show it. "Well, hello there, big guy." A wicked smile grows on her face as she raises an eyebrow at him. "Craving some company?"

"Not yours," Micah snaps.

"Shame," she croons, reaching out to run her hand down my arm, an absentminded movement while her focus sweeps between Micah and Solomon. Her fingertips linger on the gold lattice covering my forearm. "My beautiful Night Sky and I are dying to hold a grudge tonight. Aren't we, Night Sky?"

When Callan first inhaled my scent, he told me I smelled like a clear night sky after the rain falls. Beatrix thought so, too. She took to calling me *Night Sky* because of it.

She leans in to bump my shoulder with hers before she

breaks into a light laugh. "Hold a Grudge. Get it? No?" She rolls her eyes before she takes a step forward and positions herself in front of me like a shield.

Her voice becomes cold and sharp. "Maybe we'll bury a few Grudges instead."

Solomon snarls at her, backing toward his clan members, who have peeled away from the wall where Felix perches. The angels also take up a defensive formation, with the Serene Commander and Aria in front. They remain at the closed end of the alley as far away from the Lamonte cousins as they can get.

Atop the opposite wall, Felix snickers into the sudden silence, the sound of his laughter sending a shiver down my spine.

Beatrix throws a quick glance back at me, the dark lashes of one eye lowering in a wink. "We've got you, Night Sky."

Well, that's either comforting or incredibly terrifying.

My relationship with Beatrix is fraught at best, the shrewd woman's motivations remaining a mystery to me. Her presence brings the tang of sour lemon to my tongue while the heavy scent of cloves fills my chest. She's a liar and a thief, but not a killer, although judging by the emerging scent of copper clinging to her right at this moment, she fully intends to draw blood tonight.

Solomon growls a response, but I don't hear what he says because a wash of calm suddenly rushes over me, making my ears buzz. It isn't the sensation of rage and peace I felt before, but a bone-deep warmth, as if the sun suddenly came out and all my worries are melting away.

There's only one dragon whose presence makes me feel this way.

Gasping at the intensity of the warmth that rushes through me, I moan out my dread and my pent-up anger, not caring that my sigh draws Solomon's attention.

I let go of all the rage.

I don't have to feel this anger anymore. I don't have to take on the violent intentions of those around me any longer. I'm released from the relentless compulsion to finish this fight, even if I can't win it.

Because he's here.

Callan is here.

I rapidly locate him on the rooftop above the angels. It's the same spot where they'd gathered to watch me die before they dropped to the alley to join the fight that followed.

He must have scaled the wall on the other side of the Cathedral's grounds and crept around the myriad of buildings within its perimeter. Or perhaps *run*, not crept, given that his heartbeat is a fierce, rapid thud within my hearing.

I am the center of his attention.

Even at a distance—even standing alone with the clear night sky as his backdrop and the moonlight flooding his form—he seems to tower within his surroundings. His hair is slicked back and charcoal-black in this light. Normally clean-shaven, his jaw carries a shadow of growth that only serves to highlight the slight cleft in his chin. He's wearing dark-gray sweatpants, but no shirt, his sculpted chest and enormous biceps glistening with sweat. His feet are bare, which would have allowed him to move silently across the rooftop.

Ribbons of dragon's gold circle the air around him—at least ten of them—twirling in sync with his heartbeats. Other dragons may mistreat their gold, but not Callan. His gold radiates out from his body as if it's linked to him by invisible threads that will never break.

Behind him, his dragon shadow dominates the rooftop. The giant, golden dragon lifts its head and stretches out its wings, as if it would take flight and soar down to me. Its wingspan is so wide that the tips of its wings nearly reach each side of the roof. Its golden scales gleam and its eyes are full of flames as it whips its tail across the roof tiles. If it were flesh and blood, it would have ripped the structure apart.

Callan is taking a huge risk revealing his dragon like this. His clan has gone to great lengths to hide themselves from identification and detection. But now he's here, and it's because of me.

Just yesterday, he told me that if I wanted him in my life, he would find a way to make it happen.

We would find a way.

Even if it meant him giving up his position as alpha of the Dread and disappearing with me. Now, he stands on top of the Cathedral, a pinnacle of power, as if he would tear it down to get to me.

He rapidly takes in the lattice wrapped around my arm, my broken bra strap, my bleeding face…

The tension in his shoulders and the flex of his biceps is already intense, but when his focus stops on my bleeding neck, where I'm sure ugly bruises must be forming, his jaw clenches and his breathing becomes harsher, audible across the distance. Laced with snarls. His eyes are pure juniper-green, as cold as jade daggers. The color they turn when he's angry.

At the same time, his dragon focuses in on Solomon. Its nostrils flare and fire burns more brightly in its eyes. For a second, it looks as if Callan's dragon recognizes Solomon, but I'm not sure how that's possible, given that Callan and Solomon haven't met before this moment. At least, not to my knowledge.

Callan's dragon shadow bares its teeth in what appears to be a growl and, if it could make sound, I'm sure its roars would shake the air around us.

Solomon glares at Callan and, for the shortest moment, I imagine the dark flicker of a shadow around his form, a vast beast whose shape is gone too quickly for me to see it clearly.

On the roof, there's a moment when Callan appears to look

for the dragon shadows of Solomon and his men. Callan's eyes narrow, and his brow furrows with confusion that he quickly hides. I imagine I wore the same disbelieving expression when Solomon stepped into moonlight in front of me and didn't cast a shadow.

In the alley below Callan's position, the angels have startled at his sudden appearance. They spin, tipping their heads back to see him. Several of them shout in alarm, while the Serene Commander has frozen, the color draining from her face.

She has never met any Dread dragon before now, least of all Callan. A week ago, she didn't even know what he looked like. She sent me to find and kill him because I was the only one who could.

Now, he barely gives her a glance, his focus swinging directly from me to Solomon. The air glows around Callan's silhouette, a hint of the inferno burning within him, as he steps to the edge of the roof.

A single touch from another supernatural will trigger Callan's dragon and his flames will ignite.

The angels scatter to the left side of the alley—the same wall that I'm leaning against. The Serene Commander and Aria order the others backward, where they take up a new defensive formation.

They also retract their wings.

The Serene Commander knows about Callan's fire, and angel feathers are highly flammable. The Serene Commander saw fit to keep Callan's fire-breathing ability from me, but she must have revealed it to the other angels at some stage, judging by the speed with which they hide their wings.

Solomon, on the other hand, has taken a step forward, with Micah and Leon close on his heels, while the other three dragons form a defensive line behind him.

Despite the way Callan's presence scorches the air, making

the sky shimmer with heat waves, his voice is so cold that I shiver as if winter has come.

"Solomon Grudge, that angel belongs to me."

CHAPTER FOUR

"Callan Steele." Solomon gives Callan a brief nod. "I acknowledge your claim on this angel."

"Then you will give her to me," Callan says, the heat waves increasing around his silhouette.

Solomon takes a deep breath. "I will not." His own voice becomes a growl, filled with a chill that defies the warmth of his forest scent. "I will take her life as payment for the deaths of my people."

Callan crouches, catches the guttering with his right hand, swings himself over the edge, and drops all the way to the alley, landing lightly.

A ripple of alarm runs through the angels, and the Serene Commander actively looks in the direction of her spear. She's practically vibrating with tension, and I'm sure she's fighting the compulsion to spread her wings and fly to her weapon while Solomon is distracted by Callan. Wisdom must stop her. If she makes an actively aggressive move, it will only put her in the line of fire. Literally.

Callan rises from his landing and squares his shoulders, prowling toward the group of dragons. The bands of gold dropped with him and now they whip around his shoulders, snapping at the air like snakes waiting to be given permission to strike.

"You assert the right to end her, but her life belongs to me," Callan says. "I have the greater claim."

He stops five paces from Solomon and to the older dragon's credit, Solomon doesn't flinch. I suppose I didn't really expect a dragon like Solomon Grudge to cower in the face of imminent destruction.

"How do you figure that?" Solomon asks. "She hasn't killed any Dread."

"Because I was the one who captured her," Callan says. "I was the one who stopped her from killing any more of your people." His eyes are cold and his voice colder as he enunciates his words. "By my calculation, you owe me."

The tension around Solomon's eyes increases. He doesn't have an immediate response, instead giving an unhappy growl.

"Her life is my price for keeping the dragon clans safe," Callan says. "Without her strength, the angels are no threat to you."

The last declaration is said with a sharp glance at the Serene Commander, but Callan seems to be avoiding making eye contact with me, and I understand why. He can't be seen to care about me as anything other than property. An entitlement. Possibly a burden.

When he first captured me, he intended to use me to draw the angels out. He wanted to kill them one by one until they learned that attacking him or his clan meant death. Once his message had been received, he planned to send my charred heart back to the Serene Commander to prove, once and for all, that the angels should fear him and never threaten his people again.

Then I survived his fire and our relationship changed. In private, we became equals. We came to an agreement under which I promised to stop hunting dragons for a time—that I would wait, and judge him for who he is, not what I'd been *told* he is.

After that, we played a game in front of his clan where I allowed myself to be seen as a captive, to maintain the appearance that I had submitted to Callan's control. Last night, I told his clan that I agreed to be bait to lure Solomon out so that Callan could kill him. That part was not a lie.

If the Grudge dragons—or the angels, for that matter— discover that Callan cares for me on a personal level, it will shift the power of this interaction away from him. As for his clan, last night, Callan handed over the leadership of the Dread to his sister, Zahra. He promised his clan that he'd deal with Solomon Grudge, and then he planned to leave. He wanted me to come with him, to help him find a way to control his dragon. For us to start a new life together. He was willing to risk his clan's hatred to have a life with me.

Before Solomon can respond to Callan's claim, Micah steps up to Solomon's side—but not before his cedar-brown eyes flash at me.

"If you want the right to kill this angel, why haven't you done so already?" Micah asks Callan.

Micah's arm, where I cut him with my weapon, has healed. His question could be inflammatory—rhetorical, even. But he sounds curious. I suppose he's wondering why I let him live, let alone why Callan let *me* live.

Seeing Micah standing closer to Callan, it's easier to gauge Micah's age. Callan is twenty-seven. I'm twenty-three. Micah must be around twenty-two—not much younger than I am, but he's a darn sight more reckless than Callan is. Granted, Callan is one of the most well-reasoned dragons I've ever encountered.

Callan's expression barely changes, remaining as hard as stone. "I didn't say I wanted the right to kill her. I want her alive."

Micah splutters. "Why the fuck would you let her live?"

Callan responds smoothly. "Because she will hunt for me." His eyes narrow at Micah. "Lana Harlowe is a weapon in a new master's hands. *My* hands."

Solomon takes a risk shifting his focus to me across the distance, his expression wary. He's quiet for a moment before he says, "You don't know what she is."

It's true that Callan doesn't know I was born an Avenging Angel. Hell, I didn't know before tonight.

"I understand her well enough," Callan replies, staring Solomon down. "Will you relinquish your claim on her, or will you risk the lives of the remainder of your clan tonight?" He glances at the other men. "If this is all that's left of your people, then you should think carefully about their chances of walking away from a fight with me."

Callan could have used his fire already. Could have killed them all, but for Callan, fire is a last resort. He sees it as a liability, not a strength. Particularly as it carries the risk of exposing the supernatural community, as well as the existence of his clan. Standing in the moonlight is a large enough gamble. Using his fire in a place like this, where human firefighters could converge within minutes, is a huge risk.

Solomon doesn't answer Callan's question, continuing to stare at me, and the longer his focus lingers on me, the more I sense the rising electricity in the air—his anger. His breathing increases, his enormous chest rising and falling more rapidly. "I can't let her go again."

The "again" makes Callan's brow furrow. He doesn't know that Solomon took me and gave me back when I was a baby.

Callan seems to quickly dismiss his confusion. His furious green eyes finally rake across me. I read his fear for me within his anger, and it hits me hard. I'm visibly injured and barely standing upright. He may talk of using me as a weapon, and about making me hunt for him, but he hides the truth: He won't force me to do any of it. He will allow me to choose.

Callan's jaw clenches. He takes another step closer to Solomon and his dragon shadow follows close behind. "I'm offering you a truce, Solomon. It's a better deal than you could expect from any other member of my clan." His voice lowers, but it's more forceful. "Give me Lana and we can all walk away alive."

Again, Solomon pauses, but Callan's patience seems to finally be at an end.

"Do you understand what I can do?" His voice rises to a roar and the shimmer of heat that fills the air around him makes me gasp. "I will burn you and your men until you are nothing but ash."

"Release your fire and you'll kill your own people—and the angel, too," Solomon says.

"Will I?" Callan asks. "Are you sure?" He begins to pace back and forth along an invisible line that keeps him five steps away from Solomon. A safe distance. For now. "Perhaps my people have discovered a way to survive my fire. Maybe they'll shield the angel while your men burn."

To some degree, it's a bluff. Felix and Beatrix have strong enough wings that they can protect themselves to survive Callan's usual fire. But he warned me that no dragon can withstand his flames if he wants to use his fire to kill. He burned the heart of the former Dread alpha to ash. This alley may be wide, but there's nowhere to hide.

In response to Callan's threat, Solomon's breathing grows more rapid. Micah edges forward, as if he's determined to fight.

As the buzz of electricity around Solomon builds, there's once again a flicker of darkness around his form—the hint of a beast that would rival Callan's dragon in size.

Callan's shadow has remained an angry presence behind him, but now it lurches forward, its head lowered and its teeth bared, as if it's waiting in anticipation for Solomon's beast to emerge.

At that moment, Leon steps up to Solomon's other side. His murmur is soft, but my sensitive hearing picks up his gravelly voice. "This is not the battle you've been preparing for, old friend."

Solomon swings to him, his lips drawn back in a snarl, his pupils becoming jagged, and his claws extending.

Leon remains calm in the face of his alpha's rage. "I have my issues with this angel, but her death should have been clean and quick. Overseen by her people, who, despite their obvious hatred of her, would have given her a proper burial. If you persist, her death will not be clean." Leon's eyes are suddenly hard. "There will be consequences if you don't let her go tonight. You know this."

"Mercy is not in my nature," Solomon retorts, the hard edge remaining in his voice.

I exhale quietly. It's painful to understand his motivations. His need to finish the fight. I feel it too. As if a part of me will be restless until this battle is finally resolved.

"A family trait, perhaps," Leon says, causing Solomon's focus to snap to him sharply.

Solomon's jaw clenches, but then his shoulders slump. "Fuck."

His glittering gaze swivels to me again and I suspect that the hunch of his shoulders doesn't indicate defeat. Not resignation or acceptance, either. I recognize the suppression of an impulse to fight, which he's controlling with all his might.

"The Dread can have her," Solomon announces, his lips twisted with discontent. But before he signals his men to back away, he points at the Serene Commander. "You," he says. "Our truce this night is at an end. Any angel who tries to follow us will meet a bloody end. I will kill them just as I killed your favorite angel: Melisma."

The Serene Commander gasps and her breathing becomes rapid. Melisma was her strongest warrior. When I was a girl, the Serene Commander told me that Melisma asked to be sent after the dragons, to hunt them, but, like so many angels before her, she never returned. It was Melisma's death that caused the Serene Commander to decide, once and for all, to stop sending angels after dragons.

That is, until she sought permission to send me.

Solomon lowers his hand and steps back.

I let out a slow breath of relief as the Grudge dragons form an arc, facing the rest of us while they move as a group toward the alley's entrance.

Callan steps to the side of the wall where Felix crouches. Their dragon shadows remain side by side, both a threatening presence overseeing the Grudge dragons' retreat. The golden bands are elevated in the air at Callan's side, although they twirl more slowly now that Solomon and his men are retreating.

Within moments, the Grudge reach the far corner. Solomon pauses there.

Goosebumps rise on my skin as he turns back one last time, his gaze clashing with mine, before he disappears into the shadows.

Beatrix doesn't waste any time slipping her heels back on her feet. "Okay, thank you," she says loudly, directing her speech at the angels. "We'll be taking our Night Sky with us now."

The muscles in my neck are seizing up and turning my head to keep the angels within my sights is painful. I allow Beatrix to hook her arm around my waist, grateful that she doesn't try to hold me anywhere near my shoulders and neck, although the muscles in my legs and arms scream at me when I take a step toward the other side of the alley.

I'm acutely conscious of Callan's gaze on me, and this time, he doesn't conceal the worry in his eyes. His interaction with Solomon could have gone very differently and we still need to get out of here without a fight with the angels. When he focuses on my wounds again, the air around him heats, the rate of his breathing increases, and he casts a fierce glance back at the Serene Commander.

I assumed Callan wasn't looking at me before because he didn't want to be seen to care. Now, I wonder if it was because it was the only way he could control his rage.

"Quickly now," Beatrix whispers to me, urging me into hurried steps. "Before Callan loses it."

We've barely moved five paces away from the wall when the wintery scent of fog washes over me. Even while Callan stands across the alley from me, his presence dulling my senses, the Serene Commander's anger hits me hard.

She strides toward me, her boots smacking the cobblestones. Aria follows close behind her while the other angels also mobilize, moving up and forming two neat rows.

"Stop!" the Serene Commander cries. "Lana Harlowe will not leave this place alive. Her death has been sanctioned by the Celestial Ascendant. We are honor-bound to put an end to her corruption."

"Oh, fuck." Beatrix murmurs beneath her breath before she rolls her eyes and declares more loudly, "*Now* they get involved. And I thought angels were smart."

Aria surges forward, overtaking the Serene Commander, possibly emboldened by the fact that Callan has been so careful about summoning his fire. Maybe she thinks he will be as reserved with the angels as he was with the Grudge. She may not realize that he's reluctant to destroy dragons, given their dwindling numbers. He doesn't feel the same way about angels.

"How dare you set foot on Cathedral grounds?" Aria snaps at Beatrix while carefully avoiding looking me in the eye. "Filthy shifter."

Still supporting me, Beatrix tips her head to the side, squints, and cups her palm near her other ear, as if she's trying to listen to something.

"Can you hear that, Night Sky?" she asks me in an overly loud voice. "It sounds like a delicate little wind chime that doesn't understand the violence of the hurricane she's caught in." Her voice turns into a snarl as she glares at Aria. "Back the fuck off, little wind chime, unless you wish to be torn apart."

Aria plows toward us for another few steps before she seems to rethink her current course and stops in her tracks.

The Serene Commander is quick to turn to Callan, but I don't miss the way her gaze darts to her spear where it's embedded in the wall behind me and to my left, not far from where Aria has come to a halt.

The Serene Commander needs her weapon back. She's a Sentinel—one of the angelic warriors who are the strongest and purest. Each Sentinel is given a spear made of angel's gold. A single scratch from one of those spears can kill the strongest supernatural within minutes.

It was only because Solomon drove her weapon into the wall that she didn't kill me—or him—with it. With a flick of his hand in the air, he directed its flight away from me. I'm not sure if he would have been able to physically touch it, though. I tried to use it against her during my fight with her, and she said I was lucky to hold it for as long as I did.

"Callan Steele, you may think you can control Lana, but I know her better than anyone," the Serene Commander says, her lips twisted in a cruel sneer. "She will turn on you the moment you show weakness. She'll tear out your heart like the vile creature she is."

My blood boils to hear the Serene Commander speak about me that way, but it doesn't surprise me. She kept me caged for as long as I can remember, and she never once showed me kindness. To her, I'm nothing more than a means to an end. I was never a child. Not even really an angel in her eyes. She was burdened with the task of raising me and she saw me only as a creature whose rage she could manipulate to do her bidding.

Callan is surprisingly quiet. I thought he might respond with anger, but instead, he scrutinizes the Serene Commander as if he sees right through her. "Nobody controls Asper. Her destiny is hers to choose."

The Serene Commander's eyes widen. I can't tell if it's because Callan used my true name or because he said he doesn't control me. Beatrix also has frozen beside me, but Callan gives her a sharp tilt of his head, as if he's telling her to get a move on.

Beatrix pulls me another step toward Callan, but once again, the Serene Commander gets in the way.

Her scream of rage makes my ears ring. "Stop them!"

I'm surprised to see that she's pointing at Callan instead of me.

At her command, the rows of angels spread their wings, rise up behind her, and lean forward as if they're preparing to fly at Callan.

Beatrix's whisper is harsh and quick. "Do they have a fucking death wish?"

If any of them touch Callan, they'll trigger his dragon, he'll burst into flames, and he'll kill them all. The speed with which they retreated from him before indicated that they know this. It makes little sense that they would risk his fire now.

Callan responds immediately, on the defense. The golden bands twirling in the air at his sides fly toward the angels as efficiently as the bands in his home would halt me in my tracks. They wrap around the angels' waists and push them toward the alley's back wall, pinning them there.

The problem is that there are only ten bands and too many angels—fifteen at a brief count—and, sure enough, the remaining five angels fly straight for Callan.

Felix leaps from the top of the wall, batting away the first angel to reach him before plowing into the second.

"Let them burn!" Beatrix says to me. "We can meet Callan at the rendezvous point. It's time to fly." Her wings extend and she attempts to pull me toward the wall.

I dig in my heels. I can't fly, but that's not why I'm hesitating. I force my damaged vocal cords to function. "Something's not right. The angels should be attacking me, too."

Aria and the Supreme Commander are the only angels not joining the fight.

My focus shifts to them just in time to see the Serene Commander give Aria a signal.

The younger angel extends her wings, but she doesn't fly toward Callan. She heads for the wall behind me instead.

It only takes me a moment to realize her intentions.

She's the closest to the Supreme Commander's spear. In fact, when she approached me and Beatrix under the guise of insulting us, she was probably positioning herself closer to it. Now that Beatrix and I have moved away and Callan and Felix are distracted, Aria has the chance to pull the weapon from the bricks and throw it to the Serene Commander. The Serene Commander can then take a shot at Callan. All it will take is one scratch and he'll die within moments.

Aria has already reached the weapon. Her hand closes around its golden hilt, but I'm shocked when she screams, a sound of raw pain, and the awful scent of burning skin fills the air. It makes me even more surprised that I was able to hold the weapon for as long as I did during my fight with the Serene Commander.

I don't have time to wonder about that—or to tell Beatrix what I need to do.

I throw myself out of her arms and toward my glaive, which I was forced to abandon when Solomon overpowered me. It has remained, five paces away on my right.

Beatrix shouts with alarm, diving after me. "Lana!"

I'm faster than she is. I duck and roll, coming up beside my spear and wrenching it out of the ground in the next moment.

Behind me, Aria is still screaming with pain as she pitches the Sentinels' spear to the Serene Commander.

Now there are two weapons in play.

One flying across the air above me, a deadly spear headed back to the hands of its master, and my glaive, which I deftly rotate so the pike on the back end is pointed forward.

The Serene Commander has already released her wings in preparation for catching her spear. She takes the risk of turning her back to Callan to dart into the air and deftly catch her weapon.

Without stopping, she spins toward Callan, draws her arm back to release her weapon, and aims it right at his heart.

CHAPTER FIVE

*T*hud.

The deep sound of impact mingles with my scream of rage, and it feels like my heart has stopped.

Above me, the Serene Commander arches in the air, her gasp of pain and shock audible within the sudden silence around us.

My glaive protrudes from the back of her right shoulder.

Her weapon slips from her fingers and clatters harmlessly to the cobblestones a moment before her wings fail and she spirals downward. She hits the ground awkwardly and lands half on her side and half-facing the ground, her feathers spread across the stones while my blade juts up from her shoulder.

Opposite her, the other angels are suddenly darting away from Callan and Felix, no longer needing to cause a diversion, their wings beating furiously in their effort to retreat.

A quick glance behind me assures me that Aria has dropped to the ground in a kneeling position, holding her injured palm to her chest. Her quiet sobs now fill the silence, and she doesn't make a move toward me.

I'm also aware of Beatrix having frozen only a few paces

away from me, and of Felix, who remains like a guard in front of Callan.

And Callan himself, whose eyes have turned from cold green to warm, cinnamon brown, a color that calms me and tells me I only need to get through these next moments and everything will be okay.

I'm poised with my arm still raised, my chest heaving with effort. My pain levels have increased beyond endurance, but I know I can't stop now.

The Serene Commander is trying to push herself up with her left arm. I can't see her right arm, but she isn't moving it, so I assume she's partially immobilized while my weapon's blade remains in her shoulder.

Just as she gives a grunt of effort and begins to crawl, one-handed, toward her spear, I launch myself up to my feet and into a run, speeding to her side.

I leap across her and snatch my glaive from her shoulder as I fly past.

Her scream of pain is real. Possibly the first true sign of pain she's ever revealed in front of me.

I land at a crouch beside Felix and in front of Callan.

"No," I say, my voice stronger now. "I told you. You won't kill him."

She looks up at me but focuses on a point past my eyes. Her face is screwed up in discomfort. "You don't know what you're doing! You will regret this moment—"

My roar cuts her off, raging across my strained vocal cords. "You. Will not. Kill him!"

"Traitor!" Her pain vanishes and hatred disfigures her face. "All dragons will pay for this. The Celestial Ascendant will send the Sentinels now. I'm sure of it." She nods to herself and struggles to rise, making it up to her knees, no longer reaching for her weapon. Her shoulders hunch and her arms hang at her sides, but a cold smile grows on her face. "The Sentinels will come. They will crush you first, Lana, and then they will crush the dragons."

I lost count of the number of times she told me she'd begged the Celestial Ascendant to send the Sentinels to eradicate the dragons. The Celestial Ascendant always refused because the Sentinels can't leave their posts, where they guard the angels' treasures. But now... The Celestial Ascendant has already decreed that I am to die. The impossible has happened: Angels have been given permission to kill another angel.

Anything could happen.

I grip my weapon tightly as I cross the short distance to the Serene Commander. I snatch up her spear with my free hand and point both weapons at her.

Across the way, Aria gasps when the spear clearly doesn't hurt me like it hurt her, and a ripple of surprise runs through the other angels.

Holding both weapons—one in each hand—I crouch to my former master. "You needed Solomon Grudge to kill me because you're not strong enough to do it yourself," I say. "You can send a hundred Sentinels after me, and maybe... eventually... they'll succeed. But before I die, I make you this promise: Come after Callan or his family, and *I* will crush *you*."

The corners of her lips turn down. Her brow is furrowed with pain again, although I expect her shoulder will heal fast enough. She does her best to continue avoiding my eyes now that the magic of the painted wings on her face is broken. "Remember what I told you, Lana. Don't mistake your compulsions for love. You're incapable of the purity of that emotion."

If I wasn't already in so much pain, the ache within my chest might hurt more.

"Maybe," I whisper. "But that's for me to find out."

As I rise to my feet, I glare at the Serene Commander's spear where I grip it in my left hand. If only I could impose my will on it, I would turn it to putty and rip it apart. The best I can do is to take it with me, although that carries other risks. I'm wary of its blade and the deadly magic infused into it. The Serene Commander carried it safely by transforming it into the shape of a hairpin that she tucked into her hair, but no matter how much I glower at the spear, it doesn't retake that harmless shape.

It seems my influence over gold is exhausted for the night.

Keeping the spear's blade pointed safely down, I take a step back while keeping my own weapon steadily aimed at the other angels.

"You will let us leave," I say to them. "Or I will kill your beloved Commander."

Beatrix darts to my side. "Time to fly, Night Sky. I'm right behind you."

She gestures to the wall behind me, clearly indicating that I should fly over it since it's the nearest exit out of here. The other option is the alley's entrance, the same way the Grudge dragons retreated.

"I can't fly," I say, my voice strained. "One of my wings is broken."

Saying it out loud makes it somehow worse.

"Fuck," Beatrix whispers as her focus flicks to Callan.

His presence is suddenly like an inferno at my back. I can't risk turning to see his expression, but I'm not prepared for the heat that buffets me. I sense the same anger that he once directed at me for coming after his people.

My chest fills with the scent of burning grass, an endless field of it, glowing red with embers amongst the ash.

"Felix, watch our backs," he says in a deep growl, his dragon's voice finally breaking through his iron control. "We're taking the long way out."

With wide eyes, Beatrix tugs on my arm, pulling me in the direction of the alley's entrance. Her wings are out and the heat dancing around us makes the blood-red membrane shimmer and sparkle. "Quickly now."

I keep the Sentinel's spear tucked safely at my side and my own weapon raised as I back away, staying close to Beatrix.

Callan's heat circles from my back, radiating around me as he steps forward and positions himself between me and the angels. I catch only the briefest glimpse of his face, his juniper-green eyes and tense jaw, before his dragon shadow steps between us. Its golden head swivels in my direction, its eyes glowing, before it focuses on the Serene Commander and her warriors.

Felix aligns himself with Callan's position, both men taking careful steps backward while they keep our enemies in their sights. In the distance, the ten golden bands that Callan used to immobilize a number of angels against the back wall release our enemies and return to Callan's side.

I inhale the Serene Commander's pristine scent as I go. It is, once more, crystal clear and as calm and still as a pond. It's overlaid with the scent of spring flowers when we pass Aria's position on our left. She's glaring at me where she remains kneeling on the stones, and even though it's becoming more difficult to move my neck, I peer between the sweaty strands of my hair directly into her bright, blue eyes.

She gasps and winces, and I take the smallest satisfaction from reminding her that she should fear me. Even as broken and injured as I am.

As soon as we reach the end of the alley, Beatrix puts away her wings and hurries into the streetlight. Artificial light makes it nearly impossible to see a dragon shifter's shadow and true enough, Beatrix's shadow disappears immediately.

Without her wings or her shadow, she appears human. Granted, she has the appearance of a beautiful and sinister human with her dark eyes, pale skin, and perfect posture, but human nonetheless.

I step into the light with her and wait the seconds it takes for Callan and Felix to join us. Most of the golden bands that had floated around Callan's body converge and pile around his waist like a heavy belt while the remainder wrap around his forearms. They aren't exactly camouflaged, but I guess it's better than magical gold floating in the air, where humans could be startled by it.

At the far end of the alley, there's a flurry of wings as several angels fly to the Serene Commander, scooping her up in their arms and rushing her through the door at the side of the Cathedral. Another group of angels hurries to help Aria, while the remaining angels disappear up and over the Cathedral's rooftop at the far end of the alley.

That's all I see before we finally turn the corner.

"They'll follow us," I say as I take the final steps away from the mouth of the alley.

My heart is sinking with the knowledge that not only has Callan revealed his face and his identity to an entire legion of angels, but they could track him to his home and compromise the safety of everyone who lives there. A few nights ago, Aria saw me with his clan, but she didn't know which one was Callan. Now they all do.

"That's why we're splitting up," Beatrix says, tugging on my elbow while avoiding the weapons I hold. "Night Sky, you're coming with me. Felix and Callan will lead the angels away—"

"No." Callan swings to us. Now that he's standing in the streetlight, his dragon shadow vanishes, but its burning eyes remain for a moment. Two bright spots burning into my soul. "Lana's coming with me."

Beatrix digs in her heels. It's dangerous to stop moving, but her protest is instant. "The angels are after you and Lana. You need to split up. You have to make it harder—"

"No." His dragon's voice is a clear, harsh growl, cutting across Beatrix's protest.

46

She drops my elbow and takes a quick step back, putting a safer distance between her and Callan. Felix also inches away from Callan's position. He and Beatrix are both fierce dragons, but they're wise to keep their distance from Callan right now.

"Fine." Beatrix's teeth are gritted. "Felix and I will run interference." She hurries to her cousin's side where she pauses, some of her anger vanishing. "Be careful, Callan. Remember that your actions won't only endanger yourself, but our whole clan."

"I'm fully aware," he says, his shoulders tense.

Beatrix's dark eyes flash to me. "Stay safe, Night Sky. I'd hate to lose you." Her serious expression vanishes as she and Felix back away. A smile dances around her lips. "Who would I play with then?"

They spin and disappear along the street, keeping to the streetlight so their shadows don't reappear. Within seconds, their lithe forms have vanished into the dark.

Callan's voice is low. "We need to keep moving."

"Callan, I—"

I turn to find him standing much closer to me than is wise. Between his dragon and the two weapons I'm holding, neither one of us is particularly safe for the other to be around right now.

"There's a lot to talk about, but it has to wait for now," he says. "You're hurt. I'm taking you home."

Even though we should be running already, getting the hell out of here as fast as we can, he pauses. "Will you come with me?"

A sudden, unexpected ache spreads through my chest.

After I survived Callan's fire, he started giving me choices. Small ones. Then bigger ones. I was no longer his prisoner when I emerged from his home last night. I didn't escape from him. I *left* him. I even lied to do it. A stupid lie that I was going to get coffee. I told him I'd be back in a few minutes.

Callan gave me choices. *Real* choices.

He hoped—but didn't expect—that I would choose him.

I did.

I chose him with more of my heart than I'd thought possible.

Then I chose to protect him. I didn't tell him about the Serene Commander's ultimatum because I knew he would go after her. I knew that if I fought her and won, her death would not be attributed to the dragons. The angels would come after *me*, not them.

If I lost the fight, then Callan would not be complicit. I hoped that both the Serene Commander and Solomon Grudge would view my attack as mine alone and leave Callan out of it. Life would go on for him and his clan.

All of that has changed now.

I failed. Spectacularly.

The danger faced by Callan and his clan has only increased.

And yet he's giving me another choice.

My gaze flickers to the other side of the street and the shadows pooling around the buildings there. I could leave Callan, find a dark corner of this city to hide in while I tend to my wounded pride and my injured body, and then strike out on my own. It's the option that would keep him and his clan safe.

Or I can go with him. Accept his help and whatever safety he has to offer, knowing full well that it would be better for him if he never saw me again.

How can I be this selfish?

Is my heart so corrupted that I can't walk away from him now? That I would choose to bring upon him the very danger I was trying to protect him from?

The war within my mind rages for a moment before I silence it.

My head and neck hurt too much for me to nod. My voice is still hoarse, but I manage to respond. "I'll come with you."

The tension around his eyes and lips eases. He gives me the

same smile he gave me when I returned to his home after he'd set me free. It's genuinely happy and it makes my heart feel warm. An instant balm for my fears.

"My car is two blocks this way," he says. "Can you make it?"

I'm not sure what he plans to do if I say I can't walk that far on my own. It's not like he can carry me. Then I notice Felix hovering in the darkness along the street. I thought he was long gone already, although it's not such a surprise that I didn't realize he was still around. Dragon shifters register as humans within my senses. It's only their dragon shadows—or the act of shifting—that betray them.

When it comes to the choice between using my own two feet and being carried by Felix... well... I'll choose my own legs. Not least of which because I'm not sure how either of the weapons I'm carrying will react if Felix touches them.

"I can make it," I say, even though my muscles are screaming and I'm only moments away from tears of pain. I tell myself that if I have to let the tears fall, I will. My pride be damned.

Callan gives Felix a quick nod and the other dragon disappears into the darkness again.

Callan doesn't try to touch the weapons I'm holding or to take them from me. He spins in the direction opposite to the way Beatrix and Felix went, and I follow at a quick jog.

It's incredibly awkward running while carrying two polearms, although my glaive is easier to hold since it's shorter. I'm just lucky it's early morning and the street is deserted.

Callan moves fast, throwing quick glances back at me as he darts between the streetlights and the shadows along the footpath, avoiding the moonlight as we leave the Cathedral behind. He manages to run without his dragon shadow making an appearance, but keeping to the streetlights puts us in a vulnerable position. Our path is easily visible to anyone trying to follow us.

I want nothing more than to shut down my senses and

conserve my energy, but I listen carefully as we run, taking note of every distant noise, every small whisper of sound.

We are most definitely not alone, but Callan's presence stops me from sensing the intentions of the beings following us. Strangely, I can't tell what species they are, which is confusing, since I was expecting to detect the shimmer of energy that belongs to angels.

I wonder if my own energy levels are so depleted that my abilities are dangerously inadequate now. Or, more alarming, if creatures other than angels are also tracking us.

Callan races around the final corner and down a narrow side-street where a two-door sports car is parked in the full artificial light emitted by a tall lamp post. I don't recognize this vehicle. It's not one of the cars that was parked in the garage under his home, although it's just as sleek. A deep, dark blue with a streamlined body and angular lights.

The vehicle unlocks as soon as he brushes his hand across the door of the trunk. When it opens, he grabs two blankets that are neatly folded at the side of the trunk. He spreads one of the blankets out across the base of the storage space.

"For your weapons," he says.

I'm already shaking my head, but not because the weapons aren't technically *mine*. "The spear is too long. It won't fit."

He arches an eyebrow at me. "The trunk is bigger than it looks. I can fit rifles in this car. I bought this model for that reason. Trust me."

I'm doubtful, but when I lean forward, I discover that the space may be shallow but it extends far enough that I can lay the weapons diagonally to fit them both in. I'm wary of the blades touching each other, since they're both made of living metal, so I fold one side of the blanket in the trunk over the spear before I place my glaive on top of it and then fold the rest of the material over them both.

My hands are shaking by the time I finish. I take a beat to

rest my palms on top of the weapons, taking another breath and trying to steady myself before I straighten.

Callan stood guard while I worked, and the tension hasn't left his posture.

I sense the proximity of multiple beings in the distance who are all gaining on us. This time, I distinguish two separate groups: the shimmering energy of angels approaching from the direction of the Cathedral, and another group approaching from the other side, a species I still can't identify.

Closing the trunk, I turn to follow Callan's line of sight in the direction of the group I can't recognize. "Callan? What's going on?"

"The angels aren't the only ones tracking us," he says, confirming my earlier fear. "The Scorn are after you, too."

CHAPTER SIX

I jolt at this news and then suck in a sharp gasp of pain, since sudden movements are not in my favor. Neither is speaking, but I've been forcing my vocal cords to function all the same. I resist the urge to press my fingers to the side of my aching neck, my groan of discomfort coming out as a hoarse snarl.

"Fuck." I squeeze my eyes closed for a moment. "The Scorn?"

They're the third dragon clan. While Callan's clan, the Dread, have assimilated themselves into the elite of human society, the Scorn are part of a thriving underground of supernatural thieves, assassins, and enforcers for hire. I once believed I was close to wiping them out. But that was back when I thought I'd succeeded in annihilating the Grudge. How little I knew.

"I'll explain in the car. Take this. You need to stay warm." Callan hands me the other blanket from his trunk, taking care not to brush his hand against mine before he gestures to the passenger door.

I slip around to that side and slide into the front passenger seat, trying to move as little as possible now. I take deep breaths as I settle into the vehicle, click my seatbelt into place, and pull the blanket over myself.

Callan pauses outside the driver side door and I'm curious why until the bands of gold slip away from his body. They glide smoothly toward the vehicle's hood. They curve across the front of the vehicle and flatten themselves against the metal frame, blending in as if they're part of the car. It's the same mechanism they used to attach to the ceiling of Callan's home.

While Callan settles behind the wheel, I quickly catalog my injures, trying to be clinical and detached about them. Luckily, I'm not too bloodied. Only the small cut above my right eye and the nick across my neck are bleeding. My ribs are tender from where Solomon crushed me against his chest when he first seized me in the alley. My chest and torso are covered in bruises from multiple punches. Pinpricks of blood remain in rows down my sides from his claws.

The burn across my back from the noose doesn't hurt anymore. It felt painful enough at the time that I suspect it might leave a scar, but it would be just another mark to join the ropey scars the Serene Commander gave me when I was younger.

The worst injury is to my neck, which is affecting my mobility, and the pain from the bruising is clouding my thinking. I close my eyes and breathe through the moments, actively reducing my worries to one singular goal: get through each minute.

My eyes fly open when I sense Callan lean toward me. He reaches for the corner of the blanket that has slipped from my shoulder, but he stops, seeming to think better of it. A raging fire within this vehicle would not help us right now.

A mere touch from another supernatural is all it takes for Callan's dragon to be triggered. If that happens, his scales and wings manifest against his will, and he breathes fire hot enough to kill anyone who doesn't have dragon wings to protect themselves. As long as he remains in his shifted form after his fire is spent, he can safely touch other supernaturals, but he can hardly stay in that form forever. Once he shifts back to his human form, his dragon will once again be triggered by touch.

I set off his dragon twice in the last week. After the second time, Callan remained in his dragon form and fell asleep with me in his arms. During the night, while he was still asleep, he shifted back to his human form and woke up like that. It was the one time he could touch me in his human form without igniting his dragon's fire, and it felt like a small miracle. As long as we remained in contact at that time, his dragon remained subdued, but as soon as we let go of each other, the connection was gone.

If he touches me now, his dragon will trigger like usual, and this car will fill with flames.

"It's okay," I whisper, finding it easier to make softer sounds than to try to speak normally. "I'm okay."

His jaw clenches as he withdraws his hand, puts the vehicle into gear, and quickly pulls away from the curb. His focus on the road is intense while he takes frequent glances in the rearview mirror.

"It's not okay," he says, and it feels like he's talking about so much more than my injuries.

My choice to fight Solomon alone. My lie when I left him last night. Or, far worse, the threat of the Sentinels that I've now brought to his door. I want to tell him that I'm sorry, but it feels horribly inadequate. As if that single word can atone for the danger his clan now faces.

"You came for me," I whisper.

"I'll always be there when you need me."

It's such a simple statement, but it floors me.

No... He can't say that. He can't believe that.

Before I can voice a denial, a hint of a smile grows around his lips and his gentle glance silences me. "I knew right away that you were lying about where you were going."

I'm startled. "Last night?" I thought I'd crept out without him being any wiser. At least for a few minutes. "How?"

"You hate coffee."

I bite my lip. I told him I was going to ask his human body-guard to get me a coffee. My brow furrows. "If you knew I was leaving, why didn't you stop me?"

"Because I made you a promise." He looks across at me again, a longer look this time before he refocuses on the road. "I told you that you were free to leave, and I meant it."

My lips part a little as I draw a quick breath. "You thought I wanted to leave?"

He's quiet as he keeps his eyes on the road. "Everything that happened last night." He shakes his head. "My fire. Killing Byron. The plan to use you as bait to draw Solomon out. It was too much. I sat there watching over Sophia, thinking about how fucked-up everything was, and I knew I had to let you go."

Yesterday, Callan learned that Byron, one of the Dread drag-ons, had killed the sister of his close human friend, Jada. Callan's mother was human, and he has a strict rule against harming them. The fact that it was someone he'd known and cared about had made Byron's treachery a thousand times worse.

It was Byron who triggered Callan's fire last night and endangered every dragon present, including Callan's niece, Emika, who was defenseless while her wings were clipped. Byron had known the fire would kill her. It was only because Sophia shielded Emika, and I swallowed Callan's fire, that Emika made it out alive.

"You thought I wanted out," I say.

His hands tighten on the steering wheel. "I thought you *deserved* to get out. I wasn't going to stop you."

"Even though I might come for your people? Hunt them again?"

A soft smile plays around his lips. "You saved Emika's life last night. You won't hurt me or my people."

Again, he floors me with the simplicity of his trust.

Struggling to process the storm of sadness his faith in me elicits, I deflect a little, humming in the back of my throat. "Well, I'm not so sure about Beatrix..."

Callan snorts and returns my smile before he becomes serious again. "I sensed you were in trouble when your bracelet called to me." He's focused on the road, but his chest rises and falls with a deep, indrawn breath. "It was beating like your heart. Rapid and uneven. That's when I sensed you'd stepped into danger."

Instinctively, I reach for the ruby-heart charm beneath the blanket, remembering how it glowed when I was trying to escape the noose. Callan originally gave me the bracelets because they allowed him to track me. That stopped when they switched their alliance to me.

A little of Callan's previous fury bleeds into his eyes, his cinnamon-brown irises flecked with green again. "I need to understand why you would choose to fight Solomon Grudge and a legion of angels on your own."

"And a Sentinel," I murmur. "Although in fairness, I didn't know in advance that the Serene Commander used to be one."

"Lana?"

I meet his stern eyes, my smile fading as I face his need for answers.

"Why?" he asks.

My voice is small. "The Serene Commander gave me a choice: Kill you or be killed. I refused the first and accepted the second."

Callan is incredibly quiet. So quiet that the silence buzzes in my head, the purr of the car's engine not enough to fill it.

I'm shocked when the air around me grows too warm for the blanket, waves of heat rising off his bare chest and his face. "You can't ever endanger yourself like that again," he says. "Not for me."

I stare back at him. I wish we weren't having this conversation in a car while dragons and angels are on our tail. "It was my choice. I made it."

"No," he says, pure gold flecks glistening within his eyes. "That's not a choice you should have to make alone."

My heart squeezes. "I had to. I couldn't involve you."

"Why not?" he asks, taking his eyes off the road for a dangerously long moment.

I snarl back at him. "Because then I couldn't protect you."

"And what about you?" he asks, a sharp question, his fury hitting me so hard that I'm stunned. "Who was going to protect you?"

I blink at him. "No... You can't ask that..."

I wish I could back away from this conversation, but there's nowhere to go. No way out of this vehicle. I can't even shake my head at him. All I can do is grit my teeth and try to hold back the tears springing to my eyes.

"This was my choice," I whisper, my vehemence growing stronger. "I brought this on myself. The consequences for me were always going to be the same."

"Death?" he asks, a harsh growl. "Where is the choice in that, *Not*-Lana?" The heat waves beat around him as his voice grows harsher still. "Kill me or die. Where is the choice in that?"

"There wasn't one," I cry, my voice breaking, and I'm not sure if it's because of my injuries or my emotions. "Only the choice to protect you or not."

"What about protecting yourself?"

"No!" I press my fingers to my temples, dislodging the blanket, but I'm no longer cold because of his anger. It's a building inferno that's dangerously close to igniting. I repeat, "You can't ask me that!"

"Why not?" he asks.

"Because it hurts too much."

He casts me a glance that's suddenly stricken.

"It hurts too much to think that you care about me..." I press my fingers to my temples. "I can't accept... Because I'm not..." My voice breaks hard. My feelings are in turmoil and I can't make sense of them, can't pull apart anger from hope from fear from warmth...

I wish I could reach out and touch him. Anchor myself somehow. But I'm stuck in this injured body, stuck in this seat. Even if I wasn't, I wouldn't be able to reach out to him. Not without triggering his dragon.

His response is quiet, and it's the resurgence of calm around him that gives me focus. "The idea that someone could care about you enough to risk their life for you is challenging," he says. "I faced it when I met my human friends. It took me a long time to realize that they didn't judge me based on anything in my past—who I used to be —only on who I was right then. They trusted me, despite not really knowing me. But that's what trust is. It's not knowing everything about someone and loving them anyway."

"Trust can be broken," I say.

He nods. "It can."

"But you trust me not to hurt your family."

"I do." He pauses. "I also want to trust that you'll ask for my help when you need it."

I press my lips together. "That will be hard for me."

"Then let's take it one step at a time. Will you tell me where you're hurt?"

"In case I'm about to die?"

His silence speaks volumes.

"I'd tell you if I had any life-threatening wounds." I try to sound convincing, although the lie is like sour lemon on my tongue.

His focus is on the road again. "I'd like you to tell me, if you can."

My lips press together. Now that my turmoil has faded, those damn tears of pain are about to make their presence known. Solomon might have told Callan he doesn't know what I am, but Callan certainly knows me well enough.

My voice is stiff as I try to stop the hot tears from starting. Once they begin, I'll have a horrible time making them stop. "My neck has taken a beating. I have bruises pretty much every-where. You probably saw the burn across my back. That's from when the noose fell—"

"*Noose?*" Callan's voice is sharp enough that it could slice Solomon's heart open if the Grudge dragon were here. "A fucking *noose?*"

Callan's eyes are pure juniper-green as they clash with mine. "Made of dragon's gold?"

"Yes," I whisper. "But…" I hesitate to tell him what I did with that noose. "I pulled it off me and turned it into the glaive I put in the trunk."

His brow furrows, but it's a softer expression than before. "You stole Solomon's gold."

"Yes."

"I assume that includes the web on your arm?"

Self-consciously, I brush my fingertips along the protective armband beneath the blanket.

He continues. "And you transformed both pieces of gold into something else."

He's only repeating what I already told him, and I'm worried about the questions that might come next—questions for which I have no answers—so I deflect instead. "You said you'd tell me about the Scorn."

He isn't quick to accept the new path of our conversation, taking the next corner of the road before he responds. "My clan doesn't have any direct conflict with the Scorn. When I became alpha of the Dread, I sent a message to Sienna Scorn to tell her that if her clan stays out of our way, we'll stay out of theirs."

Sienna Scorn is the female alpha of that clan. To my knowledge, her family has held on to the leadership through generations. Of course, I've learned in the last week that my knowledge of dragons and their history barely scratches the surface, so I can't take my prior beliefs as a certainty anymore.

What I do know is that Sienna is as clever as she is dangerous.

All I have is her name. I don't know what she looks like or where she lays her head at night. The only way I could distinguish a Scorn dragon from a dragon of another clan was by the insignia the Scorn have etched into the handles of their weapons. A dragon, naturally. They didn't hide themselves from me like the Dread did, but that's because of their skillset.

Trained killers and fighters. All of them.

When I was hunting the Scorn, I hoped to take Sienna out first, but unlike other members of her clan, she constantly eluded me.

"I take it you're not friends, then," I say.

Callan's voice is hard. "Staying out of each other's way was the best arrangement I could make with a dragon who sells her clan's skills out to whichever gang or mob will pay the highest price." Callan glances in the rearview mirror again. "Do you remember that wolf shifter pack I told you about? The one that owed a debt to a Scorn dragon?"

"I do." It's hard for me to forget. I assumed the Dread had annihilated that shifter pack, but actually, Callan had paid off their debt and relocated them for their own safety.

"That dragon was Sienna Scorn herself," Callan say. "She was ready to take her payment in blood when I stepped in."

"You didn't have to help them," I murmur.

He lets out a soft breath. "I'd like to say I did it out of the goodness of my heart, but it wasn't completely altruistic. There are wolf shifter packs outside the city who would have taken a dim view of the city pack suffering harm at the hands of dragons. I didn't need that kind of exposure."

"But the Dread aren't the Scorn." As soon as I speak, I see the problem. In fact, I should know better than most. "Other supernaturals don't see it that way."

"Dragons are dragons." He gives me a sideways glance, and the frustration in his voice is clear. "One dragon's crimes are attributed to all dragons."

I swallow hard. "If you have a truce with Sienna Scorn, why would she break it now?"

He peers at me for a few seconds, and the look he gives me is laden with meaning. Before he can speak, I answer my own question.

"Because of me," I whisper. "She wants revenge for the deaths I caused, just like the Grudge do."

"True, but it's more complicated than that," Callan says. "Sienna Scorn may want you dead, but as long as you're with me, she was prepared to keep her distance."

"Then what changed?"

"Solomon Grudge came out of hiding because of you." Callan's gaze clashes with mine for a second. "Sienna Scorn was watching the concert hall like Solomon was. She would have become aware, even sooner than I did, that Solomon was still alive."

It was outside the concert hall that Callan captured me. He left my purse and my hairclip on an elevated window ledge in the alley beside the concert hall and then asked his human bodyguards to watch that spot and report back if they saw anyone take the items.

When Callan first told me about Solomon, he showed me pictures of the Grudge dragon in that alley. But before then, I overheard Jada and Brock telling Callan that a woman had also visited the alley multiple times. Callan didn't show me the woman's picture, only the photos of Solomon. At the time, I assumed they were talking about the Serene Commander. I didn't imagine it would be Sienna Scorn.

"What business does Sienna have with Solomon?" I ask, hoping the answer is that she wants him dead.

"Someone put a bounty on his head. A large one." The tension around Callan's mouth increases. "She wants to collect. Given that you drew him out of hiding, she thinks following you is her best bet at finding him."

None of what he's telling me sounds like hypotheticals on his part and it unsettles me that he seems so certain.

"How do you know all of this?"

He's quiet. Far too quiet. My instincts prickle and I really don't like the nasty sensation that mingles with my physical pain and seems to make it worse.

"Callan? What aren't you telling me?"

He remains focused on the road, taking another turn. I'm surprised when we exit onto the Delaware Expressway that runs parallel to the river on this side of the city. It would seem far too exposed, but then, it will also expose anyone who's following us.

"I took care of a lot of things yesterday," he says before he gives a heavy sigh. "At least, I tried to. Not as successfully as I thought, as it turns out."

He said the same thing to me when he returned after being gone all day yesterday. I greeted him at the door. Waited for him to come in. His shoulders were hunched over. He told me about some of the things he'd taken care of, but nothing that related to Sienna Scorn.

"I asked you to trust that I know what I'm doing," he says.

"Okay?" I say, waiting for him to continue.

It takes him a long minute, during which time, my awareness of all the other beings on the expressway increases. Sunrise is less than an hour away and the road is becoming busier. There are humans in vehicles driving alongside us and also traveling in the opposite direction.

But it's the quiet purr of motorcycles behind us that really worries me. At least three of them in a group.

"I spoke with Sienna Scorn yesterday," Callan finally says. "It was my first meeting with her face to face. Before then, I trusted Tyler to liaise with the Scorn in my place. He has contacts within their clan. But I couldn't trust him with this."

Tyler Dalton is the Dread dragon I mistook for Callan when I first met them both. At that time, I thought Callan was Tyler's human bodyguard. How wrong I was.

Like Beatrix and Felix, Tyler is also a member of the ruling Cohort. Only hours ago, I defended myself against him when he came at me during the Cohort's meeting.

Right from the start, I sensed the heaviness, the shadows, in his nature, and the tension between him and Callan. The reason for the friction became clear when Callan told me that Tyler had expected to take over the role of alpha before Callan took that position instead.

"What happened?" I ask.

"I told Sienna I knew she'd tracked you to the concert hall and I asked her to be straight with me about her intentions."

"And?"

"Now that Solomon is in play, she isn't willing to honor our truce."

My brow furrows. Callan must have thought he'd brokered some kind of deal with her if he thought he'd taken care of the threat she posed. "But?"

"I told her you were under my control. That trying to track you would only lead her to my home and into conflict with me. I also told her that I'd take care of Solomon. I'm one of the few dragons with the strength to kill him."

His hands tighten on the steering wheel. "When she still didn't back off, I told her that she might not like it, but she'd welcome my fire even less. She finally agreed that, as long as you remained a prisoner in my home and didn't go out without me, she could accept that you weren't a threat to her clan. But she wasn't going to wait for me to kill Solomon. I told her that was fair enough, provided she leaves you out of it."

A chill passes down my spine. "I went out on my own last night." I also left his home yesterday morning, but that was before he made the deal with Sienna.

"You did."

"Damn." I chew my lip as those tears burn again behind my eyes. I had to go without Callan to keep him at arm's length from my actions. I didn't know I was opening the door for Sienna Scorn to become a threat to him and his family.

"What are you going to do?" I ask quietly.

"First, I'm going to lose the dragons and angels who are following us. Then I'm taking you home."

CHAPTER SEVEN

*C*allan slows the vehicle down, watching carefully in the rearview mirror at the same time.

"There are the dragons," he murmurs.

I can hear the motorcycles more clearly now and I assume he can see them behind us.

Motorcycles are the mode of transport favored by the Scorn. By covering every inch of their bodies with leather motorcycle suits and wearing opaque helmets on their heads, they're able to conceal their dragon shadows, and if a glimmer of a shadow forms, it's easily mistaken for a reflection from a nearby streetlight.

While I was hunting them, the city's artificial lights were my greatest frustration. This expressway is flooded with light, so there's no way for me to tell if the motorcycles following us are ridden by Scorn dragons or humans.

"But where are the angels?" Callan mutters to himself, leaning forward to peer through the front windshield.

"In the sky," I murmur. "To the north."

Four shimmering forms blaze within my senses. They're flying above the glare from the streetlights, which conceals their positions, but even so, it's bold of them to fly where they could be spotted by humans. I guess the night's events have made them angry and less prone to caution.

"Good." Callan's jaw clenches and his lips set in an uncompromising line as he speeds up again, changing lanes as if he's preparing to exit the expressway.

Up ahead, I recognize the way toward an old power station that rests at the edge of the Delaware River. I've hunted within the buildings around the power station. They're abandoned and full of old machinery. There's a wide, concrete parking lot outside the main building that's flooded with artificial light so even on a clear night when the moon is at its fullest, it's the perfect hideout for dragons.

Behind us, the motorcycles speed up but maintain their distance, and above us, the angels follow closely.

Callan's driving so fast now that I'm sure I've mistaken his intentions and he's not going to take the exit after all.

At the last possible moment, he veers off the expressway and speeds down the deserted stretch of road leading to the abandoned buildings. His sudden move forces the dragons to speed up again, the rumble of motorcycle engines growing louder as they close the gap between us.

Callan gives a smile a second before there's a flurry of movement across the car's hood.

The golden bands peel off in unison. Four fly directly upward while the rest shoot past our windows, soaring backward.

The awful crunch of shrieking metal meets my ears seconds later. I can't look back, but I imagine the golden bands cutting through the motorcycles like scythes.

In the sky, the angels' shimmering forms are wrenched away from us. It's as if they're plucked from the sky by the hand of a giant and flung in the direction of the river. I picture the golden bands looping around their torsos and driving them into the water.

"I hope angels can swim," Callan says.

He takes the next entry ramp back onto the expressway and then, very soon after that, the next exit back to the city. His golden bands haven't yet returned but I expect they will make their way back to the vehicle soon.

I slump in my seat, my adrenaline well and truly exhausted. Despite the cozy blanket, I'm feeling colder by the minute. "Now what?"

"I'm taking you to my new home. One that has more protective wards around it than the last."

"New home?" I probably shouldn't have to ask. When he took me to his club, the Hollow Rose, I pointed out that letting me out of his home meant revealing its location. He told me it wouldn't matter because he had other homes and he could move at a moment's notice.

"My old home isn't safe anymore," he says. "Not for anyone."

My heart squeezes in a way I wasn't expecting. Callan offered to make his home *my* home. In only a short time, I became attached to his tree-filled library, his training room, and even the little café that served green vegetable smoothies.

"I'm sorry about your home," I say.

"It's just a building. What matters are the people in it. I sent my human bodyguards ahead to our new place already. As well as Sophia. Jada and Brock are taking care of her."

Jada and Brock are two of Callan's human bodyguards. He met them when he was in the human military and fought beside them in a human war. Jada is trained in combat medicine, and she cared for me when Callan first took me to his home.

As for Sophia, she's Tyler's wife—or was until last night when she told him to stay the fuck away from her. The last I saw of her, she was lying injured on a stretcher in Callan's home with severe burns across her back after she protected Emika from Callan's deadly flames. Until last night, Sophia had no access to her wings, but after the fire, for the briefest moment, her skin glimmered a luminescent shade of cerulean blue.

I turn my mind to Emika's mother, Zahra. She is Callan's half-sister. "What about Zahra and Emika?"

"Zahra's home isn't compromised. She'll stay away from us for now. It's safer until the heat dies down."

"Okay," I murmur.

Now that we're not being followed, I close my eyes and accept my exhaustion. *Nearly there*, I tell myself. *Nearly home.*

I shake myself.

Home?

It's a dangerous thought for a creature like me.

I open my eyes to find that the vehicle has stopped.

I expect to see that we're paused at traffic lights, but when I squint into the dim light, I discover that I'm staring at a solid, concrete wall.

I can't believe I fell asleep. "Where are we?"

Callan leans across me but doesn't come too close. "Stay there," he says softly. "Brock and Dermot are coming down to carry you up."

"But..." I try to fight my deep lethargy and shake myself awake. "No, I can walk—"

Pain hits me the moment I move, and I whimper. My head is throbbing, and my neck is killing me.

Callan slips out of the vehicle and within seconds, I'm aware of footfalls on my side of the car.

The door opens, and I recognize the dark-skinned human who crouches next to my seat. Like all of Callan's human body-guards, Brock is tall, broad-shouldered, and polite.

Callan told me that he handpicked his bodyguards because

they each have a skill he can use. Brock is a sniper, and right now, his keen eyes seem to have summed up the wounds around my head and neck in two seconds.

He glances at the other man standing beside him—Dermot, the fair-skinned man with very pale blond hair, whom Callan told me is a skilled close-combat fighter.

"You got the neck brace?" Brock asks Dermot.

"Right here."

Brock takes the plastic device that's shaped like a cylinder and lined with some sort of soft material.

Finally, he greets me. "Hi, Lana," he says. "I need to put this around your neck to protect against further injury. Do I have your permission to touch you to do that?"

I stare at him for a moment, not really able to comprehend that he's asking permission to lay his hands on me. "Y-Yes."

He reaches around me carefully, clipping the device together so that it sits snugly around my neck, and I can rest my chin down on the lip at the top.

"Is that okay?" he asks, leaning around me to visually check the brace.

Immediately, the pressure on my neck has eased. It's not close to pain relief, but it helps. "Yes, thank you."

"Okay, now I need to get you out of the vehicle and onto the stretcher. But first I need to remove the blanket. Is that okay?"

He continues to ask my permission as he takes away the blanket, then reaches in, scoops his arms around me, and lifts me out as if I weigh nothing.

He says as much, and he sounds surprised.

I remain quiet since I don't think it would go down well if I told him that angels are built light.

Dermot is waiting beside the stretcher with a thermal blanket that he wraps around me as soon as Brock lays me down.

Then they're wheeling me away from the car.

I seek Callan across the way before he catches up with us, but he keeps his distance. His human friends believe he has a fear of touch—a necessary explanation for why he keeps his distance from everyone. At first, I disagreed with the representation of his fear until I realized that it's truthful. At the smallest contact, his dragon will trigger completely against his will and burn everyone around him. He lives his life separately from others, always at a distance from those he loves, afraid that he could hurt or kill them.

His expression is closed off now as we cross the garage to the elevator on the other side. So far, this new place doesn't look too dissimilar to the old one. The vehicles are different. Several SUVs sit alongside the sports car he just drove in, as well as two motorcycles. But otherwise, the layout is much the same.

The elevator is the size of a service elevator, so the men have no problems wheeling the stretcher inside it and Callan keeps to the front corner. He presses the button for the tenth floor, and I take note that there are only ten levels in this building, not fifteen like the last one.

The humans stay close and it's strange that I find their presence comforting. I never imagined that the presence of humans would make me feel safe. And yet... I also feel incredibly vulnerable.

I'm laid out on this stretcher with a sense of diminishing control over where they're taking me and what I'll find when I get there. Somehow, it was so much easier when I came to Callan's other home. I was fighting him, and it gave me some semblance of control, even if that was ultimately an illusion.

When the doors open, they wheel me into an entry room that's as austere as the one in Callan's other home, and just as closed in. There are no windows, and the air conditioning is cranked up so that the air is cold. His last home was designed with a concealed internal core while the outside appeared completely normal. I suspect this one is the same.

Callan presses his palm to the security panel next to the door. The door is painted a soft eggshell blue and the color is the first distinct difference between the two homes. Instead of swinging open, the door gives a soft mechanical whir and slides into a cavity at the side.

Callan gives me a faint smile when he steps inside.

We enter a large room that makes me blink with surprise.

The whole right-hand side wall is encased in glass that appears to sit a few feet out from the wall itself. Behind the glass is a garden filled with plants. Climbing vines drape from the top while flowers and bushes blossom along the bottom. It makes me think of a tall and narrow greenhouse.

The floor is made of what looks like polished wood, but the surface glistens, as if it's coated in some sort of transparent substance, possibly glass.

In the center of the room is a narrow wall also encased in glass, inside of which water falls. The wall leaves wide spaces on both sides, so it's easy to see the far side of the room.

Images of birds fly silently across a screen that takes up the entire width and height of the back wall, their flight graceful and calm. A dining table and chairs sit in that space, appearing to be made out of some sort of black substance, possibly also glass, judging by the way it shines.

There are three doors at intervals along the left-hand wall, each one closed and painted a shade of blue. The first two are on this side of the waterfall. The third is opposite the dining table.

This side of the room is empty, other than another stretcher.

I recognize Sophia where she lies on her stomach facing the right-hand wall. Dressings cover her back from her neck to her waist and a blanket rests over her legs. She's wearing sweatpants drawn low across her hips and a T-shirt that appears to be cut up the back to allow for all the dressings. An intravenous drip is set up at the side of her stretcher.

Her tousled, brown hair is pulled up off her neck and loosely tied, leaving visible the side that she shaved. It was the side where Callan's flames touched her on the night he first brought me to his home.

The wounds she sustained last night are far worse.

Her large, green eyes are closed, and her back rises and falls rhythmically. She was sleeping when I left, and I hope she hasn't woken up to her pain in the meantime.

I catch a glimpse of her pale skin and her drawn cheeks before Brock and Dermot wheel my stretcher up beside hers and I can't see her face any longer.

Jada hovers at Sophia's side, waiting for the guys to lock my stretcher in place before she turns and bends over me. She's dressed in the same military-style, beige pants and collared shirt that she was wearing when I saw her last. They're a lot more crinkled now, though. Her dark-brown, shoulder-length hair is pulled back into a short ponytail at the nape of her neck. It's normally neat, but it's messy right now. Her skin is light olive and the darkest lashes frame her deep-brown eyes, which are filled with concern.

"Fuck, Lana." She's already checking me over as she speaks, lifting the blanket and clicking her tongue at the bruises across my torso before coming back to my head to check the cut above my eye. "What happened?"

Her voice is like fresh air. I can't sense her presence as strongly while Callan is here, but even so, she's like a tree with strong roots that hold on during a storm. Branches under which I could shelter.

She was the first person to ever touch me with gentleness, and suddenly, I find myself telling her the truth.

A vulnerable truth.

"I went out on my own last night," I whisper. "I didn't ask for help. I thought I could handle it. I thought I was doing the right thing." My voice chokes and I try to moisten my lips. "For once."

Of course, I haven't really told her anything. Not why I left or how I was injured. But she nods, as if I've told her everything she needs to know.

"I'm going to take care of you now, okay?" she says, carefully brushing the hair out of my eyes.

Jada sets about telling Brock and Dermot what extra medical apparatus she needs and asks them to bring one of her shirts for me to wear.

Callan pulls up a chair and positions himself against the wall beside the first internal door. He hasn't bothered to get a shirt. Or shoes, for that matter. Come to think of it, he ran the entire distance from the Cathedral to his car and then drove in bare feet.

He leans forward, his hands clasped in front of himself, elbows on his knees, shoulders hunched, waiting quietly while Jada cleans my wounds.

She pauses when she comes to the gold lattice on my forearm. "Protective armor?"

I press my lips together and make a non-committal sound.

"How does it come off?" she asks, carefully turning my arm over before she gently pulls on the armband.

I'm worried that the gold might rebel against her human touch, but it simply clicks open when she brushes her fingertips over the inner edge. After placing it carefully on the stretcher beside my pillow, she moves on to check my torso and stomach, scrutinizing the healed wound across my lower abdomen that I sustained a week ago.

When Brock and Dermot return with the medical equipment, as well as a soft, blue T-shirt that I slip beneath my pillow to wear later, Jada sets to work, plastering my cuts, icing my bruises, and giving me intravenous fluids.

She explains everything she's doing. "This intravenous pole

is on wheels so you can move around to go to the bathroom. You'll need to keep wearing the neck brace until the soft tissue in your neck has healed, but let me know if it starts to feel itchy, okay? I need to check your back now."

She reaches around me to maneuver me onto my side, and I brace for her to see my wounds. Not only because of the raw burn that the golden noose will have caused, but because of my old scars.

Jada is suddenly very quiet.

I can hear the silence in the way she's holding her breath, and a sense of unease floods through me. *Is there an injury I didn't know about? Or...*

Fuck. Have my wings not retracted fully?

Trying to quell my panic, I tell myself that maybe it's just the awfulness of the burn from the red-hot noose. Maybe it's far worse than I thought. She's probably wondering why I didn't tell her about it, how I've been lying on it all this time. I probably should have said something, but it stopped hurting ages ago—

"Lana, what happened to your scars?"

Her question startles me.

My forehead creases. "What do you mean?"

"I mean... they're gone."

CHAPTER EIGHT

I'm frozen. *Not those scars. It's impossible.*

Jada supports me with one arm while the fingertips of her other hand brush gently across my shoulder and follow a snaking path across my back.

"You have a welt down your shoulder and across your back, right above where I'm touching you, but your scars ... They've faded."

I try to reach around to my back. "No, that's..."

She presses her palm against my shoulder to stop me moving while she lowers me back to the bed. "The welt should heal on its own." Her deep-brown eyes meet mine. "I'm probably misremembering. Old marks can disappear over time."

The look on her face tells me she doesn't believe her own explanation. She doesn't know about the scars' origins, but I know it's not possible for them to fade naturally.

The Serene Commander took a cat o' nine tails to me after I snuck out of the Cathedral when I was fourteen. The whip was imbued with a magical substance to make sure I was left with thick, ropey marks that would brand me for life.

There's no way they could disappear. *Is there?*

Then I remember the searing heat I experienced when the noose dropped across my back. An explosion of warmth had radiated out from the band when it landed across my shoulder. The pain in that moment... And then the instinct to keep holding on to that band...

Somehow, the dragon's gold must have healed my scars. It's the only explanation I have for why the marks have disappeared.

I should be happy about it, but my breathing is more rapid than it should be. I try to focus on the calm, blue ceiling, but the color does nothing for my growing dread.

Even if I could explain how they're gone, those marks... They may be like an awful, visible reminder of my corruption, but they're an *outward* mark, as if my defects are somehow external to me. If the scars have faded, then it's like they've sunk inward, become a part of me. When they were visible, I could quantify them. If they're gone, I can't measure them anymore.

I can't defeat what I can't see.

Of all the things that would make me panic, this is not what I expected to tip me over the edge. Maybe it's just that I've finally had enough tonight.

I've reached my limit.

My hands are shaking, rattling against the bed, and my breaths are coming fast. A stupid panic about stupid scars that I've hated my whole adult life.

"Lana?" Jada's worried face dominates my view, but it's not her presence I feel most strongly now.

Callan appears behind her, and she swings to him.

"Let me help," he says, quiet and calm.

She nods and steps aside, veering around him to stand at the base of my stretcher.

Callan's presence is as strong now as it was the first time we met. He bathes me in warm sunlight that sinks beneath my skin and curls around the very heart of me.

He lowers his big hand to the stretcher a careful two inches away from my shoulder as he bends to me, and I tell myself to stay very still, even though I want to taste the fire I know is resting on the tip of his tongue.

His eyes are cinnamon, flecked with gold, a hint of his dragon. Dangerous in the presence of humans.

"Lana?" He pauses. "*Not*-Lana. Your scars don't define you."

I stare up at him, my eyes burning. *How did he know that's why I'm afraid? How did he read me so accurately?*

"But my choices do," I say.

His hand shifts toward me an inch. A faint smile appears on his lips. "Yes. Even when you choose to take on too much."

I wasn't the only one who took on too much yesterday. Callan has chosen not to tell Jada what really happened to her sister. She believes her sister died in a hit and run, and that the human police never found the person responsible. Callan can't tell her what really happened without exposing his family and the existence of the supernatural community. He certainly can't tell her that he killed the perpetrator. To do so would put Jada in the awful position of condoning a murder or reporting Callan to the human police.

But, I suddenly realize, I can tell her more than he can.

My voice is hoarse as I look right at Jada. "You asked me how I got hurt." I swallow. "Last night, I found out who killed your sister."

Her eyes fly wide. She stumbles a little and Brock and Dermot hurry to either side of her, supporting her.

"Who?" she asks.

"A monster," I say. *Not a lie.* Byron was the one who took a knife to me and reeked of murder and guilt. "Do you remember I said that if I found out who it was, I would kill them?"

Jada's breathing is rapid now, her hands trembling where she folds them in front of herself. Brock rubs her back, murmuring. "We've got you. You can get through this."

"You found him. This monster. Didn't you?" Jada asks me, her focus traveling across my wounds with a new sense of understanding of how they might have come about.

"He's dead now," I say. *Also, not a lie.*

Beside me, Callan is like stone, but I refuse to acknowledge the shift in the air around me. Refuse to recognize the growing hues of juniper-green in his brown eyes. I might not be telling direct lies, but I've led Jada to believe something that isn't true: that *I* killed the man who murdered her sister.

He begins to speak, but to me, not Jada. "Lana—"

"Jada knows what I am." My voice is cold now, my panic gone.

In retribution, I find peace.

Even if the act of punishment in this case wasn't committed by me. "She knows what I do for a living. If she wishes to report me to the authorities, then that's her right. I won't run from this."

I look up at Callan, meeting the confusion in his eyes.

He starts to speak. "Why would you—"

My instincts tell me he's about to ask me why I'd take responsibility for a death I hadn't caused. I choose to answer him as if he asked me why I would take it upon myself to end that man.

"Retribution is what I bring. It's my reason for being." I exhale, so much calmer now. "This is my choice."

At the base of my stretcher, Jada is leaning against Brock, but the color is returning to her cheeks. Tears slip down her face. "I've spent years wondering who this person was. Wondering if they got to go home to their family at night when I lost the only family I had. But now... It doesn't matter who they were. What matters is that I still have a family. My family is here, in this building. I would die to protect them, and I know they would die to protect me, and that's what matters most to me right now."

Some of Callan's tension evaporates. He once told me that some humans have the heart of a dragon, even if they can't shift into one. My sense of it is that these humans have supported Callan through hell in the past, and they continue to support him, even when he picks up and moves without explanation. He jokes about paying them not to ask questions, but their loyalty is beyond anything I've ever witnessed.

Jada clears her throat. "I think we could all do with some sleep now. Sophia will be fine for a few hours. I can come back and check on her and Lana later." She blinks away her tears. "You need some rest, too, Callan. It's been a long night for everyone."

She hugs Brock, then Dermot, and looks to Callan as if she would hug him, too, if she could, before she leads the men to the door.

Callan strides after them. "Jada?"

She spins back to him. "It's okay, Callan. Really." She rubs her temples. "I mean, it's going to take me a while to process it, but he's dead now. There's justice in the world after all."

When the humans are gone, Callan remains where he is for a long moment.

I'm not sure what to expect when he turns back, but he's quiet. He returns to my side and presses his hand on the stretcher again. Another inch closer and our pinkies would touch.

I search for the golden flecks in his eyes, the hint of his dragon, but it's gone.

"You didn't have to do that," he says. "It was my weight to carry."

A sudden warmth burns through my chest. It takes me by surprise, but I let it come.

I rebel against the Serene Commander's claim that I'm incapable of love.

My voice is guttural. Fierce. "I did it because you're mine to protect."

Callan's lips part as if in surprise. His eyes soften and the heat waves growing around him turn to mere shimmering wisps. "How is there so much dragon in you?"

Some of the heat disappears from my throat. "Maybe because I'm full of your fire."

Last night, I swallowed Callan's flames. I won't be able to hold them forever, but last time, they took a full day to burst out of me, so they shouldn't be a problem until this evening. I have time to make sure I'm in a safe place when that happens.

I continue. "There's a storm growing around us, Callan. It's quiet here in the eye of it. That's a false sense of safety. Nothing good is coming for us. If I can bring Jada some closure and take that weight from you, then that's what I choose to do."

His hand rises, his palm resting in the space at the side of my face. "I'm starting to fear that the idea of making choices is growing like a wildfire in you, *Not*-Lana."

I attempt the smallest shrug.

"I don't want to leave you," he says, "but I need to get the weapons we left in the car and put them in a safe place."

A sense of ownership rises sharply within me at the mention of the spear and the glaive. It's a strange sort of possessiveness, given that they were both used against me at some stage.

"Don't touch them," I warn him. "They're each dangerous in their own way."

"I'll use my gold to move them," he says.

I picture the golden bands that were attached to the car. I didn't see them return to the vehicle, but I assume they must have come back while I was asleep on the way here.

"You should get some sleep while you can." He gives a heavy sigh. "You're right, Lana. Nothing good is coming for us. We need to be prepared."

His hand leaves the bed and then he's striding away from me, his feet quiet on the shiny floor.

He takes his sunlight calm with him.

When he closes the door behind him, I stare up at the ceiling. Callan told me to get some rest, but it's impossible right now.

I may have hated my cell under the Cathedral, but it was a buffer between me and the rest of the world—and all the fucking guilt that floods my senses.

Now that I'm alone with Sophia, I taste endless sour lemon across my tongue, the telltale sign of a practiced liar. It's marred by a brief tang of copper, although that's fleeting, indicating that she had the intention to cause harm but didn't carry through with it.

Worse than that, her presence feels like twisted vines, all seething and tangled, and squeezing more tightly with every second. A web from which she can't escape. The more she struggles, the tighter it gets.

It's constricting my own breathing.

And it's getting worse because she's awake.

CHAPTER NINE

"Go on, then," Sophia says, still facing away from me. "Get your gloating out of the way."

My lips part in surprise. *Gloating?*

She doesn't attempt to face me. She will probably find it difficult to move with all the dressings covering her back. "You got rid of the scars on your back, while I got new ones. I'm sure you'll find poetic justice in that, given how I treated you."

Well, I suppose there's some justice in it. Sophia took great delight in the moment at the club when I handed her the shawl that was covering my scars and bared my disfigurements for everyone to see.

"You don't have anything to fear from me," I say, opting for diplomacy. "Least of all gloating."

"Oh, right, because Callan has you under control." She scoffs. "Under control, my ass. If you were obeying his orders, you wouldn't have left."

She struggles as she presses her hands against the stretcher and lifts her chest and head high enough so she can face me. That small movement seems to exhaust her. She's breathing heavily by the time her head sinks back to the pillow.

Now that she's looking at me, I can see that her right eye is bloodshot, her cheeks are deathly pale, and there's a tremor in her bottom lip.

"The only reason I'm safe around you is because you only kill real dragons." Despite her bleak appearance, her voice is completely lacking in emotion. "I can't shift. I don't have wings. I barely warrant the title of *dragon shifter*."

I *hmm* in the back of my throat. "I think I could still find a reason to kill you."

"Because I'm a bitch?" she asks. "Because I make everyone's life miserable? You don't exactly rate high on the likability scale, either."

I remain unmoved. "I wasn't put on this Earth to make people feel better about themselves."

"No, just to kill dragons."

"Other creatures, too, as it turns out," I say, since what little I know of Avenging Angels is that they aren't supposed to discriminate between species.

Her brow furrows. "Then why dragons? Why destroy *us?*"

I close my eyes as I remember the Serene Commander's speech.

I needed you to believe that dragons are not worthy of life. I needed to control you. To steer your rage in their direction, like a river that must flow somewhere, lest it drown us all.

"So I don't kill the ones who sent me," I say.

It's an honest answer, but I don't expect it to make a shred of sense to Sophia. Even so, I sense a shift in her mood, and once again, there's a mess of vines flooding my senses, a tightening in the air, as if she's quietly struggling to escape.

"The angels were afraid you'd turn on them," she says. "They sent you to kill us instead. They knew we'd keep you busy."

I stare back at her, my lips parted and a retort on the tip of my tongue, but I'm not sure how to reply given how astutely she interpreted the angels' intentions.

She says, "You thought I was stupid? I've survived this clan, haven't I? Nobody survives the Dread without knowing how to play games."

"Games of your own making," I snap, remembering how she'd tried to undermine Callan's leadership by encouraging other clan members to fear his fire.

She gives me a cold smile. "Lana?" She pauses. "Or is it *Not-Lana*? Is that what Callan called you? Why would he call you something like that?" Her forehead creases, but it's momentary. "No, scrap that. I don't give a shit." She continues in the next breath. "Why do you think I had to play games in the first place?" Her voice is sharp. "This clan is vicious. It's bite or be bitten."

"It doesn't have to be like that."

Her eyebrows rise. "Really? You've gotten to know us all so well in the last week, huh? Found us all warm and fuzzy?"

I can't argue with her. When Callan spoke about his role as alpha of the Dread, he told me he'd fallen into that position because of an act of revenge and fury, and that he governed his clan through the threat of fire and violence, not love or connection.

He said they are not a pack like other shifters form packs. There is no loyalty among them. But I saw clearly how much he cares about each one of them. He even cares about dragons who aren't in his clan—Scorn and Grudge dragons. He said that the loss of any dragon life is a tragedy, especially given the decreasing number of dragon shifters alive today. If he didn't care, he would have burned Solomon and his men to ash without a second thought.

As for Sophia, Callan is worried about her. He cared enough to call her to the Cohort meeting last night in case Tyler reacted badly to what Callan had to say.

"I know that Callan cares about you," I say.

She laughs, and it's an awful, derisive sound. "Callan doesn't give a shit about me. Even my own mother doesn't care about me. You saw her last night. She couldn't move fast enough to save herself from Callan's fire and let me burn."

Her voice chokes. She draws her head back a little as if she's regretting moving to face me. I don't need my power to tell me she's mortified that I'll see the tears shimmering in her eyes.

She isn't wrong about her mother. In those moments when Callan's fire was rushing toward little Emika, Sophia threw herself into the path of the fire despite not having any wings to hide behind, while her mother scrambled to save herself.

But I don't think Sophia saw the way that Beatrix and Felix both threw themselves toward her to protect her.

Her voice is scathing again. "Poor, defective Sophia. She's so pathetic, her daddy had to buy her a husband."

When Callan spoke about the old alpha, he told me that the alpha had been Sophia's father, and that Tyler had married Sophia because he'd thought the old alpha would pass the leadership on to him.

Callan had gotten in the way.

Not just in Tyler's way. Sophia would have been the alpha's wife. She would have had position and respect. She'd lost out, too.

She continues with her self-derisive rant. "Tyler only married me because my father promised he'd be the alpha. My father gave everything to Tyler. Everything that should have been mine. I have nothing. Own nothing. Control nothing. I wasn't even allowed to get a job among humans, even though I'm closer to a human than a dragon. I did whatever I could to survive."

She stops speaking, and I let the silence settle, giving her the chance to blink away the tears caught in her eyes. Her anger is like...

My brow furrows because I'm not sure how to make sense of the sudden sensations washing across me.

Her anger is like water.

A whole fucking tidal wave of it, except that it's poised at its peak, never crashing down. Somehow, it's trapped within the cage of vines tightening around her.

Which makes no sense because water can't be trapped by vines...

"You don't have to put up defenses around me," I say, testing a theory that the vines are a sign of a deliberate emotional shield on her part. "I know what it's like to have nothing."

Her response is quieter than I expected. "No," she says. "You don't know. You have *power*."

Do I?

I own nothing of any material value, not even the clothes I'm wearing, but I'm physically strong. I can sense guilt. I have a reputation.

I'm *feared*.

There's power in fear.

I sigh quietly and swivel my gaze back to the ceiling. "You're right," I say. "I control more than I thought. But what is power like mine worth when it means I've always been alone?"

"I don't know," she murmurs, her big, green eyes still shimmering. "Ask Callan."

With a grunt of effort, her eyes squeezing closed, she pushes herself the smallest height off the bed so she can turn her face away again. She heaves out a sigh as she settles back to the surface, and then she's quiet again.

Within minutes, her back rises and falls steadily and the writhing vines I sensed in her have disappeared. Her shields fade away while she sleeps, but it feels like mine only grow thicker.

I try to close my eyes, but it only brings back moments from my fight with Solomon that I'm trying to forget.

My hands shake as I reach for the armband that Jada removed. She put it on the stretcher beside my pillow so it's easy enough to reach for it. I click it back around my forearm like a shield against the inevitable future.

Callan wants me to believe that death isn't my only choice, but I can't see how it won't be.

I suddenly taste fire across my tongue and it carries the scent of scorched grass. A field burning to ash beneath a fiery sun.

It's Callan's scent.

It's so distinct that I look for him, convinced he must have slipped back into the room without me noticing. I'm sure I'll see him standing near the front door, his arms folded across his chest, keeping his distance, as he's forced to do.

The other side of the room is empty. Callan isn't here, but the smell of burned ash only grows stronger.

What the fuck?

Sweat breaks out across my entire body so suddenly that I feel like I'm flailing in water. Gasping for breath, I throw the blanket off myself and press my hand against my forehead, only to find my skin is hotter than hell.

I inhale. Exhale. Try to calm my breathing. But the burning scent only grows stronger, filling my head with heat and smoke and—

Oh, no.

No, no, no...

This can't be happening now. When I inhaled Callan's fire last night, I pulled it so deeply inside my body that I knew I couldn't hold it forever. But last time I swallowed his flames, it was a full day before I faced the consequences, not mere hours like this. It shouldn't be happening now. If I'd suspected it would happen so soon, I would have taken myself somewhere safe.

I can't lose control of it now. Not while Sophia lies defenseless beside me.

Of all the mistakes I've made, this could be the worst.

I have to get out of here.

Panic rushes through me as I rip off the medical apparatus that ties me to the intravenous pole, ignoring the pain of removing the canula and the agony shooting through my neck when I jolt upright.

I don't know what's behind the doors along the wall—don't know if it would be safer to try to get inside one of those rooms or if that will only make things worse.

My only certainty is that I need to get away from Sophia before I kill her.

I throw myself off the stretcher in the direction of the nearest door. I try to push the intravenous pole out of my way, but I collide with it, knocking it to the glossy floor with an almighty crash.

With a thump, I release my wings, beating them frantically. I only manage to rise half a foot into the air before my left wing loses traction, the gaps in my feathers defying my determination.

I drop to the ground, sprawled at an awkward angle.

Oh, please.

I push myself back to my feet, preparing to run, aware that Sophia is stirring.

She pushes herself up to face me, her arms shaking, her voice sleepy but filled with growing alarm. "Lana? You okay?"

"Get down!" I scream at her. "Sophia! You have to get—"

Her eyes widen, her emerald-green irises glisten, and her pale skin shimmers in the heat waves building around us.

Her whisper is sharp. *"Fire!"*

Her pupils constrict to fine points in the sudden, bright heat billowing toward her as I lose control.

CHAPTER TEN

*F*ire as hot as hell bursts from my mouth.

I haven't stopped moving. I'm running, my legs pumping, my hands flying to my mouth to try to stop the flames, but the fire has a mind of its own, heaving out of me against my will. Rushing around my fingertips.

In the seconds it takes me to turn away, I catch glimpses of Sophia through the flames.

She's screaming. Throwing herself off her stretcher so fast that, despite what must be a lock on its wheels, she knocks it backward and it skids into my bed. Both stretchers topple and hit the ground. Her intravenous pole crashes to the floor. I expect her to dive toward the nearest overturned bed for shelter, but instead, she launches herself toward the wall in the middle of the room—the one encased in glass with water cascading down the inside.

Maybe she's hoping to smash it and find refuge in the water. I don't know, but I don't think it would work against the heat of these flames. For a second, I think her skin shimmers, the same luminescent shade of cerulean blue I saw last night, but I can't stop to watch, and I don't see more before I finish turning.

The fire is only getting worse and the horror of what's happening drives me onward, away from her.

I've never hurt or killed any dragon by accident. My actions were always controlled. Efficient. The deaths I dealt were as quick and painless as I could make them. My retribution was in death, not in pain.

But *this...*

My heart is in my throat. Sobs tear out of me. My tears evaporate as soon as I shed them. I reach the nearest door only to realise that I can't open it. It doesn't have a handle, only a control panel, and I don't know the code. I spin toward the front door instead, making it halfway there when I realize that the room is quiet behind me, and Sophia isn't the one screaming.

I am.

Violent. Agonized. Awful screams.

They peel from my mouth and, with every heave, new flames fill the air around me. The force is so great that the neck brace pops and warps around my throat. I tear it off and drop it to the floor. With every cry I make, the fire worsens. This wild force... it's tearing me apart. It's breaking me from the inside out.

The first time Callan's flames tore out of me, I was in a safe environment. I couldn't hurt anyone. I was with him, and he sheltered me.

This time, Callan isn't here to hold me while I break.

I'm nearly to the door when the next heave of fire hits me. It's so forceful that it knocks me sideways—toward the wall with the other doors in it. I extend my good wing just in time to stop my fall, ramming its tip against the base of the wall. The impact judders through me, but I manage to stay upright.

I make it another three steps before the next heave knocks into me, and this time, my wing doesn't hold. It folds and I fall heavily onto my hands and knees, my palms landing flat on the glassy floor, both of my wings like crumpled mounds of feathers at my sides.

I'm aware of a cloud of white descending from the ceiling. The fire extinguisher must have kicked in, but it's doing nothing to calm this fire.

My scream is desperate. *"Callan!"*

I curl up into a ball, facing the wall, pressing my face to my knees, trying to breathe the fire onto myself instead of into the room.

My scream is muffled and full of despair. *"Callan!"*

I don't hear the mechanical whir when the front door slides partially open, but I sense the rush of air before it cuts off again.

Callan's silhouette is a dark force within my peripheral vision. Golden bands rest around his waist and forearms while several others drape across his arm. He runs toward me.

The air around him glints with gold as the bands streak through the air and hit the ground inches from my feet.

Clunk-clunk-clunk.

They assemble between me and the rest of the room, dropping onto each other lengthways, rapidly expanding and forming a seamless wall that fits to the side of the room and curves around me. One by one, the bands build high enough that they block my view of the fallen stretchers while leaving an opening at my back.

The flames hit the inner surface of the makeshift wall, spilling across it and upward. The wall doesn't reach the ceiling —there doesn't seem to be enough gold to stretch that far, but my flames don't reach that high. The gold bubbles in the fire, but it holds steady, containing the flames.

A second later, Callan is at my side. "Asper!"

It seems fitting that he calls me that right now, since this fire is cruel.

I cry, "You have to help Sophia!"

He drops to his knees beside me within the protected area

he's created. He's within inches of touching me, but if he does, his dragon will be triggered, and that will only increase the fire in this room.

"There's nothing I can do for her." His response is a deep growl as he draws me up into his arms, cradling me to his chest.

The change in him is instant and terrifying.

A new wall of flames billows around me, cutting across my face and torso, lighting up my wings where they'd dropped at my sides.

His own wings release, but slower than I expected, held tightly so they don't hit the wall on my right or the curved, golden surface he created. His wing bones look like they've been carved from gold, and the membranes shimmer so brightly that they're reflective. Fine, golden scales cover his skin, making his face, neck, torso, arms—every part of him—glisten while his human skin is still visible beneath them. It's as if his scales are transparent armor that leaves every perfect, sculpted muscle on display while making him luminescent.

Each time he has shifted at my touch, we've crashed into each other. We've ended up in the air. But this time, the force of his shift is like an implosion. His body is bigger in his shifted form, his big arms wrapping around me, pulling me against his expanded chest, his thigh muscles beneath me feeling harder, more solid. He wraps me up in his wings, an open cocoon that lets out his fire but directs it toward the golden wall.

His features shimmer in the heat waves, his eyes pure yellow as he bends his head to mine, nestling me against him.

With every breath I take, I'm inhaling his flames, but I don't try to stop.

"Sophia," I sob.

He makes soothing sounds, his beast's voice audible through his human vocal cords. "This room is set to divide into two if there's a fire," he says. "The wall in the middle contains panels that will close off that side. It's a kind of panic room. I told

Sophia about it before I went to find you. I wanted her to know she was safe from my fire. I should have realized—"

He stops, but I know what he was about to say. He should have realized *I* was a danger to Sophia. Hell, we even talked about the fire that I swallowed before he went to put away the weapons, but I was certain I had more time. He must be recriminating himself now for not placing her stretcher far away from me.

We both know I'm a threat to everyone around me. By swallowing Callan's flames last night, I took the fire that would have killed his niece, only to rain that same fire down on Sophia.

He looks me in the eyes as he continues. "I'm sure she made it through."

"How can you know? She could be lying in this room. Right now—"

"I didn't see her when I arrived, and the wall is closed. That only happens if you activate it from the other side. I'm sure she's safe, but I've put up this gold barrier as an extra precaution."

I tip my head back to see him and it surprises me that I can move my neck without pain. Somehow, the burning heat is soothing to my bruised throat muscles, even though it's agitating to my senses.

It's a shame the healing power of the flames doesn't appear to extend to the other wounds on my body—the cut on my face still stings and my torso still aches from the bruises I sustained.

"We have no choice but to wait until our fire dies down," Callan says.

I struggle to accept that there's nothing I can do, but my cry of denial only spills new ribbons of flame into the air. The air is a mess of amber and yellow as Callan's fire and mine combine around us.

It would be beautiful if it weren't so deadly. "You have to do something—"

"Lana, I understand what you're feeling." His gaze clashes

with mine, and there's a mountain of pain behind his golden eyes. "Being unable to help someone because you'll only make it worse. Waiting to see if you've hurt them." He swallows. "Waiting to find out what kind of monster you've become. I understand this."

The heat between us is intense and it takes my breath away. "I didn't want to hurt her."

"I know." He doesn't release my gaze. "I believe you."

Despite his reassurance, I rush on. "I couldn't stop it. I tried."

His hands press across my lower back, his thumbs swirling against my sore muscles as he repeats, more emphatically, "I believe you, Lana."

He once told me this fire doesn't belong to me. That it's *his*. I feel the truth of that within every inch of my being. How easily it could break me. This angry, wild force that he hates—that he would get rid of, if he could.

I press my face to his chest, flames still spilling from my mouth, cruelly aware that if he wasn't the source of this fire, I would be hurting him right now. And yet the fire goes round and round between us.

From him. To me.

From me. To him.

I'm suddenly aware that he's fixated on a point at my side and I follow his line of sight to my broken wing. It brushes his side, curved around his torso while his wing rests outside of mine. The gaps in my feathers are so large that they're easily visible.

"Lana, your wing," he murmurs.

I immediately retract it before he can reach for it. I'm not ready to accept the extent of the damage or the reality I now face: That it takes a very long time to heal a wing.

I won't be able to fly anytime soon.

He withdraws his hand and doesn't say anything more about

it, but the rasp in his breathing increases like it did when he first arrived at the alley tonight. Fierce. Vengeful.

I disentangle myself from his steady hold and reach up to trace his jaw, waiting for his anger to ease. I press my forehead to his chin as I listen for the softening of his breathing.

My voice is small despite the fire that releases with every breath I exhale. "The Serene Commander gave me two choices, but I had a third choice. I wish I'd taken it."

When I look up at him, I find his forehead creased.

"Lana?"

"She told me to kill you or be killed, but there was another path." I try to breathe as I consider what could have been. "I could have stayed with you last night."

His lips part with a quickly indrawn breath. My fingertips reach the corner of his mouth, and his fire *whooshes* across my hand as he exhales.

"I could have ignored her threat," I say. "When I responded to her, that's when I gave her power over me. If I'd stayed with you, I would have been safe in your home. Your truce with Sienna Scorn would have held. We could have faced Solomon together. The Sentinels would not be a threat hanging over us."

I squeeze my eyes closed, but nothing stops the fierce glow of the flames behind my eyelids. "And we wouldn't be here now, waiting and hoping that Sophia is alive and unhurt."

He presses his palm to my cheek, gently brushing the strands of my hair that float outward, coaxing my eyes open again.

"Sometimes the hardest thing is to do nothing." His thumb stops on my jaw. "But, Lana, other times you have to act. My truce with the Scorn was tenuous at best. Solomon was looking for you and he would have threatened my home eventually. If you'd refused to respond to the Serene Commander, it would have elicited a retaliation involving the Sentinels anyway. And as for this fire, until we figure out how and why this happens, it will be a threat hanging over you no matter what you do. Just like my fire is a threat to everyone I care about."

He takes a deep breath before he continues.

"Everyone I care about, except you."

The pain in my heart now is somehow worse than the heat in the air around us.

His thumb strokes my cheek, but he doesn't seem to expect a response, and I'm grateful because I don't know how to describe to him just how complicated the workings of my heart are. Just how many doubts I have about myself. All emotions other than my most basic compulsions to hunt and kill are new and uncertain for me.

"A battle between the dragons and angels is overdue," he says. "You tried to stop it, and even though things didn't go to plan, the point is that you *tried*."

I rest my head in the crook of his neck and we stay like that for what feels like the longest minute of my life.

Finally, cool air slips into my mouth, and this time, fire doesn't pour back out when I exhale. I check Callan, swirling my fingertips through the smallest spirals of heat around his face.

Our fire is fading.

I can breathe. Clear air.

Callan moves at the same time I do. He quickly pulls me upright, then lowers me to my feet. "My dragon has settled," he says. "My fire can't be triggered again until I take my human form, so it's safest if I stay like this for now."

I give him a quick nod, waiting only a beat for the golden bands to separate and fly up out of our way before I hurry to the middle of the room.

I can see now that two floor-to-ceiling panels have extended from either side of the dividing wall. The waterfall continues to flow inside the dividing wall, as if nothing happened.

Hurrying toward the fallen stretchers first, I pray that we

don't find Sophia lying on the floor, injured or worse, behind one of them.

The floor is empty other than the scattered medical gear and the burned mattresses and pillows. The shirt Jada loaned me is a few scraps of blue material now. Given the obvious damage to the room's contents, I'm astonished that the floor, walls, and ceiling don't have scorch marks.

Callan strides toward the right-hand panel of the dividing wall. Both sides are opaque glass and it's impossible to see what waits for us behind them.

"How is none of this burned?" I ask.

"The glass is fire-rated. The best there is. It coats every surface in this room." As he speaks, he opens a small, easily visible compartment in the wall and presses a large, green button. Many of the controls in his old home were concealed, but I imagine he wanted this one to be easily used to help anyone in the panic room.

I hold my breath as the panel slides to the left.

I'm shocked when a thin layer of water rushes out across the tips of my toes. "What the...?"

Callan's muscles bunch and his wings lift as if he's about to grab me and jump back from the small flood pouring around us.

"Did the waterfall break?" I cast a quick glance at the wall on my left. I was certain it was still intact, and it certainly appears undamaged.

"Stay close," Callan says. "The fire extinguishers don't use water. I don't know why this is happening."

The panel finishes opening, finally revealing the room on the other side. The table and chairs sit exactly where they were, appearing untouched. Soft, white crystals float from the ceiling, and they appear to be the same magical substance that extinguished the fire in Callan's other home. Not that they helped my fire tonight. They settle onto the shallow surface of the water covering the floor before dissolving into it.

My attention is drawn to the large, glistening sphere—iridescent blue in color and nearly as high as my waist—that rests in the center of the open space between the dining table and the greenery-filled wall. Water trickles across its surface, cascading from a point at its top and running down the shimmering sides onto the floor.

I gasp as a sensation of being immersed in ocean waves overwhelms my mind. Somehow, Callan's presence doesn't diminish the sensation that rushes across my skin. It's so strong that I stop breathing for a moment, convinced that if I inhale, I'll take in liquid. Within my mind, that same tidal wave rises above me, impossibly paused, a roaring force that's preparing to crash down on me.

I take an instinctive step toward the sphere.

Always toward danger.

Callan reaches for me, a warning in his eyes, but I can't stop myself. As I move forward, the surface of the sphere starts to unfold, and its shape becomes clearer.

It's a cocoon formed from wings.

Their edges are transparent, the palest blue, providing a narrow strip that allows me to see inside the sphere.

I catch sight of dark lashes resting against pale cheeks. A face covered in snow-blue scales. A female body curled up, knees to chest, floating and immersed in water within the cocoon. Her light-brown hair is streaked with gold, the strands floating around her face in the water.

I hold my breath as Sophia opens her eyes.

CHAPTER ELEVEN

Sophia's large, green eyes blink at me through the water. Her forehead creases.

Then she glances around herself.

She jolts. Her lips part as if she gasps. Then she jolts again, appearing to choke on the water she must have inhaled.

The cocoon of her wings flies open. The tips of her wing bones scrape across the floor as they shoot wide, and the water contained within the sphere crashes to the floor, another small wave that breaks across my feet.

Sophia drops to the floor on her hands and knees, water rushing off her body as she chokes and gasps for air.

She screams with every wet cough. "What. The. Fuck?"

Callan is frozen beside me, his wingtips extending forward, as if he wants to go to her, but he's not sure if he should. "The fire must have forced her dragon to surface."

My instincts take me forward. I step carefully through the water, crouching a few paces away from where Sophia kneels. "Sophia?"

She pauses, her wet hair dripping onto the floor as she shakes her head. "That's not my name." Her brow quickly furrows. She presses her hand to her eyes. "I mean, it's *my* name. But it's not *hers*. She spoke to me. I heard her... But now I can't remember..."

I glance at Callan, startled by the way his face has drained of color.

He reaches my side within seconds and kneels in front of Sophia. "Sophia, I need you to listen to me. You heard a voice before you regained consciousness. Try to remember what it said to you."

She focuses on him, and her eyes change color, becoming as luminous as her wings, the softest blue. "She said..."

Callan leans forward and I don't dare to breathe. I don't understand what's going on or why Callan seems to understand what Sophia is experiencing, but the air around us is charged and once again, a tidal wave is rising up over me within my mind.

"She said she was grateful to live again." Sophia closes her eyes, as if she's concentrating. "Then she told me her name."

Sophia pauses and now Callan seems to also be holding his breath as if his life depends on it.

"Bella Vorago," Sophia says, her voice softer than I've ever heard it. "Her name is Bella."

I let out my breath and think quickly, sifting through my knowledge of the old language that the Serene Commander drilled into me.

"*Bella* means pretty," I say. "And *Vorago* means...?" I squint, shaping my hands like a bowl before imitating a swirling motion. "Watery chasm?"

"Whirlpool," Callan says.

"Pretty whirlpool." Sophia lifts her hands while water continues to drip from her clothing. "I guess that makes sense."

"Can you still hear her?" Callan asks.

Sophia bites her lip. "She's fading, Callan." Her eyes glimmer with what seems to be awe. "Her voice was so beautiful, but I can't hold on to her. She's slipping away from me." Fresh water brims in her eyes and I'm sure it's tears now. "I don't want her to go."

I still don't really know what's going on, but it's obvious that Sophia's dragon has been somehow activated and that hearing her dragon's voice is a rare thing.

"Moonlight," I whisper suddenly, turning to Callan, who gives me a questioning look. "You told me that when dragons have human mothers, they develop like human babies until they're born. Even then, it's not until they're exposed to moonlight that they develop as dragons. Is there a way to get moonlight in here?"

He immediately jumps to his feet. "In this home, there is."

Splashing through the water on the floor, he hurries back to the side of the room. This time, the control panel is concealed in the wall. When Callan presses his palm to it, the ceiling above the narrow garden that runs along that side of the room slides back, opening up a long skylight about a foot wide. At the same time, concealed panels that were sitting against the wall tilt so that the light shining directly downward reflects across the room.

Sophia sits up a little straighter as the light washes across her, and then her anticipation fades.

Dawn's light pours down onto us.

Callan's shoulders hunch and his voice is bleak. "It's morning already. We're too late."

Just a short time ago, I wanted nothing more than to see the sun rise, but now it feels like the dawn has robbed Callan and Sophia of something I don't properly understand. For a few moments, there was a spark of hope in Callan's eyes. A spark I don't think I've seen in him before, and now, even the calm he exudes feels flat and lifeless.

He remains with his back to us, his wings tucked in at his sides.

I approach him quietly, reaching up to press my palm to the middle of his back, a light touch since I don't want to push him for answers he isn't willing to give. "Callan? Can you tell me what's going on? Help me understand."

He reaches around to take my hand, turning and lifting his wings slightly so that I can slip my arms around his waist and rest my head against his chest.

His voice is a rumble at my ear. "When my dragon first appeared, it was the one and only time I heard his voice. The change was so rapid, and the danger was so great, that I didn't have time to think or try to hold on to the connection. It was the only time I sensed what my dragon wanted. *Felt* who he is. He didn't tell me his name, and I lost the link within seconds."

Days ago, Callan told me that dragon shifters can no longer communicate with their beasts. Seeing their dragon shadow is the closest they get to knowing who their dragon is. He also told me that the strength in his wings and the toughness of his scales are only a fraction of the beast's true strength.

Each time I've encountered Callan's dragon shadow, its burning gaze has been filled with intelligence. It isn't a mindless animal and its impulses have a purpose.

"What did you sense from your dragon?" I ask Callan.

"Pure rage. Like nothing I'd experienced before. He roared for vengeance."

My eyes widen, but Callan continues quickly. "Considering that his flames could have killed my sister, I thought I'd be happy to never hear his voice again. But there's an empty space where the relationship between me and my beast should be."

Callan told me that the first time he'd shifted, it was when his sister, Zahra, had hugged him. It had only been because of her strong wings that she'd been able to shelter and survive the onslaught. After that, Callan had left his family behind, afraid of hurting them. He'd gone where other supernaturals were less likely to be: a human warzone.

"Just now, Sophia's dragon seemed to stay much longer than mine did," Callan says, drawing the focus of the conversation back to her. "I wanted her to keep that connection."

Across from us, Sophia has remained on the floor, her cerulean-blue wings spread out on either side of her. Her clothing is sopping wet, her hair hanging in wet strands—except for the side that's shaved. The sunlight she's bathed in reflects off her delicate blue scales, making her skin sparkle like new snow.

She's eyeing us warily and I realize that we've completely let down our guards in front of her. From the way I'm holding Callan, and his quiet responses, it must be clear that our relationship isn't what we've represented to the Dread before now.

Her eyes are narrowed, and her lips pursed. Her scrutiny mustn't escape Callan, either, because his arms close around me protectively—a move that would only confirm whatever suspicions are forming in Sophia's mind.

"Yes, it's very sad that I can't hear my dragon anymore," she says, more matter-of-factly than I was expecting. "But, Callan?"

"Yes?" he asks, a hint of caution in his voice.

She breaks into a massive smile. "I have wings."

Callan's entire demeanor changes, the tension in his muscles easing beneath my hands. A smile grows on his face, lighting up his eyes. "You have wings."

Laughter bubbles out of Sophia as freely as a cascading brook. She lifts her sparkling arms into the light. "And scales! I have wings *and* scales!"

Pivoting at the waist, she brushes her fingertips along the surface of her left wing before she turns back to us. "I'm a real dragon. A *water* dragon."

She attempts to stand, nearly slips in the water on the floor, and seems to rethink her actions, lowering herself back to the ground under the weight of her wings.

Her laughter becomes ragged. Tears fill her eyes. "I'm a real dragon now."

Callan releases me to approach her, kneeling in the water in front of her again, his golden wings draped across the floor parallel to hers.

"You were always a real dragon," he says.

Sophia bows her head a little and the moment suddenly feels more solemn. If Callan were still the alpha—if he hadn't passed that role to Zahra—I could imagine this as a moment of pack bonding between them. He said that modern dragons band together only for survival and don't show each other the loyalty or care that other shifters, like wolves, do. But this silence between him and Sophia feels more real than any other interaction I've witnessed between Callan and his clan. Even his dealings with his sister are often filled with conflict.

The sunlight reflects off Callan's muscular back and his translucent scales, making him appear sculpted from gold while Sophia's wings and scales are smaller but equally captivating. Together, the beauty of their shifted forms takes my breath away and the peace between them feels... so real.

I take a quiet step back, pressing my hand to my heart because my chest hurts. I have enough insight to know that it's not physical pain I'm feeling.

"My wings are heavy," Sophia says quietly to Callan, not taking her eyes off him. "I don't know how to put them away."

Callan leans toward her, his hands raised. "May I?"

She nods and he presses the heels of his palms to the tops of her shoulders, his fingers extending down behind her back. His hands are big enough that I imagine his fingertips brushing her shoulder blades where her wings protrude. "Focus on these spots. Do you feel the pressure of my hands?"

She nods again.

"Now imagine your wings folding up neatly into those spots."

She closes her eyes. A shiver runs through her wings, but they don't budge. She wriggles her shoulders and then...

Her wings retract smoothly, sliding through the water and kicking up droplets before they fold neatly into her sides and then disappear behind her back. At the same time, her scales fade and her skin returns to its usual hue. Every hint of her dragon disappears and she appears human once more.

Like every other dragon shifter—other than Solomon Grudge—it seems that the shift is all or nothing for Sophia.

Opening her eyes, she smiles, then her brow furrows. "Oh, I thought the weight would go away. I mean, it's better, but my back is much heavier than before."

"You need to strengthen your core," Callan says, removing his hands but hovering them above her shoulders while she tests her balance. "It will get easier to carry your wings' weight, I promise, but it'll take practice and time. I can teach you."

"It's not like I have anything else to do," she says with a shrug that makes her wobble again.

Callan steadies her. "Let's get you up. I want to check the burns on your back."

"What burns?" she asks, smiling at him. "I think my dragon healed them."

As Callan and Sophia continue talking, I make it to the side of the room and to the edge of the dividing wall. Slipping around the corner, I press my back to the glass, listening to the water falling behind it. The sound should be soothing, but my breathing is harsh and my eyes are burning with tears I refuse to shed.

I don't know why I'm so emotional.

Maybe it's sheer fucking relief.

I thought I'd killed Sophia. To discover that she's not only unharmed but that the fire somehow allowed her dragon to surface is nothing short of miraculous.

Or maybe it's simply because I'm exhausted.

In the last twenty-four hours, I've fought off Tyler, swallowed Callan's flames, battled Solomon Grudge, survived the Serene Commander's attack—and discovered that she's a Sentinel—fought a legion of angels, and nearly died. I've only snatched one short nap in the car on the way here, so it makes sense that my emotions would be in turmoil.

I nod to myself.

These tears are because I'm tired.

They're not because I caught a glimpse of something between Callan and Sophia that I might never have: *Belonging.* Callan has opened his home to me and offered me his trust, but the connection between us will never be a pack bond like the one that he and Sophia just formed. My people will always hate me. So will the dragon shifters. I was built to stand alone. Any connections I make along the way are gifts that I could just as easily destroy.

I take deep breaths and fight the burn at the back of my throat. I tell myself it's for the best.

I was born an Avenging Angel, one of the first for centuries. I'm not meant to have a family or a pack. I will fight beside those I choose to support, protect those whom I choose to protect, and that's the closest I'll come to having a home.

CHAPTER TWELVE

*S*ophia's soft footfalls sound from the other side of the room—easily distinguishable from Callan's—and I press my hand to my forehead and look down to cover how red my eyes must appear.

Sophia's murmur is quiet. "Lana?"

I don't dare move my hand. I try to keep my voice from wobbling. "What?"

"I think you might need to reconsider your profession."

"Oh, yeah? Why?"

"You're supposed to slay dragons, not help them."

I clear my throat. "I guess I'll have to work on that, then."

Finally pulling my hand away, I stare at the floor, then the ceiling, and back again, finally lifting my chin and meeting her eyes.

She tips her head a little, a puzzled crease forming in her forehead. Her lips press together before she murmurs, "Fuck it."

Her arms slip around me and she pulls me into a hug. She's sopping wet and the cold strands of her hair press against my face.

I'm so surprised by her gesture that my arms fly up, a defensive move as I prepare to push her away. Even my leg muscles react instinctively, and I have to force myself to hold still so I don't kick her purely on reflex.

Her arms are strong—much stronger than the time she tried to push me around at Callan's night club. Her dragon has altered more than her ability to shift. It's healed her and given her the same strength the other dragons have exhibited.

She's a far greater threat to me now than she ever was.

A threat of my own creation.

Nice work, Lana.

And yet…

As she continues to hug me, my muscles slowly relax of their own accord. A strange sensation comes over me. It's like the moment when Callan's calm washes across me with its unexpected warmth. Unexpected serenity. My breathing evens out and I lower my arms to my sides, not returning her hug but not fighting it, either.

"Thank you," she whispers. "I don't know how you breathed fire—and you damn well scared the fuck out of me—but you saved me."

Saved her?

She releases me and steps back, her big, green eyes glistening. She must still be adjusting to the new weight within her body because she wobbles a little before she regains her balance. "I control something now."

I can only stare at her.

Callan leans on the end of the wall close to my left, watching me carefully. He's still in his shifted form and, although his features are relaxed, it feels like his golden eyes are hiding his thoughts from me.

Sophia clears her throat before she looks around at the impact of her dragon on the room. Now that the water has spread across the floor from wall to wall, it isn't much higher than a thin layer across the floor, but it'll take time to clean up.

"So, uh… Wow." Sophia rubs the back of her neck. "I guess I made a mess. Will the humans ask awkward questions?"

"I pay them not to," Callan says with an easy smile at Sophia that reminds me of the way he interacts with his human friends. It seems like his defenses are no longer up. "But it's better not to tempt their curiosity more than necessary. This floor is built to accommodate fire, not flood, but I'm sure I have enough towels to deal with this."

He approaches the door opposite the dining table, enters a code into the panel beside the door, and then disappears inside. From where I'm standing, I can only see part of the room's soft-white walls and the edge of a plush armchair. I'm too tired to move to see more. I've never felt weaker than I do right now. It's as if my strength has been scraped out of me and I've been left an empty, barely functioning shell. Conserving my energy is now my goal.

When Callan emerges with his arms full of towels, Sophia steps forward to take them while sending a meaningful look my way. "I made this mess," she says. "I can clean it up. You both need to rest."

When Callan gives her a nod, she says, "I can run interference with Jada if she wants to check on us. This level is locked down, so Jada can't just walk in, right?"

"Correct. My human friends don't know the code."

"What about liquid glamor for my back?" she asks.

Callan indicates the bedroom from which he brought the towels. "In the bathroom. Top drawer."

"Then I'm all set," Sophia says with a confident smile.

I'm not sure what liquid glamor is, or what it has to do with Sophia's back, but there's no time to ask before Callan's shadow drops over me—not his dragon shadow, although his dragon's presence seems much closer to the surface right now.

He keeps his voice low. "Lana, you need to rest. Let me help you to your room."

"I'm fine," I say. "I can help clean up."

"You've already helped more than you can imagine," Callan says. "You nearly died last night. Your body needs time to recover. It's not weakness to look after yourself."

As physically tired as I am, the mechanical task of mopping up would give me the time I need to work through the turmoil within my mind. On the other hand, I need to sleep. Desperately. Unlike Sophia, I didn't just receive an influx of new strength and energy.

With a heavy exhalation, I give Callan a nod.

He reaches for me, and it seems like he's about to scoop me up into his arms, but I lift my chin and flash a hard look at him. "I can walk."

It's so difficult to read his golden eyes, but I'm sure a hint of disappointment crosses his face. "This way," he murmurs before he leads me to the door in the middle of the room.

After keying in a code on the security panel, he reveals a bedroom that's simply, but comfortably, furnished. The number of flammable items inside the room—pillows, blankets, wooden furniture, and a wooden floor without a glass surface—indicate that it can't be Callan's room.

My toes nudge a dividing strip on the floor that sits along the door line, most likely to ensure it's airtight so that fire can't pass into this room. It's lucky that the water didn't get past it, either.

"This is my room?" I ask, giving up pretending to be fine and leaning against the side of the doorframe.

"If you like it," he says. Then he indicates the dark blue door closest to the front of the room. "Mine is next door."

The location of his room confirms that the layout of this level has the same basic configuration as his last home, although there are three rooms along this wall instead of two.

I search his eyes, but it's too hard to tell what he's thinking. Or, maybe, I'm just too tired to read him right now.

"No," I say quietly, taking a chance. "My room is next door with you." I swallow and hurry on to say, "This one is too flammable. I inhaled more of your fire tonight. I could accidentally burn this down."

The tension around his mouth fades a little. "Okay, then."

He leads me to the other door. This one requires his palm print to access it. "When you're feeling better, I'll key in your data so you can access my room whenever you like," he says, a seemingly casual remark, but it means a lot to me.

There were few places I was allowed to go in his last home. Of course, I didn't stay there long enough for him to give me further access, but even so, I see this as an act of trust on his part.

When he opens the door, he reveals an interior that I wasn't expecting. His last bedroom had black marble floors and gleaming, gray walls designed to hide scorch marks, but this one is much lighter. It appears lined with the same glass as the main area, behind which the walls are a soft, linen color with white trimmings. The floor is pale oak. On the left-hand side of the room is a large dressing room with an adjoining door through which I can see a bathroom.

The only furniture in the bedroom area itself is the bed, which is topped with a mattress, a fitted sheet, two pillows, and a soft-looking blanket in a cream color.

A raised dividing strip beneath the door keeps the water at bay, and I'm happy to finally step out of the liquid, not least because the bottoms of my toes are turning into prunes.

The door closes behind Callan when he follows me inside.

"Treat everything in here as yours," he says.

I cast him a quick glance, intending to take him at his word.

All I can think about, now that the chance has presented itself to me, is to get out of these clothes and take a shower. I don't have the energy to properly articulate what I need, so I mumble, "Clothes. Shower," and head straight to the dressing room, leaving wet footprints in my wake.

I'm not surprised that the shelves and racks already contain clothing. When Callan told me he could move at a moment's notice, I assumed that means all of his homes are fully furnished and functional in preparation for hasty relocation.

The dressing room contains a bench seat in the middle and a large mirror on the wall near the door, but I head straight for the drawers on the other side.

Callan leans against the wall behind me, remaining silent while I riffle through his shirts. I find a large, gray T-shirt of the softest cotton and draw it to my face. It's so soft, I could fall asleep with my face pressed against it right now, but I'm disappointed that it doesn't smell like him. Yet. I'm sure that will change.

Turning my back to him, I pull off my broken and scorched bra and tattered jeans, and finally my underpants. I pitch the ruined items into the washing basket at the side of the room and groan with relief now that the clothing is off my body.

I can finally let go of the battle.

More reluctantly, I take off the golden armband, placing it carefully on the nearest shelf.

I stretch my neck, grateful to have full mobility again. Callan's fire didn't only benefit Sophia, it also healed my throat, but I wish it had extended its healing properties to the rest of my body.

Naked other than the bracelets around my wrists, which I don't feel the need to remove, I grip his shirt and step toward the bathroom. I only make it halfway there before I sway on the spot.

My legs feel like they have weights attached to them.

Damn it. I'm so tired, I could fall asleep right here on the floor—

There's a rush of air at my back, a single beat of wings, and

Callan's arms swing around me, lifting me off my feet and up against his chest.

"Lana," he murmurs as he gathers me against him.

I settle against his chest, resting my head to his heart and listening to the steady beat. His nearness is tantalizing but also comforting, and two conflicting *wants* war within my body and mind.

I want to lift myself in his arms and press my lips to the corner of his mouth.

I also want to fall asleep right here.

His shirt is scrunched against my chest, but getting dressed has fallen further down my list of priorities, along with showering.

"Lana," he murmurs again.

My eyelids droop, and I fight to stay awake. "Mm-hmm?"

The corner of his mouth rises at the edge of my vision, and I manage to lift my fingertips to brush them across his lips. It's the closest I'll get to kissing him right now. The tip of my forefinger lingers on the smile he's giving me.

"Tell me what you need," he whispers, his golden eyes warming me. "Ask for what you want."

Well, I did need a shower, but now a different kind of *need* is edging forward. If only I had the energy to act on it...

He turns his head just enough to plant a kiss on the ends of my fingertips. It's extraordinarily gentle. Not demanding. Not even seductive.

It surprises me.

My forehead creases because his kiss doesn't feel like a gesture that's asking for more. It feels... solemn somehow.

Important.

He nudges his lips against my fingertips once more and, again, it feels like he's coaxing something from me...

With what little is left of my capacity to think clearly, I reconsider his question. He asked me what I need and want, *really* need and *really* want, and I already know the answer, but speaking it is too difficult.

I need your help. I can't do this on my own anymore. I want to tell you all my fears. I need to belong, but I fear I never will...

I'm not able to express any of that. Not yet. So I start small.

Bend instead of break. Whisper instead of shout.

"I need a shower," I say, a soft mumble, but he seems to hear me all the same. "I can't sleep without washing off the battle, but I'm too tired to do it on my own."

"All you need to do is ask," he says, dropping a kiss to my forehead—above my left eye, where there are no wounds. "I want you in my life, Lana, but I need you to let me in."

Without another pause, he carries me into the bathroom, his footfalls quiet and steady.

This bathroom is larger even than the bathroom at his old home. It has a long bench on the right-hand side that looks like it's made out of oak wood, a set of shelves full of towels, and two sinks with black taps. The walls are covered in gleaming, white tiles. An enormous white bath sits on the left-hand side while an open shower is situated in the far corner. It has two shower heads, both round and as large as dinner plates.

Callan keeps me close, using his left wing to support me while he takes the shirt I chose and drops it onto the bench. After pulling several towels from the shelves, he carries me to the shower.

Seconds after he turns on the water, steam rises up in wisps around us. The heat from the spray is as soothing across my back as his heartbeat is against my ear. I relax fully, trusting him when he eases us under the water and sets me back onto my feet under the warm waterfall.

It's like standing in the rain, except that it's the perfect heat and pressure. The water flows across the front of Callan's chest and the steam glistens across his wings, which he tucks to his sides.

He's still wearing sweatpants and they're quickly soaked, but he doesn't seem to mind as he soaps up one of the towels and takes care cleaning my body. His touch is soothing. Soft and tingling. It makes my body hum with a sense of comfort. At all times, he avoids the worst of my bruises, as well as the little cut on my forehead.

When he runs his hands through my hair, pushing its weight to the side to clean my back and hairline, I find myself arching against his touch and tipping my head to the side, giving him better access.

After he turns off the water, he dries me as carefully as he washed me, only breaking the contact between us to set me down on the bench so that he can remove his drenched sweatpants and wrap a towel around his waist.

Then he crouches to me, his fingertips brush my jaw, and some of my contentment fades as I consider the new tension around his mouth and eyes. His focus has fallen to my neck and his scrutiny is more intense than I was expecting, given how carefully he was touching me.

I'm aware of the increasing heat rising off his body, the way the water droplets are evaporating around us. Barely touching his shoulders before they become steam. The golden hue in his eyes brightens and fades, and I recognize the emergence of his beast in his harsh growl.

"I should have burned them all to ash." He pulls me up into his arms again, his left wing pressed against my back. "Every last fucking one of them."

I allow myself to rest against his wing. I should probably be afraid of his beast, but I'm not. "Callan," I whisper. "Shift back into your human form."

He seems to consider it, then shakes his head. "I can't risk it."

The one time he was able to touch me in his human form and not burst into flames was when we fell asleep together—him in his dragon form, his wing curved around me. We woke up to find him transformed into his human form and his dragon didn't react to me despite the fact that he was holding me in his arms. It was as if, because he fell asleep with me that way, his dragon remained asleep. He didn't burst into flames.

"I'm already touching you," I say, my fingertips tingling with heat when I press them against his chest. "You asked me to tell you what I need, and right now, I need to fall asleep next to your human form. Not your dragon. *You.*"

His thumb grazes my lips. It's a soft, unhurried movement while the heat rising off his body curls around me softly.

He gives me a slow smile. "Your hair is wet. Let me try drying it first."

"First? Does that mean you'll shift back?"

He doesn't confirm that, pursing his lips and exhaling gently. The slightest breath of heat washes across the top of my head. It feels as if he ran his hands through my hair, the warmth soaking across my scalp, and I can't stop the moan escaping my lips.

He leans in, his lips above my shoulder as he gently blows across my upper arm, then across my chest and the tops of my breasts. The deliciously warm air makes me shiver with plea-sure as he crouches to whisper across my hips and my thighs.

My toes curl. Heat grows between my legs, but before I can ask for more, he lifts me into his arms. On the way back to the bedroom, he scoops up the shirt for me and a pair of shorts for himself from the dressing room.

Setting me down on the edge of the bed and supporting me with his wings, he carefully pulls the T-shirt over my head. I do the rest, tugging the shirt down over my arms while he dresses.

Once my head is on the pillow, he leans across me, the edges of his wings pressed to the bed on either side of me.

I reach up to press my palms to his chest.

"Stay with me," I say. "I want to wake up with you."

I'm surprised by how easily I express my wish. Asking for what I want is becoming easier every time I do it.

His smile makes his golden eyes glimmer, but a hint of tension appears around his mouth. "Don't let go."

"I won't," I promise him as I keep my hands firmly connected with his body.

His wings retract and his shimmering, translucent scales disappear, rippling away across his hard muscles as he returns to his human form. He blinks and his eyes are once again brown, his jaw shadowed, although his arms are just as warm around me as they were before. Warmer, maybe.

The golden shimmer no longer hides how tired he appears. The darkening shadows under his eyes. The stress lines around his mouth and the tension in his jaw.

He hovers above me, looking down, but with every passing second, the worry fades from his face. His shoulders relax. His breathing evens out.

It worked. His dragon hasn't woken up.

He scoops me up against him and rolls us onto our sides. Reaching down to pull up the blanket, he draws it over us. My eyes are closing, sleep is pulling me down, but just as I sink into it, the Serene Commander's threat returns to me.

The Sentinels will crush you.

My eyes fly open, an unwelcome shot of adrenaline surging through me. "The Sentinels!"

Callan's arms are like an anchor around me, keeping me grounded. His rumbled response soothes my anxiety. "It's okay. You're safe now. Nobody will find us here."

No, I tell myself. *I will find them first.* I will heal, and then I'll do what I do best: *hunt.*

When I relax in his arms, he murmurs, "Good night, *Not-Lana.*"

His upper arm grows heavier as his breathing deepens.

Within seconds, my eyes close again and this time, I fall into a deep sleep.

CHAPTER THIRTEEN

I wake to kisses on my cheeks and forehead, and the scent of ash on the tip of my tongue. A soft light gleams behind my eyes, the same amber hue as the sinking sun, and I imagine that this room is much like Callan's last bedroom, its light mimicking the changing light of the day.

It must be early evening, which means I've slept through the entire day. No matter how long it's been, I feel energized. Not exactly healed, but whole and safe.

It's a rare feeling.

The bristles across Callan's jaw brush my lips as he plants another kiss on my chin, making it impossible for me to slip back to sleep.

My eyes flutter open as I inhale a deep breath, drawing his tantalizing scent into my chest. Exhaling it with a smile.

"You're still human," I say, stretching against his hard muscles before relaxing into his arms again. My lower arm is curled between us, while my upper hand rests on his bicep.

"Not human," he growls.

I smile against his mouth when I press my lips to his. A light kiss. "Far from human."

Both of his hands reach around me, slipping beneath the hem of my shirt—*his* shirt—and stroking up my back. The action serves to draw me closer to him, and I'm aware of how naked I am under this shirt, and how much I'd prefer I wasn't wearing anything at all right now.

His touch makes my skin feel alive and draws a sigh from my lips. I lean into him, welcoming the heat in his expression. "Can I tell you what I want?"

His answering smile is lazy and warm, his focus dropping to my lips before he nudges forward to brush his mouth against mine.

"Tell me," he says, a low rumble that carries the growl of his beast. "I'll give you everything you want."

A shiver of anticipation runs through me. "I want to stay here all night and forget that the outside world exists."

"We can do that."

With a heated glance at me, he eases me onto my back and rises up over me. Starting at my left knee, he plants kisses up along my leg, his tongue swirling against my inner thigh, skipping across my center to my other thigh, circling back up to my stomach and then down again.

I moan when his mouth finally closes across my center, the warmth of his tongue against the most sensitive part of me creating a burst of pleasure that sets my body on fire.

I want so much more already, but he seems determined to take it slow, his tongue stroking me as if he can't get enough of me. Heat strikes through me with every press. Every caress. Building. Making my muscles tighten low in my stomach like a coil.

I'm trembling when he lifts his head with a satisfied hum, his gold-flecked eyes glittering at me as he draws his tongue up the side of my thigh.

His hands find my hips, then rise higher, stroking up my sides and pushing the T-shirt up with them. The air rushes across my skin as the material bunches under my arms, and I manage to draw it off me without lifting too much off the bed or breaking the contact between us.

Callan works his way up to the underside of my left breast, tasting my skin with slow swirls before he draws my nipple into his mouth, his tongue flicking across the sensitive skin.

Pure pleasure makes my head swim and my thighs clench.

I nearly scream when he stops.

His mouth crashes against mine as he wraps his arms around me and rolls over so that he's on his back and I'm on top, my knees on either side of his hips. Hungry for his kiss, I stay low, letting gravity press me against him, even though I want nothing more than to take control and ease the ache inside me.

I draw the scent of his body deep into my chest with every inhale, feel his stomach muscles shiver as I press against him, taste the embers on his tongue. A burning field. A world of ash. It fills my head with a kind of fury that's intoxicating. Seductive. Could easily consume me.

When his hand slips between us, the back of his forefinger rubbing against my center, I nearly explode, nearly lose control. *Nearly.*

Helping him pull off his shorts, I rise up and position myself over him, responding to the heat in his eyes as I draw him into me. I make myself take it slowly, even though I want nothing more than to drive him hard into me.

His grip on my hips tightens as his length fills me. I take my time enjoying every spike of pleasure from the initial pressure to the intoxicating heat of the outward slide.

It's like dipping my hand into liquid fire, withdrawing it, and thrusting it in again. The intensity builds instantly, but still, I hold back, watching the desire build in his eyes, sensing his near loss of control, the ripple of his stomach muscles as he seems to fight his instinct to take over.

My breathing is ragged. The rise and fall of his chest is

erratic. The tension in his body tells me he's seconds away from giving in to his instincts. But it's not in the way I expect, not by rolling us over and taking control of our speed.

Instead, he brushes his thumb across my center in time with my downward push.

Heat explodes through my body.

My hands land on his chest and I abandon all inhibition, propelled by pure pleasure and the heat in his eyes. My movements become faster, moans tearing from me, as I quicken the pace.

Every plunge, every stroke of his hand across my center, is like striking a match.

I need him. Want him. Want his fire. Want this spark to ignite.

Let it burn.

I tip my head back and let go, the orgasm splintering my sense of reality. As I crash, Callan takes hold of my hips, finally taking control, thrusting and drawing out my pleasure until he crashes with me.

I drop to his chest, shivering in his arms as he pulls me close and maneuvers us back onto our sides.

We lie like that for what feels like a luxuriously long time.

Flecks of gold appear in his eyes when his focus drops to my lips again. He doesn't seem aware of the way his skin is shimmering, a slight iridescent sheen that ripples across his shoulders and neck and reminds me of his dragon's scales.

It's a subtle change.

I draw my fingertip along his temple and to his jawline, studying the minute alterations in his expression. "Do you know that you partially shift sometimes?"

His eyebrows rise. "That's not possible. Dragons can't partially shift anymore." He seems to rethink. "Well, Dread dragons can't. Solomon Grudge seems to be a law unto himself."

His eyes crinkle at the corners. "But why do you say that about *me?*"

"These little gold flecks in your eyes. The sheen on your skin." My fingertips play across his neck and down his chest as I speak. "It's like your dragon is pushing forward."

His forehead creases. He seems genuinely puzzled. "When did you first notice this?"

I think back. "It was at dinner the other night. When I agreed to stay with you." I give him a crooked smile. "You fed me lasagna. I told you I'd like it for dinner each night."

The corner of his mouth rises. "I remember." His expression becomes more serious as he continues. "So, it was after I met you."

I'm more than a little distracted by the way he's stroking my lower back. "I guess so. Assuming you never noticed it yourself before then?"

He shakes his head. "It's like Sophia's dragon."

I consider him carefully. "What do you mean?"

"Sophia didn't show any signs of having a dragon until she met you. It was your fire that brought her dragon to life."

I immediately shake my head. "*Your* fire. I merely borrowed it."

"If my fire was going to trigger her dragon, it would have happened the night I scorched her hair. Last night's flames belonged to you."

"But that's…" I give another shake of my head. "I don't make the flames."

His hand continues to stroke my back, easing the sudden chill passing through me. "I know I told you that when you take my fire, it still belongs to me, but there's something different about the flames when you breathe them, Lana."

"How so?"

His expression becomes faraway. "It's like your scent. The rain has stopped. The sky is clear. The moonlight is pure." He shrugs, although it's a subdued gesture while he's lying down. "That's the only way I can describe it."

Slipping his other arm beneath me, he pulls me on top of him again. My black hair falls to either side of his face, casting him into shadow. It only makes the flecks in his eyes appear brighter.

"How can I do these things?" I ask him.

He tucks a length of hair behind my ear. "There's only one way to find out for sure."

He said a similar thing to me once before, but he didn't elaborate on it, except to say that it was a dangerous option.

"Tell me."

"It's a last resort," he says.

I try again. "I need you to tell me what it is."

For a moment, I don't think he's going to answer me. Then his lips rise in a smile. "Asking for what you need is good."

"Answers would be better," I say, glaring hard at him, since we've been here before. Me asking questions. Him evading.

As we've been speaking, I've sunk further toward his seductive lips. The constant swirl of his hands across my back and down the sides of my hips is scattering my thoughts in wild ways. I'm not sure how much longer I'll be able to sustain this conversation without exploring his body like he's exploring mine.

"There are whispers about a series of four very powerful books," he begins. "Each one is dedicated to a type of magic: light, dark, elemental, and old magic. Each of the four books is said to contain all possible knowledge about that type of magic: the heart, soul, and answers to all of the mysteries of that magic."

"Dragons and angels are both creatures of light magic," I say.

He nods. "Which means that if we could find the Book of Light Magic—and survive reading it—then we'd have all the answers we seek. About your power. Why the dragons are dying out—"

"Survive reading it?" I ask, latching on to that part of his explanation.

"It's said that these books can destroy you. Only the strongest supernaturals can survive reading them, and even then, the information within the books can consume someone to the point that they're never the same again."

I'm not deterred. Not yet anyway. "Let's find it. The Book of Light Magic."

"It's impossible."

"Why?"

"Because it's rumored that each book is being kept within the veil between our world and the heavenly realm."

I exhale heavily. "That means it's guarded by Sentinels." My shoulders slump, but my deflation only serves to take me closer to his chest.

When Callan first told me that Solomon Grudge had found one of the Sentinels' secret locations within the veil, killed two of them, *and* stolen an object from them, I told him it was impossible; nobody finds the Sentinels' strongholds, let alone survives the encounter.

Somehow, Solomon did.

"I've often wondered if that's what he stole," Callan continues. "The Book of Light Magic would have to be one of the most precious objects the angels own. More even than the other three books because it contains the secrets of their own power. If that's what Solomon took, then maybe it's hidden somewhere outside the veil where we could get to it—"

"It's not." My voice is wooden. "He didn't take a book."

Callan searches my eyes. "Lana?" His hands pause on my back. "The look on your face right now—"

"It was me." I nearly choke as I speak. "He stole me."

Callan immediately sits up, keeping me close so that I

straddle his hips. "What are you saying?" His brow is fiercely furrowed. "That the Sentinels kept you within the veil?"

"I'm saying... that I'm not what you thought." I follow that quickly with: "I didn't know until Solomon told me. It was when I was a baby, so I don't remember any of it."

Callan's eyes narrow at me. "Solomon said I didn't know what you are."

I press my palm to Callan's heart. "I'll tell you everything that happened between me and Solomon during our fight, everything he told me, but I need you to listen and let me finish. Can you do that?"

Callan gives me a firm nod.

I nestle in his arms, completely naked, and start from the moment I left his old home. I tell him about my fight with Solomon, including Solomon's surprise when I told him that the Serene Commander had never mentioned him to me. The way I led him to the Cathedral, hoping I could orchestrate a fight between them.

Callan remains quiet, his hands stroking my back and arms, but when I rush over the moment when my wing nearly broke, he leans forward to press his cheek to mine. A gesture of solace.

I continue my story with Solomon's revelations about my history and his claim that I'm an Avenging Angel. Even then, Callan respects my wishes and stays silent, although he doesn't hide the surprise this news causes him.

I tell him about the way I manipulated the dragon's gold, my focus shifting to the dressing room where I left the golden lattice.

Finally, with a deep breath, I say, "Solomon spoke about my mother. He said there was something she told him, but he didn't believe her. He didn't say what it was, and he didn't tell me anything more about her."

I lower my eyes, blinking away the unwelcome burn behind them. "I've never had any information about how I came into existence. I would give anything to know more about my mother."

Callan strokes my hair from my forehead. "You're an Avenging Angel with the ability to swallow dragon's fire and steal dragon's gold. I think you can assume that your mother was extraordinary, whoever she was. Or *is*."

"She could be alive or dead. I don't know. All I'm sure about is that when Solomon took me from the Sentinels, he somehow doomed me. I don't know how, but I'm not an Avenging Angel anymore. I'm not pure enough. I'm... corrupted."

"Like fuck you're corrupted," Callan says, such a sudden ferocity in his eyes that they glitter and a golden sheen washes across his skin. "If you're one of the first to be born in centuries, how would the angels know?"

"Well... the Celestial Ascendant..."

"Is how old? A hundred years?" Callan asks, accentuating his point. "If the last Avenging Angel existed before her time, then how the fuck would she really know?"

My lips part with surprise. My corruption was never something I questioned. I know in my heart that I'm a hunter to my core. "I'm angry and violent. Angels don't want to destroy life like I do. They want to save it."

Callan gives me a wry smile. "Destroying the world sounds exactly like the kind of thing an Avenging Angel would want to do," he says. "Burn this whole fucking place to the ground."

"Like your dragon," I whisper. I press my palms to his shoulders. "Is this why you calm me? Because your dragon's anger matches my own? A sort of equalizing force."

"Maybe," he murmurs. "Why don't we see?"

He scoops me up, wraps my legs around his waist, and carries me into the dressing room.

I'm not sure exactly where he's headed, but I trust him. I distract myself along the way by lifting myself high enough in his arms so I can trace kisses across his shadowed jaw. It makes my lips tingle against his sandpaper-like bristles, a strange sort of pain and pleasure that keeps me enthralled until I reach the softer corner of his lips.

I'm sure he was headed somewhere, but as my kiss intensifies, he groans and veers suddenly toward the wall inside the dressing room. He takes control of our kiss, a demanding heat in his touch as he pushes me up against the cool surface.

Wrapping my arms around his neck, I welcome all of the sensations spiking through my body—the press of his hard muscles between my thighs, the graze of his chest against my breasts, the hitch in his breathing that makes my heart beat faster, the contrasts in the pressure of his lips as he deepens and softens our kiss.

I break the contact between us only long enough to give voice to my curiosity. "Where were you taking me?" *Before I distracted you so thoroughly.*

"To see this partial shift you were talking about," he says, still kissing me, snatching breaths between long kisses before he draws back with a rough smile. "The mirror's too far away."

I take a sideways glance.

The mirror is little more than three paces to my right on the very wall I'm leaning against. "It's right beside us."

Callan returns to my jaw, kissing his way around my chin to my earlobe and down the side of my throat.

"Too far," he growls without raising his head.

Laughter bubbles up within me, but it comes out as a moan as he repositions me so that his hard length presses against my core, increasing the growing ache between my legs.

He lifts me upward so he can kiss his way across my breasts. It takes me away from the press of his body against my center, and I protest until the warmth of his mouth on my nipples sends my head into a spin.

Damn, don't let it ever end.

My body is ready for more, but I don't want to lose this

unhurried moment, not when he seems determined to love every inch of me. Finally, his mouth hovers above mine, his breathing ragged. "I want you to see what I see when I look at you," he murmurs, his gaze moving like a caress across my cheeks, eyes, lips, chin.

I search his eyes for his meaning. "What do you see?"

"Someone who's not only determined and purposeful, who sees the world in black and white, but who also notices the perfect small moments and treats them like the rare treasures that they are." His thumbs brush across my hips where he holds me. "The way you listened to the music at the concert hall. The look of wonder on your face when you try new food. The way you studied the waterfall in the living room."

He noticed all of those things?

I know him to be perceptive, but it's somehow healing to my heart to know that those moments mean something to him too.

Using my stomach muscles to lift myself, I brush my nose to his and then nudge his cheek. It's the instinctive gesture I've shown him before, and I still don't know why it feels so right. "You have all of me."

The golden flecks in his eyes brighten as he positions himself at my core, his length filling me with his first thrust. I cry out at the intensity of the pleasure striking through me, my hips jolting forward, gravity assisting me to take him deep inside.

He doesn't hold back, responding to my moans, his body igniting a storm of heat between us.

Without thinking about it, I release my wings, using them to brace against the wall as my hips rock forward, meeting every thrust.

I drown in his groans and revel in the heady rush of giving and taking control. Aware of the heat waves beating around his chest and the way his skin glimmers with sweat and iridescent power.

Ripples cascade through my wings as the intensity builds.

The orgasm hits me hard, punching through my body.

Instead of screaming, I inhale. Tip my head back. Ride the wave as if I'm tearing out of my own body and lifting away from everything that ties me down.

Callan follows me into the crash, groaning as he shudders against me.

Sliding one arm around me, he pulls me away from the wall, and I keep my legs wrapped around him. The heat in his eyes is just as bright as it was moments ago. His breathing is as out of control as mine, but his focus shifts to my left wing. To the gaps in my feathers.

Fuck. I hate that he can see how broken it is.

"May I?" he asks.

When I nod, he turns and places me on the bench in the middle of the room.

Keeping one hand on my waist, he reaches for the damaged section. It's jagged, zigzagging where the Serene Commander's spear caught the feathers, all the way up to the bone.

He traces the gaps, his fingertips brushing the edges of my feathers. After surviving Callan's fire the first two times, I noticed that the surface of my feathers had changed. An opalescent shimmer has appeared on their surface that gives the effect of a rainbow of colors when they move in the light.

Callan's hand slips from my waist to rest on my knee, maintaining the contact between us so he can kneel in front of my wing. He turns his palm so that one of the feathers at the edge of the gap can rest in his hand. He appears to study its shape and size, turning his head a little to see it from different angles.

It's a quiet scrutiny that makes me curious. "What are you doing?"

"Thinking," he says before he runs the feather between his thumb and forefinger. "About possibilities."

A smile plays around my lips. "Possibilities for… what?"

He returns his focus to me. "I'm thinking you should show me this partial shift you were talking about."

It's a curious deflection on his part, but I don't push it because I'm keen to put away my wings and set aside the glaring problem that I'm facing: how to fight without them. Somehow, I'll have to learn to function without flying until they heal. However long that takes.

He scoops me up again, and I let him carry me across the room, even though I could just as easily walk to the mirror on my own.

He sets me down in front of it, my back pressed to his chest, but keeps one arm wrapped around my waist.

I lean my head against his shoulder as he studies me in the mirror. His gaze follows all the curves of my body, from my lips to my shoulders, breasts, hips, and all the way to my toes. His forehead creases. "I don't see a partial shift."

I let out a laugh. "That's because you're looking at me, not yourself." Half-turning in his arms, I slide up onto my tiptoes, and kiss the underside of his chin.

At my touch, a golden sheen washes across his torso and gold flecks appear in his eyes, but he's still not looking at himself in the mirror.

The renewed heat in his eyes consumes me.

"You're missing it," I whisper, unable to break his gaze.

"Partial shifts can wait," he says, an unmistakable dragon's growl in his voice. "I never want to miss a moment of you, *Not-Lana*."

I didn't think I could orgasm again, but when he turns me back to the mirror, his hands stroking all of my most sensitive spots, I discover it's very possible.

By the time we return to the bed, I have no idea what time it is or how long we've stayed in his room. It's only as I'm falling asleep again, nestled in Callan's arms, that I remember the book he spoke about.

If there's a tome with all the answers in it, then I need it. Even if finding it is nearly impossible—let alone retrieving it. A sense of renewed determination pushes at the edges of my drowsiness. No matter how long it takes, I will find that book.

If Solomon Grudge can break through the veil between Earth and the heavenly realm to steal from the Sentinels, then I can, too.

CHAPTER FOURTEEN

I awake to a soft, swishing sound. The light behind my eyelids is gentler than before. It's morning, perhaps. I stretch languidly, only to realize that Callan isn't lying beside me.

Rolling over to face the direction of the swishing sound, I find him sitting in a chair opposite the bed. He must have brought the chair in from the dining area since there wasn't any other furniture in here before. He's dressed in jeans and a T-shirt that conforms to his broad chest, and his hair is slightly damp, as if he showered already.

His left hand rests, palm up, on his knee and three small golden squares rotate in the air above his hand. They seem to be the source of the soft *swoosh-swoosh-swoosh* that fills the air, but he pays them no mind.

I'm the focus of his attention. "Good morning, Not-Lana."

"What time is it?" I ask, wondering if I should be asking what *day* it is.

"It's nearly 9 A.M. Sophia ran interference as long as she could, but Jada wants to check on you. I told her I was letting you sleep. You looked too peaceful to wake."

"Me? Peaceful?" I give him a skeptical look, which he returns with a raised eyebrow.

"I guess I can't be upset about someone caring about me." I hurry to slip out of the bed. "Do I need to get out there before she busts down the door?"

He leans back in his seat, a heated smile growing on his face while he takes in the full view of my naked body.

"If I had a choice, I'd say *no*," he says. "But I told Jada you'd be out soon."

I smile. *Soon* is a relative term. It means I don't have to rush out there.

I take a moment to stretch my neck and shoulders and to catalog my state of health. My muscles ache in delicious places, although some of my soreness is certainly from the battle. My torso is still bruised, but the pinpricks along my side from Solomon's claws have nearly healed and the cut above my right eye doesn't sting anymore.

While I remain at the side of the bed, checking myself, I'm increasingly aware of the warmth in Callan's eyes. Shimmers of heat curl around his face and arms, seeping through the material of his shirt. The squares of gold spiral outward, their path extending around his torso as he rises to his feet, but he doesn't move any closer to me.

I've never been aware of my body as something that would attract attention. I've only ever viewed it as a kind of machine. I'm more concerned about whether or not I can function properly, the mechanics of movement, than how I look. After all, I don't need to be pretty to break someone's neck.

But now, as Callan's focus intensifies, I'm aware that my body carries a power I never attributed to it before. I remember him asking me why I undressed so easily in front of him, and I told him it was because I hadn't thought he'd take any notice. He told me, in no uncertain terms, how wrong I was.

But as much as I'm conscious of the power of my body, I'm also aware of his equal power to elicit a response from me.

Damn. My stomach is tightening, my breathing is becoming more rapid, and keeping my distance from the storm of desire growing in his eyes is becoming very difficult. I have to remind myself that, because he's not already in his shifted form, touching him carries the consequence of igniting his dragon's fire. Of course, it would be worth it...

"It's a shame you can't touch me without setting this beautiful bedroom alight," I say.

"I'm not sure that would be a big problem. It's fireproof." He glances at the bedding. "Mostly."

He reduces the gap between us to a tempting distance. So close that I could reach out and trace my fingertips down his chest to the waistband of his jeans. Luckily for the unburnt status of this room, the golden squares are revolving around him at such a distance from his body that we're forced to stand apart from each other.

Trying to distract myself from his nearness but not prepared to step away from him just yet, I ask, "Is that dragon's gold?"

"They're training squares." In response to his speech, the squares slow their rotation, each one beginning an individual spin on its axis while continuing to revolve around him. "We use them to train young dragon shifters. I'm planning to start teaching Sophia this week."

I follow their path with my eyes, my fingers twitching at my sides as they catch the light in mesmerizing ways.

The casual way in which Callan is manipulating them makes me want to see if I can snatch them from him.

Mine.

The thought rises unbidden within my mind, the urge to take the gold becoming more powerful with each passing second.

Come to me.

One of the squares wobbles on its axis, but I quickly shake myself, fighting my impulses and forcing myself to focus on Callan instead. It's certainly not a hardship. In fact, visually tracing his features is a powerful distraction when memories return to me of the way he kissed me, touched me...

I shake myself again, a flush creeping into my cheeks. I'm sure he sensed the tug on the gold, and I should probably be concerned in case he's unsettled by what I did, but I find him appraising me with a growing smile.

I clear my throat, my fingers falling to my bracelets while I incline my head toward the training squares. "It's beautiful gold."

Stepping lightly to the side of the room, I head for the dressing room so I don't give in to my temptation to take the gold, scatter it to the side, close the gap between Callan and me, and welcome the fire that would follow.

It's only when I reach the dressing room that I remember I don't have any clean clothes. I'm about to turn back and ask Callan what I should do when I catch sight of an open bag, brimming with clothing, that's sitting beside the bench in the middle of the room.

A small pile of clothes has already been taken out of it; a pair of black jeans is folded neatly beside a black T-shirt together with a pair of underpants and a bra. The neck brace sits beside them. More than a little puzzling is a small vial of bright-blue liquid that rests on top of the T-shirt.

Callan moves up behind me. "Beatrix brought the clothes. The shirts are shaped to accommodate your wings across your shoulder blades. That vial is liquid glamor. It's from my stash."

"Liquid glamor?" I ask, recalling that Sophia mentioned it before.

"It allows me to hide my healing ability from humans by creating a glamor that mimics whatever wound I suffered. I have vials in every home. The witch who puts the protective wards on my buildings provides it."

Callan steps around me to pick up the vial. "If I'd realized the scars on your back had faded, I would have given you some of this in the car. But it's too late to worry about that now."

He passes me the vial, careful not to brush his hand against mine. "You need to use it carefully. It's highly volatile. Speak clearly the kind of wound you want it to imitate as you apply it. You don't want to end up with a cut where there should be a bruise. Sophia has already used it to imitate the burns across her back. For you, it will need to mimic the contusions around your neck."

"I guess I don't need it to fake my other injuries," I say wryly. "Since they heal slowly like human wounds anyway." My brow furrows as I think it through. "Will I need to reapply it to my neck every day?"

He shakes his head. "It's designed to replicate the appearance of the healing process that humans expect. The bruises will yellow and fade without raising questions. I had spare vials of it ready when I first brought you to my old home in case my human friends saw your wounds and questioned how fast you healed."

I give a harsher laugh than I intended. "Except I didn't need a glamor because I don't heal quickly." I pause. "Well, except for my throat."

"Another mystery," Callan says, lifting his hand and running it across the air beside my face. "We will find answers. Somehow. In the meantime, I'll do everything I can to keep you safe here."

"Keep *me* safe?" I ask, arching my eyebrow at him. I don't know how to tell him yet that I won't be able to stay cooped up here for long. The Serene Commander might have manipulated me into hunting dragons, but my need to hunt is real.

"Keep all of us safe," Callan acknowledges, holding his hand out for the vial again. "I told Delaney—the witch who works for me—that I'd pay her millions if she could come up with a glamour strong enough to hide a dragon shadow, or better yet, subdue my dragon's fire, but so far, she hasn't succeeded."

"Your dragon is too fierce for that," I say.

Callan doesn't deny it. "I'll wait for you in the bedroom," he says before leaving the dressing room. The training squares fly ahead of him and land in a neat pile on the bed, clinking against each other.

I hurry to shower and dress, double-checking my wounds in the mirror. When I reach for the vial of liquid glamor and remove the cap, I discover that it has a little roller ball at the top of the vial like a deodorant bottle.

"Bruises," I say as I roll it across my neck.

Mottled color appears where the liquid touches my skin, and I'm startled by how realistic the marks look.

My conscience twinges when I think of Jada's genuine concern for me, but I tell myself I don't have any other choice. At least I'm not faking my other bruises, and this way, we won't have a repeat of the moment when she saw that my scars had faded.

The removal of my scars by the hot band of dragon's gold is a mystery I hope to solve. Just like the mystery of why any injuries to my neck are healed when I exhale Callan's fire. Both are instances of localized healing directly connected to an aspect of dragon's power: dragon's fire raging through my throat; dragon's gold hitting my back. I wonder for a moment if the common factor is heat—the flames were scorching and the band of dragon's gold was burning hot—but it's merely a theory for now.

My goal is to survive for long enough to find answers.

I fix the neck brace around my throat and head out to join Callan.

When we exit the bedroom, I'm immediately aware of a

figure standing in the shadows in the near-right corner. Felix Lamonte leans up against the wall, dressed in black, appearing engrossed in whatever he's looking at on his phone. The way his sharp gaze flickers to me before returning to his screen tells me his nonchalance is an act.

Soft voices reach me from the other end of the living area, along with the heavenly scent of a hot breakfast. I recognize Jada's voice, along with Beatrix's, before I catch sight of them, both hugging coffees at the dining table. Sophia must be in the bedroom opposite the dining area because I don't see her.

Callan allows me to approach first and my stomach growls at the sight of the plates covered in silver domes that promise a warm breakfast.

"Well, look who finally emerges," Beatrix says, arching her eyebrows at me. I'm surprised to see her wearing a long-sleeved dress, since she's usually in jeans, but I'm not surprised that it's black.

Jada immediately jumps to her feet. She doesn't give me the chance to sit down, checking me over right where I stand. "How are you feeling today? How's the neck? And your pain levels?"

Despite her visible concern for me, her entire demeanor seems lighter and I want to believe that the closure about her sister's death has lifted a weight off her.

"I'm much better," I say. "My neck is healing. And, as you can hear, my vocal cords are doing much better. Pain levels are fine. I'm sorry I worried you. I just really needed to sleep."

Behind Jada, Beatrix smirks at me, her focus flicking between me and Callan. I can practically hear her snarky thoughts. *Sleeping? Is that what you were doing?*

"How is Sophia?" I ask Jada. I already know the answer, but Jada would expect me to ask.

"She's in much better shape than I was expecting," Jada says, gesturing to the closed door on her right. "She's sleeping now. Whatever caused her burns, she's healing well."

It's a testament to how loyal Jada is to Callan that her brow doesn't furrow when she speaks of the mystery of how Sophia's wounds came about.

"Well, I need to get back to work. Let me know if you need anything," Jada says to me before turning to Callan. "We're keeping up surveillance around the building like you asked. So far, there hasn't been any suspicious activity, but we'll keep you informed."

"Thanks, Jada."

As soon as Jada's footfalls recede and the front door closes behind her, Callan takes a seat at the far end of the table, farthest away from Beatrix.

Felix quietly approaches the dividing wall, his phone no longer the center of his attention.

I settle down opposite Beatrix and begin to eat, determined not to let the growing friction around me detract from my enjoyment of the meal.

"Okay," Callan says, focusing on Beatrix. "Spit it out."

She leans forward, her coffee forgotten, her black nails tapping the tabletop. "Zahra says *hello*."

Callan removes the silver dome covering his plate and starts to eat, but his shoulders betray his tension. "That's all my sister has to say? Just *hello*?"

Beatrix gives him a smile that looks like a snarl. "Actually, she wants to know what the fuck you were thinking putting an angel's life before your clan, but I can see exactly what you were thinking and why, so there's no judgement from me. Oh, and she said to tell you to do what you do best while she sorts out the mess you made."

I find the "do what you do best" comment curious, uncertain what it means, but the tension leaves Callan's shoulders when he hears it, so I guess it can't be that bad.

"Nothing surprising, then," he says.

"Do what you do best?" Beatrix arches an eyebrow at him as

if she can't believe he's so relaxed. "She's telling you to stay hidden. She may as well have put you under house arrest, Callan."

He shrugs. "What's new about that?"

My forehead creases as I observe the small changes in Callan's expression. While Beatrix grows more frustrated, Callan seems more focused.

She leans back in her seat with an exasperated groan. "Why the fuck would you give Zahra the leadership? If you were still the alpha, you could summon the Cohort and sort this all out. You could control the narrative around what you did the other night."

Now Callan's jaw clenches. "I needed my freedom."

Beatrix stares at him. "You thought you could be free?" A hint of bitterness creeps into her voice. "Freedom is for other supernaturals. No dragon can be free. Not until someone finds a cure for our fucking shadows and our inability to fully shift and the fact that none of us seem able to have children, no matter who we screw."

She takes a noisy breath and focuses on the ceiling while her outburst sinks into the silence around us.

Callan considers her quietly, his food appearing forgotten. "Beatrix? Are you okay?"

She gives herself a little shake. "Oh, don't worry about me, I'm just peachy. It's this fucking mess with the angels that I'm concerned about."

Callan nods but says, "It only looks like a mess from the outside. Zahra knows what she's doing, and she knows what I do best." His expression hardens. "She'll take care of the unrest within the clan while I deal with the threat of war."

Beatrix's lips purse in surprise, but now I understand why Callan seemed so calm. His sister wasn't asking him to stay put. She was asking him to take action while she's busy dealing with clan politics.

It's at that moment that Felix shifts from his lean against the dividing wall. He moves like a panther, graceful in the way of a predator.

I've never heard him speak before, but when he opens his mouth, his voice is a mesmerizing rumble.

"The Sentinels are already arriving," he says.

CHAPTER FIFTEEN

*C*allan leans forward. "Tell me what you've seen."

"A steady stream of SUVs have arrived at the Cathedral over the last twenty-four hours," Felix replies. "Now that the angels have seen my face, I can't get close enough for a better look, but the supernaturals getting out of the vehicles were all men."

"Men?" I ask, surprised. "There are angelic orders in other cities comprised solely of men, but the Sentinels are women."

Felix gives me a sharp glance. "I know what I saw. There were at least twenty of them, as tall as dragons, and they carried duffel bags—the kind you'd transport weapons in."

I tap the table lightly. "I don't understand. Male Sentinels?" I search my memory for every mention of the Sentinels, every scrap of information the Serene Commander gave me.

Before I found out that the Serene Commander was a Sentinel, I believed I'd never met one. I'd also never fought one. I wasn't sure if I'd survive such a fight, and I nearly didn't. I'm not any more afraid of male Sentinels than I am of females, but it feels like a dangerous gap in my knowledge.

"Could it be an advance guard?" Beatrix asks.

Felix gives a shrug. "It's possible. But I don't wish for it. It would mean there's still a legion of Sentinels to arrive, in addition to the firepower they already have."

"We need to know what we're dealing with." Callan turns to Beatrix. "Beatrix, did you bring the object I asked for?"

"That thing that's so precious to you?" Beatrix smirks, seemingly back to her old self. "Of course I brought it." She gives Callan a coy smile. "But what am I going to get in return for my troubles?"

Callan's eyes narrow at her and the hint of juniper-green flashing through them is somehow comforting to me.

"What do you want?" he asks.

"Five minutes alone with Night Sky."

Callan's eyebrows rise. It's clearly not the bargain he was expecting to make. "Why?"

"That's my business."

"Then that's up to Lana," Callan says. "She chooses what she does with her time."

I'm more curious about what Beatrix brought with her than why she might want five minutes alone with me. "What did Callan ask you to bring?"

Beatrix retrieves a bag from beneath the table and produces what looks like a snow globe. She sets it down on the glass surface in front of her but doesn't let it go.

It contains four trees set in a diamond formation, each one with the strangest-looking leaves. They're too small to make out their shape properly until Beatrix shakes the globe. Then the leaves rise up off the branches and float around the inside of the globe like tiny pieces of paper.

My eyes widen as I suddenly recognize the scene within the globe. "That's Callan's library. But how—?"

"I retrieved it from his old home. It was fucking difficult—"

"Deal," I say, not needing any further convincing that the library is worth my time.

Beatrix's eyebrows shoot up. She casts a glance at Callan. "Looks like someone else likes your library, too."

I could never forget it. Instead of bookshelves, the library was made up of four leafless trees positioned in a diamond shape, each branch lined with books in such a way that it appeared as if the trees sprouted books instead of leaves. The trees felt alive, even though they weren't planted in soil, and their branches had swayed as if in a breeze.

Magical.

"How the hell did you get it in *there?*" I ask, pointing at the globe.

"The library is one of a kind," Callan interjects. "I can't replace it, but it can be compressed and transported."

"Provided you can get *in* to retrieve it," Beatrix points out. "It took me most of the day yesterday while you two were *sleeping.* It was hard enough to get in to the building unseen, let alone make sure nobody tailed me afterward."

She pushes the globe across the table and leaves it there for Callan to retrieve.

"I appreciate this," he says. "These books are irreplaceable. And they'll give us some of the information we need."

I'm not so confident. I only spent a short time in Callan's library, but what I read about the Sentinels wasn't anything I didn't already know. Certainly nothing about men. That's assuming that these newcomers aren't some sort of advance guard preparing for the Sentinels' arrival like Beatrix suggested.

Callan pushes back his chair. "I need to install the library and after that, I have something I need to attend to. Felix, you know what to do. Beatrix, you asked for five minutes with Lana, but Lana will determine how long she gives you."

His voice softens when he turns to me. "I'll put the library on floor five. There's a gym on floor four." He gives me the codes to enter those levels and then continues. "Feel free to move about the building, but keep the neck brace on. There are security cameras in the elevators and at the entrance of each secure floor. I don't want Jada and the others asking questions."

Felix steps in beside Callan, keeping a careful distance away, although the Lamonte dragon doesn't seem nearly as wary of Callan as other dragons are.

Callan pauses one last time. "Beatrix?"

She's already focused on me but glances his way. "Yeah?"

"Has Sophia's mother asked about her?"

Beatrix's long silence is an answer in and of itself. "Martha's more concerned about shoring up her own interests right now."

Callan gives a heavy sigh. "That's what I thought. Let's keep Sophia's new dragon form to ourselves for now. She can share that news with others when the time is right for her."

Beatrix and Felix give nods of agreement.

When Callan and Felix leave, I'm struck with the heavy scent of cloves that clings to Beatrix. The scent of a thief. It doesn't sit quite right with the somber image she currently presents.

"Callan won't tell you this, so I'm going to," she says. "The Dread clan is about to splinter."

I blink at her. "What do you mean?"

"I mean exactly what I said. The clan is about to split into two. There are those who support Callan and Zahra, and there are those who are about to rebel."

"Who?" I ask, although it isn't hard to guess, and I quickly answer my own question. "Tyler. Martha. What about Davison?"

Davison is the final member of the Cohort, the one who literally knows where the bodies are buried.

"He was loyal to Callan," Beatrix says. "But too many clan members support Tyler now, and Davison will be swayed by that."

"Why now?" I ask, although I can guess, and it makes my stomach sink and swirl.

The press of Beatrix's lips speaks of her frustration. "Callan can't hide his feelings for you. He convinced everyone at the Hollow Rose the other night that you were under his control, and as long as you remained in that state, the clan could accept that he was letting you live.

"But then he rescued you when he could have let you die. He could have let Solomon kill you and you would no longer be a threat to us. You demonstrated very thoroughly that you are not under his control, and worse, that he will risk everything to keep you alive. There are many who consider him a traitor now. Zahra is trying to distance herself from Callan's actions, but she's tainted by association."

"What about you?" I ask quietly. "Do you think he's a traitor?"

Beatrix gives a wry laugh. "Oh, honey. I think he's the smartest damn dragon who ever had the fucking nerve to wrap an angel around his little finger."

A trickle of cold passes down my spine. "You think he's using me."

"No," she whispers. "Fuck no. I think he's as wrapped up in you as you are in him. It's going to get you both fucking killed."

I lean back in my chair, wary of the vehemence in her expression.

"It might be Sentinels," Beatrix says, her dark eyes flashing at me. "It might be dragons. Could be Scorn, Grudge, or even Dread. Could be the Celestial-fucking-Ascendant herself. Someone is going to kill you, Lana, and Callan with you. You have too many powerful enemies now."

Maybe I should be afraid, but without Callan here to calm my impulses, there's a part of me that's coming alive with every word Beatrix speaks.

Let them come. If I go down fighting, then I will have died true to myself.

Rather than focus on the threat itself, I find myself curious about Beatrix's motivations. "Why are you warning me?"

"Because I know something about switching alliances. I understand better than most that it's never as clear cut as it appears from the outside."

When I narrow my eyes at her, she folds her arms across her chest. "Did Callan tell you that I was born into the Scorn clan?"

I'm startled. "I didn't know that."

She gives me a cold smile. "Felix and I were born in the same week. Our mothers were sisters. It was like we were twins somehow. Our dragons both manifested at the same time—when we were five years old—the earliest manifestation for any Scorn dragon in decades.

"There were a growing number of Scorn who believed that Felix and I would one day be strong enough to challenge for alpha. The trouble was, we weren't born to the original Scorn line. Sienna Scorn's father had just given her control, and she couldn't risk a threat growing right under her nose."

"What happened?"

"She attempted to have us killed. Not by sending assassins to slit our throats in our sleep. No. At the ripe old age of seven, she sent Felix and me on a mission to steal from one of the most dangerous dragons alive at that time. She was sure he would kill us and her problem would be solved."

At Beatrix's mention of the most dangerous dragon, I immediately think of Callan, but he wouldn't have been more than nine years old at the time and his dragon hadn't manifested yet.

Beatrix's gaze is far away. "Callan's father was a good man. A good alpha. He presented a fierce image. Built himself a vicious reputation. But he loved his family. When he caught us, all he saw was two scared kids." She bites her lip and blinks hard. "Sienna didn't count on him giving us a home."

Beatrix is suddenly quiet, and I don't break the silence.

She takes a shaky breath. "When he died, and Zahra's mom with him... Well, let's just say that we lost the only people we could trust." She lifts her chin. "Until Callan came back."

She leans forward. "Now the sands are shifting again. If Zahra wants to retain control and keep her daughter safe, she'll have to renounce her alliance with Callan. She'll have to align with Tyler. She might not see that yet, and she'll fight it, but it's inevitable.

"When that happens, I'm not sure if Callan's prepared for how hard it will be. He's already lost his parents. I don't think he realizes how much it will hurt to lose his sister and niece, too."

I asked Sophia what power is worth if it means being alone, and she told me Callan would know. He's already so distant from other dragons that I can't allow the final threads between him and his sister to be broken.

"As for me," Beatrix continues, "if you get Callan killed, then you and I will have a problem. Do you understand?"

She glares at me, and I acknowledge her vehemence with a nod.

"I understand." So much more than I think she wants me to. I understand now why she wanted me to warn Callan when she approached me in the bathroom at the Hollow Rose. I understand why she and Felix came with him to rescue me, even though it's now clearly put them at odds with their adopted clan.

Callan is her family.

I look her straight in the eye and it seems to surprise her. It surprises *me* that she thought I'd worry about her threat. I've heard far worse from the mouths of Grudge dragons I killed.

"I left Callan the other night for the sole purpose of protecting him," I say. "I had no good choices, but I was prepared to die to defend him and his family." My jaw clenches and my gaze hardens. "If *you* hadn't come for me, I would have succeeded."

I let that sink in for a second, watch the shadows play across her face.

"All I have are my choices," I say. "I can't control what someone else does. All I can promise you is this: I will hunt anyone who comes for Callan. Be it angels or dragons."

Her lips part and her voice is filled with confusion. "But... *why*? Why him?"

"Because there's power in kindness," I say, the tone of my voice anything but kind. "Callan was the first person to show me that."

"But do you love him?"

She's pushing me for an answer I don't have. If I believe that I'm capable of love, then my answer is *yes*, more than I thought possible, even though that surprises me. But if I believe what I've been told... that my heart can't feel what others feel...

"I love him more than someone like me should love anything," I say, a truthful answer.

Beatrix takes a shaky breath and retrieves her bag, holding it to her chest. The air around us feels to me like small tornados are swirling in every direction. Each one carries a different emotion. One contains the fury of fear. Another a storm of anger. Another the heaviness of sadness. Yet another, bright swirls of hope. My senses tell me she doesn't know what to feel, but I can't help her with that.

She clears her throat, takes a deep breath, and the swirling tornados around us soften and vanish. She puts a block around her emotions so fast that it tells me she's practiced at compartmentalizing her feelings. I suspect I've seen more of her true self in the last few minutes than she may have even shown Callan.

But her emotions are under control now and whatever she thinks of my answers, her thoughts are indiscernible.

She gives an exaggerated huff as she arches an eyebrow at Sophia's closed door. "Tell Sophia to get her lazy ass out of bed. She needs to get used to the weight of her wings sooner or later."

Beatrix's heels click on the floor and moments later, the door closes behind her.

I'm left in silence. Peace. Finally.

Sort of.

There's a strange buzz of energy coming from Sophia's room.

Crossing to her door, I focus on the energy, sensing its darkness.

Something's wrong...

I quickly tap in the code I saw Callan use the other night to gain access. The door swings open. Soft lighting comes from a lamp on the far side of the room, but the bed is empty.

Sophia sits, curled up in the armchair on the right-hand side of the room, her knees to her chest and her face pressed to her knees.

I'm immediately struck with a cloud of dark energy, the kind that pulls relentlessly downward.

Misery.

CHAPTER SIXTEEN

"Sophia!" I rush to her side, but she barely responds, even when I crouch to her.

She's wearing a new shirt, but it's been cut up the back like the last one, and I can see the edges of the fake burn marks.

After another moment's hesitation, I lower my palm to her shoulder, finding it stiff and her skin cold. "Sophia?"

Her voice is muffled. "My back really hurts."

"I thought your burns were healed?"

"It's my wings." She lifts her head a little. Her big, green eyes appear over her knees, her forehead scrunched with pain. "They *ache*. Really badly."

The way she's sitting allows me to run my hand across the nearest part of her left shoulder blade. Unlike the rest of her, it's burning hot.

"Why didn't you tell Callan you were in pain?"

"I didn't want him to think I'm weak."

"Oh, fuck, Sophia. This isn't about weakness. It's about your wings' development. You need to tell him when—" I stop myself before I become a complete fucking hypocrite. "Yeah, okay.

Come on. You need to come out and release your wings. They're burning because they need to move."

I slip my arm around her and help her up, supporting her to walk into the open area past the dividing wall.

The slit up the back of her shirt means she doesn't need to take it off, which is just as well because lifting her arms would be agony right now.

I adjust my position so that I'm facing her but am still supporting her with my hands on either side of her waist. "Wings," I order her. "Let them out."

Her wings thump out so hard that they lift her backward and out of my hold. Water droplets come with them, spreading across the air like diamonds. Little ones. Not the torrent I imagine was released the first time her wings appeared.

She groans with relief, falling forward onto her hands and knees, her wings stretching out on either side of her across the floor. "Fuck, that feels better already."

She stretches her back like a cat and then arches so that her wings lift off the floor. They're a gorgeous, iridescent blue that sparkles in the muted light.

"You can't keep them subdued all the time when they're first developing," I say.

I remember the way five-year-old Emika had told me the clip hurt her, but she had to hide her wings from humans. I'm sure Zahra allows her to spread her wings in private when it's safe.

Sophia looks up at me. "Callan must have done it."

"Kept his wings hidden?" I sigh. "Yes, he must have. And I'm sure it was agony."

I kneel opposite her. "Here, I'll show you some stretches you can do every day. They'll strengthen your core and give your wings a chance to function properly."

For the next hour, I take Sophia through my routine of stretches and gentle exercises. Even though they usually involve spreading my wings, I keep mine restrained since I'm not prepared to face the damage again. Rather than demonstrating, I talk her through each move. By the end, the heat in her shoulder blades has faded and the pain etched on her face has eased.

"I want you to train me," she blurts out when we finish. "I need to learn self-defense, and there's no better person than you to teach me. Will you help me?"

It takes me a moment to catch up with her request. "Uh... Me?"

"Callan can't teach me because it involves physical contact, and Beatrix will only ridicule me."

"Well, I'm not sure about that—"

Sophia gives me a hard stare, and I'm already tasting sour lemon on my tongue since I suspect very strongly that Beatrix *would* ridicule Sophia. She'd certainly teach her, but not without a lot of friction.

Sophia continues. "I'm sure Callan's human bodyguards would help me with combat and weapons training if I ask, but they can't show me how to use my wings. There's nobody else, Lana."

"I'm not sure I'm the best person to teach you anything."

"There's nobody else," she repeats, more insistently this time.

My resolve softens. "I won't go easy on you."

She breaks into a smile. "I won't ask you to." She leans forward. "Can we start now?"

My brow furrows. "The gym would be a better location, but the humans will ask questions if they see you going there so soon, so this will have to do. Grab as many pillows as you can and meet me back here."

I expect Sophia to tire quickly during the workout I give her, but we end up training for the rest of the day. I start small, focusing on her balance first. We're limited by the hard floor, so it's impossible to safely teach her how to tumble, but she's determined to learn, and by lunchtime, her awareness of her body has improved exponentially.

I'm not really sure how the food situation works in this building, but Jada brings lunch up for us, speaking through the intercom first so I can let her in. She stays for the meal. My conscience prickles multiple times, first when I have to snap the neck brace back on before she comes in, and then when Sophia has to retreat to her room and make herself look unwell again. It's an awful façade to present to someone who genuinely cares about us.

After lunch, I focus on Sophia's wings. The high ceiling gives us some leeway and it means we aren't hitting our knees on the floor. Her determination to learn doesn't waver and, as evening approaches, I challenge her to more difficult moves.

When I ask her to jump, release her wings, and kick—using me as a target—I'm not prepared for how fast she moves.

I narrowly evade her foot and release my own wings without thinking. I intend to propel myself backward, only to lose my balance and crash to the floor when my left wing gives way.

"Fuck, Lana! Are you okay?" Sophia drops to my side, stopping at the edge of my wing, her jaw dropping a little. "When did this happen?"

"The angels did it," I say.

Her lips press together into a serious line. "They really want you dead."

"I'm their enemy now."

It's a simple truth.

She nods. "You betrayed them."

I consider that as I remain sitting on the floor, my wings at my sides. "Did I, though?" My forehead creases. "I'm not sure they didn't betray me first."

I shake myself and retract my wings, taking care to do it slowly while Sophia is leaning close to me. "Enough talk. Let's keep going."

By dinnertime, Sophia has progressed far beyond what I expected her to achieve in one day. I tell her that, tomorrow, we should find a way to train in the gym. Even if we have to make up a story about her needing a change of environment.

Jada doesn't stay with us for dinner, telling us she's needed downstairs, but she gives me a smile when she places three covered plates on the table—one of which I assume is for Callan. I'm not sure why Jada gave me such a big grin until I remove the covering to discover a plate full of lasagna, which I quickly devour.

Callan returns as Sophia and I are cleaning up the last delicious smudges of sauce from our plates. He's carrying two cases —one that's long and looks like an instrument case, and the other that's the size and shape of a briefcase.

He looks tired, but his calm footfalls and the warm cinnamon of his eyes tell me he's relaxed.

"Hey," is all he says as he takes a seat, pulls the cover off his meal, and begins to eat.

I'm curious about the cases—and so is Sophia. She stops mid-bite to stare at them where he placed them against the wall. "What's in those?"

"It's good to see you're up and about, Sophia," he says, neatly sidestepping her question.

"Okay," she grumbles. "Keep your secrets."

I'm not quite as relaxed about it. The last time he returned with a briefcase, he wrapped me up in gold that I was led to believe would kill me.

It seems he doesn't plan to keep us in suspense for too long. "I have something for each of you," he says after quickly finishing nearly half of his meal. "The cases are for Lana and I'll show her the contents later, but Sophia, you need a place to call home."

She stiffens a little beside me. "I'm okay here," she says

quickly. "I don't need more than a bed, and if I can help out with food preparation—"

"I'm not kicking you out. I just thought you might want a little more space."

Her tension remains. "But I'm happy *here*. With you and Lana."

Even with Callan's presence blocking my senses, I can discern Sophia's fear like sharp knives. Those protective vines are gathering around her energy again and it strikes me that her fear is not of being oppressed, or controlled, but of being cast out. Dismissed like her mother has dismissed everything about her.

To his credit, Callan seems to pick up on her feelings quickly. "I'm glad you're happy here," he says. "Because I want you to stay. I'm giving you the floor below this one. It will need some adjustments to account for your dragon's power over water, but it's yours."

Her lips have parted in surprise. "You're giving me..."

"Each floor of this building can be separately owned. The apartment below this one is now in your name. If you want it."

The vines around her energy vanish. "I don't know what to say."

The corner of his mouth twitches up. "Say you'll take it."

"I'll take it."

"Good."

Callan returns to his meal without any fuss while Sophia sits back in her seat, appearing to struggle with processing it all. She quickly leans forward again and asks, "I can stay here tonight, though, right?"

I understand her struggle. It's a lot to take in—and also a very empty apartment to suddenly move in to while also dealing with significant changes to her body. Too much change is not necessarily a good thing.

"You'll need to stay on this level until Jada clears you," Callan says. "And that will give me time to figure out how to accommodate your dragon in your apartment. I might need Delaney's help to rework some of the plumbing so there's drainage in each room, but we'll see."

I recall that Delaney is the witch Callan mentioned.

"Okay." Sophia rises to excuse herself. She's wide-eyed and looks as if she needs some space to think. If Callan weren't blocking my senses, I'm sure her emotions would, despite her controlled demeanor, have been like a freight train. "Thank you, Callan."

He acknowledges her and quietly continues to devour his meal at such a fast pace that it makes me wonder if he ate anything during the day. Jada also brought one of his favorite green drinks for him and he swallows it down in one go.

Once Sophia's door is closed, Callan stops eating for long enough to say, "I've offered Beatrix and Felix each a level of this building, too. They only have one home and if it's compromised, I want to make sure they have somewhere safe to go."

I contemplate him as he finishes his meal. The moment between him and Sophia when her dragon first appeared seems to have had an even more profound effect on him than I first thought. His last home was entirely his, with a single level allocated to his human friends out of necessity. He kept to himself. Kept his clan at arm's length. The last few days seem to have changed that.

"That's good," I say. "They're your family." I hesitate but plow on. "They're your pack."

A small pack. But it feels more real than the bonds between Dread dragons have felt to me before.

A small smile rests on his lips as he looks up. "I want you to stay, too."

"Of course," I reply quickly. "It's not like I can just stroll out of here—"

"No, Lana." He takes a deep breath and puts down his fork, as if he wants me to really listen. "*Not*-Lana. I want you to stay."

My eyes widen as he continues.

"As family. As pack."

I try to catch my breath. "I don't know if…"

He lifts his hands as if he's asking me to pause. "I know," he says, his expression suddenly solemn. "I know there are limits."

He pushes back his chair. "I have some things for you that I hope will make it easier."

The cases have remained at the side of the room and now I eye them warily as he picks them up and asks me to follow him.

Once we're inside his bedroom, he places both cases on the bed.

He opens the long case first.

My glaive nestles neatly within its velvet lining, the sharp blades on either end glinting brightly. I feel its pull immediately and cross the distance to run my fingers across its surface.

"I wanted to return this," Callan says. "I stored it in the vault in the basement of this building when we first arrived, but when I went there this morning, it had lifted off the shelf I'd put it on and was hovering in the middle of the room. It was agitated." He gives me a wonky smile. "Damn near impaled me."

"Really?"

"Really. You should keep it with you at all times. The gold it's made from is volatile, but your presence will keep it calm."

I nod. "The gold its made from wasn't treated well. I sensed it the moment I touched it."

"I'm not surprised," Callan says. "Although, in fairness, the fault might not lie with Solomon. Grudge dragons have never owned a lot of gold, so in the past they would share it around. There were rules about what it could be used for, but of course, the rules would have been bent from time to time and even broken."

I grimace, but the sense I get from the glaive now is that it's at peace. "What about the Serene Commander's spear?"

"I locked it in a reinforced steel box within a separate compartment within the vault. It will need to be approached carefully, but it's not getting out on its own."

He turns to the other case and my curiosity peaks when he pauses and says, "This is what I spent most of today working on." He opens the lock and lifts the lid. "These are for you."

As he turns the open briefcase toward me, its contents become clear, and my eyes widen. "Callan, how did you...?"

He lifts his hands into the air and the contents of the case rise with his gesture.

Intricately formed, golden feathers. At least thirty of them.

Each one is fashioned from the finest central shaft while delicate gold webbing extends on both sides, perfectly curved to match the shape of my feathers.

I remember the way he'd studied them, turning his palm so that he could size up their shape from all angles. I'd asked him what he was doing, and he said he was thinking about possibilities.

"You can attach these to your wing," he says. "In place of your lost feathers."

"If they work, I'll be able to fly." I don't touch them yet, simply admiring the detail on each surface and the fineness of the webbing.

"They're perfect," I whisper, but reality quickly rushes in. "How will I keep them attached to me? What about when I close my wings? They don't belong within my body. They'll fall to the ground."

When I retracted my wings during my fight with Solomon, the bracelet that had wrapped around my wing bone was forced to return to my wrist. But it was already loyal to me.

As Callan holds the feathers in the air, he says, "If you want them, you need to accept them and make them your own. Carry them with you. Teach them to cover your wing when you need them, and to stay with you when you close your wings. It won't be easy, but if you want them, they will help you."

I remember the way he brought the training squares of dragon's gold into the room this morning, as if he wanted to test my ability to control the gold midflight. It's the only way this will work.

Relaxing my shoulders, I prepare to test the process, but Callan warns, "One step at a time. They're loyal to me and I've asked them to accept you, but you can't force it."

I carefully release my wings. It's not like the gold can sense the gap I need to fill, but I want to be in my true form when I hold them for the first time.

Callan turns his hands in the air so that his palms are no longer facing up, but rather toward me, as if he's pushing the gold away.

"Come to me," I whisper, crooking my forefinger.

The nearest feather shivers in the air, lifts a little, and then wafts toward me, settling down on my palm. It's the smallest of them all, the fine detail making me gasp.

"You created all this?" I ask Callan, marveling at the intricacy and the feel of the feather against my skin. It barely feels like metal, more like living material.

He smiles and shrugs, as if it's nothing, but it can't have been easy. It certainly explains why he looks so tired.

A well of hot tears suddenly burns behind my eyes.

Not furious tears for once. Not angry.

I press my lips together, unable to put voice to how much this means to me. My heart feels like it's bursting with warmth.

"Try it," Callan urges me, and I sense his need to know if this will work.

Curving my wing to make it easier to reach, I slip the golden feather between two of my black ones so that it will interlock and overlap with them. Then I close my eyes and take a deep breath while I keep the feather in place, sinking into the same meditative state that lets me sense my surroundings.

I need the feather to stay in place when I remove my hand.

The energy within my bracelets strikes me first. It's familiar and calm. Ready to respond to my needs. The essence of my nearby glaive reaches me next, stronger than I was expecting. Fierce. Vengeful. Wanting to be put to use.

The feather's energy is much gentler. Whisper quiet. As if Callan firmly imbued it with the essence of a gentle breeze while he was crafting it, the kind of wind that wafts through emerald-green leaves, softly enough to soothe but powerful enough to lift me from my feet.

Keeping my eyes closed, I exhale gently and remove my hand, hoping that the feather will remain where it is. As I turn away from it to straighten, the feather's energy ripples down my wing and a moment later, there's a soft clatter as it hits the floor.

My shoulders slump.

Damn. I was sure it would stay put.

I tell myself to open my eyes. Try again. *I'm not defeated yet.*

"Lana." Callan's voice carries a warning that makes my eyes fly open.

I gasp. Freeze. Can't believe what I'm seeing.

All of the feathers are attached to my wing, every single one of them perfectly filling the gaps.

I replay the ripple of energy within my mind, along with the clattering sound I thought was the feather hitting the floor. The ripple was the gathering of the other feathers, and the soft clatter must have been the sound of them interlocking across my wing and filling the gaps.

Callan smiles, his eyes bright. "They want to fly."

Very carefully, I move my left wing, concentrating on the

energy flowing through the gold, sensing it tighten, cling, but also create a buffer against the air like my black feathers do. I move my wing a little more and then take a chance and give it a careful beat.

I lift off the floor, my feet an inch above it.

The feathers hold.

Tears spring to my eyes as I lower myself to the floor again. "Callan, I..."

He's already turning to the briefcase, pulling a soft-looking leather harness from it. "You'll need to experiment with ways to store the feathers when they're not in use. Around your waist or arms maybe. Even your legs. Multiple places probably. But for now, they should fit into these pouches. And you can carry your glaive at the back."

He holds up the harness, which comes together nicely at the back to allow for my wings, and he points to its various parts. There's a long scabbard at the back for my glaive and two pouches that sit on the left side of the harness for my feathers.

I take the harness from him, struggling to focus past my tears.

I wish, more than anything, that I could hug him. A real hug.

His expression, beyond my watery gaze, is serious.

"I know you need to hunt. And I know I can't go with you," he says. "Who you hunt—and *when* you hunt—is up to you."

I give him a nod, not trusting my voice until I can get my emotions under control. I don't want to take off the feathers, but I need to practice, so I focus on their energy again, willing them to float off my wing and into the pouches. It mostly works. A few of the feathers get stuck at the edge of the pouch, but it's nothing that practice won't fix.

When I retract my wings, reality kicks in again because only by staying in Callan's home can I protect him and those who live here, so I'm not sure how I can leave to hunt. "I can't come and go from this building. If anyone sees me, I'll compromise everything again."

"Not this building," he says with a mysterious smile. "There's another way out. Get ready, and I'll show you."

CHAPTER SEVENTEEN

I hurry to shower and dress in fresh black clothing before fitting the harness across my torso. I release and retract my wings a few times to make sure I'm confident they aren't hindered by the harness, and then I retrieve the glaive from its case, slipping it into the scabbard at my back.

I have a moment's indecision about putting the neck brace back on for the cameras, but I decide I've continued that façade for long enough. The bruises are still visible and that will have to be enough. The humans know I'm an assassin and Callan pays them not to ask questions. They won't be surprised to see me in battle gear.

Ready now, I follow Callan out to the elevator.

Once inside it, Callan presses his palm to a panel above the floor numbers and then asks me to do the same.

"Your palm print is now in the system," he says. "You'll be able to access all the levels and rooms that I can access. One of which is a sub-level my human friends don't know about."

The elevator descends. Just like his old home, which had a hidden level at the top where the Cohort would meet, it seems this one has a hidden level at the bottom.

Callan keeps his distance from me within the elevator, and when the doors open, he leads me into a wide waiting room.

There are two doors set apart on the opposite wall.

One is painted red, like the door into the Cohort's meeting room at his last home.

The other is painted black.

He leads me to the black door and then gestures to the control panel that sits on the wall beside it. "Your turn."

I press my palm to it and in the next instant, the door clicks open.

A long hallway lies beyond it that's wide enough for me to release my wings but not big enough for me to completely stretch them out to either side—or to fly. It's brightly lit and stretches into the distance as far as I can see.

I step carefully out of the way to allow Callan to go in first.

"Beatrix and Felix already have access to this tunnel," he says. "I'll give Sophia access, too, as soon as she's ready."

"Where does it lead?"

"To a safe exit located two blocks from our home," he says, giving me another mysterious smile.

Our home. I let that settle within my thoughts as I set off after him.

It's a good five minutes before we reach the end of the tunnel, where there's another black door and another control panel. This time, Callan isn't so quick to ask me to access it.

"This door lets out into the basement of a bar I own. The humans who work here are paid not to pay attention to anyone coming or going through this door, but that doesn't mean they won't notice you—or your weapon." He glances at the top of my glaive, which is fully visible over my shoulder. "You'll need to move quickly and quietly."

It's not lost on me that he's referring to *me* and not both of us. "You're really not coming with me?"

He shakes his head. "I'll be preparing for this war in other ways. If it's necessary, I can use this path, but the bar above us is crowded at night. I don't want to risk walking through it unless I need to. You can follow the staff exit to the service alley at the back of the building. From there, you can go anywhere."

Anywhere?

I was always sent out with a purpose. Someone else's purpose. Not one of my own making. A thrill passes through me at the idea that this time, I'm heading out into the night for reasons of my own.

Hunting the angel elite.

Callan leans back against the tunnel wall and folds his arms across his chest. Until now, he's been focused on getting me here, but now, an edge of tension appears around his eyes. Where he stands, the tunnel lights don't quite shine, and when he turns his face, one side is bright while the other is shadowed. A duality that reflects his nature. Reason versus fury. I'm reminded that he controls his dragon's volatility with an iron will.

"I want to ask you to be careful," he says, "but I can't fucking get the image out of my mind of you flying at Tyler that first night."

I'd waited only long enough to verify that Tyler was a dragon shifter. Within seconds, his head was in my hands, my wings were spread, and I lifted him off the ground, preparing to snap his neck.

"You were single-minded," Callan says, the shadows deepening across his features. "Focused only on your goal, not on your own safety."

"It's who I am," I whisper.

Callan gives me a nod, rolling his shoulders a little as if he's trying to release his fears. He turns back into the light, his gaze roaming across my face, lingering on my eyes, then my lips.

He takes a step back, still facing me, seeming intent on imprinting my image on his mind. I try to quiet my own memories of more recent days—the way he looked at me when he first arrived at the alley outside the Cathedral, the way his dragon's snarls would have filled the air if it could make a sound.

"Come back to me," he says before he spins and strides away.

I hover for another moment, tempted to follow him back through the tunnel. Find a way to sleep beside him. Hunt another night. But the farther he walks from me, the sharper my focus becomes.

The faint thump of music filters down through the ceiling. Beyond this door, a deep hum of guilty consciences draws my attention.

To hunt angels at night, I could start at the Cathedral, but they won't simply be milling about there. They're looking for me and Callan within the city, just as I'm now looking for them.

What I need to find are the pristine souls. Sift through the mud of guilt to the purity of thought and mind. That's when I'll find the Sentinels.

Pressing my hand to the access panel, I prepare myself for the onslaught of guilt from the mass of humans above, and from the supernaturals who are no doubt hiding among them. I expect the assault on my senses will be somewhat gradual since the basement will be a buffer for the heavier environment of the bar itself. But as soon as I enter the bar, I'll have to move fast.

I step into the basement. With a glance behind me, I ascertain the location of the door and make sure it closes properly, noting the sign that declares it's for authorized personnel only.

Remaining aware of my surroundings, I ascend the staircase to the next door. Then I curl my hands into fists and press my fingernails into my palms, a sharp, pricking sensation on which to focus when I push open the door and enter the corridor beyond.

Keeping to the wall, I quickly ascertain the location of the staff exit on my left. From what I can see in the distance, the bar is packed.

I'm aware that, although the Sentinels are my focus, the Scorn dragons are also searching for me. I'm their best bet at tracking Solomon, although it would be reckless for him to come anywhere near me so soon after his encounter with Callan. Even so, I have to treat every person who appears human as a possible dragon.

All I can say for certain, as I expand my senses to scrutinize the patrons in the bar, is that there are no angels here. A heavy fog of guilt fills the room. There is the simple guilt of lies, both little and big. And then there is the more complex guilt of choices that led to harmful consequences, both anticipated and unexpected.

It's a relief that I don't taste copper on my tongue. Nobody here is a killer and that reassures me that at least there are no Scorn here.

I focus all of my strength on controlling my intentions, and on putting one foot in front of the other, slipping toward the exit and the service door.

It closes behind me, and then the pall of guilt fades.

Quickly jogging to the end of the alley, I locate the nearest street sign and ascertain that I'm south of the Cathedral. If these new angels are smart, they'll each choose a point equidistant from each other and work their way inward, looking for me.

It won't be as difficult for the Sentinels to find me as it is for them to find Callan. They simply have to look for my telltale energy. How quickly they locate me depends on the strength of their power.

No matter what, I plan on finding them before they find me.

I set off at a quick pace, sifting through all the sensory input around me: the city's night life, and the various super-naturals going about their business, although there aren't as many different species here as I imagine there are in other cities. The conflict between angels and dragons seems to have driven many out of the city center itself. Then there are the humans. I keep my senses peeled for the taste of copper, knowing it's my best indicator that a dragon in human form is nearby.

Soon, it's time to find a higher vantage point from which to hunt. Five blocks toward the river, I stop in a dark alley.

I can safely release my wings here, but it's only the second time I've called the feathers, and I have to quell my nerves.

Closing my eyes, I imagine the soft breeze that pulled the golden feathers to my wings earlier, picturing it rushing past the pouches that rest against my left hip, lifting the feathers out, and carrying them to my wing.

There's a bright flash of energy and then a soft clatter. This time, I sense the added weight to my wings when the feathers interlock. I missed it the first time because of the slump of my shoulders.

Opening my eyes, I test the feathers' hold and position by folding my wings in and out, grateful when they accommodate the movement of my wings.

Confident that I'm unobserved, I give my wings a strong beat and fly up to the rooftop three levels above me. I crouch in the shadows, wary that the golden feathers could catch the light. Carefully, I prowl to the next alley, then fly across it and up to the roof of an even taller building, finally able to see out across the surrounding streets.

I close my eyes for a long moment and stretch my abilities as far as I can, forcing myself to ignore all the darkness and seek only the purest souls. The faultless ones.

My heart thumps when I locate two of them.

One is located farther north, closer to the Cathedral.

The other is in a park near the river's edge.

There must be others, but they're too far away for me to sense them.

Of the two locations, I won't go near the Cathedral again—not yet, anyway—so I focus on the angel in the park. Their energy is as pristine as a snowflake, but I have no doubt they will be nowhere near as delicate or easy to crush.

Retracting my wings, I test the speed with which I can relocate the feathers to the pouch. This time, only one catches on the lip of the pocket, and I tuck it in before I set off at a run across the rooftop, keeping the bright spark of the angel's pure soul within my sights.

I don't stop for the alleys, leaping off the edge of each rooftop with all of my might and landing silently on the other side, reveling in the wind rushing across my body and the sense of freedom in running.

Glorious freedom.

Fuck, it would be easy to keep going and never stop.

But the fight ahead of me keeps me focused.

Approaching the next street and the wide gap between rooftops, I release my wings and leap without hesitation. The air rushing across my body is all I need to call the golden feathers to my wing. My body dips for a second before the feathers interlock, and then I'm flying high enough that the sound of my passing will be drowned out by the street noise.

Not a single person below me looks up.

Within five minutes, I reach the edge of the park. The brightness of the angel's soul is overwhelming. I thought the Serene Commander was the epitome of tranquility and strength, but this angel is beyond anything I imagined.

I drop to street level again in the dark shadows of the nearest alley, quickly putting away my wings as I observe the edge of the park. It's filled with lush trees, but not so many that I'll be able to creep through them, and their trunks aren't wide enough to hide behind.

The angel's silhouette shimmers through the foliage. A male silhouette. He's as tall as Callan and just as broad in the shoulders. Felix said the newcomers had the same stature as dragon shifters, but I didn't really believe it until now.

This man's energy is a bright glow where he stands beside one of the park benches that sits along a curved footpath meandering around the large park.

I don't think he's aware of my presence yet, but I keep watch on him as I step out of the alley onto the walkway. Remaining close to the buildings, I keep as much distance between me and passersby as I can before I cross the street.

As I set foot on the path that runs alongside the park, the angel's shimmering silhouette finally swings in my direction.

I can't yet see his features, but the suddenness of his spin toward me indicates he finally sensed my presence.

I take note of how close I am to him—about one hundred feet—which means that if I stay out of that range, these angels shouldn't be able to locate me. That is, assuming he isn't the weakest of them. Hopefully, my ability to locate him from a much farther distance gives me an advantage and will give me a better chance to slip away and keep Callan's home safe.

Even so, the moment his energy flares, I instinctively reach over my shoulder for my weapon. I have to stop myself from withdrawing it. Most humans are so intent on where they're going, what they're doing, or whom they're with that they don't see what's happening around them, but withdrawing my weapon would certainly change that.

Entering the park, I dart beneath the shadow of the nearest tree. The park is well lit at night, but thankfully, there are far fewer people here than there would be during the day.

Up ahead, the angel turns and saunters across the grassy expanse toward a thicket of trees on the far side.

There, he stops, as if he's waiting.

It's an interesting move, and I'm not completely sure what to make of it. Whatever his reasons, we'll be less likely to be observed in that part of the park, so I set off after him, keeping my footfalls quiet. I'm closer to the river now and I can hear the lapping water overlaid with the soft hum of traffic along the nearby streets.

Closing in on the trees, I reach for my glaive again. Then stop again. The angel has remained very still and, as I step nearer, I can make out his features and the intent way in which he studies me as I approach. He hasn't taken up an attack stance or drawn any weapons, so I put a hold on my instinct to fight.

I step into the shadowed clearing, only five paces away from him.

He would tower over me if we were standing closer together. His hair is pure white and falls to either side of his face, long enough to reach his jawline. He has high cheekbones, eyes the color of gray storm clouds, and flawless skin. I imagine that when he spreads his wings, they'll be as pure white as his hair. He has perfect lips that are pressed in an angry line, the only sign of aggression that mars the immaculate beauty of his features.

He's dressed casually in sweatpants and a workout shirt, as if he's here in the park for a jog. Both items of clothing accentuate his muscular biceps, chest, and stomach. A gold watch glints at his wrist and I eye it warily, determined not to be taken off guard if it transforms into a Sentinel's spear like the Serene Commander's hairpin did.

He sizes me up, a quick onceover during which he can't possibly miss my lattice armband or my glaive peeking over my shoulder.

It's the way he looks me directly in the eyes that really startles me. No angel looks me in the eyes like that—not without some sort of magical protection like the type the Serene Commander wore during my fight with her.

"Asper Ashen-Varr," he says. "I suspected you might seek me out first."

CHAPTER EIGHTEEN

shen-Varr. It refers to an Avenging Angel, a term I was previously only vaguely familiar with. Before Solomon's revelations, I certainly never dreamed it would be associated with me.

Now this angel is calling me a *cruel* avenging angel.

What a combination.

As for seeking him out first, he makes it sound as if I singled him out deliberately.

"I don't know who you are," I say, watching carefully for any increase in his aggression. "If you think I'm granting you some sort of honor, please know that's not my intention."

The muscle in his jaw twitches, a sharp movement. "My name is Isaac. I am the first of the *Roden-Darr.*"

I struggle with that term. *Soldier? Follower? Guard?*

His lips twist when I don't immediately respond, and his glare could take my skin off.

"I once dreamed of meeting you," he says. "Of serving you and obeying your commands. Now I must hunt you like a common beast."

I'm not offended by his reference to me as a beast. I expected no less, but what confuses and surprises me is his mention of serving me. "Why would you dream of serving me?"

"Because that was my purpose," he says.

He begins a slow pace from side to side, looking me up and down. His expression shifts as he moves, betraying his rapidly changing emotions. I sense fury, betrayal, loathing, but that last emotion seems to be directed at himself because beneath it all, as he takes me in—my black hair, my muscled body, and the unforgiving set of my jaw—there's a hint of respect in his eyes.

"I was warned that you know nothing of who I am or of your original purpose," he says.

"Then perhaps you should tread carefully," I say, remaining still as he paces back and forth. "Since I view you only as my enemy."

"We weren't created to be that way." The hard press of his lips betrays his greatest emotion, and it surprises me as much as his ability to look me in the eyes. What he seems to feel most intensely right now is... *loss*. As if I took something valuable from him.

"What *are* you?" I ask, giving in to my curiosity.

"I'm a Sentinel," he says, as if that answers everything.

I narrow my eyes at him. "Sentinels are usually women."

"Not those who were born to follow you."

"What are you talking about?" I didn't expect to have any sort of conversation with this angel, but the intensity of his bitterness toward me tells me his emotions will cloud his reason. He seems to have things he wants to say to me. And, by fuck, I'm going to let him say them. The more he talks, the more information he'll give me.

"We were meant to be your soldiers. Created in the purest fires of the heavenly realm. Our sole purpose was to assist the next Avenging Angel with the task of hunting and imprisoning the most heinous of supernaturals. For years, we waited in anticipation for the next Ashen-Varr to come into existence. We trained and prayed we would be worthy of you. Hoping for the day when your strength would help us fight back against the dark ones who use their powers to prey on the innocent. And now..."

His hatred is like hot coals in my mouth.

I struggle to process everything he said. In the seconds that I have, I distill it down to its most important points: He would have been mine to command, and he was promised a leader with the strength to help him, but it was all ripped away from him.

"Now we have been called to capture *you* instead," he says.

Only capture? I eye him warily. "Not kill?"

"We are not corrupted like you."

Callan questioned why the angels thought I was no longer an Avenging Angel. All my life, the Serene Commander told me I was wicked and that my heart was corrupted, but she never told me how I came to be that way.

"Explain to me why you think I'm corrupted," I say.

Isaac edges closer to me. "You have every strength and skill you need to identify the dark ones, to track, capture, and imprison them. We prepared the prison to hold them and would have guarded all those you brought to justice. You have the capacity to feel nothing but loathing for the guilty. You would not be swayed by threats or bribes. Or emotion."

As he speaks, I consider my ability to sense guilt. The way it floods my body like a physical force. The way my power allows me to sense my surroundings, even hear through soundproof surfaces. And how I can perceive motivations, even predict behavior. But as for being swayed by emotion... Well, where does reason end and emotion begin?

"But your desire to kill is an abomination," Isaac continues. "You should not be able to sustain the desire to take life. Avenging Angels must remain pure above all others. There can't be blood on your hands."

A trickle of anger rises within me. "I didn't take life until I was sent to do so."

He acknowledges this with a nod. "True. But you had already developed the capacity for it. When you were returned to us after you were stolen, and suddenly, no angel could look in your eyes without pain, we knew that your basic nature had been altered. You were no longer the warrior who was promised to us."

How? I want to scream at him. *Why?*

Did Solomon curse me? Did he have the help of a dark witch who stole my soul's light from me?

How, how, how?

"*You* can look in my eyes," I snap, my frustration clouding my judgement.

"Not without pain," he says, making my own eyes widen.

"But you do it anyway."

"I was created to follow you," Isaac says. "I was built to fight beside you. No matter the cost to myself."

"So you bear this pain because of duty." The heat of anger within me only increases. "Without the freedom to decide for yourself?"

"I have free will, if that's what you're asking, but I would have gladly died fighting at the side of an Avenging Angel."

"Just not this one," I murmur. I study the shifting shadows across his features, the way he's pacing around me, as if he's more on edge with every step.

He has my complete attention as I anticipate his attack.

"You should be careful that my corruption doesn't rub off on you," I whisper. "Fury is catching."

He nods, a slow, dangerous movement as he reaches for the watch at his wrist. He plucks it from his wrist as if he's going to throw it into the air before he catches it in his hand again.

I'm not surprised when the golden piece changes shape in the blink of an eye—but not into the spear I was expecting.

Instead of a simple blade at one end, it sports a gleaming axe on one side with a shining pike at the very tip. The pike looks sharp enough to impale my heart, while the axe would be strong enough to remove my head from my shoulders. That's if killing me were in the cards.

He holds the weapon ready, and I predict his next move from the way his muscles are bunching. He's going to come at me low and try to sweep my feet out from under me. The weapon is a distraction so I'll focus on it and not on his legs.

I'm about to release my wings, rise into the air, and show him how impossible it will be to unbalance me, when he says, "You can never hope to fight me with a broken wing, Asper. You should come with me willingly, and we can end this quickly. The prison we've prepared for you in the veil is not so bad. You can live out the rest of your days there in peace. Away from the darkness of this world."

I dismiss his suggestion with a shake of my head. As for my wings, I should have anticipated that the Serene Commander would have told Isaac and his men all about my present weaknesses, including my inability to fly. I decide it's best to keep my wings retracted for now. Using them when he least expects it could give me an advantage when I need one.

Without taking my eyes off Isaac, I carefully unclip my harness and lay it—weapon and all—on the ground.

He remains wary, and even more so now that I'm divesting myself of my blade.

"You may think I can't fight you with a broken wing, but I don't need my wings, or a weapon, to kill you," I say.

It draws a faint smile to his lips, the first he's given me.

Without another word, I dart forward. Both of my hands close around the shaft of his poleaxe. At the same time, his right leg sweeps across the ground—the move I predicted he would use to put me on my backside. The confidence in his eyes tells me he thinks I've made a mistake coming at him, but I use the weapon as an anchor point and his own twisting momentum against him.

Hefting myself upward and making use of his swinging leg as a platform, I leap to his left, taking his poleaxe with me.

I hit the ground, roll, and bounce back to my feet without a hitch.

He swings to me and once again, I sense both loathing and respect, clashing vibrations, in the air around him.

Now that I have his weapon, he braces for my attack, watching me even more intently, following the blade as I swing it back and forth.

I don't know if this weapon has a poisoned tip like other Sentinels' spears, but I won't take that chance.

Drawing my arm back, I twist and pitch it into the ground at the base of the nearest tree. To his credit, Isaac doesn't attack me while I do it, but he does narrow his eyes at me now that I've put down both weapons.

"You weren't going to use that anyway," I say.

"True," he replies, not wasting another moment.

He steps forward, swinging. His fists are so fast and powerful that it feels like they create friction in the air around me, sparks of energy that I'm so mesmerized by that I nearly forget to duck.

Silvery power falls around my head and shoulders as I drop, and his energy glitters in the air as I dart from side to side to avoid his follow-up punches. I can only attribute the glimmers to his soul light and... *Damn... It's beautiful.*

To have a soul that pure...

I duck, dart, and evade as he follows me around the clearing. I avoid his fists and feet for as long as it takes me to recover my rage, to grab hold of what makes me *me*.

I watch his next fist coming, drop again, and this time, I push forward, both of my own fists crashing into his chest, knocking him backward so hard that I'm sure he'll have no choice but to use his wings to stop his fall.

He flips midair, far more nimbly than I was expecting, and lands lightly, bouncing on the balls of his feet before he comes right back at me.

He adapts his next moves, more fluid and less aggressive, his palms flat, his feet fast, and I have to work harder not to end up on the ground.

He is as single-minded as I am. As fast as I am. As strong as I am. Almost like a shadow of me.

For the briefest, most painful moment, I acknowledge in my heart that I would have welcomed this warrior at my side. I believed that I wasn't meant to have a family or a pack. And now I discover that there was a family waiting for me all this time. A family who would have welcomed me.

To not be alone all these years…

I harden my thoughts.

He is my enemy now.

And I have to stop him.

I release my wings, leap upward at the same moment, and spin, the rush of air building around me like a call to my golden feathers.

They shoot up out of the pouches on the ground, a rippling cascade of metal that pours across the short distance and onto my wing even as I spin. In the next instant, they've interlocked, keeping me elevated.

Isaac's eyes widen at the sight of the feathers, but before he can speak, my kick lands on his chin. I knock him backward and this time, I feel the crunch of bones beneath my boot.

His blood taints the shimmers of his power as he's knocked to the side and down onto his knees.

He's already getting up. I'm sure he's already healing.

I don't waste a single second, beating my wings and swooping down onto him.

Gripping his shoulders, I pluck him off-balance and gain air before I throw him down again. I crash onto him, my knee pressing into his diaphragm and restricting his breathing.

My left hand rests firmly beneath his chin. My right hand presses to the left side of his face. I tell myself it doesn't matter how faultless he is. I thought the Serene Commander was faultless, too, and I found a way to move past my limitations and wish for her end.

"Give me one good reason why I shouldn't rip your head from your shoulders right now?"

He stays very still beneath me, working to breathe as he attempts to speak. "You only kill the guilty," he rasps.

His features should betray fear, but his voice carries a conviction that's reflected in his clear, gray eyes. "It's why you couldn't kill Callan Steele. The Serene Commander made a mistake when she sent you—"

I jolt at his mention of Callan. "What do you know of Callan Steele?"

Isaac gasps for breath. Without letting go of his head, I shift my knee so that he can speak.

He takes a deep breath before he says, "I know that he has done nothing to deserve death."

Isaac is speaking the truth, but his certainty unsettles me. The Serene Commander sent me to kill Callan. She knew—but didn't tell me—that Callan is the only dragon who can breathe fire. Despite that, she didn't know where he lived or what he looked like, and I assumed she found out about his fire from whispers about his reputation, even though it was a part of his reputation she chose not to share with me.

But for Isaac to sound so certain now makes me think he knows far more about Callan than the Serene Commander ever did. After all, to judge whether someone deserves death requires meeting them.

My voice is a harsh snarl. "How do you know Callan?"

Isaac lowers his voice, softer now. "I don't."

"Then...?"

"Your corruption fills you with the desire to end the lives of the guilty, Asper," Isaac says. "If Callan Steele were guilty, you would have killed him already."

My eyes widen at Isaac's reasoning, which has nothing to do with Callan, after all, and everything to do with me. "You trust in my nature so completely that you would judge another person based on whether or not I decide to kill them?"

"I would. Even with your corruption—in fact, *because* of it— the fact that Callan Steele is still alive tells me he doesn't deserve to die."

My hands tighten around Isaac's face, but his reasoning applies more broadly than it does to just Callan.

I let Isaac go, using my wings to rise off him and set myself back on the ground. An edge of despair bleeds into my voice. "Then why would the Serene Commander send me to kill him?"

Isaac rises to his feet. He rubs his throat, but there are no visible bruises. "Because we must protect the world from him. The Serene Commander wasn't wrong to send you after him, but her timing was ill-conceived. She should have waited."

My forehead creases. "Waited for what?"

"For his dragon to take control."

It's like a bucket of icy water pours over me. The Grudge dragons I killed reeked of copper and had misshapen shadows that barely resembled dragons at all. Callan told me it's a less common side effect of the dragon shifters' failing powers: while some dragons never shift, others lose their ability to reason and they succumb to their beasts.

Callan's own words chill me to my core: *There's no way to save a dragon whose beast dominates them. They're a danger to everyone around them.*

Callan's beast would be the most dangerous of all. He told

me he felt its rage when it had first manifested. It could turn the world to ash.

"No," I whisper vehemently. "That won't happen to Callan."

"Maybe not today. Not tomorrow. But soon. And sadly, when it does, you will no longer be here to stop him."

I scoff as I take a step back. "You won't capture me."

"We will," he says, his confidence unnerving. "Every time you fight us, we will learn how you move and how you think. We will find your weaknesses. Even if it takes us months. We will capture you. We have to. You have become a significant threat." He gives a heavy sigh. "Should you join with Callan, then, together, you would be unstoppable."

He edges forward and reaches for me. "Please know that I regret what must be done."

With a growl of anger, I thump his hand away and land another punch to his cheekbone, knocking him to his knees.

Solomon said he would take no joy from my death. The Serene Commander claimed she tried to save me from myself. Now Isaac is telling me he regrets that he will have to capture me.

It seems they're all fucking sorry for what they have to do, but nothing will stop them from doing it.

I snarl down at him where he remains at my feet. "You will make a mistake," I say. "In your efforts to capture me, you will hurt someone or kill someone. You won't be faultless anymore, and I won't hesitate to kill you."

"We'll see."

I spin and stride away, trying to quell my rising fear as I scoop up my harness and retract my wings. The golden feathers fly off my body in a cascade and slip back into the pouches even as I hurry through the trees.

My ears pop as I step into the brightly lit center of the park, and sounds suddenly flood in. I falter, shocked to realize that I was so focused on my fight with Isaac, I forgot to remain aware of my surroundings, wasn't checking if humans were near or other supernaturals were around. I was completely wrapped up in my interaction with him.

Recovering from my moment of surprise, I race on, aiming for the shadows at the edge of the park, putting as much distance as I can between Isaac and me.

I'm not afraid of him or his men, but I won't be put back in a cell, and, no matter how loudly I mentally scream in denial, Isaac is right.

Just as I can't kill Callan, I can't kill Isaac, either.

CHAPTER NINETEEN

I slow my pace only while I'm crossing the street and observable by humans. As soon as I reach the first dark alley, I spread my wings and ascend to the rooftops again, and then I don't stop running until I'm five blocks away from the park.

I convince myself I can escape the truth of Isaac's convictions if I run fast enough, leaping across alleys, my feet flying across rooftops.

Finally dropping to a crouch on the top of an industrial building, I wrap my wings around myself while I catch my breath.

If I can't kill those angels, how the fuck do I beat them? Waiting for them to make a mistake wastes time and guarantees me nothing.

"Nice feathers." The mesmerizing croon comes from beside the shadowed gable on my left.

I swing, ready to fight, until I recognize Felix. He remains in the darkness where the moonlight doesn't touch him, his outline revealing that he's in his shifted form, his wings tucked tightly to his sides.

I'm once again shocked that I wasn't paying attention to my surroundings. Shaking my head, I squeeze my eyes shut for a moment, forcing myself to straighten out the mess of anger and frustration within my mind before I wipe my expression clean.

"Were you following me, Felix?"

I recall Callan telling Felix that he knew what to do, and it dawns on me that Felix may have been watching me the whole time.

"I was following the angels, not you," Felix replies. "Don't worry. Callan didn't send me to watch over you."

There's no taste of sour lemons on my tongue when Felix speaks, which means he isn't lying to me.

"Good," I say. "Because that would be insulting."

I make out his smirk in the darkness. "Would it, though?" The tips of his boots rest at the edge of the shadows and I find his stillness unsettling. "Is it so difficult to accept that someone might miss you if you die?"

I'm about to voice a retort when I make out what looks like a blade resting in Felix's hand at his side.

Then I realize it *is* his hand. He and Beatrix are unique in that they have clawed hands in their shifted forms, a feature that I haven't encountered in any other dragon shifter so far. That is, other than Solomon. But he seems unique in most ways.

My eyes widen at the blood dripping from Felix's claw. It's making a little puddle at the side of his boot.

He's obviously been in a fight, but with whom? Could it have been Scorn dragons or angels?

"Felix?"

"Yes, Lana?"

"What have you done?"

He shrugs. "Don't worry. I didn't kill any angels tonight. Although it wasn't for lack of trying. I'd suggest you take backup next time so they don't catch you unawares."

His reference to backup and catching me by surprise causes

a sinking sensation in my stomach. My next question is even more cautious, my heart already beating faster. "Where was your fight?"

"In the park."

The park? But I didn't see or sense them. "How many angels?"

"Six."

I draw a deep breath, trying to calm my suddenly wild thoughts. *How did I not sense them? How could I have missed a battle happening nearby?*

I flash back to the moment when Isaac started speaking. How captivating he was, how the flickers of his power danced at the edges of my vision, enthralling me. Keeping me focused entirely on him. It was only when I put enough distance between him and me that my ears popped, and the outside world flooded in again.

I whisper into the silence. "Fuck."

These Sentinels aren't like the ordinary warrior angels I'm used to dealing with. Not even like the Serene Commander.

"You need to watch your back, Lana." Felix pauses before he steps back into the shadows. "Or maybe accept the fact that you have allies who are willing to watch it for you."

He swings away from me and disappears before I can call out to him.

I'm left with my stormy thoughts.

Isaac must have allowed his soul light to shine because it would cloud my senses and stop me sensing my broader surroundings. It would explain why he wanted me to find him, and why he was so keen to keep me talking.

I only escaped captivity because of Felix.

Snarls build in my throat. My jaw tightens. My heart hammers a harsh beat. I can't let it happen again. Can't allow myself to be so ensnared by the promise of answers about my past, or distracted by the purity of a Sentinel's power, that I lose the ability to perceive the larger threats around me.

Keeping my senses expanded now, I make my way back to the bar, but I take a circuitous route to make sure I'm not followed. I watch for observers before I descend to the basement and gain access to the tunnel.

I don't breathe easily until I'm back in Callan's home.

On the upper level, the living area is softly lit. It's past midnight and Sophia will be asleep, so I head straight for Callan's door.

I find him asleep on his bed. He's fully dressed, lying right at the edge on the right-hand side, making me think he didn't intend to fall asleep at all.

He doesn't stir, his chest rising and falling deeply. I'm not surprised that he needs to sleep after he spent all day crafting the feathers for me.

I slip into the dressing room, quickly put away my things, shower, and pull on another one of his T-shirts, and then I face the dilemma of where to sleep.

We didn't talk about it. We probably should have.

The last two times we woke up safely together, he'd been in his dragon form and had shifted back to human while maintaining contact with me—either while he'd been awake or sleeping.

I'm not sure that initiating contact while he's sleeping will overcome his dragon's triggers or if it will cause an almighty fire.

But, fuck it, I'm tired and I need him.

Besides, I tell myself that if I'm not nearby when he wakes up in the morning, it will only worry him.

I slip under the blankets on the far left-hand side of the bed, keeping as much distance between us as possible and using the material as a physical barrier to reduce the chances of contact.

I tell myself it's a risk worth taking.

∼

I awake to Callan's palm pressed against my back.

My eyes fly open.

I expect to see the room scorched, the mattress turned to ash, and to find myself inhaling his flames.

All is quiet. Including his breathing.

Tipping my head slowly back, I see that the blanket has fallen down to my hips. His lower arm is outstretched where he lies on his side, facing me. His eyes are closed, and his breathing remains deep. Yet he's touching me.

It's as if he came looking for me in his sleep.

I allow myself to relax and add it to the list of instances where we can safely make contact—while he's fast asleep.

Reaching back to take hold of his hand, I turn and move carefully toward him, checking and watching in case his dragon makes an appearance.

Callan finally stirs.

"Asper," he murmurs, and I don't mind that he uses my true name.

Settling in beside him, I pull his upper arm around me, intending to fall back to sleep, but it seems he has other ideas.

With a rumble in his chest, he rolls me onto my back, both of his arms now trapped beneath me, his hands under my shirt so that it rides up and bunches beneath my breasts, exposing my stomach and naked pelvis.

He plants a sleepy kiss on my lips that makes my skin tingle before he moves down my neck. His mouth sends warm signals to my core and makes my thighs clench.

"You're safe," he rumbles.

"Uh-huh."

That's all I can manage before he takes the bunched base of my shirt in his teeth and lifts it, flexing his hands beneath my back to make me arch. It gives him better access as he explores my body with his warm mouth.

Within moments, moans leave my lips.

His hands slide slowly down beneath me, across my lower back and under my hips, lifting me to his mouth so he can stroke my center with his tongue. Warm, languid strokes relax my muscles and make my fingers curl in the sheets.

I'm aching for his hard length, but the crash comes fast. The orgasm ripples through me in waves that leave me spiraling. Up and down and somehow still aching.

He makes a satisfied noise that vibrates against my core and my thighs clench again. Harder this time.

When he lifts his head—a mere inch above my center—and raises his eyes to mine, his irises are flecked with gold, a growing heat in them that promises to burn out of control.

Firmly gripping my hips, he nudges me over onto my stomach. At the same time, his mouth burns a path up my spine, skipping over the bunched shirt, to reach the back of my neck.

His voice is a seductive rumble at my ear. "If you don't like it this way, tell me, and we can stop. You're in control."

Shivers of pleasure thrum through me, a physical reaction to his request that only heats my core. *Damn, I love it that he asks.*

His mouth leaves my ear. His hands slip back to my hips, lifting me so that he can position himself against me.

His groan at the first thrust mingles with my moan of need. He waits a beat before moving again, the next thrust harder than the first. And then he pauses again.

I'm still wearing his shirt, but gravity makes it fall open at the front, giving him full access to my breasts. Which he makes use of, closing his arm across my chest, his left palm enveloping my right breast.

His other arm curves around the front of my hips and his hand finds my center, and now the explosion of sensations across the pleasure points in my body tips me over the edge.

I rock back against him, demanding more.

He responds to my heady cry, every movement bringing me

to the edge of a burning cliff until I'm crashing, over and over, a powerful orgasm breaking and mending me.

Callan's throaty growl vibrates in my ears as his body shudders hard behind mine and he holds me like I'm anchoring him and not the other way around.

I rock against him. Gentle. I don't want this moment to end. Don't want to return to reality.

He groans against my neck, nudging me with his lips, making little shivers run to my toes. Then he lets my shirt fall to my waist, maintaining the contact between us while he pulls his shorts back on and positions us on the bed so that we're facing each other. Still touching.

The longer we stay like that, the more his breathing evens out, but mine is erratic, and on my next inhalation, I'm suddenly aware that I can't get it under control. For a second, I think it's because of the intense orgasm I experienced, but then, when I exhale, my throat burns.

My eyes fly wide.

"Callan!" I gasp. "Fire!"

CHAPTER TWENTY

I should have been prepared for this, but with the appearance of Sophia's dragon the last time I lost control of the flames, the threat they pose seemed somehow diminished.

Callan reacts instantly, scooping me up in his arms. "Living room," he says, racing me toward it since his bedroom isn't the best place for a fire.

Rapidly navigating the door, he sets us down on the living room floor, keeping me close so that I'm not sitting directly on the glass. He keeps his arms wrapped around me, but I push at him.

"You have to go!"

"I'm not leaving you."

My body is screaming at me that I should let him stay. That triggering his fire is worth it. But I shake my head. "If you stay with me, you'll have to shift or you won't survive the flames. And if you shift, you'll breathe fire, and I'll breathe it in, and it all starts again. I have to stop the cycle."

His hands close over my shoulders, supporting me. "I don't want you to do this alone."

"She won't be alone." Sophia's soft voice breaks through my panic. She stands only a few paces away and must have emerged from her room as soon as Callan burst out of his. He wasn't exactly quiet about it. "I can survive the flames, I'm sure of it."

"No." My response is instinctive and it joins Callan's command.

"No, Sophia. You can't risk it."

"But... my dragon can help."

I consider her offer for all of two seconds.

"This is not the time to test your dragon's power." I gasp my next breath, a mess of sweat pouring down my face. "I can handle it. You both need to go."

Reluctantly, Callan releases me, his fingertips lingering on my arms before he withdraws.

"Go," I cry. "Go!"

He and Sophia race to the panic room and the walls begin to close.

They nearly don't make it in time.

The first flames pour from my mouth with my next exhale, burning up through my chest and turning the air to amber. A stronger flame follows it and I'm glad I'm not standing because it would have knocked me to the floor.

I wrap my arms around my chest and try to hold myself together.

Where was this fire when I was fighting Isaac? Where was this rage that doesn't care about whom it destroys?

As the fire continues to pour from my mouth, I've never felt so alone. I don't understand why *this* of all things would make me feel that way.

Then it hits me.

It's not the fire. It's not the fact that I'm by myself in this room right now. It's because I know now what it feels like to *not* be alone.

Dragons who were once my enemies have given me their

trust and their friendship. I know what it feels like to have someone stand beside me who cares about me, and now, the absence of those people is impossibly painful.

It was easier when the only one I trusted was myself. It didn't hurt so much when the only person I looked to for help was me.

I terrifies me that I want these dragons to remain in my life —Callan, Sophia, even Beatrix and Felix.

I don't want to lose any of them.

I'm shivering on the floor by the time the flames abate and the fire extinguisher's cold snowflakes land on my face and legs.

The far wall opens and running footfalls approach—Callan first and Sophia a few steps behind.

Callan kneels opposite me, unable to touch me now, while Sophia helps me into an upright position and wraps a blanket around me. She must have retrieved it from her bedroom, which is within the panic room.

"No more fire," I whisper, a request more than anything else.

While Sophia rubs my arms outside the blanket, Callan gives me a solemn nod.

His voice is impossibly quiet as he says, "Do you know why I call you *Not*-Lana?"

I lean heavily on Sophia, but she's strong enough to support me now and does so with ease. My forehead creases. "Because Lana isn't my name."

"It's more than that," Callan says. "You told me that the Serene Commander called you *Lana* because it means *yarn*. A simple length of string that was hers to weave. When I call you *Not*-Lana, it isn't because I know your true name is Asper. It's because you are not simple."

He takes a deep breath. "You're complicated. And important. You matter. Your life isn't anyone's to weave but your own."

Callan's words are like a quiet blade cutting through any ties that remained between me and the Serene Commander. Any concerns I had about being bound to the Roden-Darr are banished.

I bow my head while Sophia rubs my back.

I let the tears fall.

"We're at war," Callan says. "And I want you at my side."

"What if I'm not strong enough to kill the Sentinels?"

He hasn't asked me what happened in the night, or if I found the Sentinels, or if I fought them. He said he wouldn't tell me whom to hunt or when and he's staying true to that.

Now, it feels like his dragon shadow suddenly looms over me, its eyes burning within Callan's gaze as he responds. "If anyone is strong enough, it's you."

Sophia helps me stand, but she pauses as we turn toward the two doors on this side of the living area. "Which bedroom, Lana?"

It breaks my heart, but I say, "Mine."

She supports me to walk there while Callan rises to his feet and watches us go. I turn back at the door, but there's no pain in his expression. The distance won't change how he feels about me. Or me about him.

His gaze is clear, and his nod is firm. "I'm here when you need me."

Now, I need to prove to myself a new truth: that just because I'm physically separated from him, it doesn't mean I'm alone.

Once Sophia helps me inside, she murmurs, "Callan's dragon is a mystery to me. And your ability to survive his fire is an even greater one. But if I sweep all of that aside, it's clear to me that he would burn down the world for you."

She squints at me, her eyes screwed up, all glassy, as if she's determined not to let tears fall. "Don't ever give that up."

I'm too emotionally exhausted to reply, sinking to the bed, even though her wish reflects my own needs. To stay. To belong.

She retreats to the doorway. "I know I wanted to train

tomorrow, but I'd rather go to the library instead. I think we both need answers."

I nod in agreement.

I have to believe that I'll find something. Anything that will help me fight the Roden-Darr.

~

The library is just as breathtaking as I remember.

Every branch of the four trees is lined with books that seem to rustle in a breeze I can't feel or hear. Standing near them makes my skin tingle and I'm once again convinced that the trees are somehow alive, and that the books resting on their branches carry their own magical essence.

Books about each kind of magic.

Sophia told me she's never seen Callan's library before, and I sense the buzz of anticipation in her mood as she hovers at my side.

"These books are about light magic," I say, leading her to the tree that sits at the front of the diamond formation.

"Angels and dragons," she whispers, and even though there's no reason to keep her voice down, I get why she does it. It feels like sound will somehow break the magic surrounding the trees.

She brushes her fingertips across the edge of the nearest book. "It's fucked up that we hate each other so much when we carry the same kind of power. Light magic is supposed to be a source of hope, not hatred."

I sigh heavily. "I wish I knew how the hatred began." Callan believed it began with Solomon, but angels like the Serene Commander hate all dragons, not just him.

I expect Sophia to give me a snarky response about angels being assholes, but her response is quiet. "I don't think it's ever been any different. It's all I've known. It's all my parents knew. My mother told me it was because of what Solomon Grudge did, but I remember hearing my grandfather talk about how much the angels hated us before that. I don't know how far back it goes, but there's no changing it."

With that, she approaches the lowest branches, where the books about dragons are located, and reaches for a volume with emerald binding.

Satisfied that she'll keep herself occupied, I carefully release my wings and summon the feathers from the pouches on my harness. I left my weapon and armband back in Callan's room, but I've decided to carry the feathers with me whenever I can.

I aim for the highest branches, where I found the book on Sentinels last time. It's right where I left it, open to the page showing the group of women in flowing, white dresses with mahogany breastplates.

I move past the entries on the Sentinels and then the Celestial Ascendant, scouring the book for any mention of the Roden-Darr or male Sentinels.

Nothing.

I reach for the next book, and the next, with the same result.

I'm about to descend to a lower branch when a flash of gold catches my eye.

Beating my wings and rising upward, I spy a book nestled deeply in the leaves. Unlike the other books, this one is closed.

Its title leaps out at me, two words that don't belong next to each other: *Angelic Monsters*.

Settling into a clear space on the branch below, I open the book very carefully, wary since it was being stored in a closed position. The edges of its pages are gilded, which must be how it glinted at me, but they are also ragged, as if it was well-used.

The style of the text within it varies from page to page, clearly written by different people. Some pages carry annotations in different hands, as if information was added by others over time.

The illustrations are all in black ink and depict supernaturals of all kinds: wolves, wraiths, witches… All of them have misshapen forms. Bloodied teeth. Jagged claws.

I turn back to the beginning of the book, carefully sliding my finger between two pages that are stuck together at the edge. I draw a quick breath at what it says.

We, the Roden-Darr, make this record, a true account of the Legacy of the Avenging Angel, Eva Ashen-Varr. May her light return to us.

Beneath that is a list of names, and it must be the names of the Roden-Darr who wrote in the book, since I'm able to match some of the handwriting on subsequent pages to the names at the front.

The first entry is about a witch who drained the life force of an entire village of humans to feed her dark magic. The account tells of how the Avenging Angel, Eva Ashen-Varr, fought and chained that witch. It wasn't easy and one of the Roden-Darr was killed.

The next entry is about a wolf. The next about a nest of vampires.

Each account is brutally honest, detailing the moments when Eva doubted herself, when she was exhausted and struggled to fight on, even when she was filled with so much rage that she nearly killed her target. She always stopped herself, and the Roden-Darr would quickly encase the captive in light and take them away. Knowing about their ability to use their light to dull their target's senses makes my own experience with Isaac more real.

The book doesn't say where the captives were imprisoned, only that it was within the veil between Earth and the heavenly realm.

The more I read, the more the Roden-Darr's role as Sentinels starts to make sense. They don't guard precious objects like the female Sentinels do. They guard dangerous prisoners.

I can't help my wry smile as I wonder why they weren't guarding me when I was born, but of course, I was only corrupted *after* I was stolen. And it was afterward that the Celestial Ascendant gave me to the Serene Commander and told her I was now her burden. If they couldn't have their precious Avenging Angel, then I guess they decided to put me to use killing what they thought needed to be killed.

Finally, I reach the last entry of Eva's Legacy and my heart sinks when I see the illustration.

It's a dragon shifter.

His name was Atrox Imperator. The illustrations depict him in both human and dragon form. *Full* dragon form, so he might have been one of the last true dragon shifters.

His list of crimes goes on for pages. It includes the names of his victims, the places he destroyed, and the gold he stole. He was powerful and savage. His attacks on villages would happen so fast, and in such quick succession, that sometimes it seemed as if he was in two places at once.

In his human form, he's drawn wearing a full suit of armor, and the text describes it as being made of dragon's gold. He's holding his helmet in his hands, but his human face is partially obscured by his shoulder-length hair, only portions of his features visible. A hard mouth. Cold eyes. The helmet itself appears beautifully crafted with perfect openings across the front and a slit to its base that would reveal his eyes and the center of his lips. It has two sharp horns on each side that project directly backward, not like a devil's curved horns, but like a dragon's horns that would protect its head from behind.

An entire page is devoted to his dragon's face, and the beast makes me shiver even more than his human form. Its eyes are a storm of rage, and its lips are drawn back from its sharp teeth with a kind of fury that has no feeling. It's possible that the illustration was embellished, but I'm not sure that anyone could draw such a brutal countenance without witnessing it.

More than any other entry, the text for Atrox is written in multiple hands. There are numerous accounts drawn from sightings and near-misses, two failed attempts to capture him leading to loss of Roden-Darr life and then retreat. He picked them off one by one until their number had reduced to a mere five.

In the final desperate battle, Eva fought him for an hour, and in the end, when he held her beneath his claws and was preparing to rip her apart, she defeated him in the only way that she could.

She gave up her soul light.

My fingertips linger on the final words in the book. They're smudged as if by tears.

"All dragons will suffer for this."

I exhale heavily and close the book. "And so it began."

CHAPTER TWENTY-ONE

I tip my head back to rest against the tree trunk. Callan's assertion in the car after my fight with Solomon rings even more true: *One dragon's crimes are attributed to all dragons.*

But if it began with Atrox Imperator, how to make it end?

I'm not sure how much time I've spent reading when I fly down from the tree to reach Sophia. She's sitting cross-legged on the floor beneath the branches with a book in her lap, her hand resting on the open page.

She's sitting so still that I'm suddenly worried. "Sophia, are you okay?"

"She was real," Sophia says, tracing the bright illustration on the page open in front of her. Unlike the book of Angelic Monsters, which I left on the topmost branch, the tome Sophia holds is illustrated in color that seems to ripple across the paper.

I bend to the dragon she's pointing at.

It has cerulean blue wings that are transparent at the edges and its body is elegantly serpentine. It's depicted flying above a lake, droplets rising from the watery surface to sparkle in the air around the dragon's body.

The title beneath it reads: *Bella Vorago in flight.*

"My dragon was a real dragon," Sophia says. "She could swallow so much water that she helped humans irrigate their crops. The humans loved her. And look here."

She turns the page.

I sink to my knees beside Sophia, surprised by the vivid illustration showing Bella flying over a burning village, helping to put out the flames. What really makes my eyebrows rise is that angels are flying beside her, carrying buckets, helping her.

"Angels and dragons working together," Sophia says, her voice filled with disbelief. "I never thought I'd see anything like this."

"What happened to her?" I ask, although my most burning question is how she is now Sophia's dragon.

Sophia's lips press together. She turns to the next page, and this image nearly breaks my heart.

The humans and angels are attacking Bella with spears and arrows.

"It says that a dragon named Atrox corrupted her." Sophia points to the text. "She attacked a group of angels for no reason, and they were forced to kill her."

"Atrox." I mentally sift through the list of names of his victims. Bella wasn't among them, but I suppose the Roden-Darr might not count her as a victim if they believed she followed Atrox by choice.

"When I heard her voice, she said she was happy to live again," Sophia says, peering at me. "I don't know what to think of that now. Does it mean that our dragons have lived before? Is there somehow a limited number of them and that's why some of us don't have a dragon anymore? Or am I the first to experience this and it's all some bizarre occurrence?"

Her questions become more rapid as she speaks and I place my hand over hers, trying to calm her. "We'll find the answers."

She begins to protest, and I stare her down. "First, you have to train. And I have to hunt. But every chance we get, we'll come back to these books and learn as much as we can. The answers are in here somewhere."

I need them as badly as she does.

The next seven days pass quickly.

Each morning, Jada and Brock give a report to Callan about any unusual activity around the building during the night—nothing that causes any great concern yet.

Then Sophia and I train for a few hours before lunch.

In the early afternoon, Callan takes Sophia aside to teach her how to control dragon's gold. That's when I spend time in the library, searching for every scrap of information I can find on the Roden-Darr. Mentions are few and far between and are usually only by way of vague references to angels who can use their soul light against other supernaturals.

I come to the conclusion that the Roden-Darr are a secret closely kept by the angels, and that mentions of their existence have been deliberately limited.

I also focus on familiarizing myself with the dragons who lived in the past. There were once all kinds from water dragons like Bella, as well as mountain and desert dragons, each with a unique name. All powerful in their own way.

The forest dragons make me pause. If Sophia's situation isn't unique, then Solomon's deep-forest scent could indicate his dragon is one of the woodland beasts depicted in the books. He could be the warrior dragon, Magnus Grim, who was apparently a friend of the forest fae, or one of the lesser-known forest dragons, such as one named Torva Viridia, whose scales were like emerald-green gems.

Then there are the rarest dragons: fire dragons. There are many mentions of the mythical Vanem Dragon, who was revered during the time of the fae and whose fire was fueled by the power of old magic. He was capable of righteous rage while also being the wisest of dragons.

On the fourth afternoon, when Sophia joins me in the library, she brings me a book containing the majestic image of a golden fire dragon named Graviter Rex.

"They called him the 'Solemn King,'" she says, reading from the text. "He was calm and wise and it says that his flames could imbue any blade with the power of light magic."

Her green eyes are filled with hope. "Callan heard his dragon's voice, too. So I can't be alone in this." She taps the page. "What if this is his dragon?"

I would love to think that the answer to Callan's dragon lies in these books, and that maybe, by chance, a dragon like Graviter Rex could be the dragon with the burning eyes that shadows him in the moonlight. It's a romantic notion, and an overly hopeful one, because if his dragon existed once, then maybe there would be a way to reach it. Communicate with it. Calm its power and free Callan from its flames.

"Maybe," I say.

Sophia gives me a faint smile and shakes her head at herself. "Yeah, I know. It's unlikely. I'll keep digging."

Each night, I head out onto the streets, but now, I'm searching for the blank spots in my senses, not the bright ones. It takes me a few days, but I come to recognize the way the Roden-Darr can tap into their soul light to announce their locations—attempting to draw me in—or subdue it completely to conceal themselves and mislead me. Typically, one of them is fully visible while five or six others are concealed close by.

I don't fall into that trap again.

I also remain aware of the fact that the Scorn are out there, watching for me, so I remain wary of humans, keeping to rooftops and deserted alleys as much as I can.

Remaining outside the radius of the Sentinels' ability to sense my presence allows me to watch the way they work together. After a few nights, their hierarchy becomes clearer.

Isaac is their leader, but there appear to be two others who share the role of second-in-command. Although it's difficult while staying far enough away, I manage to lay eyes on ten of the Sentinels, including the two who are second-in-command, and I relay their descriptions back to Callan.

While Callan continues to avoid asking me questions, I don't withhold the information I'm gathering.

Over the course of the week, I get better at recognizing when Felix or Beatrix—or both—are along for the ride. Even though they may as well be humans in my senses, I've come to recognize their scents. The scent of thieves is heavy when they're nearby and it makes sense to me now that I understand where they came from, the act of attempted theft that changed the course of their lives.

By the end of the week, I've come to accept their presence, as well as the responsibility that comes with it; they only need to endanger themselves if I get into trouble, so I think carefully and err on the side of caution.

It's difficult.

I'm constantly fighting my instincts to step into danger, and it means holding back where before I would have charged in. I promise myself that when the risk is acceptable, I'll make my move.

At the end of the week, storms settle in over the city of Philadelphia and thick clouds block out the moon. It's exactly the kind of night I would have hated when I was hunting dragons—the kind when dragons can walk freely on the streets without risking their shadows appearing.

Heading out into the wind and rain, I'm drenched within seconds and, frustratingly, one of my pouches has a gap at the top that means it keeps filling with water, weighing me down on that side.

Making my way up onto a rooftop five blocks away from the bar, I flop into a crouch with a groan before I lift my wings and attempt to use them as a makeshift umbrella against the needle-sharp rain. Then I shake my head with a soft laugh. Outside of the extra difficulty when hunting dragons, wind and rain never bothered me before I experienced the luxuries of living with Callan. Hell, I often slept in wet clothing since I didn't have anything else to wear.

I tell myself to harden the fuck up.

Then I close my eyes and sink into my senses.

A single bright spot lights up farther south. But curiously, there are no dark spots around it. I continue to expand my senses, sifting through all the smells and sounds of the city, finally locating ten black spots like a cluster of dark chasms, all in one location.

It's the first time so many of them have gone dark in a location where they aren't also trying to lure me in.

It means they don't want to satellite their location tonight. *But... why?*

The rain suddenly stops. I withdraw my wing to look up in time to see Sophia land beside me, her gorgeous wings glistening with raindrops that somehow—impossibly—don't descend farther than her head. It's as if a transparent sphere has formed around us, sheltering us from the rain.

I'm aghast. "Sophia, you shouldn't be here."

"What am I training for, if I'm not going to help you?"

Now I understand why she seemed so keen to move in to her apartment downstairs today. It means she didn't have to sneak past Callan to leave the building.

"Where are the Sentinels tonight?" she asks, as if she doesn't expect me to argue further.

I point to our far right. "Over there. Ten of them. I'm not sure what they're doing."

She peers across the city and she's suddenly very still. "But that's where Zahra lives. And little Emika!"

Callan didn't reveal the location of his sister's home to me, and I didn't ask, but Sophia would have already known it. If the Sentinels are gathering around it, then Zahra's in danger.

"We have to help them!" Sophia cries.

Before I can stop her, she runs to the edge of the building, leaps off it, and soars up toward the clouds, her dragon form blending seamlessly into the stormy night sky.

"Wait, Sophia! No!" I gasp for breath as the rain pelts down on me again and I'm spitting water as I shout.

Fuck. I can't rule out the possibility that it's a trap. The Sentinels' previous tactics haven't been working for them, so they might be switching things up tonight to see what happens. On the other hand, they might intend to attack Zahra's home. Setting aside the question of how they located it, ten of them will be difficult to beat, even for a dragon as strong and skilled at combat as Zahra. Especially if she's trying to protect her daughter.

Without another thought, I spread my wings and leap off the rooftop, flying toward the cloud cover and into the wind. A stormy night is one of the few times I can risk flying above the city since the poor visibility gives me cover, and it's the only way to catch up to Sophia.

On either side of me, I'm aware of Felix and Beatrix rising up out of the shadows on nearby rooftops to follow me. Their dragon wings are the color of the darkest blood, and they blend into the darkness of the stormy sky.

I fly close to the clouds until I spot Sophia directly ahead. She's descending toward the rooftop of a building in the distance that sits in the middle of a block with narrow alleys on either side of it. The street at the front of the building is wider, while it looks like a narrower lane sits at the back.

The dark spots in my vision are positioned around the back and sides of the building and are closing in.

My dilemma now is that if I get too close, the Sentinels will sense my presence—unlike the dragons, who can fly right in, provided the Sentinels don't physically see them. On the positive side, I'll draw the Sentinels' attention away from Zahra's home.

Casting glances left and right, I ascertain that Beatrix and Felix are close to me in the air, but both are speeding up and verging on passing me. They've obviously seen the angels and I don't need to tell them what to do. They'll target the Sentinels on each side of the building.

Felix shoots to the right and Beatrix to the left. Beatrix follows the path that Sophia took, and I trust that she'll make sure Sophia is safe.

I focus on the back of the building and the two Sentinels creeping up on it. The narrow lane there is darker than the front of the building and seems to be an access lane with short driveways into parking garages at intervals along it. There are very few windows in the buildings opposite Zahra's home.

All doubt leaves my mind.

I was born for this.

I may not wish to kill the angels, but I can make them think twice about coming after Callan's family again.

Picking up speed, I soar down through the wind and rain, ignoring the needle-sharp raindrops as I close in on the first angel.

In the brief instant that they both turn their faces up to me, I recognize that they're two of the ten whose features I'm familiar with: both dark-haired, with bulky muscles. They aren't as lithe or as fast as some of the others I've observed. These men are built for ground combat, not an aerial fight.

So that's where I'll take them.

Into the air.

My hands close around the first angel's shoulders, and I pluck him off his feet before he has time to shout.

Tearing up into the sky with him so fast that he struggles to extend his wings—hard enough in the rain, let alone against the force with which I'm traveling—I wait a beat for the second angel to spread his wings and launch into the air after us.

Wrenching the man I hold upward with all my strength, I close my wings at the same instant so that I drop down far enough that our bodies are momentarily parallel in the air. My hands land on his wing bones from behind, right where his wings join his shoulders. Such vulnerable little handles.

He's frantically beating his wings. Shouting.

I plant my feet against his lower back and position myself right where he can't punch me, can't dislodge me, can't even whack me with the sides of his wings.

I don't hesitate.

After all, *cruel* is my name.

With a scream, I break his wings, snapping the bones at his shoulder blades.

He roars with shock, and I let him go, allowing him to plummet to ground. I don't stop to watch him hit the empty street.

I spin in time to defend myself against the second angel, who soars toward me, his fist outstretched.

Instead of hitting back, I evade the blow by grabbing his wrist and allowing my body to be pulled along beneath his for the split second it takes me to kick his stomach, using his torso as a springboard from which to somersault toward the ground.

I spear downward and then curve back into the air while he chases me.

A glance back tells me he's aiming for my left wing, and it doesn't take a genius to guess that he's going for my golden feathers. He probably thinks he can rip them off and they'll fall to the ground—and me with them. He may not realize they'll fly right back to me.

I throw myself into a spin as I fly higher, directly above the rooftop of Zahra's home now. The speed with which I whirl doesn't give me much time to take it all in, and visibility is bad in the rain, but I do get a view of what's happening on both sides of the building.

Two angels are down on each side. Beatrix and Felix are not holding back as they each fight the last angel standing on their respective sides. Sophia now hovers clear of Beatrix's fight.

I pull up, high above the building, my wings spreading wide, exposing my chest and making myself an easy target for the angel coming after me.

He's too fucking arrogant to realize the danger.

Pious angel.

The thought comes unbidden to my mind, but I don't brush it away.

He closes in, ready to tackle me. At the last moment, I spin, and my wing bone cracks against the side of his face, more effective than any punch with my fists. He tumbles to my right, this time colliding with my fist.

He flies back through the air, and I follow him, my punches flying. Chin, cheekbone, shoulder, stomach, and finally a hit that breaks his nose.

His wings slump as he loses consciousness and plummets, slowly at first, and then faster, to the ground.

He hits the paved lane on his side. The other angel is stirring, but both are seriously injured. It will take them time to heal and their brethren will need to carry them away.

I alight on the second angel's torso and prepare to land a final blow to ensure he stays down.

Blood bubbles between his teeth. "You're too late," he wheezes. "We will always be two steps ahead of you. We are... unbeatable..."

His speech is boastful, and, as he speaks, the purity of his aura mists with a sliver of darkness that allows me to quell any reservations I had about hurting him.

"Pride is a sin," I whisper before my fist lands.

But I don't ignore his warning. I jump to my feet and spin to the building.

Now that I have time to observe Zahra's home from this angle, I immediately spy the broken glass scattered across the short driveway. Seeking its point of origin, I locate the broken window on the third floor.

Damn! I should have noticed it sooner.

If Zahra's home is designed like Callan's, then it's shrouded in a cloaking spell that stops any supernatural sensing anything unusual about its occupants. The protective wards are what keep the angels from locating me in Callan's home. But those same spells have now stopped me from seeing within this building.

The Sentinels are already inside.

CHAPTER TWENTY-TWO

*R*acing to the corner of the building, I untie my harness and slip it neatly behind a couple of trash cans. The window I need to fly through isn't large, and I won't make it through with my glaive on my back, so I have to leave it here.

The weapon protests, calling to me, a tug within my mind, but I place my hand briefly on it.

I'm not abandoning you. Please wait for me.

Satisfied that the glaive will obey me, I rise into the air and fly to the window on the third floor. Without slowing down, I shoot forward, tuck my wings to make myself small, and sail through the opening without cutting myself on the jagged glass at its edges.

The room is furnished, but its dimensions are deceptive, appearing full depth from the outside while on the inside, it's clear that it's as narrow as a walkway.

Off to my left, a square that appears big enough for a man to squeeze through has been cut out of the ceiling.

I shoot up through the opening into the roof cavity, where I hover and search for the second opening that will lead inside the apartment. Zahra's home won't have the kind of fire-proofing that Callan's place does, so it would have been far easier to cut through the ceiling material.

A young girl's scream reaches me from my far right, and I spin to the sound, identifying a glow on that side of the building that must indicate the opening I'm searching for.

Emika!

My heart skips a beat, and my wings are already beating hard.

I fly straight at the side of the roof cavity directly above the glowing opening. Because the roof slopes on that side, there isn't enough height within the cavity to fly upward and get my feet under me. Not at this speed. I tuck my legs at the last minute, hit the wall feet-first and arch back, diving down through the opening.

I retract my wings midair, somersault, and land on soft, cream-colored carpet. The golden feathers cascade off my wings and hover in the air directly behind me, responding to my needs, ready for when I want them again. I don't have time to send grateful thoughts their way.

What I see fills me with rage.

One wall is decorated with a child's drawings. Another wall has fairy lights. Soft toys overflow from baskets on a nearby shelf.

It's Emika's bedroom.

She's curled up on her bed, knees to her chest, her hands over her ears, her eyes squeezed shut, trying to block out the threat standing at the side of her bed.

One of the Sentinels looms over her, his brilliant, white wings spread wide like a barrier. It's one of the men who's second-in-command. He has red hair, a porcelain complexion, and the palest blue eyes.

He stands with one palm extended toward Emika, his soul light flowing from it and curling around her face and torso.

He clutches a dagger in his other hand. "Don't be frightened, little dragon," he's saying. "I'm here to save you."

What shocks me most is that my mouth fills with the taste of copper and I nearly choke on the scent of murder pouring from him.

He's not here to capture her. He's here to kill her.

Even as I take in the bedroom, I'm aware of what's happening in the corridor outside. The door is open, and it's hanging off its hinges, cracked down the middle as if someone punched it or was thrown into it.

Zahra is a whirlwind outside it, fighting two Sentinels within the confined space. One of them is Isaac. The other man is the black-haired second-in-command. Both angels have retracted their wings and so has Zahra, but that doesn't make their fight any less brutal.

I've experienced Zahra's fighting style. The first time we fought, she was trying to capture me, and her movements were fluid, designed to disrupt my balance and allow the dragon's gold to chain me.

Her fighting style now is nothing short of furious. In the split second that my focus rushes across her, her fist collides with the black-haired angel's jaw with a horrible crunch, but it's a desperate shot.

They're keeping her from her baby.

Her eyes widen in the moment that she sees me, and I understand her plea as clearly as if she'd screamed it.

Please.

Snarls leave my lips as I swing to the red-haired Sentinel. I'm already running. Leaping. Releasing my wings. The golden feathers fly up to meet me as I run, and this time, they seem to burn, a friction in the air as the room heats around me.

The angel sees me coming, but instead of defending himself, he pivots back to Emika, drawing his fist back to drive the dagger down and kill her before I can reach him.

Oh, how he underestimates me.

My right knee collides with his shoulder, his head is in my hands, and my momentum pulls him backward. Away from her.

I exhale.

Twist.

Crack.

I hit the ground on top of him, my heart filled with ice that seems to rise up and turn to mist against the heat within my wings.

It was a clean death. I made sure that not a drop of blood fell to the floor that would traumatize Emika further.

I don't stop moving. The angel is already lying on the rug, so I ram his wings against his sides and pull the rug over him, covering him completely so she won't see his body. Then I crouch there and take a breath.

I have to get up. Have to get to Emika. Make sure she's safe.

A great storm is raging within me, but I have no time to process my actions.

"Angel." Emika speaks from behind me, her voice a whisper, as is her way.

I wipe the fury from my face and spin to her.

Her cheeks are tear-stained, her straight, black hair is ruffled, and her hands still hover next to her ears, as if she's ready for another attack, even though her large, angular eyes are clear of enthrallment and the angel light has vanished from around her.

The color of her eyes is so similar to Callan's cinnamon brown—a family trait that he and Zahra must have inherited from their father—that I could be looking into his eyes right now.

Emika carries the same depth of intelligence that Callan does.

She's seen too much for her five years.

"Angel," she whispers again, holding her arms up to me.

I hurry to my feet, notice the fallen blade, and kick it with my boot on the way past, sending it, tip first, into the skirting board at the bottom of the wall. I kick it so hard that it sticks there. I have no idea if the blade is poisoned, but I don't want it anywhere near Emika.

I scoop her up and hold her close, bending to snatch up her blanket and wrap it around her. As an added measure, I fold my wings around her, too, a black-and-gold shield.

The sound of the fight continues in the corridor for the next few seconds, but I'm not about to let Emika go. Not for anything. If the only way to keep her safe is to fly out of here with her, I will.

"Isaac!" I shout. "It's over."

There's a scream of rage—Zahra's voice—and Isaac flies through the doorway several paces away from us.

He recovers fast, looks like he's heading straight back into the fight, but he freezes when he sees the mound under the rug.

"You are not worthy of me," I say. "*Liar.* Get out. Before I end you."

His pure-white hair is bloodied, his gray eyes are wide, and he's breathing hard from his fight, but his whisper is incredulous. "You killed him?"

My response is as sharp as a whip. "He was going to kill *her.*"

"No," Isaac says. "That's not what we—"

His gaze falls to the dagger at the side of the room. He must recognize it as the angel's blade.

Isaac's cheeks were already pale, but now his face drains of all color. He looks as if he's been punched. Or possibly that someone tore his heart out. He shakes his head, apparently in denial, his lips drawn tight, but then the furrow in his brow slowly clears.

When he speaks again, it's a quiet declaration. "If you killed him, then he deserved death. We did not come here to kill her. If that's what he intended, then his death was warranted."

I study Isaac, a sense of confusion rising within me. There is no sourness on my tongue that tells me he's lying, and I wonder if it's possible that he didn't know about the red-haired angel's intentions.

But if Isaac is losing control of his men, then this situation is even more volatile than it first seemed.

"I warned you," I whisper. "Fury is contagious. There's too much hatred on this side of the veil. Your men aren't prepared for it. Take yourself and your Sentinels back where you came from and save them."

His voice rises, a deep, painful roar. "Only *you* can save them! They're lost without you!" As he speaks, he seems to hear himself, and he turns away with a frustrated exhalation. His jaw clenches, but his shoulders hunch.

"Answer me this, Isaac," I say. "Why would a Sentinel come for this child?"

Isaac pauses. Outside in the corridor, there's a crash, the wall vibrates, and I hope it was because Zahra threw the black-haired angel into it.

"That child's dragon has the power to change the world," Isaac says.

At that, he spins and shouts to the other man. "Zadkiel!"

The black-haired angel stumbles into the room, clutching his arm, which looks broken. He's so unsteady that he hits the door on his way past.

Zadkiel's eyes widen when he sees the rug. He flashes a look of betrayal at me, hesitating only another second before he launches himself up toward the hole in the ceiling, followed quickly by Isaac.

Within moments, they're gone, and all the black spots in my senses retreat from the building, disappearing into the night.

A dragon with the power to change the world.

It's already recognized among the Dread that Emika is one of the strongest dragon shifters to be born in generations—next to Callan and Zahra. It makes the Steeles a very dangerous family, but it's Emika who secures their future legacy.

The little girl is shaking in my arms and all I can do now is whisper, "You're safe. I'm here. Your mama's here. We will never let anyone hurt you."

Zahra races into the room. Her face is bloodied, but she only seems to care about her daughter. "Emi!"

I open my wings and pass Emika across to her mother, who pulls the little girl close and bends her head to her daughter's cheek.

"Mama," Emika whispers, nestling into her mother's arms.

"Emi, honey. You're safe." Zahra's cinnamon-brown eyes are filled with tears. She has light-brown skin and dark-brown hair that's currently falling out of the topknot she must have tied it in before the fight.

She's nearly collapsing, but I think it's from shock more than any injury, since she's otherwise clear-eyed, not dazed. She and I have never been friends—in fact, Zahra has actively opposed Callan's choices when it came to me—but I set all that aside and reach out to support her, preparing to tell her that we need to move, we can't stay here.

That's when a woman appears in the doorway.

She leans heavily on the doorframe, a bleeding cut on her forehead and a bruise on her jaw, both of which are slowly healing and fading.

She's much taller than me, but her muscles are just as honed. Her long hair is blue-black with a bright-indigo streak down the left side. The braid her hair is tied in is coming apart. Her eyes are the darkest blue with an explosion of amber around the pupil, a startling combination. She's dressed in black entirely, from her boots to her high neckline.

I've never seen her before, but I really don't like that she's pointing a gun at me.

"Be careful, angel," she snarls at me. "I never miss."

CHAPTER TWENTY-THREE

*T*he newcomer gives me a command. "Step the fuck away from Zahra and Emika."

"Wait! Stop." Zahra steps between me and the woman with the gun. "Put your weapon away, Sienna. Lana is with me."

Sienna? As in... Sienna Scorn?

I can't fathom what the hell she's doing here, but her identity explains why I feel like I'm chewing on a copper coin right now. She's the one who sent Beatrix and Felix to their intended deaths. She's responsible for countless crimes across the city, including assassinations.

And again, I'm asking myself: *Why the fuck is she here?*

Sienna doesn't lower her gun, but my tension eases when I take another look at it. It's an intriguing weapon that appears to be made entirely out of gold.

It must be dragon's gold.

In which case, I don't necessarily need to fear it as much as Sienna would like me to.

Even across the distance, I sense the weapon's cold heart calling to me. It feels nothing like Callan's gold. There's no warmth in it at all.

The feathers on my wing rustle, as if a chill runs through them. But the fact that the gun's heart is open to me, cold or not, makes me far more comfortable.

"I heard you were looking for me," I say to Sienna, keeping my wings ready and my torso turned slightly to the left so that I'm best placed to use the armband on my right arm if I need to deflect a bullet before I can call the gun to me.

Sienna ignores me, directing her sharp question at Zahra instead. "How do you know she's not with the other angels? She could have led them here."

"Or *you* could have," I snap back.

Sienna's lips twist and it appears she's about to snap a retort, but she pauses, as if she's reconsidering. Her forehead creases in thought. "If they followed me, their power is much stronger than I anticipated. Nobody knew I was coming here today. Not even my Cohort."

Zahra draws herself upright, her back stiff. "I invited you to my home to discuss an alliance, Sienna. I would remind you that you're currently aiming a gun near my daughter."

Sienna immediately withdraws her weapon, slipping it into a holster that sits across her torso. "I apologize, Zahra. Your daughter's safety should be your priority." Her dark-blue eyes glitter at me as she speaks, and it's as if she's suggesting that by defending me, Zahra isn't protecting Emika at all.

"I'll leave you to take care of your family," Sienna says, straightening her shoulders. "I'll give serious consideration to your request."

Zahra doesn't seem willing to let Sienna leave so quickly. "You've seen the Sentinels," she says before Sienna can turn away. "You've felt the power of their attack this very night. The only way we can survive this war is to form an alliance between our clans. The Scorn and the Dread. United against the angels."

Sienna pauses, her eyes narrowing at me before she returns her attention to Zahra. "What does your brother think of this?"

"He supports an alliance."

It's a smooth lie, and Zahra must really believe she's telling the truth because I'm not sucking major lemons right now.

"Forgive my skepticism, Zahra, but your brother could lay waste to the Scorn if he chose to," Sienna replies. "Burn this city to ash. When I spoke to him a week ago, he seemed only concerned about ensuring the safety of that monster, not of protecting his people." She pokes her finger into the air at me. "I need to hear from him directly. I need guarantees that he won't use this alliance against me."

Zahra remains tense. I can't see her expression with her back to me, but she gives a firm nod. "I understand your concerns. I'll arrange for him to meet with you."

Sienna is slow to agree. "No," she says, as if she's giving it careful thought. "I don't need carefully constructed speeches. I need him to see that my clan is worthy of protection, despite our profession. I need him to understand that we've done what we must to survive."

She takes a deep breath and appears to dive in. "Come to dinner. Bring your Cohort, including your brother, and I'll bring mine. Maybe Callan will see us differently once he gets to know us in a less formal setting."

Zahra is hesitant. "His dragon—"

"I can make arrangements to safely accommodate his dragon," Sienna says. "Believe me, carnage is the last thing I want."

When Zahra doesn't immediately disagree, Sienna continues. "Tomorrow night. When the moon is up. At a club I control."

She gives Zahra an address that's not far from the abandoned industrial area where Callan drove to shake off the angels and Scorn dragons who were following us after my fight with Solomon.

I know the club she's talking about. It's in a part of the city that houses the thriving underground. Targeting it would have been the easiest way to take out Scorn dragons, but I've avoided going there for two reasons: First, because I couldn't trust myself to stay focused on a single target and, second, because I couldn't risk being overpowered by the sheer number of potential opponents. After all, if I'd been injured or captured, the Serene Commander wasn't going to come and rescue me. I chose patience.

As soon as Zahra gives her agreement, Sienna spins and her footfalls fade as she hurries away down the hall.

Zahra nearly collapses in front of me. Emika can't be light, and Zahra held her the entire time despite her injuries. I catch Zahra, helping her stay upright. I don't dare take Emika from her, but at least I can keep her on her feet.

Emika's quiet whisper breaks our silence. "I don't like her, Mama."

Zahra's response is a quiet murmur. "I don't, either, Emi. But we need her."

"We have to move," I say, urging Zahra to the door. "We've already stayed too long. I don't trust the Sentinels not to come back." I check the corridor. "Beatrix, Felix, and Sophia are outside. We need to reach them and get out of here."

Zahra doesn't delay, snatching up a backpack from beside Emika's door and heading down the hallway ahead of me. "I'm not flying in this weather. The car's in the garage downstairs."

I follow Zahra through a windowless living area to an elevator at the side of the room and then down to the parking garage.

When the elevator doors open, we come face to face with Beatrix, who holds an access card as if she was about to use it.

An SUV revs mere steps away. Felix sits behind the wheel, apparently ready to gun it out of here. I don't see Sophia, but it would make sense if she's standing guard outside—probably not the wisest choice. Felix would have been better, but the Sentinels shouldn't be an immediate threat.

Before I ask Beatrix about Sophia, the dark-eyed dragon launches into a barrage of questions, all directed at Zahra.

"Where the fuck are your human bodyguards? What happened to your security? And why the freaking hell was Sienna Scorn here?"

"It's a long story," Zahra says, sounding exhausted.

Zahra's fatigue seems to take the wind out of Beatrix's sails. She reaches for Emika. "Here, let me help you. We're taking you to Callan's. We'll need to park a few blocks from his home and smuggle you in." She doesn't mention the tunnel, but I assume that's what she means.

Zahra doesn't object and within minutes, she and Emika are safely inside the vehicle. While they're getting settled, I retract my wings. The golden feathers hover in the air around me and I can't wait to retrieve my harness and my glaive.

I snag Beatrix's arm before she can slip into the front passenger side. "I'll go outside and get Sophia," I say. "We can head home together."

"Wait..." Beatrix glances around. "Isn't Sophia already with you?"

A growing sense of alarm builds within me. "I thought she was with you. I assumed she was standing guard outside."

Beatrix gives me a blank look. "We dealt with the Sentinels and then she went around the back to find you."

My stomach is rapidly sinking. "She never came inside. Three Sentinels were inside the building and two of them left through the back."

"Fuck." Beatrix is suddenly alert. "She would have been right in their path."

Isaac and Zadkiel's path. She wouldn't have stood a chance.

"Get Zahra and Emika to safety," I say quickly. "I'll find Sophia."

Without waiting for Beatrix to agree, I race to the garage

door. Darting beneath it as soon as it starts to open, I run back out into the rain.

I didn't think it was possible, but the downpour is worse, plastering my hair to my head in seconds. The golden feathers hover around me like loyal golden stars as I check my immediate surroundings. No Sophia, but no Sentinels, either.

Seconds later, the SUV drives past at a slow and careful pace. The rain is too heavy to see easily into the vehicle, but I make out Beatrix and Felix checking for threats. Trusting them to protect Zahra and Emika, I turn my mind completely to Sophia.

Where the hell is she?

With all this rain, and her water dragon's nature already like a tidal wave, I can't sense her. It's impossible to distinguish her from the water pounding down on me from the sky or the torrents gushing along the drains at the side of the lane.

Except... Wait...

All of the water is running in the same direction, which wouldn't be unusual except that the street is on a slight slope and the water is running *upward*, not down.

I follow the water's direction at a quick pace along the lane and then across the street where the water's path curves unnaturally in the direction of another side alley.

When I reach the opening, I pull up sharply.

Sophia lies in the middle of the alley on her side, facing me, her upper wing draped across her body. A thin layer of water swirls around her on the ground and, although the rain is torrential, it hits an invisible dome that keeps her mostly dry.

A male figure crouches, leaning over her from behind. It's impossible to sense his nature in the downpour—it's all I can do to breathe without spitting water—but I recognize him.

It's Micah Grudge. Solomon's son.

CHAPTER TWENTY-FOUR

"Get away from her!" I cry, striding toward Micah.

His focus snaps up to me, and his lips draw back in a snarl that makes him look more like a wolf than a dragon. "I won't let you kill her."

Me, kill Sophia?

I don't know how she's ended up here, but I can't trust Micah not to hurt her.

I cast quick glances around for Solomon, but I don't see him yet. He could be lurking on the rooftop above us, or on a nearby street, but it's impossible to identify any individual scent within the rain.

"Sophia is my friend!" I shout, spitting raindrops as I continue to storm toward Micah. "Back the fuck off!"

He remains exactly where he is. Water drips from his light-brown hair and down his cheeks. Counter to my command, his upper arm drops over her before he rapidly begins tucking in her wings, as if he's going to try to lift her.

The moment he cradles her head in his hands, Sophia's big, green eyes fly open.

She takes one look at Micah and screams. "Get away from me!"

At the same time, her upper wing unfurls, the movement shoving his arms off her. Her wing bone smacks him in the face loudly enough to be heard above the rainfall.

He drops backward with a grunt.

It only takes Sophia another second to see me.

"Lana!" she cries as she struggles to her feet and retracts her wings, allowing me to step to her side.

A moment later, I'm standing within the quiet of her water-free dome. My hand flies out to ward Micah off. "Back away!"

Slowly rising to his feet but standing his ground, he casts incredulous glances between Sophia and me. He's ended up at the edge of the dome and the rain is beating down his back while his face remains clear of the water. It can't be comfortable, and he looks confused about the dome, but he stays right where he is. He's shirtless, which makes me think he flew here, and once he rises to his full height, I'm reminded of just how intimidating he is.

Like father, like son.

Solomon is a hulking shadow as he slips from the rooftop on my right and lands with a thud beside Micah so that he's also partially within the dome. Like his son, his wings are put away —he didn't bother to use them to slow his jump—and he's wearing old khaki pants. The rain has darkened his blond hair and emphasizes his muscular silhouette.

"What are you doing here?" I demand to know. I'm nearly certain that Micah and Solomon aren't the ones who knocked Sophia unconscious. Micah's exclamation about not letting me hurt her indicates he found her like that. But I'd rather be certain.

"Looking for you." Solomon growls.

Before I can ask him why, Micah speaks to his father with an incline of his head toward Sophia. "That dragon is new."

Solomon's sudden partial shift is no less surprising to me than it was the first time I saw it. His pupils constrict into vertical slits with jagged edges while his hazel irises brighten. "A new dragon? Impossible."

"I swear I'm not mistaken." Micah inhales deeply and I'm reminded that his olfactory senses are as strong as mine. "She smells…" His forehead creases. "She smells wet."

Sophia gasps. She pushes out from behind me. "I smell *wet?*" Her cheeks flush with outrage. "You arrogant piece of—"

Micah backpedals and would have stepped into the rain except that the dome moves with Sophia as she plows toward him.

His hands fly up defensively. "I didn't mean—"

Water droplets rush from the sides of the dome into the space between them, each one glistening like a diamond and, impossibly, forming points that look as sharp as little blades. When Sophia screams, they spear toward Micah, hitting his chest and face.

He flinches, but it turns out that water is still water, and it merely splashes against him and runs down his body.

He blinks at her for a moment before he shakes himself in the same fashion that a dog would shake out its fur. The water flies off him, and his expression becomes stoic. "Like I said."

"Well." She edges toward him and draws an overly dramatic breath. "*You* smell like…"

She stops, and her brow furrows.

I remember the first time I sensed Micah's nature. I'm not sure of the extent to which Sophia will be able to grasp the same sensations, but I imagine her mind is suddenly filled with racing paws, the chase through a forest, a predator near to catching his prey.

Her head tips to the side, her rage vanishing. "Why do you smell like a wolf?"

Micah doesn't exactly relax, but a little of the tension leaves his shoulders. "My mother was a wolf."

Solomon, on the other hand, hasn't stopped scrutinizing me or the golden feathers floating in the air behind me. I'm painfully aware that I don't have my glaive right now. I do have my armband, and the two bracelets, and the feathers. I tell myself I can use all of them to protect us if I need to.

Although curiously, Solomon doesn't appear to have brought any dragon's gold with him. No golden bands to trap or hurt me this time.

"Okay," I say, reaching for Sophia and hooking my arm through hers. "It's time to go."

"No," Solomon says.

"Don't fuck with me, Grudge," I retort, preparing to release my wings and haul Sophia out of here if I need to.

I'm surprised when Solomon lifts his hands, palms up, and keeps them raised. "Peace, Cruel One. I have no wish to continue our fight. I only want to ask you a question."

"Her name is Lana," Sophia snaps at him, and I'm worried she doesn't realize the true extent of the danger Solomon poses to us. He could crush her head with his bare hands. She suddenly falters. "Uh... I mean, *Not*-Lana."

The corner of Solomon's mouth twitches as if a smile is lurking behind his stern expression. "Actually, her name is Asper Ashen-Varr."

Sophia falters again. She's spent enough time in Callan's library now to know exactly what that term means. She half-turns to me. It's a risky move, considering her back is partially exposed to Solomon. "Ashen-Varr? But that's a—"

"An avenging angel," I murmur, without taking my eyes off Solomon or his son. "I used to be. Not anymore."

Sophia swings back to Solomon. "If your question was that important, you could have asked Lana a week ago." Her voice hardens, now with a sharp edge it didn't carry before. "Oh, that's right. You didn't ask her because *you were trying to kill her.*"

She gives Solomon a scathing onceover and, before he can respond, she says, "I know your kind. I was married to your kind. You don't get to ask your question because you deserve nothing from us. Now. Back. The fuck. Off."

Of course, Solomon doesn't budge, barely reacting to her speech.

Sophia draws nearer to me, and only now do I get a sense of her emerging fear. "Lana?"

I grip her arm and urge her slowly backward, step by step. The dome comes with us, leaving the two men standing in the pouring rain.

I brace for an attack at any moment.

Eight steps away from them, I lean toward Sophia with an urgent command. "Fly. Now!"

She lifts off in a blast of cerulean blue wings, spreading raindrops around her as she soars into the air. I follow, urging the golden feathers to return to me as fast as possible as I launch myself upward.

My heart pounds as I soar away from the alley and swoop down to retrieve my weapon from the next street, snatching it up without taking the time to put it on. Any second now, I expect bands of gold to wrap around me and haul me back to Solomon.

Fear for Sophia makes me want to get home as quickly as possible, but I force myself to lead her on a circuitous route, since I can't risk exposing our destination.

By the time we creep through the bar, then run through the tunnel and step back into Callan's home, we're both breathing heavily. Our hair is dripping wet. Our clothes are sodden. And I can hear Sophia's heart pounding.

Once we're inside the elevator, she collapses against its wall. "Callan can be scary as fuck, but Solomon..." She closes her eyes. "Oh, fuck."

"You hid it well."

She tips her head back. "It was that damn wolf-dragon."

"Micah," I say.

"Is that his name? All I could think about at first was..." Some of her fear vanishes and a smile flickers around her mouth. "Have you ever had a moment when the air is clear, and you can hear the leaves rustling, but gently, and maybe there's a rain shower, but the sun is shining, and it's... perfect?"

Callan. He is those moments for me, but I don't say so.

She shrugs and blows out her exhale. "I had that moment." She clicks her tongue and the rapture fades from her face. "And then Solomon spoke, and it was gone."

"What happened to you before I found you?" I ask.

She grimaces. "A Sentinel with white hair."

"That would be Isaac."

"He was stronger than the others. The last thing I saw was a fist framed in light, and then I woke up where you found me."

The elevator doors open to Sophia's floor. She steps out but swings back and holds her hand out to stop the elevator closing. "I'm sorry if you wanted to hear Solomon's question."

I give it a moment's thought. More than any other dragon, Solomon has answers about my past, but the last time I was enthralled by an offer of information, my distraction turned out to be a mistake. "If someone has knowledge that you need, but they withhold that information, it gives them power over you," I say, speaking to my recent experience. "To succumb to that is dangerous. You did the right thing."

With a relieved smile, she steps back and allows the elevator doors to close.

My heart rate is slowing back to normal, but the loss of adrenaline brings a flood of unwanted emotions and there's nothing to distract me now.

An angel died at my hands tonight.

A murderous angel, but still an angel.

I don't know what I'm supposed to feel. Remorse. Sorrow. Fear that I've made things worse. Relief that Emika is safe...

Loss?

I didn't know him. Don't know his name. He was destined to be my brother and instead... Fate led me to end him.

The elevator reaches the top floor and I stumble out, carrying my harness with me. I'm desperate for a hot shower and a quiet place to straighten out my thoughts, but when I reach for the security panel, I pause.

The energy around the door makes my skin prickle.

My immediate sense is that it's not danger so much as *conflict*.

Wary of barging in on a situation where I'm not wanted, I close my eyes and expand my senses to scan the room.

Callan and Zahra are inside.

The tension between them is like explosions going off. Anger, frustration, fear. And it sounds like their conversation is just getting started.

CHAPTER TWENTY-FIVE

*C*allan's question is sharp. "Of all the places you could meet Sienna Scorn, why the hell would you invite her to your home?"

"My home was already compromised." Zahra's voice is raised enough that it echoes slightly. I judge that she and Callan must be either standing near, or sitting at, the dining table, based on how the sound bounces. "Tyler knows its location, and I can't trust him anymore. I used to think Sophia was stirring him up, but now I believe it was the other way around. He's made it clear that he's coming after me."

"Fucking Tyler," Callan growls.

Zahra lowers her voice. "I was planning to move to a new home right after the meeting with Sienna. By using my old home for our negotiations, I could give her a show of faith without any future risk. It seemed like a smart idea. Until it wasn't."

Callan remains tense. "What about your human bodyguards?"

"I sent them ahead to make sure my new home was secure. I didn't want them at my meeting with Sienna because I couldn't risk their safety. Sienna Scorn doesn't respect human life like we do. If things got heated between her and me, I didn't want them caught in the crossfire. Their strength and weapons are no match for hers."

Callan gives a heavy sigh. "That's fair."

Zahra's anger doesn't abate. It's like a bright, emerald swirl in my vision. "I can handle a dragon like Sienna. It was the Sentinels who threatened us, and I have no idea how they found my home."

"Did they follow Sienna?" Callan asks.

"It's possible. If they know what she looks like, they could have tracked her." If Zahra wasn't already gritting her teeth, it sounds like she is now. "She played innocent, but she might have been reckless about the risks. After all, she's killed angels before. She probably thought she could beat Sentinels just as easily."

Callan's snarl is a deep rumble that reminds me of the times when his beast has surfaced. "We can't trust her, but you expect me to play nice with her."

"It's our only choice." Zahra's voice is sharp again. "We need the Scorn. The Sentinels are coming for us. And they're far stronger than I ever imagined. Beatrix and Felix were able to deter the ones outside my home, but the three who came inside were unbeatable. We can't defeat them without an army."

"You *have* an army," Callan grinds out. "I have a vault full of weapons and armor ready to be used—"

"By whom?" she asks. "Felix and Beatrix? Sophia?" She scoffs. "Yes, three dragons make a fine army. Or do you mean to include yourself?" Her chair scrapes back, a sudden sound. "You're a dragon in chains, Callan. You can't help me win this fight."

I've listened for long enough. Longer than I should have, actually. I'm about to activate the panel beside the door when Callan's response stops me.

"You only *think* you need the Scorn because you aren't willing to ask for Lana's help."

The swirls of emotion surrounding Zahra's position darken from emerald-green to stormy gray, the energy I associate with danger. But if anyone would be endangered in a fight with Callan, it's her.

Her voice is low, but so angry that it feels like she shouts. "You need to justify your choices by claiming she's an asset to us because you can't face your truth."

"What truth, Zahra?"

"We're in this fucking mess because you couldn't let her die."

The tension between them now is unbearable. It's like a physical force reaching around me and squeezing my chest hard enough to break my ribs. I wish I could stop listening, but I can barely move, let alone shut down my power.

"You chose Lana over your family. Your clan. Me and Emika." Zahra's breathing is harsh. "Lana wanted to leave you, Callan."

"No—"

"She made a choice to face her people. She chose a path that was more honorable than I ever dreamed an angel would choose. And then *you* couldn't let her die."

"Lana's death—"

"You should have let her die!" Zahra's scream carries so much emotional force that it knocks me backward. I slip in the water I've been dripping onto the floor, only regaining my balance by crouching and lowering my center of gravity.

Callan's voice is cold. "She saved Emika's life."

"That doesn't make up for all the lives she's taken. It doesn't make up for the fact that Emika's life wouldn't *be* in danger if it weren't for Lana. It doesn't make Lana any less monstrous."

My fingertips brush the cold marble and there I stay, my long hair dripping across my shoulders while I try to calm my heartbeat. Try to slow my breathing. *Oh, the danger of listening to a conversation I'm not supposed to overhear.* I only have myself to blame. But the truth of what Zahra said is undeniable.

I'm a dragon killer.

I'm an angel killer.

I can count the good things I've done in my life on two fingers: Saving Emika. Twice. But Zahra's right—both times I was a trigger for the attack that had endangered Emika in the first place.

I am the monster Zahra thinks I am. She's right not to trust me. And she's right that Callan should have let me go.

Over the last week, I started to form connections. The closest to friendships I've ever had. But all I bring these dragons is danger. I told Callan that we were in the center of the storm, but I didn't want to admit that I am its source.

I was deluding myself to think that I could ever find a home or be part of any sort of pack or family and not endanger them. Callan may want me here, but no matter how strong his trust and faith in me is, that doesn't make his choices wise or safe.

I find myself focusing on the elevator doors. I could leave right now. I already have with me the only belongings I own—my weapon, my armband, the two bracelets. Callan gave me the means to fly again. All I have to do is walk the five paces to the elevator, take the secret tunnel, and disappear into the night.

I can be gone from his life within minutes.

My lips twist and my heart hardens.

Running is for fucking cowards.

But I can't step back into his home believing that I will always have a place here. I close my eyes and picture myself driving a dagger through the parts of my heart that softened in the last week, cutting them out. Leaving only the cold, hard bits.

It's surprisingly easy, but then, gentle emotions don't belong in the heart of a creature like me.

I rise to my feet and smooth out my features, ensuring I

appear unemotional. Then I press my hand to the scanner and wait for the door to slide open.

Callan spins to me first. As I suspected, he's partially shifted, a golden sheen across his face and arms, heat shimmering around his silhouette.

Zahra is poised opposite him, and I'm not surprised that she's also shifted, her skin glistening with bronze scales, her bronze wings ready at her sides. With the heat radiating from Callan, I guess she was preparing to protect herself from his flames.

Callan's jaw tenses. He knows I can hear through sound-proofing, although he won't know if I was actually listening or how much I heard.

I drag my harness along the floor even though the buckles make an awful scraping sound, but it succeeds in making Zahra wince. I'm not doing it to cause her pain; rather, the auditory disruption makes her focus on me and serves to put her on the backfoot, which is a far safer place for her than in Callan's face.

I choose to stop a few steps behind Callan, forcing him to turn so he can see me, breaking the fury he was directing at Zahra.

Not that I should care to do her any fucking favors.

My hair falls across my eyes in dark strands as I speak. "You have a choice to make, Zahra, but if I were you, I'd choose to keep this monster close."

Her lips part in surprise. "You heard that?"

My lips twitch and I'm sure she finds my smile disconcerting. "I killed one of the angels you described as unbeatable. It took five dragons and a legion of angels to bring me close to death. At what point will you stop underestimating me and realize you're only alive because I choose, with every breath I take, not to kill you?"

The color drains from her face, and her heartbeat jumps in my hearing. She didn't see me kill the angel, and she didn't see me fight Solomon. She didn't even witness the aftermath of that fight like Callan did. The time she fought me, I was already badly injured. She's barely seen the tip of my strength.

Callan takes a step toward me, and I can already hear what he's about to say—that I'm the sum of my choices, that his sister only spoke out of fear and desperation—but I hold up my hand.

"No," I say, urging him to stay where he is. He has been incredibly patient with his sister, and I know that's because he understands her fears, but I can't let their feud grow because of me. "I won't be the wedge that breaks your family apart. Your sister needs to make a choice. Either she wants my help, or she doesn't. But she has to make the choice for herself, or she will always blame you for the consequences."

Zahra retracts her wings, and her scales vanish. Her eyes are sharply narrowed as she prowls toward me. Even now, it doesn't seem that she's taken my warning seriously.

"You've saved my daughter twice," she says, circling me slowly. "You have my gratitude for that." She shakes her head as she continues. "But I can't trust you."

"I'm not asking for your trust," I say. "I'm asking if you'll accept my help."

"The two go hand in hand," she says.

"Really? Then why are you willing to make an alliance with Sienna Scorn?"

Zahra continues to prowl around me. "Because I know where I stand with Sienna. I know how she operates, and I can predict when she'll become a threat to me. I'm prepared for it."

"But I'm unpredictable," I say.

She stops right in front of me, and I don't underestimate how smart, or proud, she is. "I see it in your eyes, Lana. You have a well of anger inside you and it's like a bucket of fury that keeps on filling. There's a small space for mercy. It's what compelled you to help my daughter. But it's very small."

When Isaac described me, he said that I have the capacity to feel nothing but loathing for the guilty. I won't be swayed by threats or bribes or emotion. Maybe that's what the Serene Commander meant when she said I was incapable of love.

Even love won't stop me ending what needs to end.

"You're right," I say. "It's not in my nature to accept shades of gray. Mercy is for the innocent. But for now, that includes your daughter."

"Until it doesn't," she says. "And then what?"

"That's a question for a future you won't have if you don't accept my help."

She lets out a frustrated snarl. "We're only here now because of you!"

"Yes," I say, my tolerance for taking her blame running thin. "Accept it and move on. What do you choose?"

Her whole body is tense enough that I expect her to shift into her dragon form again at any moment. For a second, her pupils constrict, a startling, serpentine shape. A partial shift. I'm not exactly in a position to draw her attention to it right now.

"I don't have a choice," she says. "I need to keep you where I can see you."

I lift my chin. "Then I'll remain in full sight."

She takes a deep, shaky breath, as if making this decision is as much a relief for her as it is for me.

Some of the tension also leaves Callan's shoulders. Despite his conflict with his sister, I'm sure he didn't want to see her and I come to blows.

Zahra spins to him. "I know you disagree with my decision to form an alliance with Sienna, but it's the only way Tyler will back off. This way, I can maintain control of the Dread, our clan won't tear itself apart, and we'll have the army we need."

She lifts her head high and takes a deep breath. "I'm meeting Sienna tomorrow night and I need you there, Callan."

He gives her a gruff nod. "We'll be there."

She takes a step back. "I need to get back to Emika now. Thank you for letting us stay with Sophia."

Callan shrugs, his expression closed off. "It's Sophia's home. She makes the decisions about who stays with her. I'm sure she's happy to have the company."

Zahra strides to the door but pauses for another moment. "There's a vacant position in the Cohort, and since I'm the ruling alpha, I've decided to offer the position to Sophia. I need as many dragons as I can trust."

"I support your decision," Callan says. "Her dragon is growing stronger by the day. She's a worthy ally."

With a quick nod, Zahra leaves. The door hasn't even closed behind her when Callan speaks quietly to me. "You're drenched. You need to get warm and dry."

Water drips down the back of my neck, but I ignore it, even though I'm freezing from the inside out.

"I don't need to be warm and dry," I say, lifting my eyes to his. "I need to be in your bed, but that can't happen tonight. The last thing we need when we meet Sienna is for me to breathe fire and turn the whole fucking deal to ash."

Callan doesn't release my gaze. "You fought and killed an angel. You shouldn't be alone tonight."

I give him a nod. *Truth.*

But I'm not sure what he can do about it.

I swing away from him, heading for my room, trying to ignore how close I came to not returning to him tonight. Once inside the bathroom, I peel off my clothing and curl up on the tiles under the hot spray, waiting for the warmth to seep through.

It takes a long time before I can drag myself out again and pull on a nightshirt.

I stop in the open bathroom door.

Callan sits on the chair in the corner of my room, towels piled across his lap, drying off my golden feathers. The harness already lies spread across a blanket on the floor, its buckles gleaming and dry again.

As soon as he sees me, he sets everything down on the ground.

"You don't have to be alone," he says again, gesturing to the pillows and blankets set up at the base of my bed. "We won't collide there."

I want to collide with him more than anything.

"If the angels were determined to kill me before, they'll triple their efforts now," I say. "More Sentinels will come. At some point, it will be safer for your family if I leave and draw the Sentinels away with me."

His expression is inscrutable, but I don't try too hard to read him right now because I know what I'll find.

Rage and determination. Enough to set the world on fire.

CHAPTER TWENTY-SIX

*T*he rain has cleared by the following evening, although some cloud cover remains. Not a perfect night for dragons to go out, but not the worst.

After showering and putting on my now-customary black T-shirt and jeans, I have a heavy debate with myself about asking Sophia for a dress. It's supposed to be a dinner, and I'm sure I'm expected to be dressed up.

Sophia appears in the doorway of my bedroom wearing a gorgeous, satin, knee-length, one-shoulder dress in a color that matches her green eyes. The left side of her head is freshly shaved, while her hair flows in a wave to the right that touches her bare shoulder. She's wearing drop earrings consisting of a long, narrow bar at the front and a chain at the back, and the way the gold calls to me tells me it's dragon's gold.

She hovers a step inside my room, nervously biting her lip. "Tyler will be there tonight."

One of the last things Tyler said to Sophia was that she couldn't survive without him. She told him to watch her do it.

"Does he know about your dragon?" I ask her.

She shakes her head. "I asked Zahra to keep it to herself.

Tyler has no right to know anything about me anymore. Still, I'm nervous."

I appraise her choice of dress from the slit up her leg, which will allow her to run and kick in it, to the soft material flowing across her left shoulder, which will allow easy arm movement, and finally to the sash at her waist, which could be used in a fight if she needs it.

"Fuck him," I say. "You look like you could slay a god."

My declaration draws a smile to her face, and she stops biting her lip. "I can lend you one of my dresses if you like?"

"I'm fine," I say, deciding that I need to be true to myself.

I snap on my armband, adjust my bracelets, and check that the straps of my harness didn't warp in the rain last night. My glaive might raise some eyebrows, but every other dragon will be wearing weapons in the form of jewelry. Mine is simply in a more obvious form.

Before I leave my room, Callan appears behind Sophia. He's dressed in a pair of gray suit pants and a white, collared shirt that's open at the neck. I don't sense any gold hidden on his body and that's probably wise. His mere presence is a threat, and he won't want to add to the unease that the Scorn dragons will likely feel around him.

He's holding a garment bag, which he places on my bed, simply saying, "If you like it."

A smile lingers around his mouth as he leaves the room.

Sophia follows him out after arching an eyebrow at me. Her curious glance at the bag tells me she doesn't know what's in it.

I unzip it, expecting to find some kind of beautiful gown within it that I have no intention of wearing.

Instead, I pull out a two-piece garment befitting a warrior.

The top is made of a fitted bodice with straps that extend up to a halter neck, which will hide the yellowing remains of my fake bruises. The material is thick enough to protect against a knife aimed at my vital organs but will fit around me without impeding the movement of my arms or torso. The bottom half is a pair of long, black pants that are made of a more supple material that shouldn't hinder me when I fly or run.

Every aspect of the ensemble appears designed to protect me while accommodating full movement. I have no hesitation removing my jeans and T-shirt and putting the garment on. Testing my harness over it, I find that it fits nicely.

When I emerge from my room, Callan gives me a quick onceover, the satisfaction in his eyes giving way to the heat of desire. It's been days since we could be together, and my body craves his touch.

I may have determinedly cut from my heart any hope that I could find a place where I belong, but there's no way I can deny the impact Callan has on my mind, my senses, or my body.

"Zahra will meet us downstairs," Callan says. "Beatrix and Felix will join us on the way."

"Who's watching Emika?" I ask.

"I've asked Jada to stay with her in Sophia's apartment until we get back. My human friends are sitting this one out tonight."

I don't imagine Jada, or any of Callan's other human body-guards, is happy about letting Callan go out tonight without them, but their trust in Callan is absolute. They respect his privacy when he asks for it.

Fighting my impulse to move nearer to Callan's side, I follow him to the elevator and down to the parking garage.

Zahra is waiting there for us, dressed in a muted-gold, knee-length cocktail dress that brings out the cinnamon in her eyes. She's wearing the same golden armband, chain around her neck, and anklet that she wore to the Hollow Rose the first time Callan took me out.

Callan tosses her a set of keys, which she deftly catches.

She heads to the black two-door sports car parked on the other side of the garage, and Sophia goes with her, while I follow Callan to the same sleek, blue vehicle that he drove away from the alley a week ago.

Now, I sense his dragon's gold, at least ten bands of it plastered across the hood of the vehicle like last time. He can leave it there during dinner where it won't be a direct threat to anyone but use it if we have any trouble on the way to or from our destination.

I slip into the passenger seat, noting that the tinted windows will keep the moonlight out, but I'm worried that we could be spotted driving the vehicles from this building, which would give away the location of Callan's home.

I needn't have worried because, before exiting the parking garage, Callan drives to the left and along a narrow lane that extends from the side of the parking garage far enough along that by the time we approach a garage door, I surmise we must be exiting from the back of the building next door.

The door opens into a back alley, and I glance up at the building we're leaving behind. "Let me guess," I say with a wry smile. "You own this entire block."

"It seemed safest." Callan casts a quick glance in the rearview mirror. "My identity is concealed behind a string of shell companies."

The purr of the black sports car follows us from the building along the lane, and then we're on the main streets.

Within minutes, we're traveling across the city. The cloud cover is intermittent, with a sprinkle of rain every few minutes, but it clears up the farther east we travel.

Zahra follows closely behind us, and although there's a lot of other traffic on the streets tonight, I don't miss the dark-gray sports car that slips in front of us, taking the lead.

"That's Beatrix and Felix," Callan says. "This meeting with the Scorn will be tense for them."

"I'll watch their backs," I say without hesitation. "As well as yours."

He casts me a soft smile. "We'll watch each other's backs."

Our surroundings change as we near our destination. Graffiti starts to appear on the lower extremities of buildings that have fading paint, chipped bricks, and watermarks running down their sides. Trash is scattered along the sides of the streets and piled at the sides of the cracked footpaths. It's a far cry from the other side of town. A different world to the one in which Callan lives. But it's a world I'm familiar with, and in many ways, it's where I feel most comfortable.

It isn't pretty. It isn't clean. But it doesn't hide its true nature. There is no subterfuge here.

The dark-gray sports car that Beatrix is driving pulls off ahead of us, turning onto a short driveway at the side of a large, stone building that takes up an entire block. The building is three levels high, judging by the number of windows, and has stone steeples set at intervals along the top.

She pulls her vehicle to a stop in front of the garage door. Four men, all dressed in black, who are standing guard in front of the door step toward her vehicle. They're presumably dragon shifters, although they could be humans.

Callan slows down as he watches the interaction up ahead, his eyes narrowed.

Beatrix winds down her window, speaking with one of the guards.

The tension between them is palpable from here and I'm about to extend my senses to hear what they're saying when the garage door begins to open and the guards wave her through.

They're even more tense when Callan drives up.

Beatrix must have warned them that Callan is in this vehicle because they don't approach when he winds down his window.

"Drive to the back of the parking garage," the guard who spoke with Beatrix says. "Your parking space is marked in red."

When Callan pulls into our allocated space and we exit the

vehicle, Beatrix and Felix are already out of their vehicle and waiting for us.

"Nice getup, Night Sky," Beatrix says to me, appraising me from head to toe.

She's also wearing black pants, but her sleeveless, black cowlneck shirt has a sparkle in it. She's also wearing a multitude of golden bracelets on both arms, along with a belt that has a curiously-designed golden buckle with an oversized prong. I can only imagine what sort of weapon it might transform into if she needs it.

Felix isn't concealing his weapon tonight, instead carrying a dagger in plain sight on his belt. Both he and Beatrix appear as cruelly beautiful as the first time I saw them, their eyes dark and their heads high. If they're nervous about this encounter with their old clan, then they aren't showing it.

Within moments, Zahra has parked her vehicle and she and Sophia join us on our way toward a set of stairs where another group of guards waits. These men carry a variety of blades and guns, each of which is etched with the symbol of the Scorn clan. All of their weapons call to me in a way that tells me they're made of dragon's gold.

I resist the urge to tug on the gold and test my ability to take their weapons from them. Somehow, I don't think that would go down well.

They stand clear of Callan, keeping to the sides of the stairs while, again, one of them speaks. "Follow the blue lights. They provide a clear path for you to walk." His olive eyes narrow as he focuses on Callen. "Stray from the blue lights, and it will be taken as an act of aggression."

Callan responds calmly, giving the guard a firm, acknowledging nod before he heads up the stairs, while we proceed in a wide arc at his back.

Sound filters through the open door at the top of the stairs— a steady thrum of music mixed with the hum of voices. Blue lights have been attached to the wall of the corridor at the top of the stairs and are visible across the floor in the distance.

Callan keeps near to the lights but steps aside so that Zahra can enter the corridor first. As the alpha, that is her right, and it will be important that he's seen to observe the hierarchy so there aren't any misunderstandings about his status.

Sophia walks close behind me, while Beatrix and Felix flank her, becoming a protective force at our backs.

"Go carefully, Night Sky," Beatrix whispers, while Felix remains stoically silent. "Zahra may wish to make an alliance, and the Scorn will tolerate her presence, but make no mistake: You, Felix, and I are the enemy here."

"I'll watch your back," I say, meeting her dark eyes.

She inclines her head. "And we'll watch yours."

I catch the flicker of her smile before I focus back on the corridor.

It lets out into a room filled with people. Tables are scattered throughout the space and the dragon shifters are already sitting with plates of food and bottles of wine on the tables. The sound of clinking of glasses mixed with their raucous laughter grates on my nerves like a blade scraping against stone.

I walk calmly into it, expecting Callan's presence to be a much-needed buffer against the inevitable fog of guilt, but it hits me with a force I wasn't expecting.

I stop so suddenly that Sophia runs into my back, neatly sidestepping to draw level with me. She glances at me before she hooks her arm in mine, as if we're simply waiting for instructions and not frozen in place.

I'm also aware of Beatrix and Felix stepping up on either side of us, appearing austere and completely in control despite the nearly imperceptible look of alarm they send each other at my sudden halt.

Zahra is already a few steps ahead of us, but Callan pauses at the edge of the blue-lit path he's supposed to follow, as if he sensed the sudden gap between him and me. He casually turns in my direction, the golden flecks in his eyes brightening and tension in his shoulders increasing.

My feet are rooted to the ground. With every inhalation, I drag in the scent of creatures who have killed, maimed, hurt, abused, lied, stolen, deceived, betrayed...

A room full of fucking monsters that I need to kill.

CHAPTER TWENTY-SEVEN

*J*ram my fingernails against my palms so sharply that I'm sure I've drawn blood. I can't take deep breaths to calm myself because breathing only makes it worse.

A snarl builds within my throat and the room starts to blur as the fog around every dragon in this room—except the dragons I arrived with—thickens to the point where I can identify, with startling clarity, every sick, evil thing they've ever done.

I imagine myself taking control of every weapon made of gold in this room and turning it against these dragons. Guns and knives. Cutting them down with the blades and bullets they've used to destroy others.

Beatrix leans in close beside me, the heavy scent of cloves that clings to her paling in comparison to the suffocating fog around me.

"We should fit right in here, shouldn't we, Night Sky?" she asks quietly, cutting through the weight that's bearing down on me. "There's nothing like looking into the face of a true monster to put your own sins into context."

I search her eyes, the darkness in them, imagining the pathways her life could have gone down. The monster she could have become if she'd stayed with the Scorn. The death she would have suffered if Callan's father hadn't chosen the unlikely path.

Somehow, her speech is a lifeline that I use to swim up, to take control again.

I give her a nod, unable to trust my voice as I rein in my overwhelming compulsion to cut through this room with a vengeance. I remind myself that, even if the next few hours will be some of the most difficult of my life, I'm doing this because Zahra needs this army of creatures.

Placing an invisible wall between them and me within my mind, I force my shoulders to relax, and I allow Sophia to lead me forward.

Callan turns back to his sister, who has paused a few steps ahead of him—but not because of me.

Sienna Scorn approaches along the narrow path laid out in blue lights. She's dressed in a plunging, blue dress that clings to her curves while a golden chain rests around her waist. Her blue-black hair is loose and flows across her left shoulder. Her gun is nowhere to be seen, but I'm sure she's capable of strangling anyone with that chain.

She appears completely relaxed, a queen in her domain.

"Welcome," she says with a benevolent smile.

The moment she speaks, every Scorn dragon who wasn't already staring at us turns in our direction. Quiet falls over the room. I'm acutely aware, not only of the Scorn dragons' scrutiny, but of the sharp gazes from a table on our far right.

Tyler sits beside Sophia's mother, Martha, along with Davison, all three Dread dragons already holding drinks.

Tyler's glass lands heavily on the table as he rises to his feet. I expect him to stare at Sophia, but she's on my left and must be partially obscured by both me and Beatrix.

Tyler is easily six feet tall and nearly as solid in stature as

Callan. He has fair skin, blond hair, and gray-blue eyes. The paleness of his irises is accentuated by a navy-blue suit jacket. I'm a little surprised by how disheveled he looks. His hair is tousled instead of slicked back, his facial hair is a dark shadow across his jaw, and the white shirt visible beneath his suit jacket is creased. His lips carry a cruel twist, and he doesn't attempt to repress his hatred when he looks at me. I return his gaze, prepared to subdue him if he makes any sort of move toward us, but he's smart enough to stay where he is.

That's when Sophia releases my arm and steps out from beside me.

Without moonlight, Tyler won't see her dragon, but a furrow forms in his brow. He won't miss the way she holds herself taller, the changes to her physique, or the air of confidence around her.

She is remarkably relaxed as she looks right back at him with a *fuck you* smile on her lips.

"This way," Sienna is saying to Zahra. "I have a table set up for your Cohort, but you're welcome to mingle with the members of my clan if you wish. Of course, Callan will need to remain separated."

Zahra thanks her and calmly heads toward the seat beside Davison. He is the final member of the cohort and has dark-brown hair, olive-green eyes, and light-brown skin.

With a quick backward glance, Zahra indicates that Beatrix, Felix, and Sophia should join her, and they all step off the blue-lit path while I remain resolutely at Callan's back.

I take note of the way that Beatrix and Felix sit on either side of Sophia at the table so that she's not directly in Tyler's line of sight or easily accessible to him for conversation.

Ahead of me, Sienna continues to wear a smile plastered to her face. She points at the blue lights on the floor that lead to a smaller table isolated at the far end of the room. "Your table is this way," she says to Callan. "You're sitting with me."

When we reach it, there are only two places set, but it doesn't bother me. It would be impossible for me to swallow a bite in this environment, and if I had to sit down, I'd need to take off my harness. This way, I can keep my weapon close and I'm ready to defend Callan if necessary.

I take up position behind his chair like a guard at his back. I can't see his face now, although I expect his expression will be carefully closed off for the entirety of his interaction with Sienna, but on the positive side, I'm facing the room, so all potential threats are visible to me.

Including Sienna, who pulls out the chair on the opposite side of the table, her back now to her people, but that doesn't seem to bother her. She barely pays any attention to me, calling to the waitstaff who are positioned at the sides of the room to bring more wine along with her meal.

Sweeping her dress to the side as she sits, she takes up a relaxed pose, folding one leg over the other so that both are visible and one high heel starts to slip off her foot. She doesn't seem to care. It's the kind of nonchalance that tells me she might make use of that stiletto to ram it into someone's neck.

"The human who owns this building is a drug lord who owes me some favors," she says, leaning forward to pour herself and Callan each a glass of wine. "He lets me use this place whenever I want. Not that he has much choice. He knows I'll do to him what I did to his rival if he displeases me."

She takes a sip of her drink, although Callan doesn't touch his.

"I prefer more collegiate relationships with humans," Callan says, his voice monotone.

"So I heard," she says. "Your mother was a human, was she not?"

"She was."

"Mine was a dragon, but you probably already knew that. The Scorn don't tolerate any dilution of our dragon blood."

Callan acknowledges her with a small nod and nothing more. As much as Sienna's comment was probably intended as an insult, I suspect he agrees with her. Not because of anything to do with the so-called dilution of dragon strength, but because human mothers don't survive the birth of a dragon child. Callan has made it clear to his clan he won't tolerate any such loss of human life.

A young woman—possibly in her mid-teens—who is dressed as a member of the waitstaff approaches our table. She's carrying a tray loaded with plates of food but keeps her eyes averted as she places everything down on the table, staying as far away from Callan as she can.

I can't tell if she's human or dragon, but I doubt Sienna would be so reckless as to have human waitstaff here tonight, and the girl's behavior indicates she's aware of Callan's power.

The plate she sets down in front of Sienna rattles a little, and Sienna's hand snakes out to grab the girl's wrist. "Spill my food, and I'll whip you raw."

"Yes, Mother."

Mother? I take a closer look at the girl, noting her blue-black hair and high cheekbones. My focus drops to her arm. Sienna's sudden movement has pushed up the young woman's sleeve, revealing a number of yellowing bruises along her arm. The way the teen allows her hair to fall across her face now seems intended to conceal the bruise I make out across her jaw.

"My daughter," Sienna says, releasing the girl's wrist and allowing her to finish her job. "A complete disappointment to me."

She leans back in her chair and speaks again, more loudly and clearly intending for others to hear. "Without a dragon, she is weak! A fucking waste of my time."

The girl flinches, her head remaining bowed as she quickly retrieves the tray and hurries away.

Across the room, Sophia's head has risen. A furrow deepens

in her brow as she watches the girl retreat. For a second, it looks as if she's going to follow her, but Beatrix casually places a hand on Sophia's arm and keeps her in her seat.

Sienna stabs the practically raw steak sitting in the middle of her plate. "You deprived me of fresh wolf shifter meat when you rescued that pathetic pack from their own vices, Callan," she says, abruptly changing the subject.

"The debt was paid," Callan says. "I assumed you would be satisfied with that."

"It's not about the money," Sienna says. "It's about the hunt. I'm sure the angel understands."

For the first time since I arrived, Sienna acknowledges me with a sharp stare. "The hunt is what keeps us alive, isn't it, angel?"

If she intends to rile me, I'm about to disappoint her. The reality is that nothing she can say right now can compare to the atrocities committed by the dragons in this room. Her words are pale and insubstantial in comparison and hardly worth reacting to.

When I remain silent, her eyes narrow, and the explosion of amber around her irises brightens before she turns away from me again.

Sienna puts down her fork and finally cuts to the chase. "You've made it very clear that you don't approve of my profession, Callan. If I join with your sister, what assurances do I have that you won't turn on us?"

"What assurances do I have that you won't betray my sister at the first opportunity?" Callan asks.

Sienna smiles. "Finally, the beast reveals his concerns." She leans back in her chair and folds her arms across her chest. "I see we share a common apprehension. You wish to protect your family. And I wish to protect my clan."

Only the clan members who have dragons. I bite my tongue before I call out her hypocrisy.

She peers at Callan but then seems to make a decision. "Perhaps we simply need to agree that we are an equal threat to each other. We both have a lot to lose if either of us breaks the alliance. If you threaten my clan, I will go after your family. If I threaten your family, you will come after my clan."

I'm not sure that Sienna is an equal threat to Callan, but again, I'm not about to point that out.

"Then we're agreed," Callan says.

"Excellent." Leaving her steak nearly untouched, Sienna rises to her feet and swings to her clan. "We have an agreement! The Scorn and the Dread are now allied."

She beams at her people before inclining her head at Zahra. "We are all friends here."

She turns back to Callan but doesn't re-take her seat, lowering her voice as she says to me, "I look forward to hunting with you, angel."

I don't twitch a muscle, but there's no way I will tolerate having this dragon at my side. I'm more likely to give in to my compulsions and kill her than to let her go anywhere with me.

Sienna runs her finger along her bottom lip as she studies me for a moment longer. Then she swings back to her clan with a magnanimous smile on her lips. "Dragons! Let's celebrate in the garden. Bring your drinks and enjoy the moonlight."

As she speaks, several waitstaff open a set of wooden doors at the side of the room. The space beyond it is bright, although the light is mottled, possibly some sort of atrium, given her comment about moonlight.

The Scorn dragons rise from their seats and head toward the doors, many of them scooping up extra bottles of alcohol to take with them. Tyler, Martha, and Davison are quick to join them. Callan told me that Tyler has contacts within the Scorn, and he is quick to mingle and disappear with them through the door.

Sienna retrieves her wine glass, but before she sashays away, she says, "Callan will need to stay in here. There is no safe space for him in the garden. But you can come out when you're ready, angel."

I wait a few minutes for most of the dragons to leave before I edge closer to Callan's side.

"That was too easy," I murmur.

"Agreed." He folds his arms across his chest. "She barely haggled."

I sigh. "Maybe she needs the Dread as much as Zahra needs the Scorn. If Sienna has no succession plan, then her family's control might be under threat."

"True, but that gives Beatrix or Felix a foot in the door. They could take control of the Scorn more easily this way."

I'm not sure that Beatrix and Felix would want to return to their old clan, but I give it some thought. "That could be Sienna's intention. A way to save face. Call it an alliance and anoint them of her own free will. It's not a takeover or a coup if she can name her terms and be seen to choose them."

Even as I pose my theory, I'm not convinced. The way Sienna studied me at the end of the conversation was unsettling.

Across the way, Zahra and the others rise to their feet. Zahra and Sophia head toward the wooden door, but Beatrix and Felix veer toward us instead.

"Zahra needs to mingle," Beatrix says. "I'd love nothing more than to get the fuck out of here, but we can't leave her on her own. That said, it's best if Felix and I don't go into the garden. We don't want to say or do anything that might jeopardize the alliance." She turns to me. "Can you keep an eye on Sophia? I don't want her to cause trouble by looking for Sienna's daughter."

It's a valid fear, judging by the concern on Sophia's face at the way Sienna had treated her daughter. "I can."

I press my hand to the table's edge near to Callan's position. I've been fighting my instincts since we arrived at this place, but the ebbing brightness of the golden flecks in his irises tells me he has, too. Neither one of us wants to stay here any longer than we have to.

"One hour," I say to Beatrix. "Then I'm coming back and we're leaving."

"Make it thirty minutes," she answers, her dark eyes flashing. "That's about as long as I can stand being around these fucking dragons."

"Agreed."

"Lana." Callan's voice makes me turn back to him. "Stay clear of Sienna. We don't know what her game is."

"I will."

The tension around his mouth eases and he gives me a smile that floors me. "We'll make it through this," he says. "All of it."

Some of the weight lifts from my shoulders. "I'll be back soon."

Stepping off the blue-lit path, I stride toward the wooden doors and pause there, surprised by the space beyond.

I was expecting some sort of glass ceiling at least, but the atrium is open at the top and much larger than I was expecting. It's a garden with trees, vines, and dense greenery. The kind of place where you can't quite see where the paths will take you. Music comes from somewhere off to the far left and a wash of vines from a stone arch across the path creates a curtain across the way ahead.

I consider if I should expand my senses, but I'm already at breaking point. To open my mind would send me over the edge.

Carefully pushing the vines aside, I step onto a small section of diverging paths, each one surrounded by trees and plants and leading in a different direction. Craning my neck, I can see that the one going straight ahead leads to an open area where the majority of dragons are drinking and dancing. I spot Zahra among them. Overhead, the moon is obscured by clouds, and I can only imagine the dragon shadows that will become visible when the clouds roll aside.

I don't see Sophia among the dragons straight ahead, so I peer down the left path next. That one leads directly to the inner wall of the building and alongside multiple open doors. Several dragons disappear together through one of the doors, and it doesn't take a genius to guess what those rooms are for.

Turning away from the party and the music, I set off down the third, and narrowest, path, which sits to the right and seems the least frequently traveled, judging by the number of vines that crawl across the cobblestones.

The trees create a buffer against the music, and I finally isolate Sophia's voice up ahead.

"Get off me, Tyler."

She sounds angry, not scared, but Tyler's response chills me to the bone.

"You either walk out of here with me tonight, Sophia, or you don't walk out at all."

CHAPTER TWENTY-EIGHT

*W*hatever control I had over my instincts snaps.

Reaching for my weapon as I stride along the path, I hold my glaive ready as my target becomes pinpointed.

Tyler Dalton.

He comes into view just as he shoves Sophia so hard that she drops toward the small, grassy patch at the side of the footpath. Her strength has improved greatly since her dragon appeared, and she doesn't lose her balance, spinning to take the force of the push and landing at a crouch. Another inch to the left, and she would have hit her head on the trunk of the tree beside the path. I imagine that's what Tyler intended.

My blood boils, but I don't make it another step before the trees on either side of me rustle, there's a rush of wings, and a dragon drops down into the space between Tyler and Sophia.

Micah folds his silver wings, raises his head, and growls at Tyler with as much force as an alpha of a wolf pack. "Back the fuck off."

What the hell is Solomon's son doing here?

As much as I'm happy that someone is standing between

Tyler and Sophia, my back stiffens. I draw closer to the trees on the left-hand side of the path, keeping to the shadows.

Where is his father? I don't imagine that Micah is here on his own. I scan the cloudy sky above me and focus up past the tops of the trees on my right to the edge of the roof.

When I don't see Solomon—or inhale his deep-forest scent—I return my attention to Micah. Even with his wings tucked to his sides, he's such an intimidating size that he's obscuring Sophia. I can't tell if she's remained at a crouch behind him or is rising to her feet.

"You're not a Scorn dragon." Tyler seems to have enough smarts to take a breath before he lashes out, but the growl in his voice tells me he's itching for a fight and might not care whom he has it with. "Who the fuck are you?"

At that moment, the clouds clear, and the moon shines unimpeded across the path. Tyler's dragon shadow appears beside him, its glistening, black body dominating the narrow space on his right-hand side. Its sharp teeth gleam as it lowers its head in a soundless snarl at Micah.

The Grudge dragon chooses that moment to spread his silver wings, the reflection of the moonlight off them nearly blinding, but his dragon shadow remains concealed.

If Sophia's dragon shadow has appeared behind Micah, it's completely obscured by his wings, and I have no idea if Micah chose that moment deliberately or if it's purely by chance.

Tyler takes a step back, a hint of uncertainty entering his voice. "What the fuck? Where's your shadow?"

Micah only smiles. Pure menace. "It's time for you to leave."

"Like hell I will. That's my wife—"

Micah's fist moves so fast that I hardly follow it. He hits Tyler with an undercut that lifts him into the air.

Tyler manages to twist so he lands on his side instead of his back, but even so, he cracks the cobblestones.

I dart forward as he hits the path, reaching him in the seconds it takes him to recover. Before he can leap upward, my boot lands on his chest, shoving him back down.

His eyes narrow as he glares up at me, reaching for my foot to shove me off himself, but he stops when I lower my glaive and hover the curved blade above his neck.

"Think carefully, Tyler," I say. "Even if I decide not to dispatch you to hell right now, Zahra and Callan are only a cry away. Sienna stands at Zahra's side now. Nobody's going to let you destroy this alliance."

I didn't swallow a bucket-load of guilt for this night to go awry here.

I give Tyler another moment to think about it before I lift my boot and allow him to get up.

His focus flickers to Micah, and there's a moment when I think he's going to try to get past me, but he finally backs away.

"You're going to die screaming," he says to me.

"I'd like to think so," I say, making his brow furrow. "I sure as fuck won't go quietly."

He backs up another few steps before he turns away, and I wait only as long as it takes for him to disappear along the path.

I swing to Micah, ready to deal with him, only to find him stepping to the side of the path and tucking his wings to his sides. He bends and holds out his hand to Sophia, who has remained crouched on the cobblestones.

Her dragon shadow—Bella Vorago—is curled around her, the same beautiful, cerulean blue serpent that was depicted in the books we read in Callan's library. Bella's head rests on Sophia's back, and both of them have raised their eyes to Micah.

"Why did you do that?" Sophia asks, her voice filled with her dragon's strength. "I didn't need your help."

Micah continues to hold out his hand to her. Unwavering. "I know you didn't. But what kind of dragon would I be if I stood by and did nothing?"

Her brow furrows, and her glare grows. "You act like you're honorable, but you're a Grudge. You wouldn't look at me sideways if I didn't have a dragon. You'd sneer at me like all the others."

His lips press together. Still, he doesn't retreat. "I'm half wolf," he says quietly. "My dragon didn't destroy my wolf the first time I was exposed to moonlight. Not like it was supposed to. How do you imagine my clan looks at *me*?"

While Sophia's eyes widen, Bella lifts her head from Sophia's back and rises into the air so that her face is directly opposite Micah's.

He doesn't flinch. Doesn't seem alarmed. "Bella Vorago," he says. "It's an honor to meet you."

I'm as wide-eyed as Sophia when Bella touches her shadow nose to Micah's. He closes his eyes as if he can feel her touch when she turns her face and brushes her cheek to his, staying there for a moment before she draws back.

It's the same gesture I've shown Callan, and it makes me shiver.

"What the fuck was that?" Sophia whispers, suddenly trembling as if the buzz of energy in the air around us now is shaking her from the inside out.

Her hand rises, and Micah's closes around it.

He helps her to her feet. "I wish I had more time to explain it, but you can't stay here right now. You need to leave."

He's barely finished speaking when Bella Vorago jolts, her focus suddenly on a point behind me.

Sophia wrenches her hand from Micah's, but it's not him I'm worried about now.

"Lana!" Sophia cries. "Look out!"

I barely have time to snatch a breath, let alone spin to face the dragon soaring toward me at full speed. The scent of the forest overwhelms me a second before Solomon's arms close around me from behind and he snatches me from my feet and lifts me into the air.

His arms are like a crushing vise pinning my own arms to my sides as he soars upward. He veers sharply to the right so that we pass across the building on that side, out of view of the partying dragons below.

I'm still holding my glaive at my side, but it's pointed downward. I'm ready to release my wings, which will knock Solomon's arms wide and give me room to move. Every muscle in my body is tightening, preparing to retaliate. I'll spin, lift my weapon, and take his head off in one sweep—

A shadow passes across me, enveloping me from behind, bringing with it the intense sensation of flying beneath the branches of the oldest trees, not across this city like we actually are.

It's so sudden that I gasp. I struggle to breathe.

Within my mind, I'm soaring through an ancient forest. Veering left and right and circling trunks that are so large, they seem to go around forever. The sparkling city disappears and instead, I'm skimming low over glistening moss, my fingertips brushing the cool fronds, and when I beat my wings, I soar up through wide branches, dislodging raindrops that were clinging to the leaves.

I scream at myself that I'm not in a forest. I'm being carried above the city, transported away by a dragon who can only mean to harm me. But the shadow at my back only grows darker, a nearly tangible force, and its presence becomes more powerful.

It has to be his dragon shadow. If only I could turn to see it...

Solomon's mouth is at my ear and when he speaks, his voice sounds different than before.

Deeper. Quieter.

His command is like a dagger driving through my heart. "Stop fighting."

A violent shiver rages through me before my body goes limp, obeying his order. Inside, I'm shouting at myself, but no part of my body will obey me. Not my arms or legs or hands. My head tips back against Solomon's chest, and my will to fight drains away.

My grip on my glaive loosens. The weapon slips from my fingers, gravity pulling it down.

No! Stay with me!

At my desperate thought, the weapon halts in the air before it would have plummeted and then it flies after me, a glint at the corner of my eye as it catches the moonlight.

At the same time, the dark shadow retreats from around me, the forest scent lifts, and the feeling of soaring through the trees becomes a distant memory.

I groan with relief, discovering that, although my body refuses to fight Solomon—has somehow been *compelled* not to fight him—it seems I can still express my emotions.

"Fuck you," I snarl, although it sounds more like a whimper than an expletive.

"Your control of dragon's gold is impressive, Cruel One," Solomon says, his voice returning to normal again as he acknowledges the weapon that sails behind us. "You have a strong will, but it's not strong enough to disobey my dragon."

I don't know what he did to compel me not to struggle—how he somehow used his dragon shadow against me—but I promise myself I will fight him as soon as this compulsion wears off.

He adjusts his hold on me, turning me so that I'm resting more comfortably against his chest.

"Where are you taking me?" I demand to know.

Now that he has turned me around, I can see his face. His blond hair is tied back into its usual messy ponytail, the strands flying in the wind. His lips are pressed together, and his eyebrows are drawn down in their usual menacing lines.

His wings were already beating fiercely, but now they sweep us into a steep dive and his answer is nearly snatched away by the wind.

"I'm taking you to your mother."

CHAPTER TWENTY-NINE

*M*y thoughts are a storm.

My mother has always been a mere idea in my mind. Someone who must have brought me into the world but also never really existed for me. When Solomon mentioned her during our fight at the Cathedral, she became a little more real to me. But the warning I gave Sophia was real, too: Knowledge means power. I told Callan that I desperately want to know more about my mother, and I meant it, but I can't give that sort of power to Solomon. He will only use it against me.

I vow to myself that as soon as my body obeys me again, I will fight my way free of him, even if it means losing this chance.

If my mother really does exist—if she lives in this city—then I will find her on my own. Without Solomon's help.

As we soar toward the ground, my glaive continues to fly along beside me, and it gives me hope that I'll be able to use it against him soon.

Solomon lands at the entrance to a back alley, slowing his descent so he doesn't crack the pavement when he touches down.

I lost track of my location when I was immersed in the illusion of flying through a forest, and I don't recognize my current surroundings well enough to know where I am. My only sense of it is that we flew far enough that we could be miles away from where the dinner was located.

Solomon adjusts his hold on me again, this time hoisting me across his shoulder, and then he hurries along the alley. A fence sits in the middle of it, although the barrier is only waist-high and Solomon scales it one-handed, landing agilely on the other side and racing on without stopping. The alley lets out into a shadowy side street where a beat-up SUV waits. It's a vague shade of maroon in the darkness.

I recognize the dragon shifter named Leon waiting beside it. He has speckles of gray in his wavy, brown hair, his skin is light brown, and his voice is as rough as an old machine.

"Where's Micah?" he asks.

"Right behind me," Solomon replies. "We need to be ready to move as soon as he gets here."

Leon doesn't ask more questions, opening the back passenger door before he helps Solomon remove my harness so I can sit down. Then Solomon shifts his weight and slides me onto the vehicle's back seat.

My glaive floats neatly inside the vehicle and settles into the footwell.

I'm not about to follow its peaceful example.

With all my strength, I attempt to drag myself across the seat to the other door, trying to convince my body that this isn't *fighting* Solomon. It's simply moving in the direction opposite to him.

My left hand lands on the internal door handle just as the door opens, and I stare up into Leon's face.

His deep-brown eyes view me with a hint of respect. He's the opposite of Solomon, whose scent transports me to a verdant forest; Leon's presence evokes the dryness of the dessert. A rough, sand-filled wind that gusts through stone walls. The subtle scent of spices. Black pepper, cinnamon, cardamom, and cloves. Those are just the first aromas to hit me as he leans forward to block my escape.

Although his voice is low, his gravelly tones somehow convey more warning than if he'd grabbed me. "Consider your choices wisely, angel. You're an easy target in your present state and the stink of Sentinels is heavy in the air this night. I doubt they will show you mercy."

Damn. He isn't wrong. It's been a hot minute since I checked my surroundings, but the nearest flare of angels' energy isn't far enough away for my liking. I don't want to encounter Isaac or his men while I'm vulnerable like this.

I tell myself to bide my time. I will see my chance, and then I'll take it.

I edge away from Leon, only to collide with Solomon's broad chest behind me. One of his muscled arms snakes around my waist before he hauls me into a sitting position and pushes me back into the middle seat. His big palm plants on my sternum before he grabs the seatbelt and clips me in.

There's a *whoosh* outside the vehicle and a moment later, Micah opens the driver's-side door and slips behind the wheel. He's breathing heavily, as if he pushed himself to get here as fast as he could. "We need to leave. There are five Sentinels three blocks to the west."

"What of the water dragon?" Solomon asks, and I assume he's referring to Sophia, since she was with me when Solomon snatched me.

Micah glances in the rearview mirror. "She's safe, but I had to use my power to compel her to return to her friends and not to follow me. I'm sure she's told them what happened by now. It won't be long before they're searching for us."

It sounds like Micah used the same sort of power on Sophia

that Solomon used to stop me fighting him. I don't know how he did it, but I'm determined to survive it.

"Being hunted is nothing new," Solomon says. "We'll evade them as we always do."

Leon hoists my harness onto the front passenger seat before he closes that door and slides into the back seat with me. I'm now wedged between Solomon on my right and Leon on my left. As soon as Leon is settled, Micah starts the engine, and the truck lurches forward.

Solomon glances at me, and I'm shocked when his expression softens a little. It seems to erase some of the forbidding lines that make him appear as unyielding as stone. "This meeting is too important to fuck it up."

I try to see which way we're going, but with Leon's large body on one side and Solomon leaning across me on the other, I can't catch more than the flicker of streetlights. I take note of the first few turns, memorizing them, even though I don't have a reference point to know where we started from.

Solomon lowers his face to mine, demanding my attention.

"I know you hate this," he says. "I know you want to fight me. I fully expect you to attack us at your first opportunity. But your mother asked me to take this risk, and I couldn't deny her this mercy." He gives a heavy sigh. "Not after the mistakes I've made."

I promised myself that I wouldn't ask for answers. I told myself I wouldn't give anyone power over me again, but I can't stop the question leaving my lips—the question that has eaten away at me since Solomon's revelations at the Cathedral. "Why did you steal me?"

His expression hardens again. "You may believe that I'm merciless," he says. "I am not. But for a long time, life taught me that mercy brings nothing but grief. Even when hope dared to break through my darkness, danger lay within it."

My brow furrows as I try to unravel his answer, but I can't

fathom it. Am I the hope, the darkness, or the danger he's referring to? Or none of them?

"I have questions for you, too, Cruel Angel," he says, considering me carefully. "Since we're stuck together in this vehicle for at least a short while, why don't we trade answers? Perhaps, somewhere along the way, we can meet in the middle."

When he approached me during the storm near Zahra's home, he said he had a question for me, and he wasn't lying. But his offer sounds far too reasonable, and I don't trust it.

I remind myself that it was *his* fist around my neck, and *his* dragon's gold, that would have killed me at the Cathedral.

"You told me you were an instrument in the hands of a vengeful master," he begins, even though I haven't agreed to his proposal. "The Serene Commander was your master. She sent you to kill Callan Steele, but you chose to disobey her. You probably think I'm going to ask you why you didn't kill him, but that's not what I want to know."

I remain silent, waiting for his question, uncertain what he's going to ask. Equally uncertain if I'll answer.

He studies me for long enough that it feels like he's scouring out the deepest secrets of my heart and laying them out to examine them.

"Why did Callan Steele let *you* live?"

It's not the question I was expecting. At the Cathedral, Callan told the Grudge that I would hunt for him, that I was a weapon in a new master's hands. But that wasn't Callan's initial plan. His decision to let me live came from the moment when I stood within his flames and didn't burn.

I should probably lie about it, but I've been exposed to too much guilt tonight as it is. I don't need to add my own lies to it. "Because I survived his fire."

I'm aware of the sudden, wide-eyed glances Micah throws me in the rearview mirror, and the way Leon startles beside me, but Solomon...

Why doesn't he look surprised?

He lets out a deep breath, closing his eyes and shaking his head. "I should have fucking known. You stole his fire, didn't you?"

"Stole it?" I blink at Solomon. "Didn't you hear me? I *survived* it."

"No," Solomon growls, suddenly vehement, his pupils constricting and *now* the beast within him rises up. "You swallowed his fire. Took it. Made it your own. Just like you stole my gold and made it yours. You're a fucking fire thief."

I'm incredulous. "How did you know I swallowed his flames?" I ask, only realizing once I speak that I've confirmed Solomon's theory.

He lets out a gruff laugh. "Fuck, you are a marvel."

"How is it possible?" I ask him, momentarily giving in to my need for answers, since he seems to know more about the fire than he's saying. "How can I do these things?"

Solomon's jubilation fades and he leans back in his seat, allowing me to see more of my surroundings. It's the dead of night. There are only a few other vehicles on the road, but I recognize some of the buildings now, the location of which tell me we're heading northeast toward the river.

"It's not my place to answer that," Solomon finally says. "Only your mother can explain."

"I suppose that will be your response to everything," I snap. "My mother will tell me."

Solomon is silent for another long moment, and it feels like he's done talking until he says, "I didn't mean to steal you that night."

My lips part in surprise at both his answer and the fact that he spoke it. I need to know more, but I'm terrified he'll withhold that information, and then I will have given him the power I swore I wouldn't give him. "You didn't mean to steal me?"

His hazel eyes gleam, and the tension around his mouth and

eyes increases. "You weren't the only treasure the Sentinels were keeping in that location. There was another object. Something very precious to all dragons. An object with the power to heal us. My clan was deteriorating more rapidly than any other. My mother, my father, my brother... They were succumbing to their beasts, and I couldn't stand by and let it happen."

His voice is a deep growl now. "I wasn't going to let anyone stop me. But when I finally broke through the Sentinels' defenses—killed two of them, injured the third—there were *two* columns of light within the veil, not one."

He holds up his fingers. "*Two* precious objects, both concealed in light. The columns were too bright to see inside them, and I only had moments to choose before reinforcements arrived. I was so sure I'd picked the right one. So fucking certain. I reached into that light, and I pulled you out. A tiny baby. Not the salvation my clan needed."

I'm holding my breath, hardly daring to exhale. He's told me more than I expected him to and even as questions burn within me, I don't ask them. Can't risk disrupting him. I sense Micah and Leon listening intently, too, and I wonder if Solomon has ever told them this story.

"The strange thing was, you were quiet," he says. "You didn't cry. You just looked up at me, and I could sense your fury even then. Your quiet anger. The truly dangerous kind."

He pauses, but I remain silent, trying to process what he's telling me. I don't know what to think or feel. He's telling me he stole me by mistake. He had a choice between two bright silos, and he simply reached into the wrong one.

I was never his target.

"I didn't have time to put you back," he says. "They were already on me. A whole fucking legion of Sentinels. I fought my way out of there one-handed, holding you against my chest, and then, when I finally made it out and I could stop running, I looked down at you, and—"

He lets out a sudden laugh. "You were asleep." His chest rumbles. "You fucking fell asleep while I was fighting for my life."

He lifts his hand and hovers his palm beside my cheek. "You never cried. Not once in the entire seven days that I cared for you. What the fuck did I know about looking after a baby? Diapers and formula. Fuck, I muddled through, but you never complained.

"Then the angels offered me amnesty if I would give you back, and I agreed, because what the fuck was I going to do with an angel baby? I couldn't even keep my own family alive. I was never going to save them."

He stops, exhaling heavily. "But I knew, the moment I placed you into the arms of the Celestial Ascendant herself, that I shouldn't have returned you to her."

My mouth is dry, but this time, I force the question from my lips. "Why?"

"Because that was the first time you screamed." His hazel eyes are piercing. "You fucking screamed as I turned my back on you and walked away."

His snarl washes over me. "It's because of me that you became something you were never meant to be. A dragon killer. I told myself that one day, I would right my wrongs. There is no saving you from what you've become."

My voice is cold now. "You mean to kill me."

"I'm one of the few who can."

A shiver runs through me. Somehow, he compelled me not to fight him. I'm completely helpless right now. "Then why haven't you killed me already?"

He draws back again. "Like I said, I promised your mother this mercy."

I'm suddenly chilled to the bone as I work through his intentions. "You're allowing me to meet her, to speak with her, as a last act of mercy... before you kill me."

His silence is my answer.

No wonder he was willing to talk about the past. He doesn't intend to let me live long enough to do anything with this information.

My voice is constricted. "Does my mother know you plan to end me tonight?"

"She does not." He gives a slow shake of his head. "She would fight me to the death to save your life, and I have no wish to hurt her."

I consider him carefully as he turns his face into shadow, as if he's afraid that he's revealed too much already. He told me he isn't merciless, and I believe him now. If he were heartless, he wouldn't care so much about his son or about the woman—whoever she is—who brought a monster like me into the world.

"If you're not merciless, then grant *me* a mercy," I say, challenging him for the truth. "Tell me what you did to me to turn me into the monster that I am. Because something happened when you pulled me out of that light. Something changed. Before that moment, I was an Avenging Angel, and then suddenly, I wasn't."

He spins back to me so fast that I jolt into my seat. The glaive twitches at my feet, and for the first time since he compelled me not to fight, I sense a trickle of my rage returning.

"I already told you, Cruel One," he snarls. "We are mere playthings in fate's game."

Before he can say anything else, Micah's sharp warning interrupts him. "We've picked up a tail."

Both Solomon and Leon swivel to look at the road behind us. I only need to use my senses to know the nearest vehicle is too far behind us to see it yet.

My chance for answers has slipped away, and I force myself to focus beyond my deep disappointment and to prepare for yet another possible threat.

"Is it angels or dragons?" Leon asks. "Scorn or Dread?"

"Dragons," Micah replies. "I can't tell what clan while we're driving."

The fact that he can distinguish dragons from humans at all surprises me, but his wolf's senses must be beyond compare if he'll be able to tell one clan from another.

"I can hear the engine in the distance. It's taken the same turns as us for the last few minutes," Micah continues. "And it's approaching fast."

Both of my bracelets suddenly warm against my skin, and I try not to react in case Solomon notices. The last time the bracelets heated, they were calling to Callan. He told me he could sense them beating like my heart. Rapid and uneven. Just like my heart now.

But if Micah can detect the far-away purr of an engine following us, then he'll surely detect the changing beat of my heart, the way the mere thought of Callan makes my pulse thrum, along with the gentle hum as the crimson-heart charm brightens beneath my wrist.

Micah's brown eyes are piercing in the rearview mirror. "It's someone Lana cares about."

Dammit, he's astute.

At Micah's declaration, Solomon takes a long look at me. He grabs my wrists and snarls at the pulsing charm. "Fuck." His voice is a deep growl. "It must be Callan Steele himself. To assume a lesser danger would be foolish."

The sound of the other vehicle's engine finally reaches me as we exit onto the Expressway. The driver may have been keeping their distance while we were winding through the city streets, but now they seem determined to gain on us down this straight stretch of road.

If it *is* Callan, he won't risk a crash knowing that I don't heal quickly. He won't try to drive us off the road, but he also won't know what level of danger I'm facing within this vehicle. After all, if I were fighting for my life right now, he wouldn't hesitate to come to my defense.

I try to calm my breathing. Calm my heart. Indicate that I'm not in mortal danger yet. That he just needs to follow us.

I gasp, and my heart jumps again when Solomon clamps his hands around my face, roughly this time. His palms are calloused, his thumbs even more so as he brushes them across my cheeks. "It's rational for dragons to fear Callan Steele. In fact, it's wise." His voice becomes a deep rumble. "But it's also wise for Callan to fear me."

It *is* wise to fear Solomon. My fight with him taught me that he is one of the most formidable opponents I could ever face.

Callan's advantage is his fire. He took control of the Dread by burning out the heart of the old alpha.

But now that I've seen the extent to which Solomon can shift, I wonder if Solomon's hide could be strong enough to repel the worst of Callan's flames.

"I promised myself I would end you." Solomon's skin glistens with a wash of scales in the flickering streetlight. "Callan Steele won't stop me this time."

CHAPTER THIRTY

*M*icah takes the next curve faster than before, the truck's wheels screeching as we fly along the Expressway. The vehicle following us continues to purr, the sound of its engine drawing closer.

"Which exit do you want me to take?" Micah asks, as if they already had contingency plans and he's seeking confirmation of which to follow.

"You need moonlight and a place to constrain Callan's power," Leon says, staring hard at Solomon. "The location of the meet will give you both. But it will endanger Lana's mother if she gets caught in the fight."

Solomon gives a heavy exhale. Solomon's lips set in an uncompromising line. "Callan's reluctance to use his power at the Cathedral tells me he won't risk hurting others." He continues to grip my face, speaking to me this time. "I promised your mother she would see you. You will have to make the most of the seconds you have with her."

Micah's eyes flash to Solomon in the rearview mirror. "The old power plant is up ahead."

Solomon gives a curt nod. "Get us there as fast as you can. Take us inside the gates, but don't stop. I'll haul the angel out while the truck's moving. I want you to drive the hell away—"

"Fuck, no," Micah snaps. "We're not leaving you behind."

"You will obey me!" Solomon roars, making Micah's heart jump in my hearing. "The future of the Grudge clan depends on you."

Micah's hands are so tight around the steering wheel that his knuckles are blanching, but his response is quiet. "A mutt like me can't be the future of our clan, Dad. Leon knows it. The others know it. Why don't you?"

Solomon's answering growl is drowned out by the determined roar of the vehicle now edging up to our back corner. It veers close to the middle of the road, and its headlights sweep the back of the truck's cabin. It's close enough to tap our back corner.

The friction within the SUV is just as fraught.

"This is not the time for this conversation," Solomon says to Micah. "Your job is to stay alive. My job is to protect our clan. That's the end of it."

Micah casts a final fuming glance into the rearview mirror a moment before the roar of the vehicle behind us dominates my hearing again. The flash of its high beams lights up the interior of the truck's cabin for a second time, and I suspect Callan is trying to see what's happening inside the vehicle.

It won't be helping Callan's agitation levels that my heart is pounding and the heart charm is flickering like crazy. He's faced with the choice of ramming us off the road, and potentially injuring me that way, or holding back without knowing if I'm being attacked.

Up ahead, I recognize the same exit toward the old power station that Callan took the night he shook off the angels and dragons who were following us from the Cathedral. The abandoned industrial area has a wide parking lot outside it—perfect for speeding around. Rows of floodlamps are positioned at intervals around the lot.

The insides of the buildings are another story. They're dark, cramped places. Hard to fight in and mostly devoid of moonlight—except the main building that has a soaring, arched ceiling filled with glass. I imagine that's the location Leon was talking about, since it will provide both moonlight and a space within which to confine Callan's fire.

Speeding along the final stretch of road, Micah takes a hard right toward the padlocked gate. He smashes right through it and hurtles across the bright, concreted area. Zooming toward the arched building, he only slows down as he approaches it.

With a satisfied grunt, Solomon moves fast, reaching around me and unclipping my seatbelt. His arms wrap around my waist, and he wrenches me up against him so that my back is to his chest.

"Keep your wings closed or I'll claw out your stomach," he threatens me, his hands pressing against my sides.

He must be worried that the compulsion is wearing off. I take it as a good sign.

He reaches back to open the door, just as the vehicle behind us finally makes a move. It speeds up on our left side—positioned between us and the building. Its location won't stop Solomon throwing himself out of the vehicle on this side, but it will block our entry into the warehouse. Assuming that's where Solomon intends to take me.

Since I'm facing in that direction, I get my first good look at the sports car, although its tinted windows prevent me seeing inside it.

I don't need to.

I recognize its sleek form as the vehicle Callan drives.

Solomon wrenches the door open behind me while Micah

nudges the brakes and slows right down for Solomon to jump out. Callan's vehicle overshoots and he hits the brakes, his vehicle skidding another hundred feet past us.

The door behind us is already open.

We're already falling through it.

The impact against the rock-hard surface rattles every bone in my body and seems to snatch Solomon's breath away, but he doesn't stop moving, throwing us into a roll that kicks the wind out of my chest as we tumble over and over.

We're moving too fast to tell up from down, but in the split second that I still have visibility of the truck, I catch sight of Leon throwing himself sideways, wrenching the door closed again.

Micah speeds up toward Callan's vehicle. He brakes and turns the wheel at the last moment, causing the back of the truck to slide sideways. It's a deft move that allows him to turn the vehicle toward the gate while creating an obstacle in Callan's path.

Solomon doesn't waste a second, leaping to his feet and wrenching me up with him, my back still to his chest. He releases his wings with a thump and, with a single beat, he lifts me into the air.

My senses are going haywire now. My muscles are tensing, my hands are twitching, and it's as if the lock Solomon placed on me is being torn apart by such a rush of rage that I can't control it.

Glaive! I scream within my mind. *Feathers! Come to me!*

In the distance, there's a crash of glass, and multiple pieces of gold stream from the truck's now-broken windows, feathers flying toward me followed by my weapon. At the same moment, I smack my elbow back into Solomon's jaw. He releases me for the barest second before his arms clamp around my waist, and he hauls me against him again.

It's only been seconds since I fell out of the vehicle with him, and now, to my right, the car's driver's-side door is flying open.

A hulking mountain of rage bursts out of it.

Callan!

My heart stops to see him and then beats slower, calmer. Calm in the way that only Callan can make me.

Even across the distance, I can see that his eyes are pure juniper-green, the color they turn when he's angry. He's as imposing as Solomon, his dark hair appearing charcoal-black in the artificial light.

Ribbons of gold fly off the vehicle's hood, ten of them, flying past the truck and shooting toward Solomon. They're only seconds slower than my weapon and feathers, which are soaring toward me at the same speed that Solomon is traveling.

Callan is close behind them. He vaults over the truck's hood, ignoring Micah and Leon as he runs after me.

"Asper!" Callan roars, the deep caliber of his voice striking at my heart like a hammer.

Solomon soars toward the building that has the arched ceiling and, no matter how many times I ram my elbows and my boots back into his chest, face, and legs, he doesn't let me go.

The warehouse door is open. My last glance at the parking lot tells me that Micah is speeding out of here like his father ordered, and Callan is closing in.

Solomon tucks his wings and tears into the building, and I lose sight of the parking lot.

He throws me from his arms the moment he passes through the opening. I gain air and release my wings, but without my golden feathers, they only send me into a faster spin toward the floor.

I hit the concrete, my left wing slapping the ground first and cushioning my fall enough that I don't break any limbs.

Back at the entrance, Solomon drops to the ground, swings to the door, and slams it shut a split-second before a multitude of violent thuds tell me the golden bands, my glaive, and all of my feathers must have hit it from the outside.

Leaning his shoulder against the surface, Solomon grabs a thick plank of wood leaning against the wall next to the door and drops it into the metal hooks across the entrance.

He succeeds in barring the door a moment before another, harder, *thump* indicates that Callan threw himself at it.

My chest heaves as I crouch halfway across the room. I'm forcing myself to ignore the pain from all the bruises I've sustained, but I take a moment to check my surroundings.

Large, rusted generators sit idle at intervals along the floor with walkways between them. The area directly in front of the door is a clear space but not large enough to easily conduct a fight without being mindful of the nearby machinery.

The ceiling within the building is as high as I remember from the times I hunted dragons here, although there are fewer panes of glass in it. Moonlight shines right through them, unimpeded by the artificial lights outside.

The only shadowed part of the room is behind me.

Still crouched, I retract my wings and prepare to throw myself at Solomon when my senses finally normalize, the roaring in my ears quietens, and I'm suddenly—*painfully*—aware of a glimmering presence behind me.

"I can only hold this door for one minute!" Solomon shouts without looking back. "If you don't leave within that time, I may not be able to keep you alive."

"I understand," a soft voice says.

A silhouette moves in the darkness and I'm frozen where I crouch.

She's... *real.*

A woman steps out of the shadows, and I try to breathe because...

I know her.

She was the Serene Commander's favorite warrior. An angel

with the darkest hair and whitest wings. The brightest eyes and the purest shimmer. Not tall, but formidable. The strongest of the warrior angels within the Serene Commander's legion. Practically a legend among them.

Or she was, until she was supposedly killed by dragons.

CHAPTER THIRTY-ONE

"*M*elisma," I whisper. "But... you died."

She drops to her knees in front of me and reaches for my face, her eyes glistening as she takes in the bruises that must be developing across my cheek bones, my shoulders, and my arms from falling onto concrete twice. "Asper, dearest."

Her endearment floors me. I'm not anyone's dearest. Not even Callan's. But somehow, it sounds right coming from her lips.

She is like... sunflowers. A whole field of them. Golden petals and warm summer afternoons. She's wearing faded jeans and an old, sleeveless T-shirt. Her black hair is tied in a loose ponytail that rests across her right shoulder.

Her death was the turning point in my life. It prompted the Serene Commander to decide that she couldn't bear to lose another angel's life—except for mine. The Serene Commander's grief was real. She must not know that Melisma is alive. Solomon fortified the lie of her death when he mentioned Melisma at the Cathedral. He threatened to kill any angels who followed him, just like he claimed to have killed Melisma.

"I have so much I need to explain," Melisma says. "But I don't have enough time."

I suddenly realize that she's looking right at me, right into my eyes, in a way that angels usually can't. For a brief, disbelieving moment, I look for some sort of magical shield across her face like the paint that the Serene Commander wore. Then I wonder if she's simply bearing the agony like Isaac did.

I wait another moment for her to flinch and look away, but she doesn't.

"You're looking at me," I whisper.

"Of course," she says, as if there were never any doubt she could. "You're my daughter."

She pulls my hand into hers, holding it lightly, her palm beneath mine. "You're not corrupted, Asper. You're simply an angel who has never existed before." She pauses. "Someone who has the strength to do what will need to be done. No matter how much it hurts you."

I feel like I can't breathe. "I don't understand."

"I will tell you everything," she promises, her expression hardening. "But first, you must get away from Callan Steele. You need to take yourself as far from him as possible—"

"No, wait, what are you saying? Get away from *Callan*?"

Surely, she means Solomon. Or Sienna Scorn. Or even the Serene Commander.

Melisma's eyes are wide. "Now that the Sentinels are here, we're all in terrible danger. Not only the dragons, but the angels and other supernaturals, too. Please, Asper. There's no time to explain."

Her orders come swiftly, the edge in her voice reminding me that she once commanded a legion of angels. "Get away from Callan. Stay with Solomon. Don't let the Sentinels capture you." She casts Solomon a quick glance and her expression softens in a way that indicates she trusts him completely. "He'll keep you safe until I can come for you—"

She jolts when the next *thud* against the door makes the wall on that side of the building shake and a pane of glass drops from the ceiling and smashes on the floor.

"You've got ten seconds," Solomon shouts, pressing against the door with all his might, his biceps bulging and every muscle across his back straining.

"I'll come for you," Melisma promises me. "Whatever you do, stay alive."

She releases my hand before she rises to her feet, tips her head back to the ceiling, and extends her wings.

I want to stop her from leaving. I need to understand what she meant. I want to tell her that the dragon she should fear is Solomon, not Callan.

Callan won't hurt her. Or me. Not like Solomon will.

But everything she said was spoken with true belief. She doesn't carry the same crisp piety that the Serene Commander does. Her energy is open, truthful... compassionate. She has a heart that is capable of trust, and I can't break it.

"I'm grateful that I met you," I whisper, although I'm not sure if she can hear me as she shoots up through the rough opening in the ceiling and disappears from view.

I tell myself I'll see her again soon. I'll survive Solomon, and I'll find my mother on my own.

Across the way, Solomon leaps away from the door just before it splinters.

Pieces of wood explode across the floor as Callan bursts into the warehouse. He's shirtless now, the sculpted muscles across his chest and stomach gleaming with sweat. There are gashes across his right shoulder and down his arm where he must have used that side of his body to break through the door.

My glaive hurtles through the opening, along with the golden feathers, all of them flying to my side. I deftly catch my weapon and spread my wings, calling the feathers to me.

Callan's gold circles the air around him, the bands appearing linked to his body by invisible and unbreakable loyalty. "Lana!"

"I'm okay," I cry, stepping toward him, making myself stop five paces away from him. I want nothing more than to step into his arms, but I don't want to trigger his dragon. "I'm okay now."

Callan's quick gaze takes in my state of health, lingering on each of the dark patches where bruises must be forming.

Despite my assertion that I'm okay, the tension around his mouth and eyes increases. With heat waves growing around his chest, he steps out of the artificial light that pools in the doorway and into the moonlight within the building.

His dragon shadow rises from the darkness, a colossal golden beast whose lips draw back from its teeth in a silent snarl, its eyes growing more fearsome by the second.

"I have to end this," Callan says to me, his voice low but barely restrained. "Promise me you won't get caught in the fire."

Now that my golden feathers and my weapon have returned to me, there's a part of me that wants Callan to fly away with me. I could turn my back on Solomon and his threats. But he's proven that he won't stop coming after me until I'm dead. No matter what he promised my mother.

Callan backed away from a fight with Solomon at the Cathedral because of the risk of collateral damage, but he has the chance, right here, to use his fire without harming anyone else. He might not get another chance like this.

I meet his fierce gaze, and even though a flutter of fear grows within my chest, I say, "I promise."

That's all Callan seems to need. He swings to Solomon, who has soared up toward the ceiling. "Solomon Grudge," Callan says, his eyes remaining pure juniper-green. "You've made your last mistake."

Solomon's wings beat the air, the moonlight seeming to

darken their earthy color. The spikes on his wings gleam like claws, and his eyes are pure reptile. "No, Callan," he replies. "You're about to make yours."

Callan's lips twitch a split second before his golden bands shoot toward Solomon. They arc up high, their points sharpening like spears as they curve in the air, a blur, perfectly aimed at Solomon's chest.

"Stop," Solomon says.

The golden spears halt midair, their tips only inches from Solomon's torso. The projectiles hum, shivering as if two opposing forces are pushing on them at the same time.

Callan's hands fly upward, palms out, his forehead creased in concentration. At the same time, his dragon raises its head, towering above Callan as if it's preparing for war.

As the gold continues to shiver in the air, sweat breaks out across Callan's forehead, but the flare of fire in his eyes only grows. "What the fuck?"

Solomon gives a cold smile. "You're out of your depth."

"How the fuck are you controlling my gold?" Callan asks.

I saw the way Solomon diverted the path of the Serene Commander's Sentinel spear, but the bonds between Callan and his gold are incredibly strong. I only made Callan's gold mine after he chose to give it to me. Even when I tried to tug away the training square that morning, it barely moved.

But Solomon starts to turn his hands in the air, and the spears are slowly responding, their tips lifting upward and the rods starting to flatten, as if the weapons are going to fold over themselves.

"It appears that you've been deprived of important history lessons," Solomon says, while his focus on the spears remains intense. "My father was the last true Grudge King. He was the last dragon to achieve a full shift. He should have been supported, but the factions between clans had widened too far.

The Grudge had already been driven beneath the city and our heritage wiped from the history books."

Callan's brow is furrowed, his arms straining, but Solomon's speech doesn't appear lost on him. Of all the dragons I've met, Callan cares the most about the welfare of the dragon race. "You could have come to me!"

"How?" Solomon demands to know. "Nobody could find you. Not even my son. Even if we could have, you would not have welcomed me. I was the enemy. I was the one who made the angels angry—an anger they have no right feeling after what they've done to us."

Solomon's hazel eyes lift just far enough to gleam at me across the surface of the gold in front of him. "They took far more from us than I ever took from them."

On instinct, I extend my own will toward the gold in the air, but the friction around each piece is like touching a live wire. My breath catches and I hastily retreat, gripping my glaive more tightly and willing my feathers and my armband to stay with me.

"My father had a unique ability that he passed on to me," Solomon says. "A skill his mother possessed that was passed down through the generations."

In the air, the golden spears have flattened into metal plates. They respond to the push and pull of Solomon's hands by twining up toward his chest and shoulders, neatly sliding into place around his torso, conforming to his shape and size, until his right shoulder and chest are plated in glimmering, golden armor.

He hovers in the air, a beautifully monstrous dragon, every beat of his wings reminding me that he is the reason my life changed.

"My father had the power to control another dragon's gold as if it were his own," Solomon says, his features hardening. His emotions closing off. "I can, too."

Now that he's taken Callan's gold, Solomon doesn't wait another moment. His lips twist and his focus turns away from Callan and narrows on me. "It's time to end this."

With a beat of his wings so savage that it rocks the air around me, he dives toward me, his hand outstretched.

At a flick of his fingers, the glaive flies from my hand and slams into the far wall.

My golden feathers scatter.

Solomon's big fist reaches for my throat.

I don't waste time with screaming. In the second before Solomon reaches me, I snap my wings closed and brace, ready to leap up to his right, send my fist into his face, and crack his jaw while spinning out of his reach.

But suddenly, all I can sense is the inferno that's exploding toward me.

Callan tears straight at me like a bullet, his golden wings curved for speed, flames billowing around him.

The air screams with his approach and then—

His naked chest collides with mine, his strong arms close around me, and he snatches me right out from under Solomon's grasp.

The Grudge dragon is traveling so fast that he bangs into the wall, turning to hit it with his shoulder instead of breaking his outstretched hand.

That's all I see before Callan whips me into the air and curves to the side. It's too hot to breathe, but I don't care as he soars toward the ceiling and then toward the back of the building, his fire bursting around us both.

It's been days since we touched and, in these seconds, I soak up everything he gives me.

He fought to convince me that I have a place with him, showed me that I have real choices and that *he* is one of them. He warmed my body and my soul. Because of him, I found soft places in my heart that I never knew existed.

Peace. He gives me peace. Despite the fury burning around him, and despite the dragon shadow that makes my eyes widen as it rears up over us.

It's the first time I've seen his shadow within his flames. I drag in the fire, a sharp breath, because the dragon shadow seems to take on substance, as if the fire is filling its vacant spaces.

It lowers its face to me above Callan's head, and its lips move, as if it would speak to me.

Soon, it mouths.

Callan's body obscures it before I see more. He drops to the ground and places me on my feet, pressing his forehead to mine.

"Not-Lana," is all he says before he steps back, spreads his wings, and soars into the air.

The fury on his face is undeniable.

The fire around him changes color from golden to white and finally to blue, the hottest flame, as he soars toward Solomon.

The heat billowing back toward me feels a thousand times more intense than the flames I've survived in the past. I throw my arm across my face and drop to a crouch, curving my wings around myself, seeking shelter at the edge of the nearest genera-tor. I doubt the rusted metal machine can protect me. I don't think anything could protect against these flames, and I sure as fuck won't willingly step into them.

Ahead of Callan, Solomon has risen into the air, sweat glis-tening across his face, the armor he's wearing reflecting the blue inferno tearing toward him.

He doesn't retreat. His features remain set in hard lines as his focus flickers to me, then back to Callan. He soars forward, as if he's determined to veer around Callan and fly right through the inferno to get to me.

Callan adjusts his trajectory, and the two dragons collide midair in an explosion of heat that snatches the breath from my chest.

The clash between them is so savage that they crash through the air and into the wall at the side of the room. Solomon's back hits it and, using his right wing to push himself away from the surface, he curves his left to deflect some of the flames.

His right fist flies out, but Callan's flamed-tinged punch lands firmly against Solomon's side, pushing him back against the wall and putting a dint in his armor.

At the same time, Solomon's claws slash across Callan's face.

Callan barely flinches. His pure-golden eyes don't even blink. His next punch collides with Solomon's stomach, then his chest, rapid hits that finish with an uppercut that cracks Solomon's jaw.

Solomon slumps, his head lolling, indicating that he's been knocked unconscious. I don't expect it to last long and neither does Callan, judging by the speed with which he grabs Solomon's shoulders, rams his knee into his stomach, and pins him against the wall.

Just as Callan's flames intensify, a dark shadow materializes around Solomon's unconscious body.

It rears up through the fire as Callan rips the golden plate away from Solomon's chest, where it protects Solomon's heart.

I scream a warning, but the crackling fire is too loud. My cry is swallowed by the roaring inferno as the shadow knocks into Callan like a physical force, throwing him backward.

Solomon slides to the floor, his back to the wall while Callan lands at a crouch, his descent smooth despite the force of the blast, his golden wings curved around his body while his shadow rises up at his back, its teeth gnashing the air.

Solomon's dragon shadow steps through the flames and stands between Callan and Solomon. A protector shielding the Grudge dragon. It's as large as Callan's shadow, its body perfectly formed, its tail bearing spikes, and its scales—like Solomon's wings—the color of the deepest, darkest tree trunk, glistening as if it had stepped right out of a rainy forest.

It brings with it the scent of mossy undergrowth and the relentless sensation of flying. Of fucking freedom. A scent that knocks into me as hard as the heat from Callan's fire.

In a voice that vibrates through the air and seems to shift the foundations beneath me, Solomon's shadow roars, *"Callan Steele, you will yield!"*

CHAPTER THIRTY-TWO

*M*y hands fly around my ears as the dragon's roar tears through my senses.

The wind is knocked out of me, but I can't take my eyes off Solomon's beast. Can't process the fact that...

It spoke.

Not with Solomon's voice. Not *through* him.

His dragon shadow spoke with its own voice.

Despite its insubstantial form, its presence feels so real, I could be convinced that it was flesh and blood.

Opposite it, Callan rises to his feet and his dragon moves in sync with him, lifting its head when he lifts his.

"No." Callan's voice is barely recognizable, a deep growl, the intensity of which I haven't heard from him before. Even when his beast seemed to surface at times, he didn't sound so fully *dragon* as he does now. "I won't stop. I won't give her up. Not even if I have to burn every fucking part of this world to keep her."

My eyes widen when the dragon's lips move in time with Callan's as he continues. "That angel is mine. Her power is mine. And I will never let it go."

The forest dragon arches its neck, its dark-green eyes narrowing. "Callan Steele!" the forest dragon roars. "You will hear me above the din of your dragon's desires. You will regain your mind and your honor. And you will *stop!*"

With a growl, Callan steps forward and prepares to leap upward, a new rush of flames billowing around him, but just as he would leave the ground, he jolts. Falters. Shakes his head.

He drops to a crouch, his forehead creased, and his fists clenched. "Fuck! I can't... I can't think..."

The golden dragon standing at his back appears to snarl, a silent action, but this time, its head is turned to Callan and its anger seems directed at him.

Solomon's dragon roars again, taking a step closer to Callan. "You will regain your mind. You will retain your honor. You will not attack."

Callan presses his right fist to his head, his other hand landing on the ground as if he's trying to stay upright. A shudder runs through him, and he shouts again.

This time, it's a roar of pain.

He slumps further toward the floor and the blue flames around him turn white, some of the heat he's creating abates, and it's all the opening I need to launch myself to my feet and run toward him, reaching out once again for my golden feathers now that Solomon is unconscious.

The feathers rush toward me, allowing me to fly the remaining distance and drop down in front of Callan, an inadequate shield between him and the forest beast looming over him.

I nearly scream when Callan's flames hit my back, but they're already reducing to the amber fire I've survived before and within seconds, the agony stops.

Breathing through the pain, I tip my head back, facing Solomon's dragon with a vehement scream. "*You* will stop."

The beast stares down at me from above. "Asper Ashen-

Varr," it says with a deep sigh. "Your love for this dragon is misplaced."

"No!" I shout back. "My love for this man is everything good in my life."

I gasp at my own declaration. My eyes suddenly burn. I tried so hard to cut out the gentle parts of my heart, but they can't be subdued, can't be destroyed. My heart knows what love feels like now and I don't want to live without it again.

My arms are flung wide and my wings wider. Callan groans at my back, and his pain is a sharper force than his flames.

The forest dragon gives a long, low growl before it says, far more softly, "Callan Steele, you will sleep."

The scent of the forest washes over me and for three intense seconds, it fucking transports me again, as if it's reaching into the furthest recesses of my mind and dragging out my most basic needs.

There's movement behind me, and I come back to myself just in time to tuck in my wings, spin, and catch Callan before he hits the concrete.

His eyes are closed, and despite the moonlight shining around us, his dragon slowly vanishes. Its body disappears first, and then its head. Its burning eyes are the last to fade, searing me as it goes.

Callan's head rests heavily in my lap, but the creases in his forehead even out and his breathing deepens. Even though I'm touching him, his dragon doesn't reappear.

"Callan?"

He doesn't respond.

"Callan!"

With a sharp inhale, I raise my eyes to the forest dragon. "Who *are* you?"

The dragon replies in a voice as ancient as the trees that its scales resemble. "I am Magnus Grim. And you are the angel who could break the world."

I exhale softly. I learned from the books in Callan's library that Magnus Grim was a warrior dragon. A woodland beast who was a friend of the forest fae.

"Do you intend to kill me?" I'm not sure how this insubstantial beast could finish me, but, hell, it can speak. And it compelled Callan to fall asleep—compelled his dragon to disappear—the same way it forced me to stop fighting Solomon earlier tonight, so nothing's impossible.

"I don't," Magnus Grim replies. "But Solomon does."

There's movement behind the forest dragon and Solomon strides right through its insubstantial form. His wings are fully retracted. He's testing his jaw and rolling his shoulders, but his wounds seem to have healed.

I try to move Callen's head off my lap as fast as I can without hurting him, only just succeeding when Solomon reaches me.

Before I can get my legs under myself, he wrenches me up so high that I'm at eye level with him.

"Enough," he says.

His pupils are once again reptilian. His hold on me is intolerable, my chest pressed to his, my legs dangling, and my midsection taking my weight.

He scatters my golden feathers across the floor once more.

As fast as I can, I draw my fist back and punch his mouth. It's a hard hit right on the spot where Callan broke his jaw. Solomon twists in an attempt to absorb the blow, which causes his arms to loosen.

The impact of my hit propels me backward, out of his hold. I kick my legs, pushing off his chest, arching back toward the ground and narrowly missing Callen's sleeping body.

I land beside him, leap back to my feet, and brace as Solomon charges at me.

He's only three paces away when a sudden *crack* explodes through my hearing.

Opposite me, Solomon jolts to a stop, a surprised look on his face.

He looks down at his chest.

Blood blossoms across his left pectoral muscle where Callan tore at his armor, leaving Solomon's chest exposed.

The tip of a golden bullet appears, slowly boring its way through the final quarter inch of his flesh. It wrenches from his body and spins, suspended, in the air in front of him.

I'm frozen where I stand. I don't even have time to take another breath before there's another *crack*.

This time, I sense the oncoming golden bullet, even if I can't see who fired it. The cold heart of the weapon it was shot from reaches me across the distance. I know that weapon. I felt its icy nature when it was first pointed at me.

Solomon's attacker can only be Sienna Scorn. I can't see her, have no idea where she's located but, without thinking, I leap forward, attempting to catch the path of the bullet's trajectory.

It's traveling too fast for me to change it.

Solomon is also swinging in that direction, and I expect him to spread his wings and use them as a protective shield, but when he turns his back to me, I'm confronted by the damage caused by the first bullet.

One of his shoulder blades is shattered, the bone visible. He won't be able to call his wings.

The second bullet curves through the air—an *impossible* curve—to strike Solomon's chest, but this one doesn't slow down, and the impact throws him back into me.

His weight hits me hard, knocking me to the ground as he falls. I land on my backside, Solomon's heavy body sprawled across my legs, pinning me to the floor.

At the same time, Magnus Grim swings to the building's open door, a roar on his lips. I expect him to rage in the direction of Solomon's attacker. To my shock, he simply disappears, vanishing so fast, it's as if he was never here.

I struggle beneath Solomon, gripping his shoulders and trying to lift him enough that I can heave myself into a sitting position. I'm wedged between him and Callan, but right now, I can't think about why Callan's dragon hasn't been triggered at my touch.

Blood bubbles up between Solomon's lips as he coughs and chokes, his breathing shallow and strained. He's looking up at me, his hazel eyes following my movements as I lean over him.

One of the bullets must have nicked his heart, because his heartbeat is thready, and it isn't getting any stronger.

I wait a beat for him to heal, but it isn't happening. The blood doesn't stop flowing. The two open wounds on his chest don't close. His breathing doesn't even out. The damage must be too great.

I should be relieved. He was trying to kill me. He wasn't going to stop. But my eyes are suddenly burning at the thought that this proud dragon might die in my arms and I...

I don't want that.

Many times, I spoke of ending him. Many times, he was beneath my blade, but I was thwarted; my glaive was deflected by his wing or stopped by his dragon's compulsion.

But when I peel away all the anger, I'm left with a single moment in time that has nothing to do with rage or revenge.

It's the incredulous smile on his face when he told me how I fell asleep in his arms while he was fighting for his life after he stole me. The way I never cried.

There's only one reason that could have happened.

Somehow, as impossible as it seems, when he reached into the light and took me from it, I must have trusted him. Before I became what I am, before I started killing dragons, before I had any experience of hate, when I was still innocent of all death, I trusted this man.

"Were you really going to end me?" I ask him, not expecting an answer.

His breathing is ragged, and his speech is labored, but his eyes are more human in appearance than I've ever seen them. "I don't know."

An honest answer.

I'm peripherally aware of the female figure who finally appears in the open doorway. I immediately recognize Sienna Scorn, dressed in black, her blue-black hair gleaming as she strides toward us.

Her arm is outstretched, and her golden gun is pointed at Solomon. The weapon's surface gleams, and its cold heart continues to call to me.

I should probably be concerned that she'll turn the gun on me. I should probably be trying to get up, but for all his efforts to deprive me of my glaive and my golden feathers, Solomon left the armband on my arm, and I trust it to protect me. Even from a close-range bullet.

I won't leave Solomon on this dirty warehouse floor to die alone.

Sienna crouches on the other side of him, resting her gun down on her upturned knee as she studies his wounds. The ice in her voice makes the hairs on the back of my neck rise. "Don't thank me, Lana. I'm not here to save you."

"You're here for the bounty on Solomon's head."

She tips her head in acknowledgement. "Among other payments."

It takes me a moment to realize that, despite the fact she's crouching in the moonlight that streams through the ceiling, her dragon shadow hasn't appeared.

Perhaps she has a dragon as strong as Solomon's, but it's a mystery that will have to wait because a memory of the first thing she ever said to me is stirring.

She never misses.

And yet... each bullet she shot at Solomon achieved maximum damage without causing death.

"You could have killed him with a single shot," I say. "Why didn't you?"

She lifts her dark-blue eyes to mine, and the explosion of amber around her irises is even more startling than it was the first time I met her. Her lips part in an expression of disbelief. "Lana, I thought you, of all creatures, would understand. Only a slow death can satisfy a hunter's heart."

Without missing a beat, she presses the gun to the armor plating that sits across Solomon's right side. "I wonder if I'm strong enough to send a bullet through this," she says, considering the metal. "What a challenge."

Solomon hasn't taken his eyes off me. Not to look at Sienna or the two bullets that continue to spin in the air nearby like a constant threat of pain. His breathing is quieter, but not because he's healing. His heartbeat is too weak for that. He isn't fighting death now, and it will only be moments before it takes him.

I ignore Sienna as I speak aloud a truth that is barely rational, is more instinct than anything else, but I want Solomon to know before he dies. "I wish you'd raised me."

His features soften and all of the tension around his lips fades away. He exhales softly.

But while my heart is quiet and peaceful in this moment, it's also filled with an inferno of rage.

Peace and rage. They are the fucking same emotion for me.

Opposite me, the cold heart of Sienna's weapon speaks to me of all the deaths it has delivered in its lifetime. Every damn shot.

As she pulls the trigger, I catch hold of the thread of connection between me and the cold-hearted gun, and I hurl a mental command at it before the bullet can leave the barrel.

Shatter!

Sienna screams as the weapon explodes in her hand and blows back in her face. Chunks of gold scatter across her head like shooting stars, knocking her back with a thud, and then there's silence.

The two bullets that were floating in the air nearby drop to the ground with a sharp clatter and roll toward Sienna, where they stop.

Her heartbeat slows, then ends, and the awful taste of copper leaves my mouth. My mind now fills with the scent of the deepest forest and, at the same time, the warmth of the brightest sun. Solomon's heart. Callan's heart. Two dragons who should have been allies.

"Gold thief." Solomon's whisper draws me back to him in time to catch his fading smile.

"Apparently," I reply.

"Lana. Asper." He speaks both my names as he struggles to breathe again, a sudden agitation in his arms, his fingers twitching as if he wants to reach for me. "You need... to know..."

My breath catches, but I wait quietly for him to continue because there's no forcing this moment.

"When I stole you... I took you into the moonlight."

My brow furrows. Of course he took me into moonlight. He stole me at night, so the moon would have been—

I feel like dragon claws suddenly close around my heart.

How many times have I heard about moonlight? From Callan, who said that babies born to human mothers don't show any sign of their dragon nature until they're exposed to moonlight. From Micah, when he told Sophia that when he was exposed to moonlight for the first time, it was a miracle that his wolf wasn't destroyed.

Dragon babies respond to moonlight. *Dragon* babies.

I'm choking. Drowning. But worst of all is that I think, deep down... I knew.

I fucking knew it every time I survived Callan's fire. I knew it the moment I pressed my nose and cheek to his—a dragon's gesture of faith. I knew it the first time I loosened the golden bands that were chaining me, and the moment I realized that the bracelets Callan gave me had become mine.

I knew it the first time I inhaled Solomon's scent and it felt like coming home.

But still, I deny it. "I'm an angel."

"You're my... half-sister."

"No. I'm..."

His arms tremble, his fingers twitch, and he closes his eyes, but in the next moment, the silhouette of his dragon appears, although it's faint and weak despite the bright moonlight.

Magnus Grim's wise face lowers to mine. "Solomon can no longer speak, so I will express his final thoughts before I, too, am gone."

His energy flickers, but he holds on. "You are the daughter of the Grudge King. A thief of fire and gold. Born an Avenging Angel. The only creature strong enough to overcome a dragon. When Solomon stole you, your angel had nearly finished destroying your dragon; there would have been no trace left. But Solomon took you into the moonlight before the process was complete."

Magnus Grim's voice is faint and his form fades in and out. "He wants you to know that he has finally decided..." The forest dragon's expression softens as he gazes down at Solomon, who lies still in my arms now. "He wasn't going to kill you."

A sob bursts out of me, a pain I've never felt before flooding my chest.

"Don't..." I whisper. "Don't die."

"Goodbye, Asper Ashen-Varr."

CHAPTER THIRTY-THREE

*H*ot tears escape down my cheeks.

My heart has been scoured out from the inside. I can't process what I've learned or what I feel. I could compartmentalize the loss and the confusion, but that will only push it into the dark corners of my mind, where it will strike back when I least want it to.

I have to break down what I now know into small pieces and accept that each one is true.

Solomon was my enemy.

He was also my brother.

I have... a dragon.

Without realizing it, my free hand has rested down on Callan's chest where he lies on my left. His heartbeat is a deep thud in my senses. A calming sound that helps me focus.

I need to think in terms of action, instead of emotion. I need to get Callan home. I need to find a way to wake him up. I need to tell Micah what happened to his father, and I need to find my mother.

I had questions for her before, but now they've multiplied.

Instinctively, I tip my head back, as if I might find her again in the stars shining above me, but as I stare upward, I realize...

The sky is wrong.

A white glow fills the air above me. It's a strangely beautiful light, but it's not moonlight, and it's not the glitter of stars.

I gasp at the knowledge that while I was consumed by the events within this building, I lost awareness of my surroundings. A mistake I swore I'd never make again.

Fuck, fuck, fuck!

Rapidly extending my senses into the strange, white glow filling the night sky above me, I reach through it, and then—

Bright light blasts through my mind.

It knocks into me like a physical force.

At the same time, angelic forms crash through the glass ceiling and drop into the space around me.

They land on the tops of the rusted generators and on the floor. All Roden-Darr. All armed with blades of various kinds. Each man extending his right palm toward me in an outpouring of soul light that instantly blinds me.

Within seconds, I'm surrounded.

I kick myself because it suddenly makes sense that Sienna's dragon shadow didn't appear. It couldn't manifest because the light shining through the ceiling was no longer moonlight. It also explains why Magnus Grim disappeared so suddenly and why his outline was so faint at the end. I thought it was because Solomon was dying. But the Sentinels must have arrived above me, shining their soul light to camouflage their presence, at the moment when Sienna fired her first shot.

It's impossible to move quickly while Solomon rests across my legs, but I swivel at my waist, blinking hard and trying to plot a course between the men—a course that will be very difficult to travel once I'm trying to carry Callan out of here. He's still fast asleep and my heart is pounding rapidly because, hell, I don't know if I'm strong enough to move him.

Fear of failure strikes through me, but that won't stop me from trying.

I'm sliding Solomon away from me, preparing to launch myself at Callan and hook my arms beneath his shoulders, when another blast of light explodes across me.

This time, it knocks me into Callan's side.

I look up, only to see a golden net falling onto me.

I flinch at the sudden weight of the net and the strange feeling of the metal, but I'm not overly concerned.

I've fought off worse.

Seeking this new metal's heart, I try to sense its nature and connect with it, to control it, only to discover that it's nothing like the living gold I've encountered before.

It has no heart.

It's simply... metal.

But it's certainly enchanted.

I leap to my feet, heaving and pushing upward while the weight of the net drives me down as if it weighs a ton, drawing tighter across my back and forcing me into a kneeling position again. Then onto my side, where my back presses against Callan. I grunt with effort, gripping the webbing and trying to pry it apart, pulling with all my strength.

With every passing second, it presses me closer to Callan while the edges of the net draw closed beneath us.

Fuck!

Isaac drops to the floor at Callan's feet, his pure-white wings tucking neatly into his sides. Five other Sentinels, including Zadkiel, the dark-haired second-in-command, land behind him.

Isaac kneels outside the perimeter of the net, his palm extended toward me, his power even stronger than the other Roden-Darrs' light. I want to scream with rage when his soul light slows my thoughts and makes my movements sluggish. The angels won't be concerned that I'm pressed up against

Callan. They will have seen that I was already touching him, and that his dragon wasn't triggered.

Isaac's white wings are blindingly reflective, and so is his pure-white hair, but there's a storm of determination in his gray eyes. "It's over, Asper," he says quietly. "It's time to come home."

His power dances around me, a glittering force as I fight the net.

My whisper is vehement. "My home is not with you."

Four of the Sentinels who descended with Isaac produce small metal rods that they shake once within their hands. The rods extend at the movement, elongating into poles, each forming a hook at the end. Once again, the metal is not alive—I can't connect with it—but it must be enchanted. The angels take up position at intervals around Callan and me, and I imagine the hooks are how they intend to latch on to the net and carry us out of here.

Zadkiel steps away from Isaac and moves quickly around the space, crouching beside Solomon and then Sienna. He runs his palm through the air above each of their bodies, pausing longer beside Sienna. Bending close to the ground, he picks up the two bullets, along with the largest remaining chunk of her gun— what appears to be a mangled piece of the barrel that has turned back on itself and now resembles a fist-size stone.

Isaac rises to his feet when Zadkiel returns to his side.

"What of our informant?" Isaac asks, indicating Sienna.

Zadkiel holds up the chunk that remains of her gun. "Sienna Scorn is dead. It appears she was killed with her own weapon. Solomon Grudge was slain with these two bullets."

As Zadkiel speaks, I taste the strangest flavor on my tongue. It's bitter but also sweet. Light but also heavy. It's like a field of violets, but instead of growing on a sunlit plane, they're flowering in slimy mud that oozes up between their stems. It's not a scent I'm familiar with and I'm not sure what to make of it.

Isaac gives a heavy exhale. "Magnus Grim was an honorable

dragon. It could be millennia before he lives again. I pray he will be born to a wiser shifter next time."

"If he is ever born again," Zadkiel replies and, again, my mouth fills with mud and violets, a confusing mix.

Isaac gives a nod, his lips pressing into a solemn line before he seems to refocus. "We need to move quickly. We must reach the veil before Callan Steele's dragon wakes up or we risk his dragon's fire. He may not be as in control of his beast as he once was."

Isaac crouches to me again, this time with a sigh. "From what I've learned of Callan Steele in the last week, I believe he has attempted to live a worthy life, but he is no match for his dragon's rage. We can't risk his dragon being unleashed. It falls on me to imprison you both."

Isaac's emotions are open and easy for me to read. His anger at me has been replaced with the heaviness of responsibility. Vibrations of loathing and respect no longer clash in the air around him. He has trapped me, and now it's his job to see that I'm securely imprisoned.

"Please say your goodbyes, Asper. Your home in the veil will be far from Callan's. We can't risk caging you near each other."

When I first met Isaac, he told me that I had become a significant threat but if I joined with Callan, then, together, we would be unstoppable.

Isaac reaches out and presses his palm to my shoulder, and I discover that it's not a conciliatory gesture when the heat beneath his palm grows so intense that I flinch. The warmth makes my head spin, and my vision starts to fill with light. It's as if he's injecting me with enough warmth to force me to fall asleep.

"Don't fight it, Asper," he murmurs, continuing to press his palm to my shoulder even as I try—weakly—to push his hand away.

His face blurs and his perfect lips settle into a line that seems to multiply into many lines in my warping vision. "You will soon wake up in the veil."

For the briefest moment, I close my eyes, focusing on the calm that Callan's presence gives me. I tell myself to let the Roden-Darr take us. I will conserve my energy and find a way to escape.

I open my eyes, but it's increasingly difficult to focus, and I have to squint to make out the shapes of the angels. Some of them are rising up into the air. The four who were standing at intervals around us are hooking their poles into the net and lifting us off the ground.

I can still make out Isaac and Zadkiel, but now, Zadkiel's form is as murky as the mud I taste. It seems that the brighter the light within my mind becomes, the darker his silhouette grows. So do the silhouettes of the angels who are carrying us, and half of the others who are taking to the air.

The breath catches in my chest as I suddenly realize what the muddy taste in my mouth means.

Betrayal.

Never before have I sensed such cold-blooded treachery in the hearts of so many angels at once. Not even when the legion of warrior angels attacked me at the Cathedral.

A cry of warning rises to my lips when the darkness around Zadkiel grows so intense that it looks like a shadowy beast rising up at Isaac's back.

Just as Isaac lifts off the ground to follow me, Zadkiel leaps forward and grabs Isaac's wing bones, wrenching him back to the ground.

Isaac shouts, stumbling as he turns. "Brother?"

Zadkiel's arm swings and the rocky remains of Sienna's gun glints as he smashes it across Isaac's temple.

Suddenly, all around me, the darkened angels are attacking the bright ones, their violence so frenzied and sudden that they overcome their brothers within seconds.

I can't do a fucking thing to stop it.

Copper floods my mouth and I gag on it, struggling to breathe. All the while, the angels carrying us toward the open door don't flinch and they don't stop.

Isaac is a fading form in the distance, his once-glimmering energy flickering weakly. My heart lurches in a way I wasn't expecting. These Sentinels—the Roden-Darr—were created to be my warriors, to stand at my side, and protect my back; but now they've turned on each other. I don't understand why, or what they intend to do with me, but I know that Isaac doesn't deserve this fate.

Swallowing hard and closing my eyes, I extend my senses toward him, using the last of my energy to listen for his final breaths and the slowing beat of his heart.

His voice is faint. "Why, brother?"

"We needed a new master so we found one," Zadkiel replies. "But don't worry. We will take the Avenging Angel and the Fire Breather into the veil just as you wanted."

He gives a cold laugh, and the taste of slime thickens across my tongue, layering over the tang of copper.

"We will take them to Atrox. He is our master now," Zadkiel says. "He will use Asper's power to free himself from the veil and soon his fire will cleanse the world of all evil."

I try to hold on, but my energy fades.

With my final coherent thoughts, my mind fills with the image of the last Avenging Angel, of her body crushed beneath the claws of the most fearsome dragon to have existed. The dragon she gave her life to imprison.

Atrox Imperator.

CHAPTER THIRTY-FOUR

I open my eyes to darkness.

Endless darkness.

It stretches in every direction, left to right, up and down. I can't tell what I'm lying on. Only that it's cold.

My breath frosts in the air, a little puff of white that lights up my hands when I lift them in front of my face. Goosebumps rise on my skin, but it's the prickling across the back of my neck that alarms me most.

I rise to a crouch and spin to the presence behind me.

A throne sits not more than ten paces away. Like everything around me, it's inky black, but its outline is surprisingly clear. It appears to be fashioned out of the blackened bones of an enormous creature's ribcage.

The man who sits on it leans forward slowly, his eyes gleaming and silvery like a cat's eyes in the dark.

He's bigger than any dragon shifter I've encountered, as large as Callan in his shifted form, his shoulders taking up the width of the throne. His entire body gleams and it takes me a moment to realize it's because he's wearing armor.

It's the same suit of metal that Atrox Imperator was depicted wearing in the book of Angelic Monsters.

Unlike the drawing, where he was shown holding his helmet in his hands, he's wearing it on his head so that it obscures his features. The perfectly crafted openings across the front of the helmet, and the slit that runs to its base, reveal only his cold eyes and a portion of his hard lips. Two sharp horns on each side project directly backward.

His voice is a low rumble that thrums through me. "Have you ever seen a dragon hunt a thunderbird, Asper Ashen-Varr?"

I remain crouched where I am, horribly aware that my golden feathers are gone and so is my glaive, but my armband remains.

"What is a thunderbird?" I ask.

"Ah." His lips purse. "You've never seen one." He continues in the next breath. "They were beautiful creatures. Nearly as large as dragons. Their hearts were powered by lightning and when they beat their wings, it sounded like thunder."

Atrox leans further forward and this time, when he moves, there's a soft, clanking noise. "It was such a thrill to chase them." He gives a soft chuckle. "There was no greater ecstasy than to rip out a thunderbird's beating heart, sink my teeth into its lightning, and swallow its heart down, power and all."

My stomach turns, but I snap back at him. "I take it I'm the thunderbird in this story."

"Clever girl," he says, rising to his feet and stepping from the throne.

With each step he takes, vibrations spread through the surface we're standing on, and his body lights up a little. It's as if sound creates light in this place. I make out little details that I couldn't before. His armor is golden. The ends of his hair that extend from beneath his helmet are the darkest brown. His eyes are green.

He's dragging something beside him and the heavy, grinding

sound it makes casts flickers of light up over his legs. As the noise grows louder, the object's shape becomes visible.

It's an enormous hammer. Its shaft appears to be made of the same black bone that forms Atrox's throne, but the hammer's head is a thick block of gold that's decorated in runes.

He stops at a point equidistant between me and the throne. With an almighty heave, he swings the hammer up into the air and then down onto the floor.

It hits the surface in an explosion of sound that lights up the space around us, revealing a white, marbled floor that stretches in every direction, but it's the area in front of Atrox that draws my attention.

My breath stops to see Callan lying on the floor right in front of Atrox. Callan is resting on his back, completely still other than the steady rise and fall of his chest. His hair is a dark mess against the white marble, his face and chest glistening with sweat as if he's fighting a battle despite his stillness.

But what strikes fear through my heart is that the hammer hit the floor right beside Callan's head.

He could have been killed, but he didn't stir. Not even a twitch of his fingers. He's completely vulnerable while Atrox towers over him holding a weapon that could crush his skull.

Atrox lets the hammer's head rest on the floor as he gestures at Callan. "I'm holding your heart in my hands, Asper Ashen-Varr."

As the sound of the hammer's first strike continues to radiate around us like an echo, the throne, Atrox, and Callan remain fully visible.

My fear for Callan clouds my thoughts but I try desperately to push through it, to buy myself time while I figure out how to get Callan to safety. "What do you want, Atrox?"

Atrox lifts his hands and stomps his feet. The clanking sound he makes sends smaller vibrations through the air, so that the shapes of his restraints can be seen. Shackles rest around his wrists and ankles. The chains that are attached to them extend all the way back to the throne with enough slack that Atrox could walk to my location and back.

"You will break my chains," he says.

Still focused on Callan, I divert my attention briefly to the gold that binds Atrox. It *feels* like dragon's gold, its heart is living, but it isn't like any I've sensed before. It's harder. *Much* harder.

All of the dragon's gold I've encountered has been malleable and flexible, its shape able to be manipulated. These chains are set, as if they were forged and then fixed in these perfect, unbreakable ropes.

"If the Sentinels imprisoned you here, why can't they free you?" I ask. After all, Zadkiel said that Atrox was their new master. "Surely, they can unbind those chains."

"These restraints can't be broken by angels. Not even by Sentinels. They were tempered by the Vanem Dragon, who served the Twilight Queen. Once they were placed on me, they couldn't be removed. It was a measure to ensure nobody could release me from this place."

"Then what makes you think I can break them?"

"You are no mere angel." His fingers twitch around the hammer's hilt. "Are you, Asper? Or should I call you *Daughter of the Grudge King*?"

I narrow my eyes at him, watching the way he grips the hammer, ready for any indication that he intends to swing it again. "How do you know about that?"

His lips stretch into a cold smile. "I remember the night the Roden-Darr returned to the veil after they discovered you were corrupted. Zadkiel stood where you're standing now. His heart was in tatters. His hope was gone. He told me he went with Isaac to oversee your safe return, but when he looked upon your face, he felt only a terrible need to tear down the world. Your corruption was intoxicating."

Atrox's sneer broadens. "He said that looking into your eyes was like standing in the heat of my flames and being burned alive. In that moment, I knew two things. First, that I could turn him against his people. And second, that you carry a fire dragon within you."

The knowledge that I have a dragon is so new and raw that I flinch. But a fire dragon? Solomon thought I stole Callan's flames—and maybe I did—but Callan said that I changed his fire and made it mine. And maybe I did that, too. If my dragon is a fire dragon, and I also inherited the Grudge King's skills, then it could explain how I survived Callan's fire *and* how I stole it.

"Of course," Atrox continues, "it took longer to find out whose daughter you were. Imagine my joy when Zadkiel sent me a message that you stole the Serene Commander's spear and transformed Solomon Grudge's noose into a weapon of your own making. Only a gold thief could do that."

His voice deepens to a rumble that adds to the vibrations of sound radiating around me. "You were born with the strength of an Avenging Angel and the power to bend gold to your will. You, alone, can break my chains."

"Atrox," I growl, knowing in the very depths of my being that I've never wanted to kill anyone as much as I want to end him right now. "I will never help you."

Atrox's focus drops to Callan's sleeping form. "You have far too much to lose if you don't."

My breathing seethes through my lips, but my anger is laced with fear. When Isaac first met me, he told me that I have every strength and skill I need to track the dark ones, and to then capture and imprison them. He said that I have the capacity to feel nothing but loathing for the guilty, and that I can't be swayed by threats, bribes, or emotion.

Perhaps that's true. But the threat is not to my life, it's to Callan's. Even with the full force of wild rage burning through me and the undeniable need to kill Atrox, my need to protect Callan comes first.

I have to find a way to get to him and pull him beyond the reach of Atrox's hammer. Then he'll be safe, and I'll fight this monster to the death.

My heart pounds as I judge the length of Atrox's chains and plot a course to Callan.

Atrox watches me carefully as he lifts the hammer again, hefting it above his head. "I'll enjoy sinking my teeth into your heart, Asper."

I don't waste another second. My feet fly across the smooth floor, every footfall vibrating around me and lighting up my path. As the hammer descends toward Callan's chest, I throw myself into a dive toward Callan's feet, my hands closing around his ankles, pulling him so sharply at an angle that his body slides clear of the hammer's descent.

The weapon hits the ground where Callan's body lay only seconds before.

As Atrox quickly lifts the hammer once more, I throw myself toward Callan's head, hook my arms under his shoulders, and heave as hard as I can, dragging him away.

I'm confused when Atrox drops the hammer onto the same patch of empty floor instead of adjusting his aim.

"Wake up!" he shouts.

The explosion of sound splashes across the marble, bringing out the striations in its surface and revealing all the little cracks, as if every new sound exposes another detail of our surroundings.

"Wake up!" Atrox screams again, this time staring at Callan.

I can't stop to figure out why Atrox would want Callan to wake, or why he isn't coming after me. I continue to pull with all my might, heaving Callan's sleeping body another few paces.

Atrox watches me struggle, his green eyes sharp.

The sudden smile on his lips makes me cold.

"There you are," he says, a soft but triumphant declaration as he lifts his hammer again, holding it high, the strain on his massive arms showing as he keeps it aloft.

Callan groans.

He stiffens in my arms a second before he wrenches himself around to face me so fast that I lose hold of him and fall backward.

His eyes are clear, but his irises are startlingly golden. Heat flares around his naked chest in a shimmer that makes it difficult for me to breathe.

I'm shocked by his intense fear.

"Lana! No!"

I was already on my backside, but he launches himself at me, picking me up and throwing me across the floor. I get my feet under myself just in time to land at a crouch. It's not so much his sudden attack, but the dread in his voice that freezes me to the spot.

"Get away!" he roars. "Get the fuck away from me while you still can!"

"Callan... what?"

He drops to his knees only three paces away from me—close enough that I could lurch forward and grab him again.

His shoulders hunch, and he slaps his hands over his ears. "I can hear my dragon, Lana. *Fuck.* He wants vengeance, and I can't control him." Sweat pours down Callan's face as he squeezes his eyes closed. "I can't control him, Lana. I don't want to hurt you. You have to run!"

In the distance, Atrox drops his hammer.

This time, the *crack* is earsplitting. A scream tears from me as the sound vibrates through me so hard that I feel like I'm made of glass that's about to shatter.

Callan's roar of pain mixes with the deafening sound.

Behind him, Atrox is also shouting. Although this time, he leaves the hammer on the ground and both of his hands are outstretched, as if he has caught hold of the vibrations rippling between him and Callan, and now he's controlling them.

"Fire dragon!" he roars. "Show yourself."

Callan's eyes fly open, pure gold now, just like they look when he shifts. His dragon shadow appears behind him, materializing within the light, its body covered in brilliant scales, each one sparkling like a jewel, its teeth bared like blades, and its eyes burning with flames.

Its focus is purely on Callan.

"Dragon," Atrox growls. "*Strike.*"

To my shock, the dragon shadow swipes its claws across Callan's back and, even though its body should be insubstantial, Callan arches with another roar of pain.

Blood splatters the marble floor behind him, a garish spray of sudden color.

No! I jump to my feet, preparing to throw myself between Callan and his dragon shadow when Atrox snarls his next command.

"*Bite.*"

The dragon shadow closes its jaws around Callan's shoulder, savaging his arm and that side of his body so violently that my heart feels like it stops.

I launch myself at the beast, right over Callan's head, my fist pulled back, ready to punch the dragon shadow right in its burning eyes.

Instead of meeting a solid form—despite the damage its teeth are doing to Callan's body—I fly straight through the shadow's form, landing on the other side and slipping in the blood spreading across the floor.

I skid to a stop, one arm outstretched to balance myself, a scream of fear rising into my throat.

How can I stop something I can't touch?

My hatred overwhelms me as I swivel to Atrox. His hands

remain outstretched, the vibrations connecting him and Callan continuing to thrum.

I may not be able to fight Callan's dragon shadow, but I can kill Atrox. I run at him, launching myself into the air. I don't dare send a command at his golden armor, even though I sense its living nature, in case I inadvertently damage the chains that bind him.

Instead, I throw myself toward the hammer that rests at his side. At the last moment, I somersault and kick my feet across into Atrox's chest, knocking him a few steps from his weapon. My right hand drops to the hammer's hilt.

I know it's going to be heavy. I know that taking hold of it and trying to lift it as I fly past will wrench my shoulder so hard that I'll dislocate my arm, so I focus my weight down, using the hammer's hilt like an anchor point and rotating around it.

I land at a crouch on the other side.

With a heave, I wrench the hammer off the ground and swing it at Atrox's side with all my might, intending to smash through his armor and break his ribs.

His left hand snakes out.

He snatches the hammer right out of my hands.

His other fist crashes into my face, pain rockets through my bones, and I fly back across the floor, landing heavily.

I hate the whimper that leaves my lips. *Fucking hate it.* But it's not my pain that scares me the most, or even Atrox's incredible strength. It's Callan's silence.

He's quiet, and with every breath I drag into my chest, it feels like *my* heart is being savaged. I'm the one being torn apart.

Callan convinced me that I have choices, and I do.

I can choose to run and protect myself. Or I can do what Atrox wants and save Callan's life.

Callan once asked me why I didn't think about protecting myself, and I told him it didn't matter. I am a wild thing with a single purpose: to hunt those who deserve to be hunted. Somewhere along the way my purpose changed. Protecting Callan became my goal because he brings me peace. He is my calm. He is my love.

"Beat your wings as hard as you can, little thunderbird," Atrox whispers. "You won't stop me."

In the distance, Callan's dragon shadow takes hold of Callan's other shoulder and prepares to rip him in half.

"Stop!" I scream, reaching out toward Atrox, as if I can compel him to obey me. "I'll do it. I'll unbind your chains."

Atrox lowers the hammer to the floor. This time, it lands softly, and it's similar to the effect of a gentle finger on a ringing bell to calm it.

The vibrations ease. The hum quiets. And then complete silence falls.

In the distance, Callan's dragon shadow rises into the air, its wings beating before it lands between me and him. Its head swivels to me and its lips stretch into a smile.

Callan slumps where he kneels, his back remaining to me. He's bleeding badly, but his heartbeat grows stronger in my hearing, and I need to believe that he'll heal now that the attack has stopped.

I stumble to my feet, sensing his dragon shadow's sharp gaze while I approach Atrox.

My breathing is short and shallow, my heart pounding, as I reach for the shackle around Atrox's left wrist. I push away my fears and the knowledge that I'm about to unchain a monster. I tell myself that I will fix this. Even if I release him now, I will capture him again. I won't stop until I do.

My fingers brush the golden shackle, and the power within the metal rushes through me so fast that I gasp. The heat from this gold fills me with the sensation of standing in a flaming field. Inside my mind, I feel a blast of light, the purest magic contained within these restraints.

"Break," I whisper.

A small crack appears in the golden surface, but it goes no deeper.

"Break!" I say, louder this time, willing the metal to obey me.

The fracture remains hairline and surface deep, resistant to my command.

Digging deep, dragging up the rage that lies within me, I scream. *"You will break!"*

The shackle cracks apart beneath my fingers, and it's like a ripple effect. Every other binding snaps, and the chains slide away from Atrox's body and fall to the ground.

He shakes them off with a deep exhalation before he slowly removes his helmet. His hair falls across his face, masking his features so that I catch only the hard lines of his lips and his sharp, green eyes.

"Stay there, little bird," he orders me. "Or you won't live long enough to regret it."

I'm on edge as he strides right past me to reach Callan's dragon shadow. He doesn't stop there, walking onward until he reaches Callan.

I'm about to disobey him and run to Callan when Atrox drops to a knee on the bloodied floor and bows his head.

"Brother," he says. "Forgive me for the pain I caused you."

My eyes widen and I pause, even more wary now.

Callan rises to his feet, his back still to me. As he straightens himself, he appears taller, his shoulders broader, his muscles even larger, as if he shifted without releasing his wings or triggering his fire.

He turns slowly.

His eyes are pure golden. Heat waves shimmer around his body and his skin is covered in golden scales that appear to be rapidly healing the remainder of his wounds.

When he glances at me, his expression is cold, and his voice is a sharp growl. "The pain was necessary to destroy the shifter's mind. You freed me, Audax."

Fear strikes at my heart and confusion makes my thoughts spiral. My rising anxiety makes it difficult to process what I'm hearing and seeing.

Pain... Callan's mind... Audax...

The dragon that Callan called *Audax* holds his helmet up like an offering. "I've been waiting for millennia to give you back your armor, brother."

Callan takes the helmet, running his hands over it. "You took my place in this prison when the angels tried to trap me. Our ruse was successful, but it came at a cost to you, my brother. Your loyalty and suffering will be rewarded a thousand times over."

Audax rises to his feet and turns to face me. His features are fully visible and even though he looks nothing like Callan, I suddenly realize why his green eyes seem so... fucking... familiar...

They're the same color as Callan's eyes when he's angry. Juniper-green. A color change that always struck me so intensely.

"You should kill her, brother," Audax says in a low growl, his gaze raking me from my head to my toes.

They keep calling each other *brother... Dragon brothers... With identical eyes...*

My scattered thoughts settle on a single piece of information I read in the book of Angelic Monsters. It seemed like an exaggeration when I read it—an embellishment of Atrox's skills—but now, it's a critical fact. *Atrox was so fast and so strong that, sometimes, he seemed to be in two places at once.*

Callan shakes his head. "Not this one. She will choose to join me. I'm sure of it."

I can't seem to breathe, can't seem to control the rapid beat of my heart or the dread that threatens to swallow me. "Callan?"

He strides toward me, a towering inferno whose presence no longer calms me.

I inhale his savage heat and the scent of ash.

A world burning down around me.

Every muscle in my body braces to run, but his big hand closes around my arm, his palm burning my skin.

"Callan Steele is dead," he says. "Call me Atrox."

Find out what happens next in Lana and Callan's story in Slay the Dawn (Supernatural Legacy #3).

Then complete the series with Claim the Light (Supernatural Legacy #4),
the final book with no cliffhanger.

SLAY THE DAWN (SUPERNATURAL LEGACY #3)

**The hunt is mine.
But now I'm hunting the man I love...**

Content information: Slay the Dawn is a dark paranormal romance, the third in the Supernatural Legacy series. Recommended reading age is 17+ for sex scenes, mature themes, violence, and language. NO cliffhanger.

Complete the series with Slay the Dawn, the final book with no cliffhanger.

ALSO BY EVERLY FROST

SUPERNATURAL LEGACY - COMPLETE

(Angels and Dragon Shifters)

1. Hunt the Night

2. Chase the Shadows

3. Slay the Dawn

4. Claim the Light

DARK MAGIC SHIFTERS

(Dark Urban Fantasy Romance)

1. Wolf of Ashes

2. Bond of Flames

3. Crown of Fate

KINGDOM OF BETRAYAL

(Fantasy Romance)

1. A Sky Like Blood

2. A Sin Like Fire

3. A Storm Like Iron

4. A Soul Like Glass

BRIGHT WICKED - COMPLETE

(Fantasy Romance)

1. Bright Wicked

2. Radiant Fierce

3. Infernal Dark

STORM PRINCESS - COMPLETE

(Fantasy Romance)

1. Book 1

2. Book 2

3. Book 3

ASSASSIN'S MAGIC - COMPLETE

(Dark Urban Fantasy Romance)

1. Assassin's Magic

2. Assassin's Mask

3. Assassin's Menace

4. Assassin's Maze

5. Rebels

6. Revenge

7. Rogue

8. Assassin's Match

SOUL BITTEN SHIFTER - COMPLETE

(Dark Urban Fantasy Romance)

1. This Dark Wolf

2. This Broken Wolf

3. This Caged Wolf

4. This Cruel Blood

DEMON PACK - COMPLETE

(Dark Paranormal Romance)

1. Demon Pack

2. Demon Pack: Elimination

3. Demon Pack: Eternal

MORTALITY - COMPLETE

(Science-Fantasy Romance)

Mortality Complete Set: Books 1 to 4

1. Beyond the Ever Reach

2. Beneath the Guarding Stars

3. By the Icy Wild

4. Before the Raging Lion

<u>Stand-alone fiction - dark romance</u>

Corrupt Me: Immortal Vices and Virtues

ABOUT THE AUTHOR

Everly Frost is the USA Today Bestselling author of fantasy romance, urban fantasy and paranormal romance novels. She spent her childhood dreaming of other worlds and scribbling stories on the leftover blank pages at the back of school note-books. She lives in Brisbane, Australia with her husband and two children.

a amazon.com/author/everlyfrost
f facebook.com/everlyfrost
o instagram.com/everlyfrost
BB bookbub.com/authors/everly-frost
g goodreads.com/everlyfrost